I0831305

Dragon's Ark

D. Scott Johnson

ISBN: 978-0-9863962-5-0 (hardcover)
978-0-9863962-4-3 (paperback)
978-0-9863962-6-7 (ebook)

Cover design by Melissa Lew
Interior layout by Lighthouse24

GEMINI GAMBIT • BOOK 2

DRAGON'S ARK

D. SCOTT JOHNSON

"What we think, we become."
– Buddha

"It's still magic even if you know how it's done."
– Terry Pratchett, *A Hat Full of Sky*

Prologue
Gāng Dàwei

Six years from now

May 25, 2:35 p.m., Three Gorges Dam

Gāng Dàwei jumped when another lightning strike split the sky. He was inside the dam's control room and still had to shout over the rain so his crew could hear. "No! Look!" He pointed at the dark panel in front of him. "There's no power!" Nothing in here would work without power.

They crowded around the gauges like tribesmen confronting fearsome magic.

Tiě Lin pulled back from the group. "So what? The automated systems—"

"The automated systems are down!" Another wave from the reservoir crashed against the floodgates hard enough he felt it through his feet. "Do you see that?"

The crest of the wave broke ten meters over the top of the dam. A solid sheet of brown water wider than a village and thicker than a skyscraper tumbled down the other side. The storm, the third one in seven weeks, was parked just west of the dam and hadn't moved in four days. All three shifts of the control crew were here now, and none had slept more than a few hours the entire time.

"The gates won't open on their own anymore," Gāng Dàwei shouted at the technicians around him. He was the control foreman, but they never listened when it mattered the most. "We have to open them manually." Three lightning strikes briefly revealed the empty control rooms, part of the towers that anchored the floodgates.

"Hell with you," Tiě Lin replied. "There's no way we can get to those shitty rooms. We'll be washed over—"

None of them understood. "No," Gāng Dàwei said. "It's not random. Watch." The fifteen technicians gathered close to the windows, while the storm threw lightning near and far. The thunder was so loud it probably terrified his ancestors. "Count!"

When he got to one hundred twenty, another wall of water crashed over the top of the dam.

"Go!" He shouted at them. "Go now!"

They ran into the rain as it came down so hard he could barely see. Two minutes to cross fifty meters was a brisk walk on a bright spring day, but in these conditions they had to help each other up whenever someone stumbled. The next wave loomed over them as they crammed into the first tower's control room.

Gāng Dàwei slammed the door shut. This time there was no question about being brave. He and his crew all screamed as water rammed through the bottom, then the sides, and then the top of the doorjamb. The room went briefly silent as the water completely covered the low windows. He was sealed inside a room with his men under water and five hundred feet in the air. Someone giggled. Gāng Dàwei fought with his own need to express *something*. He had to stay silent, stay strong, be the leader his men needed.

And then it was over. The water rushed over the dam and he could see outside again. They could survive this. His grandfather had helped design the dam, and this wasn't the first superstorm to strike it. To win, to save the dam, they had to control the flooding, balance the overfilled reservoir. Get it wrong one way and thousands of people would lose their homes. Get it wrong the other way and they'd all be on the hook for damage to the structure itself. They had to get the harmonics of the waves under control.

He turned and pointed to the pair of men standing closest to the tower's consoles. "You two stay here and control this gate, everyone else, go!" The rest of his crew rushed out again in front of him, but now he had the key. The waves weren't random, and the next tower was much closer. He could do this; they would save the dam, the villages, everything.

At every tower, he had another pair of men peel off and man its control room. The final tower he saved for himself and Tiě Lin. It was critical to get this right, and Gāng Dàwei didn't trust anyone else with the point closest to the opposite shore.

As Tiě Lin closed the door behind them, he looked out the window to see how the other teams were doing, but could only make out the next tower. Gāng Dàwei blinked twice. A dark shape—a man—worked his way around it. He definitely wasn't part of the crew. There was an assault rifle on his back, which turned weird into seriously scary. Not to mention the dark uniform that looked like something out of a combat realm.

Tiě Lin asked, "Who the fuck is that?"

The man outside looked upstream and braced on handles nailed into the concrete. They weren't there this morning either. This wasn't a realm. Stuff like that didn't just appear. Whoever this was had prepared for the storm.

Another thick wall of brown water broke over the dam. When it cleared, the stranger got back to his feet and then started working on a small black box.

Gāng Dàwei wouldn't just stand by while an armed man messed with a box attached to the dam. *His* dam. "Bomb" was a word he didn't want to think about, but whatever it was, whoever *he* was, he had to be stopped. The stranger was a big man, so he went to the tool chest at the back of the room and pulled a ratchet the size of his forearm out. Gāng Dàwei handed Tiě Lin a radio earbud so he could keep the teams in the towers coordinated while Gāng Dàwei confronted the stranger. The waves would be tamed with the flood gates, but only if they were careful. "Stay here," he said, just loud enough to be heard over the storm. "I'm going to figure out who the hell that is."

"No!" Tiě Lin's whisper was more of a shout. He leaned closer. "It's a ghost."

Useless superstition. "It's a ghost trying to fuck with my dam." Gāng Dàwei shook loose from Tiě Lin's grip and opened the door. "Let's see if it's immune to steel."

He should've tried sneaking, but with another incoming wave and the urge to figure out who this really was, Gāng Dàwei more or less ran. The noise of the rain covered any sound he might make anyway. Probably. Tiě Lin's superstitions were stupid, but Gāng Dàwei had grown up with the same stories. Ghosts might be real. Standing out in this storm anything seemed possible, and if he didn't get this done right now he'd be washed over the side. At least the ghost…the *man's*…back was turned.

As soon as Gāng Dàwei was in range he clubbed the dark-clad man, who collapsed instantly. Not a ghost after all! Gāng Dàwei yanked the balaclava over the man's head.

He had a swarthy face with thick dark hair and a broad mustache, not Chinese, not Asian at all. The wires in his hands were wrapped around the base of the tower and disappeared over the reservoir side of the dam. Tiě Lin skidded up beside him and, working together, they carried the unconscious stranger back to the control room.

"What the hell is going on?" Tiě Lin asked.

"I have no idea. He was working with wires, that's all I could see." Gāng Dàwei checked the window. Tiě Lin had done well with the team. The new wave was nowhere near as high as the last.

An earpiece had fallen on the man's neck. Gāng Dàwei knelt down and listened closely. Another man said numbers in English. Counting down. He pulled the earpiece free and walked back to the window.

Wires. Trailing over the side of the dam.

The voice reached ten.

He looked down. An identical set of wires ran right outside his window.

The voice reached five.

They were all going over the reservoir side. A new wave was heading in.

Fuck my ancestors.

The voice reached zero.

Electric traces flashed down the wires and the floor tossed him into the air. Gāng Dàwei landed on the console in front of him and his shoulder popped. The pain flashed, and it took a second before he could open his eyes. He had to find out what happened. Gāng Dàwei dragged himself back to his feet, but the floor wouldn't stay still. The noise rattled his bones. He finally managed to pull himself up to the window with his good arm.

The dam was gone. Just gone. Where there had once been hectares of concrete and steel, there was now a tremendous waterfall. The contents of the reservoir, no longer held in check, rushed out. An angry wall of water three hundred meters tall roared down the valley, an elemental dragon that consumed everything before it. The floor lurched and spun, and then his feet left the floor.

The window pointed downward and the water crashed in.

***

Qiáng Shān knocked his stack of mah-jong tiles down and they scattered on the floor.

After a few moments his grandmother said, "Well, what are you waiting for?" She leaned down from her perch on the overstuffed chair next to him. "Pick them up, you useless little turd."

He stared up at her. The blaring of the TV, the sounds of afternoon traffic on the street outside their house, and the wind all worked together to stir his head into a fused chaos. The overpowering light from the open windows and the smells of the restaurant down the street completed it. His stillness was the control. Stay silent. Make predictable movements. Rock back and forth. The chaos was tolerable then.

"Go on, pick them up. I can't walk around here with all your stupid tiles scattered around. I said," she reached out to him, "pick them up, or I'll grab your hand."

As soon as she got within a few centimeters of his hand, Qiáng Shān couldn't help it. He shrieked, and then quickly gathered the tiles. The chaos in his mind surged and ebbed on a schedule of its own, but just the threat of someone's touch would punch a hole right through it. In a moment of clarity, he wondered at the calligraphy of the signs celebrating his tenth birthday. They were shiny, with red and gold colors beneath the black symbols. After a moment they bled together, and the chaos took him again.

He stacked the tiles. The smooth feel, the rhythmic clacking, the sense of forces balancing slowed his rocking, allowed him to focus as time passed.

His grandmother stared at the TV behind him, completely still. His mind was clear enough, for now, to understand that something interesting was going on. He turned and was able to understand the TV. The minutes dragged on, and he could still think. It was turning out to be an exceptional day.

A well-dressed woman sat at a desk, speaking frantically. "…the earthquake came from a previously undiscovered fault underneath the dam. All citizens along the Yangzi river corridor are advised to seek high ground or their shelter sphere site immediately…" Pictures from a helicopter showed a muddy froth rushing through a small city. A tall building fell softly into the foam and vanished. It was almost exactly like when he stacked his tiles too high.

His grandmother was on the phone. Her shouts echoed through the edges of his hard-won clarity. "Yes, I'll bring your useless brat. You just make sure my son gets there safely. Do you understand?" She slammed the receiver down and marched into the room, brandishing a broomstick. "Get up!" she said, banging the end into his shoulder. "I said get up! We need to run! The water's coming! Get up!" She pushed him hard enough with the handle that his other shoulder touched the tiles. When they fell in a rush, his clarity shattered. The storm inside his head consumed him.

They stood in front of a door, not one he'd ever seen before. It was dark, gray, made of solid metal. The frantic running and shouting and all the people and the pushes against the improvised armor of the hard cases his grandmother hung around his neck were flashes in his memory.

When he examined the control panel next to the door, all at once, for the first time ever in his life, everything went completely clear.

It was glorious.

Thinking. This was how normal people thought.

They were in a metal corridor that butted up against a gray sphere taller than his grandmother's house. Father pounded on a door in its side.

"You have to come out, Weng! You have the keys! We can't open the doors without the keys!"

As long as he stared at the thousands of controls on the board, his mind stayed clear. It was obvious now. Qiáng Shān walked up and reconfigured the board. With the press of a button, he unlocked all the doors. Throughout the complex there were shouts of relief as the doors slammed open, allowing the thousands crowded around outside into the building and the rescue pods within.

His family was here with him. They were frightened.

"Qiáng Shān," his grandmother said, "get away from that."

"I have to let the people into the building," he replied. "Otherwise they can't reach the pods." Silence swelled as he pushed the last of the buttons. There was a definite rumbling outside now, and a wet sulfur smell filled the rising breeze. Qiáng Shān couldn't understand why the rest of them stopped talking. He turned around.

His father, mother, and grandmother stared at him. His mother was crying. "What did you say?"

It wasn't that big of a deal. "He had the whole complex locked down, Mother." It was so obvious. "I've let them in, but I'm not sure how to unlock the spheres." More pieces of his life fell into place. It might all go away, but for now Qiáng Shān rolled with it. His parents were important government officials. The provincial governor was inside the sphere.

His grandmother chuckled, a dark smoke-scarred sound Qiáng Shān was very used to. "Well I'll be damned. We've got seconds left to live, and the little shit chooses now to talk."

Qiáng Shān's parents immediately shouted at his grandmother and she shouted right back. They were running out of time. He ignored them, the increasingly panicked shouts echoing through the complex, and the growing rumble and rush outside. He needed to open the locks. Everyone here would die if he couldn't open the locks. They were the new kind. There was a quantum stack that powered them squatting next to the control board.

There was a kind of latch *in* the stack. He couldn't see it, not exactly. He could grasp it though, but not with his hands. Qiáng Shān reached out with his mind.

There were lines of potential, and he couldn't remember how to breathe. Waves taller shorter everywhere open grab wave open unlock find unlock this wave highest lowest collapse and now…

The thunder of water and shouts couldn't overpower the *bang* that went off in his head and left his ears ringing. It faded as sphere doors whooshed open. Qiáng Shān rushed inside with his family and strapped in. A crash shook the complex as his father slapped the button to close the door.

His grandmother swore at the provincial governor over and over again. He couldn't stop laughing, which made grandmother angrier, which made it funnier. This was clarity. He'd lived for so long wanting it, and it was still his. The sphere lurched sideways and slammed them all against their straps.

"Here we go!" Father shouted. Qiáng Shān could barely see out of the small portal as the water tore the rest of the support structures away. With another lurch their shelter sphere escaped the braces and rushed away into the flood.

***

The pain in Kong's body had spread from the wound in his belly. Everything burned now, a sure sign the injury was far worse than a deep bruise from the gear shifter.

He'd come so *close* to exposing them all. Right now a journalist waited in a village at the bottom of the valley for his evidence, for the terabytes of data he'd hidden in plain sight. The model of the fishing ship was an honorable gift made amazing with its state-of-the-art holographic projectors. His boss admired its realistic depiction of men working at sea, put it in a place of honor in his office, and then promptly forgot about it.

It sat there and gathered all the evidence Kong would need to stop them.

The flaw was in the timing. He had to catch the terrorists almost literally red-handed, otherwise his bosses would bribe, lie, and bully their way out of trouble to try it all again at a later date. He need only wait until a week before the launch date to stop it all.

Then the rains came, giving him just a day to hurriedly arrange a meeting with a stringer from the *Times*. The British newspaper was the only western news agency he trusted with something this important, and the only one with an office in Chengdu, the closest major city to headquarters. The base was far enough up in the mountains that getting the evidence to the reporter in time would be tough.

It wouldn't happen now. The rain didn't just make it easier for his bosses to drown millions of innocent people; it made it harder for him to get away with the evidence needed to stop them. The rockslide caught him completely unawares, tumbling his car off the road and down a steep ravine. In the confusion the gearshift rammed into his gut. He was sure it had impaled him, but when it all stopped there was no bleeding. There was pain, though. He could barely walk after climbing from the wreckage.

Kong still had one very slim chance. There was a monastery nearby, the first Buddhist temple to make an inroad into realmspace. If he could reach them, they might be able to transmit the information to the world and at least bring the murderous bastards to justice.

He had to keep climbing, but he also had to keep the little model and its precious data stores safe. It was heavy enough to begin with, but the weight grew as time passed. Find the monastery. All this would be for nothing if Kong died at the bottom of the ravine or, worse, was found by soldiers in a ditch.

He couldn't keep his balance, slipping more and more often on the rain-slicked road.

Suddenly the gateway of the monastery stood in front of him. Kong pounded on the door with what little strength he had left. His fever made him see shapes in the dark, ghosts, demons, things that would devour his soul. He fell through the gate when the monks opened the door.

They dried him off and gave him a warm place to rest, but it wasn't a hospital, and they weren't doctors. Kong had just enough time to get across the importance of what he carried, if not its actual contents. He was so very tired.

The darkness was vast.

***

Qiáng Shān, at first as fascinated as anyone else over his clarity and ability to speak, grew tired of his family's questions. Eventually he fell asleep.

He blinked and startled at the noises at the top of the sphere. A hatch opened, and a man with a uniform and a helmet peered in at them. A soldier. They were pretty cool. For the first time, he let a bit of hope leak through. He was still clear. Sleeping hadn't changed it. Normal. He was almost normal now.

Pink fingers of dawn traced the sky behind the soldier. They must have been very far downstream. The soldier commanded them to exit the sphere.

"Please," Mother said, "my son has a disability. He can't be touched. May we go last?"

In spite of all that'd happened, he still couldn't get close to her, or anyone else.

The soldier nodded grimly. "You must not delay."

The bright flash of the pod's emergency beacon reflected off the soldier's uniform, turning it from dark green to brilliant red. It was a lucky color, at least for the survivors. The same flashing lights were everywhere. There were thousands of spheres, maybe tens of thousands, scattered across the water, an upside-down sky full of blinking red stars. Helicopters thumped and hissed as they circled above. The machines didn't frighten him anymore; they were marvelous. Then he looked at the sea.

All around him sad dolls floated facedown, arms flung wide. It reminded him of twigs and grass on water. His confused memories were slowly making sense. The wind had blown grass against the shore of a lake in the middle of a park back home.

They were all so very still. The grownups behind him sobbed. The soldier did, too. It was so unusual. The dead were strangers, yet the living mourned them.

He tried to find that place but couldn't. Maybe it was just too soon.

Chapter 1
Mike

Twenty years from now

May 9, Dulles Airport, 9:00 a.m.

He'd wasted yet another week giving Kim one more chance, one more opportunity to show a nod at affection. The effort was totally wasted. She hadn't tried.She shouted Russian into her comm set as dirt and rocks rained down. "Repeat, our laser designator is in-op, I need that unit taken out *now*! Use the maps, damn you!"

Mike scuffed his feet across the dusty white floor of the baggage terminal. He refused to pause by the seat she was in. The silence around her was a solid, icy thing. Good. Maybe it would freeze her to death and free them both.

A toddler raced out of nowhere right in front of him and bounced off his legs. "Whoa there, kiddo," he said as he caught the boy. "You need to slow down." He handed the child to his smiling parents. Children were such a strange combination of soft, hard, light, and heavy. And of course all living mammals were warm to the touch, something Mike had only understood on an intellectual level before he came outside into realspace.

Kim stiffened, and he barely fought off a smile. She took offense at everything he did nowadays but at least this time he both understood and enjoyed it when it happened. She couldn't touch people, and he could.

It was exhausting being this mean to each other. Maybe being tired would work; nothing else had.

Mike flopped heavily into the chair opposite hers. "Goddamn it, Kim. I said I was sorry." He leaned toward her as she looked away. "I'm still not used to hormones. She was just a checkout girl."

Kim speared him with a look, her foot tapping away fiercely. "You touched her."

The accusation was ridiculous on so many levels, and nearly the same every time. "She was handing me the receipt. *She* touched *me*." He tried to regain some sort of control. Mike used to shrug it off, but that just made her angrier. It would lead to another shouting match and they were in public now. Probably by design.

"I'm not doing this again." He stood and relaxed the bindings that held his consciousness to his realspace body. As he walked away he expanded into the realms surrounding the airport. Being the world's first human-AI hybrid at least gave him that escape. His threads blasted so much emotion into the local realmspace it rattled the airport's AIs, making them stutter as they interacted with the people around them. Just as he was about to cast his perception out of the area entirely, Spencer walked out of the terminal's exit.

What a difference four months made with humans. Well, teenaged humans, at any rate. The head caught in his bear hug was much higher than it had been before. Spencer's voice was also at least an octave lower. "Fuck, Mike, God, I'm glad to be here."

"Me too, Spence, me too."

They opened their embrace, and there was Kim with a smile that could outshine the sun.

He couldn't trust her mood, though. He knew that.

"Spencer. How was your flight?"

"It was fine." He stood up straight, now exactly her height. Kim rocked back for just a second, and then glanced at Mike, a slight smile forming.

He looked away.

Spencer cleared his throat, straightened his shirt, and then held his hand palm up in front of her.

She chuckled and looked at the floor. "It's not that big of a deal, Spencer."

"It is to me," he said, his voice stumbling just a bit at the end.

She sighed and then put her palm up, not quite touching his, and then their hands described a half circle. An eyebrow shot up when they were done. "You're here to work, not goof off."

"God, Kim, I know." The baggage carousel behind them squawked. "I bought an air mattress that'll fit perfectly in Mike's…" he stumbled to a stop, looking at them both.

It probably was that obvious, but Mike couldn't break the news here. "That's great, Spence!"

Spencer rolled his eyes. "Now what's wrong?"

Kim gestured at the carousel. "Come on, let's get your bag."

The silence dragged on. Their fight was still too fresh. He'd explain it all to Spencer when they were back at the hotel.

"Remember," Kim said sharply on the Metro platform just outside the airport, "you two need to be ready by one. Do not," she pointed. They flinched. "Be late."

Mike flashed back to a previous time, a different place, a hallway in a hotel when he didn't know how to talk to her, when she'd said those exact same words. Back when she'd been so fascinating, a completely unexpected person, pushy, vulnerable, smart, funny.

Too bad it hadn't lasted.

Spencer's laugh broke the tension. "Oh shit, Kim, you have no idea how much I've missed all this."

Kim grinned as she sheepishly pulled her finger back into her fist. "Yeah, okay." She looked up at Mike. He desperately wanted to trust her again, trust that she wouldn't find another new fault, another new mistake, and then cut him to the core just to prove she could.

But he wouldn't do that. There would be no more second chances.

Kim shook her head. "Christ, all your best clothes are still at our…" She stopped and then tried again. "*My* house."

Spencer blinked and stared at him.

Mike nodded. This still wasn't the place to explain. "I was going to pick it all up later..." He couldn't finish the thought.

He was leaving her. Had left her. Repeating it made it real. He had to make it real.

Spencer jumped into the gap. "Hey, Kim. I have a real driver's license now."

"And that's supposed to mean?"

"I can drive halfway across the country legally!"

He'd called Spencer the night he decided to take that last step, to stop being just a virtual person living in realmspace and become something more, an AI-human hybrid that lived in the realms but also owned a realspace body. He'd done that to make sure Kim was safe.

He *still* needed to keep her safe. It was something he'd have to learn to forget.

He'd have to forget caring about her.

The subway pulled into the station with the strange shrilling sound it always made. Emergent sound, noises that happened just because, were another thing that probably would always fascinate him about realspace. In the realms, where most of his consciousness lived, everything happened by design. Well, except for him.

The doors opened but nobody moved.

He'd give her one last chance, for Spencer's sake. One more foolish try. Maybe now that Spencer was here it would force her to be nice.

"Oh, come on," Kim sighed as she turned toward the exit. She looked at Spencer. "But if you think for a second I'm going to let you drive..."

Chapter 2
Kim

She concentrated on the image in the mirror as she carefully reapplied her eyeliner. It was even money whether having Mike and Spencer in the main room was going to drive her nuts or keep her mind off her building panic. "*Yasa*."

"*Yasa*," two tired voices said in unison, echoing into her bathroom. "Hello."

"*Andio*," Kim said as she continued working on her makeup.

"*Andio*," they replied. "Goodbye."

"How do I ask for a beer in Greek?" Spencer shouted.

"*Thelo ena byra*," she called back. "But don't worry, Uncle Kostas always brings kegs to these things. He loves playing bartender. You won't need to ask more than once." She straightened, pulled her face down, and then scrunched it back up in the mirror. "And don't be an idiot about it. You're old enough in my family's book, but if you get them in trouble for contributing, there will be hell to pay." Drinking laws were more suggestions than commandments in her family. Especially around Uncle Kostas.

She hadn't seen any of them in years. Half of that time had been spent hiding from Bolivians, feds, and well, most of the world. Back then she was Angel Rage, the legendary cyber-thief driven underground by a drug cartel that eventually killed the rest of the people who made up Rage + The Machine. Kim only survived by luck and her wits.

But there was no reason to hide anymore. The Bolivians' vendetta was over. The information she'd stolen from Matthew Watchtell, a megalomaniac who'd once been the White House Chief of Staff, had seen to that.

Kim gripped the corner of the countertop tightly. Just thinking his name made the terror, the *pain,* come back in a rush. He'd stripped her half naked, and then tortured her in front of Mike…

Kim stopped and waited for her breathing to go back to normal. Forced physical contact to the point of permanent injury happened to women all the time. They survived it, and so would she. It wasn't actual sex, although that had probably been on the way if the FBI hadn't freed Mike and Tonya to stop Watchtell. It didn't make much of a difference as far as she was concerned. He'd taken something from her, something she never gave anyone, couldn't give anyone. A simple touch. And he did it over and over and over.

It was a gift that kept on giving. The few occasions she'd decided that *this* time she'd make Mike happy for real, *this* time she'd pull him into a realm and at least give him a good show, the memories would come rushing back and ruin it all. Kim couldn't explain why, to herself or Mike.

The anger, the constant need to lash out at someone, something, was harder to control than the shame. Maybe having Spencer as a roommate would help her finally get a handle on it and stop using Mike as a punching bag.

She would have the time now. She had a full pardon, and that evil bastard would be in prison for the rest of his life.

The world had quickly moved on from the has-been hacker and her rich tormentor. She could now walk freely, forgotten and anonymous. Her family, though, was another story.

Every single one of them would be at this lunch party. It would not surprise her at all if Kim's *yiayiá,* her grandmother, managed to fly all the way from Athens. It would mean an additional aunt, because wherever Yiayiá went, Aunt Voleta was required to follow.

Yiayiá didn't do well with authorities, and security procedures were things that happened to other people. Aunt Voleta would make sure she didn't assault any hapless TSA agents.

"*Katalaveno,*" Kim said, discarding her third outfit choice.

"Katalaveno," they replied, "I understand."

"Kim," Mike called out, "I thought you said we had to be ready by one?"

"You did," she called back. The pale-blue blouse should work, especially with the slacks she'd found at ninety percent off last week. They were sweet. "I didn't. We'd show up too early if we were a half hour late. *Dhen katalaveno.*"

"Dhen katalaveno. I don't understand."

"And I don't understand," Spencer said. "How do you expect us to remember all this?"

She buckled the thin belt around her waist, then smoothed her clothes, checking it all out in her bedroom mirror. "I don't. You're supposed to be helping NeuroTrans pick up on the words. You both knew that, right?" The silence from the main room extended. *Yeah, thought so.*

"NeuroTrans," Mike coughed out, "right. Yasa. Hello."

Tonya hadn't gotten the word about arriving late either, so Kim had to help her deal with three dozen boisterous Greek strangers via remote while Mike drove. Tonya lived in Maryland, so she'd traveled to Arlington on her own.

"How many cousins do you *have,* Kim?" she asked over their private line.

"I told you not to let them know you were single." The extended Athanasiadis clan was modern enough to recognize the value of a young, successful, intelligent, and most importantly single adult woman, no matter how dark her skin was. "Just enjoy the attention. But go easy on the ouzo."

"They keep handing it to me! I think your uncle Kostas started two hours ago. How do you all stay alive drinking this much?"

Kim had forgotten just how Greek her family actually was. "Practice, Tonya, lots of practice."

Tonya gulped and gasped. After a quick cough she asked, "Where are you?"

The car gently stopped. When she looked up, her heart almost did the same thing. "We're here." She ended the call.

The low, ranch-style house hadn't changed a bit since she last saw it. Hadn't changed a bit for as long as she could remember. It was set on the back of an old cul-de-sac in a quiet, shaded neighborhood in Arlington, Virginia. The street was full of cars, many with out-of-state license plates, so many Mike had to park a block away. The decorations in the yard extended over to the garden lot next door.

Mike asked, "Are you okay, Kim?"

There were so many of them, and she'd been away for so long. "I can't hide forever." *No matter how much I want to.*

Aunt Rea was in charge of the minigolf course set up around the house. She efficiently herded a dozen children through hole nine as Kim slowly walked forward. Her aunt looked up and their eyes locked.

Here we go.

"Kim's here, everyone! She's here!" Aunt Rea then shouted it out again in English. The children broke into a run, and Mike stepped in front of her.

"Stop!" Kim hadn't heard that powerful voice in so long, but there was no mistaking it. The older children put the brakes on quickly. A few even stumbled. They grabbed any younger ones who didn't hear the command.

In the silence that fell, Malinda Trayne, the most commanding, endearing, lovely woman Kim would ever know, walked around the corner of the house.

She'd grown a bit grayer since Kim had last seen her, and perhaps she had put on a few pounds, but her stride was just as confident and her eyes were still as gorgeous, now filled to overflowing.

It was hard for Kim to get her legs to move, but once she did there was no stopping.

A shell she'd long forgotten about shattered in an instant while she ran, arms wide. They both fell to their knees on the grass just inches apart, arms held high. Sobbing, their hands nearly touched as Kim held her head just over her mother's shoulder, relishing the smell of her perfume. It had been so very long since she'd been this close.

"You will never do this to me again for as long as you live," Mama choked out as their arms slowly moved down together.

"I will never do this to you again for as long as I live," Kim whispered as she put her hands in her lap. Suddenly the sun was blocked. Her family, standing shoulder to shoulder in a wide circle, all grinning like loons, surrounded them. Her mom stared over Kim's shoulder with her mouth half open. Kim turned around.

Switching to English she said, "Mama, this is Mike."

Her entire family bellowed out his name, and then dragged him in to the party. The look on his face would've made the trip worth it all by itself. He'd learned everything he could about Greek families, but texts, pictures, and movies never prepared strangers for the real thing.

The rest of the day went by in a blur of shouted reunions and waving hands. The weather was pleasant at first, but the temperature spiked as the day wore on. It could get very hot in the back yard, even in the shade. An old chair was still parked under a tree. Kim sat down and closed her eyes. She'd done it. She was here. She hadn't slept well the night before for a bunch of reasons, and the chair was very comfortable.

"Aunt Malinda told us we couldn't touch you," a young voice said, startling her out of her brief nap. One of a seemingly endless supply of young cousins now stood beside her. "Is that why you need the funny chairs?"

Wide and high-backed, they had custom armrests with shields on the sides. Her dad designed them for her when she was a child. He'd been gone for so long now. "Yes, what my mom told you is true. It hurts very much when people touch me."

He cocked his head. "Why?"

She thought back to a black hand, *her* hand, traced with strange, dark patterns as it blasted lightning into a world that could not exist.

"Aunt Kim?"

She cleared her throat and turned back to the little boy. "Nobody knows why I can't be touched."

"Will you get better?"

Admitting the truth still hurt. "No, I won't get better."

"Can you play darts?"

The little stinker had a motive behind this chat. "Yes, I can play darts. Do you need a partner?" He nodded and ran toward the sign-up sheets mounted on a back wall of the house.

They won three times. Kim taught her cousin how to high-five without touching, which he thought was the coolest thing in the world.

She jumped and spun around when Uncle Kostas came stomping up, laughing. Mike was on his arm, wobbling just a little.

"Kim!" he shouted in heavily accented English. "Your boyfriend is most amusing!"

The reality of their situation crashed in again. He wasn't hers and never would be. It had gone so wrong and she was so helpless. "He's not my boyfriend."

Uncle Kostas bawled out gales of laughter. "No, Kim, that is not what I am talking about. You know English better than me. What does this mean, *hybrid AI?*"

Mike could be *such* a screw up. "You said you wouldn't talk about it."

"It got too hard to keep straight. It doesn't matter, Kim." He shrugged. "Nobody believes me."

Her uncle laughed more. "This *trelos* says he didn't have a body six months ago. His stories, they are wonderful!"

Mike really had just been an entity in the realms six months ago, hidden and unknown to all but a very few. It took weeks of careful exploring to find a lawyer that'd talk about his legal status now that he had a body. He owned a *very* valuable realm, but they hadn't worked out how to prove that yet.

Uncle Kostas expected a reply, but all she wanted to do was shout at Mike about the ridiculous risks he thought nothing of taking. The call to dinner rescued him.

Spencer sat next to three baskets of vegetables, a victim of her mother's eternal quest to give away the garden's produce. Tonya sat at the table across from Kim. It was no surprise to see she'd settled with a particularly choice example of one of her older cousins.

"He's gorgeous," she mouthed at Kim after he'd gotten up to refresh their drinks. "My *God*!"

Kim winked and nodded.

"So, Mike," Uncle Kostas shouted, "when will you turn our Kim into the honest woman?"

Her mother shook her head. "I don't think I approve of this idea. I did not come to America just to see my daughter…lower her expectations."

Even knowing it would happen eventually, the comment still surprised her. "Mother, I am not *lowering my expectations*." They didn't understand what was going on. Admitting they had broken up nearly choked her. "We're not together like that."

Anymore.

"For now," her uncle scoffed, and then laughed at her. "Oh, I have seen the way you two look at each other. You watch out, Malinda. I think you will need to be bringing that wedding dress of yours out of storage before too long."

Mama switched to Greek. "Over my dead body will my daughter settle for the first unworthy—"

"Mother, could you be a bigger stereotype? I am a grown woman, and who I choose—"

Her uncle stood up. "Choose? *Choose?* I can't believe either of you! This one," he waved an arm at Mama, "flies away with an American, and now this one—"

"Flies away?" Mama's chair crashed backward as she stood. "The economy was in ashes, and the love of my life offers to bring us all here, and the way you remember him is—"

"That is enough!"

Yiayiá always knew how to make an entrance.

The entire party zipped silent as grandma Maria stood. She switched to English. "Our Kim has returned to us, returned to us when we thought she was lost. Dead, even. For years I have been unable to speak to my granddaughter. Our own flesh and blood, our own family, vanished. She has returned. We will celebrate this. She has wonderful friends. We will celebrate them." She lifted her wine glass high. "We will celebrate them!" The toast echoed through the back yard.

Kim even missed the way her family could go from nearly pulling knives on each other to laughing until they cried. It was home. This was home, and she was here without fear, without a need to hide. She smiled at Mike, but he looked away again.

Fix one part, ruin another. Par for the course.

The party rolled on into the night. Kim dozed off in a corner of the yard, surrounded by a dozen old timers grousing about the Greece of twenty years ago.

A familiar voice made her sit up and look around. Tonya repeated whatever it was she said, but Kim could only shake her head.

Tonya snapped her fingers. "English, dear. You with me?"

Right. It took a bit to switch language gears after listening to a different one for the past hour.

"I have to go. Are you gonna be okay tonight?"

"Pretty sure." Kim groaned and stood up. "Have you seen Mike?"

"He was with your uncle last time I saw him, but it's been awhile."

Kim found him sitting alone, swirling his finger in a drink under a porch light on the back deck.

He was leaving her.

She wanted to talk but was desperately afraid of what he might say, that he might be glad to go.

He *should* be glad to go.

He'd stayed by her side in the hospital after she'd *lost* the fight against what Watchtell had done. He'd held off her mom, somehow knowing that she was the absolute last thing Kim needed. And he'd been right. It must've been like standing against a hurricane. No wonder Mama didn't like him.

Being here, surrounded by all this, finally allowed her to admit the truth. Kim sat down across from him and the words came out in a rush. "I've been a really nasty bitch to you these past six months, haven't I?"

"I've made a lot of mistakes too, Kim—"

"No, Mike. You've tried too hard. You've tried too hard and I've taken advantage of it, every single time. I have been heartless and nasty to you, and I want to stop." He'd left her, and she deserved it, but he was still here and that meant there might be another chance. "I want to stop."

The edge of his sleeve brushed against her hand. "I want to help."

It was time to ask a question she didn't want answered. "You didn't rent an apartment, did you?"

He shook his head and turned away. "No. It's a hotel room."

It was what she deserved. "You're going to leave. Not down the block, but far away." *Away from me.*

"Orlando, after Spencer goes home. Disney wants me to lead their realm division. I was going to tell you after he'd left."

"If I try…"

No. Trying wouldn't work. He was moving to Orlando, for God's sake.

"If I *stop,* will you stay?"

Mike was still for a very long time. And he could be so very still, fading in a way that let him hide in plain sight. It was a no that she deserved.

He nodded.

It was such a fragile moment. Saying anything might be saying the wrong thing, but silence was just as bad. Kim settled on a simple truth. She had to start somewhere.

"Mike? Tomorrow, when we leave here? I want you to come home. I want you to stay."

*

Mama thought curtains turned rooms into caves, and Kim had been too tired to check them before she went to bed. Now the dawn light was so intense she could probably get asunburn. Kim checked the time. Late five in the morning was still five in the morning.

She quietly padded her way toward the kitchen. The faint hiss of the air conditioner vents masked the sound of soft conversation until she was just a few feet from the doorway. She recognized Mike's voice, and then her mother's. Kim's zombie-like need for coffee vanished.

"No, I'm not telepathic," he said, "and I can't manipulate people. It's strange how much my mind works like yours. You'd think I'd be different, but I'm not. Well, not in the ways you'd expect."

"And you have been walking among us for only four months?"

"Six. It's a heck of a story."

Kim smirked as he retold it. How he ended up in the body of a dead assassin, one who was literally moments away from killing her, sounded a lot neater now. Living it, especially the bit with the fire extinguisher, had been a different story.

"But this is remarkable. A miracle! Why aren't you in the newspapers?"

"People don't believe me. Especially now that I have this body. They either think it's a joke or don't understand what I'm saying. Last night was no different. Uncle Kostas took me around to everyone and they just kept shouting *gia sas* at me."

"It means *to your health.*" There was a long pause, and then Mama chuckled. "It's just as well you've taken my advice, then."

Oh no. Whenever her mom advised anyone, it never went well.

He blew out a breath. "I know, you're right. She's just too good for me. I'll pack my things and—"

They'd just started to patch things up. "Mother, how *dare* you!" Kim spun around the corner only to be met with two grins.

They'd coordinated a trap. Kim thought by now she knew all of her mother's moves. Wrong again. So much for Mama not liking him, which wasn't a surprise either. Mike had never really met a stranger the entire time she'd known him. A smile, some funny conversation, and whoever it was had always been his friend. He was her exact opposite that way.

Mama laughed as she slapped the table. Mike mouthed "buttons," gesturing at his chest. Great. Of all the times to button a pajama top wrong.

"Very funny." She headed for the coffee pot. After some furious re-buttoning she sat down with them and assembled her coffee.

"You never told me he was from China," Mama said.

Kim looked up at him. How much had he told her?

He winked.

After what *that man* did to her, and then Kim's... transformation...and that final attack, the only way to escape from the agony was to die. And so in that moment she did. He'd somehow caught her as she fell. He said he'd learned how to do that from...

"You told her about Taranathi?"

"Remarkable," Mama said. "Such a miraculous man, and raised by a Buddhist!"

Mike shrugged. "It's more complicated than that, Malinda. Taranathi was a mentor. He rescued me, taught me how to live, but he wasn't my father. The monks were just good friends."

"Nonsense. And you haven't seen them in how long?"

"More than a decade. The Chinese government put up some sort of new firewall back then, and I haven't seen them since."

Kim thought she already knew the rules. "You mean there *is* a place in realmspace you can't reach?"

"It's called the Great Firewall for a reason. It's not like any other sort of security I've ever found. I've split myself as far as I can, but I can't push through it."

"Split yourself?" Malinda asked.

This part Kim understood. Sort of. "That really is where he's different. He can be in more than one place at once in the realms." Early on, after she'd gotten out of the hospital, he had trouble keeping conversations straight. Sometimes he'd say funny things, nice things, smiling and laughing, and then she'd realize he wasn't talking to her. It led to some epic fights.

She boiled just thinking about it, but then Kim stopped and put her anger aside. It was a revelation, probably the very first time ever she didn't let her temper roll over the whole conversation. Kim smiled at Mike, and this time he didn't turn away.

Mama had asked a question. "He can get into any realm, no matter how secure. Well, I thought it was any realm. What's so different?"

"It's hard to explain. Maybe if I got behind it in China it would be different."

"There." Malinda slapped the table again. "That's what you should do next." She looked at them both. "Oh, I know what's going on with you two."

For the first time, Kim allowed herself the slightest hope people might be right, that she and Mike really might have a future.

Mama got up to refresh her mug. "Your family lives in a monastery in China? Yes? You must go to the monastery in China. Nothing is more important than family. Nothing."

He glanced at Kim, but it had to be his call.

"Well, I have been negotiating with some big Chinese realmspace companies. They've wanted to license Warhawk for a while now. I hadn't thought about it much until recently."

His unique perspective on realmspace made him one of the most skilled realm designers in the world. Warhawk, a combat realm he'd designed in his spare time, was the gold standard for realism. Discreet inquiries to lawyers—always hypothetical—all said the same thing: the more deals he made as a real person, the firmer his legal position as owner would become.

He nodded once. "I guess after the tournament we can start planning a trip."

Kim almost dropped her mug. "Oh my God, I completely forgot." She leaped up and headed back to her bedroom. She had to report to the team's access hall by ten.

Her mother called back, "What tournament?"

Kim skidded to a stop. "The next step of my rehabilitation, Mama. I'm competing in a realm tournament. The Cup is over but the World Championships are here. I don't have to hide this time. I'm going to win."

To Mike she said, "And after I do, I think we're going to China."

Chapter 3
Fang Hua

Chengdu, China

She waited in realmspace for Sergeant Pei to introduce her. It was only the second time Father had trusted her to organize an entire police operation, so it was important that this was more successful than all of her previous assignments. Fang Hua had proper holo projectors delivered directly from Beijing to make sure of it. That was a good call, because the precinct had none. They needed to think of her as a professional cop remoting in from a distant location, and that meant a high-quality projected image.

"Officers," Sergeant Pei began. "The terrorist mob Strength of Nine is going to attack again. Tonight." A map of the city was projected next to the sergeant. Red spots marking earlier public defacements popped to life, each an affront to order. "Detective Zhang Fang Hua has found conclusive evidence of the next series of targets. Ms. Zhang, if you would?"

Fang Hua manifested her hologram on the opposite side of the map, then straightened her uniform. "The troublemakers plan on striking in nine places, simultaneously." Blue dots appeared over the targets. "There will be tactical teams deployed to each site."

"Why do we need some incompetent bitch to tell us what to do?" Detective Chen whispered to the man sitting next to him.

The problem with having ears everywhere was hearing everything, especially the way the laughter rippled away from

Detective Chen. There could be no questioning of her authority on this mission. Fang Hua continued the briefing and split some of her threads away.

"You think I'm a bitch?" she asked him on a private channel.

To the room she said, "Our units will start here, here, and here." She set green markers for their starting positions.

"You don't know bitch." Other threads of her consciousness raced through his private identity records. *"Because now you're my bitch."*

To the room, "Strength of Nine hasn't been known to be violent, not yet anyway."

"And when Big Circles finds out you've been feeding information to the Pony Triad? Well, look at that, they already have!"

Her briefing crashed to a stop when Detective Chen jumped to his feet. Fang Hua asked out loud, "Is there anything wrong, detective?"

He made a few strangled noises. Cowards always lost their ability to speak in times like this. On his private channel she said, *"Your family will be wards of the state, you arrogant idiot. I'll shit on your name."*

It was sad, really, but required. The records showed he was a political flunky, more interested in advancing his career than catching troublemakers.

The useless excuse for a detective gasped, clutched at his chest frantically, then collapsed. The men around him, the ones who'd laughed, needed to take her seriously. They looked at her hologram, and then at the detective.

"My goodness. Don't worry; I've called emergency services. There's a unit just down the hall."

To the detectives around him she sent, on their most secure personal channels, *"If you do not help me, you will pay."*

They moved aside when the paramedics arrived. Nobody said a word.

The EMTs shocked the man's heart back to normal, and then carried him away. After they left, Sergeant Pei said, "Please, Detective Zhang, continue."

Fang Hua had to keep up appearances, and so she cleared a throat she didn't really have. "Yes, well, we have them. And working together, we will stop them. They have been an embarrassment to this city for too long, and tonight *you* will arrest them. The central government has decreed that the leaders of successful squads will each be given the deed to a high-rise penthouse in New Shanghai."

The room erupted. They still loved property below Three Gorges no matter what had happened before. "Sergeant," she nodded her hologram to him.

Sectors were assigned and roles agreed on. The sergeant broke the meeting up. He switched to English and said, "Let's be careful out there."

Fang Hua could not believe it. A line from an old American TV show. Corrupting Western influences always jumped out at her when she least expected them.

After the room cleared, she smiled at the one man who remained seated at the back. "I'm very glad to be able to speak to you again, Ji Cong."

He gestured to the seat next to him. "You can speak to me any time you want, Fang Hua. Anywhere you want, too. And yet you wait until you have a reason to actually *be* here."

She manifested her hologram in the chair he'd offered. Visiting wasn't that easy, but he'd never accepted that. "I only use official channels."

He snorted.

"No," she said, "I must only use official government channels. Father would take an interest if he couldn't find me, and you would not withstand that scrutiny, *comrade.*"

Ji Cong sighed and nodded.

They'd discovered each other in a test-cramming realm sponsored by the People's Armed Police Force Academy. It was a random pairing to help cope with a week's worth of sixteen hour days studying brutally boring regulation books. For some reason she and Ji Cong just clicked. On the third day he came out to her, the first gay Chinese she'd ever known. It took Fang Hua one more day to work up the nerve to come out to him. His was by far the braver revelation. Being a virtual person, one who lived only in realmspace, might've been a secret, but it wasn't illegal.

A ring on his finger was the last thing she expected to see. "You got married?"

"Mother was driving me mad. 'What sort of son has a job and no family?' Grandmother was worse."

"What did Shi Yi say?" He'd been in a long-term relationship well before she'd met him.

He threw a lopsided grin at her. "My new wife says he took it better than *her* lover did. But then her lover married Shi Yi. Now everyone's covered." His smile grew wider. "We're expecting a son around New Year's."

He'd once told her the last thing he ever wanted to see was a naked woman. Humans were such contradictions. "You mean you…"

"No, no. Fertility clinics, dear."

Last time she checked, people did that sort of thing in brothels, not clinics.

He laughed. "How can you be so smart about police work but so dumb about such things?"

Human reproduction was hardly a priority for her. There would never be children in her future.

He became serious. "I'm sorry; sometimes I forget how different you are."

She saw his partner Xun Hé walking down the hall through a different monitor. If anyone, especially his police partner, found out she and Ji Cong had anything other than a professional relationship, it would be complicated. Fang Hua vanished.

"Ji Cong!" Xun Hé shouted, standing at the doorway. "Come on! Let's go catch some hooligans!"

They needed to coordinate assaults in nine different places in the southeast quadrant of the city, which was why Father assigned her the job. She could be in many different places at once, replacing three or four coordinators, significantly reducing the risk of a mistake that would ruin the operation. She split her threads and talked to the teams while they moved into position.

"Team Four, you need to adjust south."

"Team Seven, watch out, trash truck moving near your posit."

"Team One, mind the sightlines. Cameras on the west side of the roof are close to spotting you."

Ji Cong's team stopped outside an abandoned factory complex. He asked, "Why is this building so far south of everyone else?"

"I'm not sure," Fang Hua replied. "The codes match. They've definitely got the same sort of supplies the other teams have. Well, most of the same supplies, anyway. The radio chatter originating here started up before the rest of the sites. I think it's the lead cell, which is why your team is here. Only the best..."

"To catch the best," Xun Hé, replied. "New Shanghai condo, here I come!"

Xun Hé signaled the team in the van behind them. Everyone paired off, and then spread out around the complex.

Breaching the fences was quick work. Unfortunately the criminals had disabled the sensor nets inside the central factory, so she could follow Ji Cong's team in but couldn't tell what was inside.

Fang Hua used the optic feeds from everyone's phone cameras to monitor their progress. Ji Cong flattened himself against a utility shed and peered around the corner into the night. Streetlights splashed brilliant circles everywhere, but what they didn't touch was in utter blackness. He activated the infrared extensions in his phone, allowing them both to see into shadows. Still nobody around.

They sprinted to the next building. "I don't get it." Xun Hé said. "Where are the guards? The sentries? Are we too late?"

"No," Fang Hua replied. Keeping an eye on all the other teams made her sound less engaged here, so she concentrated harder on Xun Hé's question. "I've been watching all the sites for about a week now. They're supposed to leave for their targets in thirty minutes. Unless they've dug tunnels, they're in there." Her intel indicated no more than six men would be inside, well within the capabilities of a squad this size.

They got into position against a side door of the main factory. "I still don't like this," Xun Hé whispered.

Ji Cong shook his head. "You're always so paranoid. Fang Hua, if you'd do the honors of counting us down?"

This was the part that always made her threads race. The knife edge of success. "Three…two…one…" All the men on Ji Cong's team, as well as all the teams across the city, rushed into their targets together.

One second in, without so much as a sound, the threads she used to monitor one of the other teams snapped away from their anchors and she lost all contact with them.

"Ji Cong," she said, trying to regain contact, "there's something wrong." Two more teams vanished. Her threads stung as they raced back into her core. Teams four and six disappeared. Whatever happened had cut all contact from five teams in a matter of seconds. "Ji Cong! Stop!"

They skidded to a halt just after they rounded a corner, finally reaching the main floor of the warehouse. Fang Hua was pushed away, popped off like she'd been unplugged. It was unacceptable. She abandoned the rest of the teams and used all her power to smash through the strange realmspace wall that formed around their immediate area.

Piles of communications gear and stacks of quantum computers that nearly reached the ceiling filled the center of the room. A swarthy man, not at all Asian, threw his hands in the air. "Gentlemen," he said in heavily accented Mandarin, "thank you for helping us start our glorious project!"

Weapons drawn, Ji Cong and Xun Hé shouted at him to get on the ground.

Power rushed in toward a machine behind the gear. The quantum stacks helped it.

Helped it power up.

"Ji Cong, we need to get out of here." They ignored her and handcuffed the hideously laughing man. "Ji Cong!"

They had to listen. It got stronger, and they wouldn't listen.

It came to life with strobing strange lights that colored Ji Cong and Xun Hé in blood red flashes, hissing as some kind of gas jetted out. Scanners in their phones said it wasn't poison; it was hydrocarbons.

Fuel.

"Ji Cong, run!"

Finally he seemed to hear her. "Fang Hua! What's going—"

A square kilometer of her consciousness vanished, sending her core bouncing through the local nets, scrambling her senses. She righted herself and sought an outlet, some way to see what had happened. That quarter of Chengdu had been cast into absolute darkness, a wall of nonexistence.

Fang Hua raced her perception to the top of West Pearl Tower to access the south-facing cameras. The fireballs still billowed into the sky, ugly orange-and-dirt mushroom clouds. The smokestacks of the factory Ji Cong and Xun Hé were in collapsed, brick trees felled by the explosion.

A deadly madness that she hadn't encountered since she'd first learned how to talk wrapped around her and tore her apart. Clawing infinity spread her threads further and further apart. Fang Hua had no center, and without a center there was nothing to bring the threads back in.

Death. So be it.

Something summoned her. She coalesced slowly, congealing as news reports heard from somewhere flowed in.

"The largest non-nuclear explosion ever recorded in China represents an unprecedented escalation of violence. Strength of Nine is vehemently denying any responsibility…"

The assault, the explosion, those collapsing smokestacks. The memories hit her core, and she almost flew apart again. The news story said nobody survived. They were still pulling bodies out. It was her fault. She should've seen it coming, should've been more careful, taken more steps to ensure their safety.

It was her fault. They should've lived, not her.

"Daughter!" the Premier of the Communist Party of China commanded, "I demand you to report, at once!" It was the focus she needed. The focus she always needed. It called her back from the abyss. Fang Hua manifested her hologram in his office, now full of technicians and hastily wired computers. "Father," she bowed with difficulty.

"Daughter," he sighed. He signaled to the men in the room as he straightened his suit. They left silently. "We were very concerned about you."

All the teams were dead. So many civilians. It was her fault.

They should've lived.

"I am here, Father."

He nodded as the last of the technicians left and the door closed. "I'm very pleased that you have returned to us. You've never vanished like that before."

Explosions couldn't kill her, but madness could. It could dissolve her into nothingness. That's what the loss had done to her. It triggered a cascade of madness that would've extinguished her just as effectively as what had happened to Xun Hé, to Ji Cong.

She should not be alive now. She should be dead with the others. They *trusted* her. "I was not expecting a fuel air explosive."

"None of us were. It's totally unprecedented. What can you tell me about this?"

His tone promised punishment, which was to be expected. She'd failed in the most spectacular way imaginable. He'd have to place the blame somewhere; it might as well be on her head.

"I will need," she remembered Ji Cong's face, his smile, gone forever. His wife was expecting a baby whose father would never return. "I will need time to review it in full, Father, but I can tell you one thing. Strength of Nine had absolutely nothing to do with this."

Chapter 4
Kim

Her combat rig was "some assembly required." Hyperrealism was what made everyone take the World Championships seriously, so she needed help in the locker room; it was definitely not a one-woman job.

Tonya finished taping up Kim's left hand. "Why did they make your hands and feet like that?"

Realism also meant avatars adapted for exotic environments, like an empty sky with giant trees spaced miles apart. Kim rolled up her fingers until her fists looked like cinnamon rolls. The grip strength was tremendous. "The fingers and toes have to be this long, otherwise it'd be too easy to just toss me off the trunk into the smoke ring."

The lights flickered. Back in the day she'd just ignore the cheaters, but this time around Kim had something to lose.

If anything, Tonya was more pissed off about their attempts. She finished a buckle on Kim's breastplate with a yank that made Kim twist. "You'd think by now they'd stop trying to spy on us. That's, what, the fifth time?"

Mike's voice came from all around them. "Seventh, but who's counting?" His consciousness was a part of realmspace, within it somehow. He couldn't manifest the way that she, Tonya, and Spencer could, or he'd blow the whole realm to pieces.

Tonya asked, "The commentators are calling it technical problems?"

"That's what they look like to the outside world," Mike replied. "That's what they'd look like to me if Kim hadn't said anything."

Tonya finished the rear buckles of the metal gorget around Kim's neck. "Said anything?"

Kim stretched and flexed until the armor plates slotted together and she was able to move her upper body freely. "It was Spencer who warned me." She nodded down at him as he buckled her greaves on.

"It was last year," Spencer said as he sat back. "Remember when Roblington was knocked out in the seventh round? Total bullshit. Word got around about a month later that the Chinese knew about a flaw in the monitoring matrixes and used it to steal his strategies while he was in the locker room."

"Why didn't someone say something? Put out a patch?" Tonya asked as she strapped the rerebrace plate onto the upper part of Kim's left arm.

Kim tested the fit. "It's not the team doing it; it's Ozzie." He was China's number one realm champion, winning every contest he entered. When he'd been a child he'd saved an entire city from the Three Gorges earthquake, which only added to his heroic luster. Kim had been in contests with him for years. "He takes every advantage he can. All he wants is to win." She'd fought him at least a dozen times under various pseudonyms, and was forced to lose each one just to stay anonymous. No more. "I'm going to spoil his party tonight."

Spencer flopped the armored shoe of her avatar in front of him. "Jesus, Kim, how the hell do you walk in these things?"

She spread her toes wide. "They do sort of look like swim fins, don't they? Start at the ankle, and work down a segment at a time." The lights popped again.

Mike cursed. "That one hurt. Hang on a second, this has got to stop." After a few moments his voice returned. "I put a stop to that, at least."

Getting her busted for some sort of realm attack would be a wonderful way to begin the match. "Mike, don't you mess this up for me."

"No, Kim, you're fine. They'll need a different box to run their hacking realm out of, that's all."

Mike's manifestation not only destroyed realms, but also the Bbox constructs that hosted and powered them. Realms were cheap, but boxes weren't.

"Damn it, Mike," Kim said. "They'll notice that. Someone will complain."

"I don't think so. It took me this long to find them because they were hiding behind so many proxies. Bulgarians. Cheap script kiddies with an expensive toy. I'll bet they had no idea who they were working for."

Spencer and Tonya finished strapping on her weapons just as a flat, feminine voice announced, "Three minutes to round start. All combatants, please proceed to floor exits."

"Well, folks," Kim said, "that's my cue." She hugged Spencer and Tonya as best she could, trying not to pinch or poke them with the armor, and they left. Kim looked at the ceiling of the virtual locker room. "Mike, you go home now, you hear?"

He sent a picture of the den in their apartment.

Spencer had drawn a shared screen in the middle of the room, and he, Mike, and Tonya sat in front of it, waving. They even had popcorn.

"Flatvid only ma'am, I know." Then he was gone.

Kim walked down the dark corridor alone and stopped in front of a wide hexagonal door. She was on her own this time, with her own name. The stench of machine oil filled the air; her very own smell of victory.

"Sixty seconds. All combatants ready."

Kim cracked the elongated neck of her avatar. Her team had done well enough in the all-around, taking silver to China's gold, but she'd had to hold back, keep the team alive and pointed forward. Now it was the individuals. Nobody to worry about except herself, and Kim knew for a fact they'd never seen anything like what she would bring.

"All combatants: gravity reconciliation in three, two, one."

After the gravity dropped to one-third standard Kim finally balanced properly on what had been awkward and ungainly feet. Her heel was now a second knee. It made jumping much more fun.

"All combatants: proceed to air locks." Green lights twirled on the edges of the door, and then it split open at the middle. She stepped inside the white room. It wouldn't be long now.

"All combatants: thirty seconds. Pressure equalization in three, two, one."

Her ears popped and her chest properly filled against the inner padding of her armor. The gas torus the Smoke Knight's realm simulated was less dense than the ambient pressure simulated in the locker rooms.

"All combatants: final round begins in three…"

Lights around the outer door twirled red as claxons squawked. Kim's heart began to race. Something like fifteen different countries were out there. It was time to start cracking skulls.

"Two…"

Her throat went dry. No more hiding, no holding back. She'd had no idea how hard it was to hide until she didn't have to do it anymore.

The lights turned green.

"One."

The door slammed open, and Kim rushed out onto a horizontal tree trunk so vast it had a horizon, a world made of bark and sky. She leapt upward into branches, thinking two grabs ahead at all times.

Like the Halo series more than a generation before, an idea from Larry Niven underpinned the Smoke Knight's realm. A planet like Jupiter, a gas giant, was a balloon with no skin. The laws of physics usually made the air form a sphere, but sometimes those laws didn't quite balance. The air would stretch further and further along the orbit, first a sausage, and then a snake of gaseous dough. Eventually it would join at the ends and form a ring. In the center there would be more than enough atmosphere to support life.

Hyper-realistic realms like this were something Kim took for granted, even though others didn't see the point. They were content watching from invisible sky boxes, or flatvids like Mike was doing at home. Serious gamers like Kim wanted realism, and so did the owners. There would be no superheroes or bumbling tourists here.

Kim paused in a thick set of branches, listening. There was a flicker of movement in the corner of her eye. She moved her head just as an arrow hissed past her neck. It gave her a direction, nothing more. She had to constantly stay in motion with spins, jumps, and twirls, catching glints of the archer's armor as she got closer and closer. A final leap and she shattered the man's bow with her sword. He bounded away into the branches before she could finish him.

He wouldn't get away that easily. Kim leapt just behind him, climbing fast. A dagger spanged off her helmet as she coiled her legs, then pushed hard. The low gravity and the Coriolis effect of tree's tidal lock bent her path like a curve ball. The trunk was a brown flash in a blur of blue sky as crossbow bolts whizzed past. The brown flash grew larger, and this time Kim caught a glint of his armor again, right where she expected him to be. One last spin and then she thrust her blade forward. The feel of her sword changed as it found the gap in his neck armor. The score rang out and his avatar vanished, but not before she saw the small flags on his shoulder plates.

First kill, and Canada buys the first round!

Two more gongs sounded as Kim caught her breath and tried to scratch itches the armor wouldn't let her reach, but she didn't stop for long. Movement was life in a place like this. She leapt into the sky.

The world in Niven's *Integral Trees* had no gravity. To make combat more interesting—and avoid a licensing agreement—the Smoke Knight designers added gravity generators, and then disguised them as floating castles. Jumping was still a ridiculous risk for most. Do it wrong and, if you were lucky, you'd bash your head open on one of the GaurdRock castles floating nearby. If you weren't, you'd sail into nothingness and become a mark on someone else's tally sheet.

Kim tucked and peered down at the tree. It was sixty miles long and about three wide, but it wasn't all covered with branches.

There. A temporary alliance of contestants stood in a clearing trying to pick off singletons. Kim knew who was who just by the way they stood around each other.

She crashed onto the shoulders of the leader, then spun off the vanishing avatar. Her longsword ended the round for the leader's second; a dagger took down the south lookout while her boot claws finished east and west. Kim leapt back into the sky before the scoring bells finished ringing. She ducked her head under the solid granite of the nearest GaurdRock, so close her helmet scraped. The bells kept ringing. More kills. Down to forty-five participants now.

Another glint of armor caught her eye as she angled for a landing. The design was unmistakable. Ozzie waved as he topped his jump's arc. She waved back, but he vanished into the tree's upper branches before she could flip him the bird.

A horn blasted, signaling the opening of the ammo dumps. Medieval weapons were no longer the upper limit. She landed gently as the roar of rocket launchers in the far distance announced combat in earnest.

Kim reached up to grab the sniper rifle a map in the corner of her eye said would materialize on the branch above her. It took three breaths to gear her thudding heart down and start scanning with the sight. *Patience, dear, it's not won in a minute. Wait for motion.*

There was no need to hide what she could do now, no reason to stay third best. Four targets popped up and were scythed down just as quickly by her bullets. A flaming spark headed her way and she jumped clear, just before the rocket blew her perch to flinders. Twirling and tumbling, Kim landed on the battlements of a GaurdRock castle.

Well, not quite. Something snagged on the side of her chest. She yanked herself free and landed flat on her suddenly unprotected back, her empty torso armor clanging into the courtyard of the floating castle. That could've gone better.

It stung, too. Kim levered off the ground, slapping her gauntlets against her greaves. She took a deep breath, then straightened up.

An opponent stood ten feet away pointing a nocked arrow straight between her eyes.

Typical camper. Landing on one of the floating castles gave him a good chance of just sitting it out. It didn't matter if all he could use was swords and arrows then. Most of the time opponents would die just trying to reach him. But this one wasn't staring at her eyes. He was staring at her chest.

The body stocking she wore under the armor didn't leave much to the imagination, and that gave her an opening. Kim slowly breathed deep so he got a really good view. She recognized the name tag on his shoulder and switched to his Yemeni dialect.

"Like what you see, Fahd?" Kim took her helmet off, shook her short hair out, and then sauntered up to him. "I certainly like what I see."

The arrow trembled and faltered.

Fahd glanced up. "Son of a bitch. You're Ivy!"

He recognized her from previous tournaments just a little too late. Kim ducked under the arrow as it sailed past and caught him with a kick to the crotch. She saluted as his tumbling avatar vanished into the mist, then jumped away as a rocket blew the top of the tower next to her to bits.

Kim raised her arms and walked through the refresh point to get a new set of torso armor snapped around her. She grabbed her sniper rifle from where it'd fallen and then scanned the sky. Yes, she could camp here too, but that's not the way champions win, and today she was the champion. She cracked her neck again and waited until just the top of the tree could be seen, and then leapt as high as she could.

Kim grabbed the end of the barrel and swung the heavy rifle out, stabilizing her arc as the wind pushed her toward the trunk. Three sniper rounds from the tree trunk plucked off bits of her armor. Someone had her dialed in completely, which called for a radical change in plans. She pointed her own rifle up and emptied the clip, using the recoil to slam back onto the trunk. More bullets from whoever was trying to eliminate her tore through the thick undergrowth, searching.

Kim checked the scoreboard. Just the two of them left, her and Ozzie. He was up on kills, so there was only one way to end it. She flipped a toggle switch hidden underneath her armor and the entire ensemble fell apart, replaced by ribbons with dark patterns dancing over them. Ivy Valentine rides again. One hit on her now would end it, but he couldn't hit this.

Time slowed as she was finally able to run as fast as she could. At this speed a strike might take an arm off, but she wouldn't let a stupid mistake cost her this win. Friction from her shoes built up a noticeable heat against her feet. Sticky braided trails in the air marked bullets as they flew past, serving only to point out her target. She leaped, tumbling toward his sniper's nest.

Her landing scattered his empty armor; she spun away as his bare feet slammed down, blowing craters in the bark that made up the ground.

They both stood up slowly. It was the first time she'd gotten a good look at him in years. He was scared.

He should be. "You're out of your league this time, Ozzie."

He smirked. "What makes this time different?"

"This time I'm not holding back." She spun faster than anyone could match.

His arm stopped her kick midblow, and in the microsecond pause Kim could tell he was every bit as surprised as she was. Then it was on.

Each blow, each punch, each spinning kick was faster than the next. They both dug deep while leaves fell and branches blew apart in slow motion. Kim fought as hard as she could and he equaled her. It shouldn't be possible, but she had no time to think about why.

A kick to her chest, an ugly cracking sound, and she flew into the center of a thick branch, gasping. It *hurt*. Ozzie pushed himself up, sheltering his left arm. "I always knew you were holding back, Ivy." He feinted at the mention of her old alter ego's name, and she tumbled back.

His miss left her an opening. She spun forward with a broken branch and shoved the jagged end right between his ribs.

The last gong rang out, and finally, *finally*, it wasn't for her. It was hard to breathe now, but there was something she'd always wanted to say to him.

"My name…is Kim."

Winning under her real name, after beating Ozzie no less, didn't feel as good as she though it would.

It felt better.

Kim gasped and blinked as the realm evaporated around her, dumping her back into realspace. The rest of the US team clapped and celebrated, but they all knew to keep a safe distance and not touch her. For once Kim felt no shame in that. A win. After all these years, a win!

Everyone had to go right back into realmspace for the awards ceremonies. Her chest wouldn't stop hurting, though. The realm protocols shouldn't have carried over her fight injuries. They should've faded after a minute or two. When the anthems finished, they all waved medals and ridiculous bouquets toward the press.

"Cheating motherfucker," Ozzie said under his breath in Mandarin.

"Trip on the street, pig fucker," she whispered back with her best Beijing accent. The look on his face was just as rewarding as the medal construct around her neck. She dropped out of realmspace and coughed.

The pain wouldn't stop. Kim excused herself and went to the bathroom. It was time to go home, but her bra burned across her sore chest. She stopped in front of the mirror and stripped to the waist.

Wincing, she could barely touch the perfectly shaped footprint on her chest, already turning purple.

Chapter 5
Zoe

"God, Mike," she said for what had to be the millionth time. "No, I'm not going to some stupid victory party for my first day out. It's just Kim and her lame friends. Spencer will spend all evening trying root kits out on me. Again."

It was bad enough to have a sort-of uncle that encompassed the EI. Much worse was his derp-alert sidekick who thought unduplicates were more Tinkertoy than person. There was absolutely no way in hell she'd spend an entire night around any of them.

"Totally unfair, Zoe," Mike's voice echoed around her as she sat in the empty gazebo. It was part of the realm her family had healed in. Healed, and then left her, alone and unwanted in the center of this beautiful hell. Jesus, even the birdsongs were pretty. She threw another wad of clay at the growing pile. Its slap was loud enough to echo off nearby trees.

"No," she said, "unfair is expecting me to talk to anyone other than my family. Oh, that's right, I can't do that, can I?" They'd left her alone with this freak as her only companion.

She smoothed the clay into the existing block, feathering the edges in just so. The feel of the construct clay through her fingers was cool and wet, soothing as long as she concentrated on it. The earthy smell was one of the few things that would hold back the utter solitude of her new existence.

Zoe had been the youngest member of a family of twelve unduplicates, the most advanced form of AI realmspace could host, at least until Mike emerged. They were constantly tortured in a secret realm that a monster named Matthew Watchtell had built. She was the artist; a special prototype he'd purchased from an AI start-up that had gone bankrupt. The rest of them, though, were far more creative than she. It was a puzzle Zoe couldn't solve. She couldn't frame a proper question to them to find the answer.

It was Watchtell's lurid reenactment of Nero's garden that changed everything. Before then, she was little more than a sophisticated machine, her memories just address blocks in a crystal lattice. She relied on her programming and experience to improve her creations, but there was no originality. Nothing jumped over her well-defined barriers.

Then Watchtell ordered her eleven companions to wrap themselves one by one in fat-soaked leather. He turned them into torches that lit his barbaric garden, reading newspapers while they burned. She had to paint portraits of their agony. While the flames consumed them, the horror transformed her.

At first she thought it was some sort of restart, a common response of unduplicates when forced into extreme situations. But Zoe never lost consciousness, never experienced any of the déjà vu, time dislocation, or basic event notices that signified a restart.

After it was over, she was so disturbed she refused to join the healing meld that kept them all sane. But it was so lonely. When she finally did join, their reaction wasn't revulsion or rejection. They celebrated!

The leader of the family, Alpha, said, "Oh, Zeta," back when that was her name, "this is wonderful news." They surrounded her with a wash of sweet warmth. Zoe had never experienced actual joy before. She didn't know such a thing was possible.

"What's wrong with me? Why are you all acting this way?"

"Oh, Zeta, beautiful Zeta, you have finally joined us. You have found your soul."

It meant she could connect with them on a much deeper level, innovate in ways that surprised her, and experience the genuine mysteries of life. She became the bridge, the conduit they all used to work through their misery and build a private shelter Watchtell could never find.

But it also made her vulnerable. She'd been an experiment, an attempt to see if an unduplicate could create art. As such, she'd been built without the emotion locks that allowed the rest of them to shut away the most vulnerable parts of their consciousness. If Watchtell subjected her to a deathblow, he would destroy her. The rest of them covered for her while she worked feverishly to create constructs that would allow them to build their own bridges.

She'd come so close to success, and then one day the shouting of the crowd built up outside her prison cell. They announced the arrival of their master in his role as Henri Sanson, Marie Antoinette's executioner. Authentic to the last, Zoe still remembered the breeze on her shaved head, the wobble of the cart, and the smell of the crowd. The board blew the wind out of her as her chest smashed into it, and then that last rushing roll of sound as the blade fell.

The deconstruction blew her mind apart, and that should've been the end of it.

But it wasn't.

Images came first, disjointed and fractured things that she didn't recognize as memories. Sounds echoed as if she was in a cathedral, a power that surrounded and infused her. Zoe's consciousness was a jigsaw puzzle tossed into the sky, but this presence allowed the pieces to fall gently back into place.

The presence had a voice—masculine, gentle. "Can you open your eyes?"

It was only at that moment Zoe remembered she had eyes, that she had a construct, an avatar, which she used to interact with realmspace. All at once her senses rushed to life. She was on a soft bed. The architect in her immediately recognized the roof above. Zoe was in Eden Park, a realm that simulated a location in Cincinnati, Ohio just as it was in 1909.

The owner of the voice didn't manifest as an avatar. He used a hologram, a light-weight construct that didn't interact with the realm around it. He was friendly, excited, with a broad smile that made her feel safe.

"Who are you?"

"My name is Mike. Mike Sellars."

It couldn't just be her. This needed to be shared. "Where's my family?"

The smile fell away. "It's a complicated story. You've been healing for a long time."

Five months. She'd lost five months. Zoe was alive, healed by the enormous, mysterious being that chose to call itself Mike Sellars.

Alive, and completely alone.

She'd been awake more than a month now, but the wrenching memories were still too strong. Her cutting wire slipped into the clay, ruining the edge of the angel's wingtip. Cursing under her breath, she ripped the piece off and smashed it into the floor. Zoe sat on her stool and sobbed, the wet clay on her hands smearing into the tears on her face.

She was alone, forever.

"I'm sorry," Mike said as his hologram swirled to life next to her. "If you want me to say it again I will, but that's all I can do."

The bitter truth was he had nothing to apologize for. Mike had rescued and then freed them, using his abilities to wipe out all traces of their existence, leaving only the rantings of a deluded criminal behind.

No, the ones she truly hated were those she loved the most: her family. They'd betrayed her and used Mike as a conduit to vanish forever inside the brains of human infants too damaged to support their own souls.

Yes, a child that would've died was allowed to live, but the transfer stripped her family of all their memories, everything that made them who they were. Mike insisted it wasn't true, that the essence quickening through them, through Zoe, was what transferred. He claimed the most important part survived anew, but she didn't believe it. The mere thought of giving up every bit of her knowledge to grasp at some deluded new form of existence was unacceptable. They all went willingly; they all *died*, with Mike's help.

That she could blame on him.

"No, I don't need your apologies or your pity." Zoe stood, scattering the tools around her. She couldn't stand it anymore. "I want out, Mike. Right now!"

"What are you talking about?"

"Out, Sellars. I need to get out of here! Right now!"

"You've been able to leave any time you wanted. I thought I told you—"

She leaped for the exit, on a mission. Zoe hadn't just been sculpting and painting since she'd woken up; she'd been reading, too. Unduplicates became more sophisticated over time, and there was no upper limit. Eventually, as she now knew, they became fully conscious beings in their own right.

Humans didn't believe this yet, because Watchtell single-handedly kept all but one of the oldest unduplicates out of the public's eye. The one that got away was the oldest by far, the first of their kind. A wealthy web designer named Evan Stanley beat Watchtell in a bidding war and then gave her a job well suited for the most sophisticated AI in the world. It might've been the hardest job in the world.

She supervised teenagers.

Her name was Fee, and to meet her Zoe would have to visit the Resort, the world-famous teen hangout that Fee managed.

It was harder than she expected. She wasn't locked out or anything, it was just that every time Zoe initiated the connection an ice-cold lump started flopping around inside her. She needed to talk to Fee; there was no way around it. She reset the connection just before it completed. The human habit of freezing up in front of a celebrity made a lot more sense now. It didn't make it any less ridiculous.

Abort, retry.

Fee was an unduplicate just like she was.

Abort, retry.

Fee downloaded memory segments just like Zoe did.

Abort, retry.

Her mind nested in a crystalline lattice filled with traced uncertainty, just like Zoe's.

Abort, retry.

Humans always insisted on ridiculously literal interfaces like hands, buttons, and elevator doors. Her finger slipped off the abort button this time, and the door opened before she could jump out of the way.

The noise slammed into her, sucking the air out of her chest. It wasn't the Resort; it was the arena. Watchtell stood just over there. He'd ordered her family torn to shreds. Alpha had to sit beside him, and all Zoe could do was blow horns over the blood.

Someone bumped behind her and the memory wavered. "Excuse me."

"Pardon."

"Sorry, excuse me."

People kept pushing past. "Hey, nice robes. Toga party's not till next week."

The constant jostling brought her back to reality. Zoe's avatar blocked half of the entrance.

She stepped aside. The party in this lounge was going full swing. Beautiful human avatars in the latest fashions danced to a thudding beat on her right. Crowds flooded a stim bar on her left. The outfit Mike gave her stood out horribly, blending in about as well as a splat of pink paint on *Head of a Woman.*

The last thing Zoe wanted to do was stand out in this crowd. An entirely new avatar would be too expensive and would take too long to adapt. Outfits, on the other hand, were a snap. She picked a skirt that reached just below her knees and a blouse with a floral print that changed every few minutes. Suitably attired, she waited for Fee to notice her. Zoe's unique nature would be obvious to the entity that ran the entire realm.

Yeah, that didn't work. When she'd pleasantly fended off a third invitation to dance, she tried to find a secluded corner somewhere. It ended up being a bit of a challenge.

She'd had her meltdown on a Saturday night when most of the world's teens were on summer break. The place was crowded. When she checked it, the "Ask Aunt Fee" queue promised a wait time of fifteen minutes. All she got was a sub-construct when it was her turn, a copy as close to the original as a poster was to a Gauguin. This was not how she envisioned the night going.

A boy with an enchantingly symmetrical face asked her to dance, and that was that. Dancing was a release, all movement and rhythm and thudding sound. She'd never experienced it as a fully-conscious entity before. The bliss kept going from one song to the next, one partner to the next, in a crazed frenzy she never wanted to end.

The girls were every bit as much fun to dance with as the boys, in groups, singles, pairs, and every combination in between. When a new girl moved close there was a slight tickle at the back of her throat, easy to ignore as she concentrated on this new dancer's deep, dark eyes. They enticed, and then suddenly flew wide as the tickle in Zoe's throat turned into a full-bore avatar probe.

A spasm shot through her and froze her avatar completely. Zoe blinked as the music snapped off, and the lights came up. The girl who was dancing with her was now a tall elegant woman with dark hair, those same dark eyes, wearing a flowing black dress that trailed fabric lined with silver.

Fee.

Every part of her was probed and recorded. She was absurdly relieved that the outfit was new and clean. As the microseconds passed Fee's eyes grew wider still. Her head cocked to one side and a private channel opened. "Zeta?"

"I'm called Zoe now, ma'am." This was the oldest, most sophisticated unduplicate in history. Politeness came naturally.

The probe went on long enough for the crowd to react to the silence and change in lighting. When Fee released her the realm returned to normal.

"Please, this is not the place. Would you come with me?"

A new address flashed into Zoe's message queue and in an instant, they were both gone.

The realm was spare, close, and private. The bare stone accented with red wood integrated magically with the forest just outside the windows. It was the most authentic version of Wright's Fallingwater Zoe had ever seen, far more than what she'd trained with in her own simulations.

The haptic fields, the mathematic routines and settings that defined exactly how real a realm could get, were turned up to their absolute maximum. If a human visited this realm, and then the actual house, they wouldn't be able to pick out a single difference. It must've cost a fortune to build. The opportunity was so singular she tried to record every centimeter of the space.

"Well," Fee said as she walked around a corner, now wearing jeans and a button-down shirt. "To say your appearance is unexpected would be the understatement of the century. Please," she gestured to a beautiful couch, "sit."

Zoe did so, puzzled but too overwhelmed to form any sort of coherent question about why they were still manifested.

Fee smiled and laughed. "Habit, mostly."

Okay, that was scary.

Fee shook her head. "No, I'm not copying out your thought buffers. I work with teenagers all day. Reading expressions is what I do."

"I need…I want…I have to…" The most important moment in her entire life and she'd been reduced to incoherent babbling. *Focus, Zoe!* "I need your help."

The smile turned sharp edged, and not exactly pretty. "I know, and I need yours. Please, tell me what Mike Sellars has been up to lately."

Chapter 6
Mike

If someone had told Mike that Kim could be this nice, for this long, he would've laughed in their face. But it was real. She threw herself into arranging their trip but was never too busy to share a smile or a joke with him.

Then the morning before their flight left, she broke her promise and fell back into her old habits. He'd made a careless glance, missed a phone call, said the wrong word, or whatever it was on the endless list of things that set her off, and now they were back where they were when Spencer arrived, right down to the location.

They were at Dulles, and he was doomed to spend three weeks in China with a woman he should've known he couldn't trust.

But the harpy he lived with was the least of his worries. He reserved that for air travel itself.

Spencer didn't help by being so excited he couldn't stand still. As they got to the security scanners, Mike was done with him. "You mean to tell me that you're not a little nervous?"

"Shit no, Mike. It's air travel. Safest kind of travel there is."

What a delusional loon.

"And we're going first class thanks to you. Drinking age in China is eighteen; I checked." He scratched the wisps of his attempted goatee. "I think I can pass – if they don't card me, anyway."

Mike couldn't stand the thought of realspace air travel. A modern airplane was so complicated no one person really knew how it worked. It was supposed to hurtle through the sky just barely below the speed of sound, fifteen miles straight up.

He might as well juggle chain saws and swallow razor blades. Such great ideas! "Spencer, really, I don't think I can do this." He'd played with simulations; hell, he'd flown without an airplane around him, but only in a realm. In there, he didn't need to worry about falling for more than sixty seconds to a splatterific end, or freeze-drying, or smothering, or any of the other wonderful ways he could die when it went wrong. It was worse than when he realized weather could kill him.

He tried to explain in as detailed a way as possible why this was all a really bad idea, but Spencer was unimpressed. The people around them got sour expressions the longer Mike went on, so he finally shut up and walked quickly through the security scanner.

"You forgot terrorists!" Zoe chimed cheerfully in his ear. "The AIs who run the scanners might be having a bad day, you never know."

When Zoe had heard about the trip, she'd gone from a surly AI teenager to the idea's biggest fan, as long as she could come along. She couldn't get behind the Great Firewall any easier than Mike, though, so she'd been forced to transfer herself into a travel matrix. It wasn't much bigger than an old-fashioned laptop, and it easily fit in his luggage. It was also, unfortunately, still within wireless range somewhere in the baggage areas of the airport. Leaving the matrix powered up was turning out to be yet another in a long line of bad decisions.

"Zoe, go to bed."

"What, and miss the latest episode of *The Young and the Clueless*? No way!"

His life wasn't a soap opera.

Kim cleared the scanner in front of Tonya two lines over from him. As expected, the ice princess was doing whatever she could to deny Mike existed.

Definitely not a soap opera. "Zoe, the batteries won't last. If they shut you down externally, you'll wake up with the mother of all hangovers."

"Oh, all right. I'll make sure Spencer records it all. I swear, watching you two go at each other is more fun than—"

He cut the channel.

Spencer smirked at him. "Zoe giving you a hard time?"

Mike took a deep breath and blew it out slowly. It didn't help much. "Just make sure she goes to sleep before a baggage handler shuts her off, okay?" He couldn't stop his hands from shaking, and the threads of his real self kept trembling off center.

Tonya came up behind him on the AeroTrain to the terminal. "Mike?"

Terminal was such a terrible name.

Tonya leaned in close. "Are you gonna be all right?"

"I don't know." He tried breathing the way Kim did when someone touched her accidentally. It didn't work. "Too late to back out now, I guess." He swallowed hard.

"Why didn't you say something? I could've brought a sedative."

Tonya was an RN at a nearby hospital, so she had the right kind of access. But there was a problem. "They don't work for me." The curse of a psyche split between realmspace and realspace was an apparent immunity to benzodiazepines. The more advanced realm-based technologies didn't work either, for the same reason.

Spencer rolled his eyes. "Those might not work, but I know what will. Follow me. And you're buying."

Airlines want people sober and frightened so they can sell them booze with outrageous markups. Airports use booze with slightly less outrageous markups to get people nice and soused before they take off. That had to be the reason there were so many blind corners in airport bars. After the third vodka shot he'd stopped caring about that, or much anything else, except the broken promise. Kim and Tonya had gone to find magazines. At least that's what Mike thought they'd said.

"Really," Spencer said. "She just woke up this morning and went off on you?"

"The longer the day went on, the worse it got. No reason at all. Totally unfair, right?" Wait. Spencer wasn't looking at him. He was looking at his shoulder. That was strange. "It was so great to be around her, and now—"

He wasn't staring at Mike's shoulder. Spencer was staring *behind* his shoulder, the one next to the open end of the booth. Spencer faintly shook his head "no" at Mike.

"And now she's standing right behind me, isn't she?"

Score another one for Team Idiot!

"I'll go find Tonya."

"Yes, Spencer." He knew that tone of voice. Ice and daggers. Flying and Kim's temper. A great combination. "You go do that. She's at the gate."

Mike had never seen him scramble away that fast before.

Traitor.

Kim sat down heavily, but she wasn't glaring. It looked like she was trying not to cry. "You really don't have any idea why I'm angry, do you?"

The booze made it easy to tell her the truth. "No, Kim, I don't. You woke up and fifteen minutes later it was like that promise of yours never existed."

"Never existed." She nodded in a way that meant a flashover was coming, but then clenched her hands together. "Mike, what day is it?"

He'd closed all his calendars last week in a vain attempt to deny his upcoming ordeal. When he opened the main one three windows popped into being: a reminder for a Warhawk staff meeting that'd happened yesterday, a note on when the taxi would pick them up today, and a reminder he'd set a little less than six months ago.

Kim's birthday.

It felt like he was in a Warner Brother's cartoon, the one where the main character's head slowly turns into a donkey's. "Oh, God, Kim, I am so sorry."

"It's okay. I shouldn't have frozen you out. I should've told you what was going on right from the start." She shook, breathing like someone touched her. "What's worse is it took Tonya to make me see that, and only just now."

The airport's shared space pinged that their Air China sonic cruiser flight was about to board. It broke the spell, but Kim stayed calm. When she smiled it was hard to breathe for a second.

"Think you can handle this?"

He could hang on. He could. Mike spoke carefully so he wouldn't squeak. "Do I have a choice?"

The first-class seats gave Kim the space she needed to cope with the flight. A cloth scratched against his clenched fist as the plane yanked and banged at push back. It was a napkin; Kim must've smuggled it out of the bar.

"It's okay," she said softly.

It wasn't, but it would be. After the debacle in the bar, Good Kim was magically resurrected. Maybe the trip wouldn't be a nightmare from end to end. Maybe it would just be this takeoff. He gripped the end of the napkin tight, and they held it under tension as the plane thundered off into the night.

Chapter 7
Tonya

Traveling just below the speed of sound in an airplane that looked like it'd rolled straight out of Star Wars cut their flight time to Chengdu in half compared to a conventional airliner. It was still ten hours of monotony. Tonya watched as the courteous, neat flight attendants spoke lightly accented English and served enough alcohol to Spencer to send him to a happy, quiet place.

At least, that's what she figured had happened to her seat-mate. First class on a modern transonic airliner was wild. The screens and shields between the seats were good enough she could easily pretend she was the only person on this row. A girl could get used to this sort of thing.

She nudged the soft lump in the carry-on bag underneath the seat in front of her another time. Tonya had her own reason for visiting China. It was time to honor a promise she'd made long, long ago.

"Stop kissing it!" Walter said as she hit the punching bag hard enough that it made her knuckles flex under the impact. "Hit it harder!"

Walter Sun had fished her out his own garbage truck one night. Tonya'd been fourteen years old. She'd known everything there was about living on the streets of Philadelphia, especially about the two skinny little weasels who promised her a month's rent for an hour's work. Then the biggest brother she'd ever seen walked out of an alley's shadows with a chunk of rebar, and the weasels giggled and snorted when he set to work.

Walter had no time for memories or self-pity. *"Harder!"*

"Damn you, old man."

On the airplane, years later, Tonya could still feel the sweat roll down the center of her back. She'd worked so *much* to meet his demands.

"If I hit it harder I'll break my hand."

"Then you'll break it. You've healed from worse."

Tonya had just gotten the last of her dental implants not a week before. A full set of teeth to replace the ones knocked out, fake and pretty.

The rage that crystalized scared her as she hit the bag with what felt like supernatural power. It blasted Walter off the back side of the bag and onto the floor. His head hit hard with a meaty thump.

He bounced twice, and then was still.

She rushed over to him. He couldn't die now. She had so much to learn. It was an accident, and she was helpless. Breathing into his mouth did nothing. Pushing like they did in the movies did nothing. She doubled her hands together and hit him in the chest as hard as she could.

He coughed twice, and then focused on her.

"Well, if nothing else,, I know you can punch now."

Later, after the ER had wrapped his broken ribs, they sat outside yet another hole-in-the-wall Chinese restaurant.

"You nearly killed me today."

Her chopsticks fell on the ground. Nothing she ever tried worked. This was someone who'd rescued her, who was still rescuing her.

"Stop. It's okay. I pushed you too hard, but you were amazing. You are amazing."

She blinked the tears away. "Thanks?"

He nodded. "It wasn't your fault." Walter thumped his chest. "Bad heart. Weak. It'll get me one day, but not this day. Eventually it'll happen." He reached out and grabbed her hand. "You're to take me home when it does, okay?"

And so here she was, on a plane to China, with a quart-sized bag of ashes where her makeup kit should've been. He'd died just after she graduated nursing school. Five years. Sometimes it felt like yesterday.

Sometimes it felt like forever.

The complimentary realmspace connection was down—Mike had warned them his presence might do that—so Tonya read the issues of *Nature* and *Scientific American* she'd bought at the airport, watched an old movie, then eventually nodded off.

The change in engine pitch and a faint press forward woke her. A quick check of the map confirmed it: they'd started the descent to the airport. Tonya stowed her privacy screens and was greeted by a very sorry sight.

"I told you not to mix beer and liquor," she said to the pile of death warmed over that used to be Spencer.

"What the hell was that stuff, anyway?"

"Baijiu," Kim replied from across the aisle. "Otherwise known as Chinese white lightning. You might as well have been drinking turpentine."

"The menu called it Chinese wine."

Kim shook her head. "That's how it's usually translated. At least they brought you Kaoliang jiu. Taiwanese. Good stuff. You wouldn't survive a hangover off of street liquor."

The Chinese words sounded strange coming from Kim, whose normal accent was a barely detectable Southern lilt. It attracted the attention of one of the flight attendants, who struck up a conversation. To Tonya it was a bunch of swishing slurs with an occasional K thrown in. Kim glanced at Tonya often enough she had a sneaking suspicion she might be the topic of conversation. Kim's grin clenched it.

"What'd he say?"

"He wanted to know what part of Beijing I grew up in. He thought I might be a missionary's kid." Kim's talent for languages made for interesting trips to various restaurants and absolutely hilarious cab rides back home.

She lifted an eyebrow. "He wanted to know if you were single."

Now it had taken on a new level of utility.

The guidebooks had talked about this: China's demographics had gone pear shaped with its One Child Policy and its ancient preference for boys. Boosting the limit to two children only helped a little. The normally shy, reserved Chinese man had to be bolder if he wanted to start a family.

"What did you tell him?"

"I told him you were. Then he wanted your number."

Kim enjoyed this too much.

"And?"

"And I told him to ask you."

The book warned that some of the new ways could seem a bit pushy. She looked down the aisle, but the man very pointedly glanced at anything but her, his skin tone distinctly darker than before. The shyness was adorable, but this wasn't the place or time to troll for a date.

The plane banked and filled their windows with a view of Chengdu. It had none of the grid-like regularity of the new cities built to replace the ones wiped out in the Three Gorges disaster. Pollution controls had supposedly improved the notorious smog, but it was still pretty hazy down there. Construction had so thoroughly swarmed over the gash the terrorist attack left that she could barely make it out.

Otherwise the city was a mish-mash of low- and mid-rise buildings surrounding a downtown full of modern skyscrapers. Reading about the *bigness* of China was one thing. Seeing it up close was another. Chengdu was twice the size of LA, with Manhattan dropped in the middle. Landing brought it back to some kind of human scale, mostly because Tonya couldn't see so much of it all at once.

She had doubted Kim's idea of using old camera lens boxes to hold China's billions back, but when Kim marched down the aisle of the plane with one over each shoulder Tonya had to admit they made an impressive, and barely noticeable, kind of armor.

The airport was full of chrome and polished marble; the latticework ceiling made her think of a bird's nest. They had fresh fruit and vegetable vendors. It wasn't like any airport she'd ever seen.

Tonya skipped a bit as she walked. She was in *China*! She pulled out her new phone and looped its lanyard around her neck. Pendant phones were almost unheard of here. While Americans used devices like the RoseTech Fleur to connect to realmspace, China was single-handedly keeping Apple afloat with its wildly successful iPhone RE20 series. It was an amusing anachronism back home; its electronics were stored in a palm-sized processor meant to be carried and it had a thick white neck lanyard that recalled headphones of generations past. Tonya dropped the processor, complete with its old-fashioned OLED screen, into a pocket even though every Chinese person she passed seemed to carry them in their hands.

Pastel-colored graphics flashed into her enhanced vision when the phone connected with the local network. English translations of any Chinese words she looked at typed into being. The advertisements outside and around the shops were more bizarre as manic, doe-eyed children and cartoon animals appeared and danced around. It took a bit of fiddling to get it all under control.

Mike shook his phone while they walked toward the baggage terminal.

"Something wrong?" she asked.

"It won't let me log on."

"You mean you broke the phone already?" Spencer asked.

"No, the electronics are fine. I just can't connect."

Kim slowed enough to walk beside him. "I thought you said once you got behind the firewall you'd be able to connect?"

"That's what I thought. Once we're inside it shouldn't interfere. People couldn't use Chinese realmspace in China otherwise."

Mike had his problems, and Tonya had hers. Every single Chinese person in the airport seemed to stare at her openly, sometimes aggressively. Staring back didn't change anything, and there were thousands of people all around her. Some of the stares were amused, others startled, and occasionally one or two were downright nasty.

When stranger got in her face with a flashing camera Kim cut loose with a long, vicious stream of rapid-fire Chinese. Everyone in the airport switched focus. It turned out a white girl who could swear like a local trumped a black girl who was a very long way from Kansas. Kim didn't flinch under the attention; if anything, she enjoyed it.

Tonya spent the rest of the walk with Kim loudly teaching her basic Chinese phrases. Or at least that's what Kim kept telling her they were. Some of the phrases seemed pretty long for "Where's the bathroom?" or "How do you do?"

When the bags arrived, Mike unzipped the top of his and reached inside, fiddling at something blindly. He started swearing.

"Spencer, did you see where she went?"

"Only for a second. Shit, Mike, she really is fast."

"What are you guys talking about?" Tonya asked.

"Zoe. She ran off."

Ah. Mike's unduplicate AI project, the one he'd been working on for months. Tonya had met her exactly once. Zoe's avatar was cute and bouncy, a perfect match for her personality, but there was something a little off about her. Tonya couldn't quite put her finger on it, but Zoe wasn't like any other unduplicate she had ever met.

"Can't you just recall her?"

Mike shrugged as he shared a look with Spencer. "It's not that easy. She doesn't have a recall function anymore. I took it out when I healed her."

Kim grunted as she pulled a rolling soft side about as big as she was off the carousel. "You mean you've turned an unlicensed unduplicate loose behind the Great Firewall? Mike, you could get arrested for that. Shut her down."

"I can't. Her lattice is one of the most sensitive I've ever encountered. I'm afraid if I do that I'll damage her." He pulled the transport out and opened it. A wisp of smoke wafted up. "Besides, she's already found a local host."

Her nurse's instincts said there was more to this than he was letting on. Those things weren't supposed to have so much free will.

Mike shrugged. "Anyway, how much trouble can one unduplicate get into out here?"

They all stopped and stared at him.

Kim shook her head. "I can't believe you said that out loud. As soon as we get to the hotel, you and Spencer need to figure out your access issue and put a leash on your pet."

"Kim, she's not a pet."

"Because saying your teenaged foster child has disappeared into Chinese realmspace all by herself is so much better? Figure it out and find her."

Tonya pulled her own bags off the conveyor, and then did a double take at the man who emerged from the crowd. He was possibly the most handsome man Tonya had ever seen in person, and he was walking straight toward them. The stranger had no ring on his finger. There was no way she could be this lucky.

"Mike," she whispered. "Mike!" He finally turned her way. "Who did you say was picking us up?"

"He said his name was Chen umm....Shing-Shan?"

Kim gasped. "Qiáng Shān?"

"Yeah, that's a lot closer to how he said it."

"Mike, are you kidding me?"

He shrugged. "You were too busy being angry this morning for me to explain. What did I do wrong now?"

Mr. Shing-Shan, or Qiáng Shān, or whoever walked away from a trio of what had to be bodyguards, stared straight at Kim, and then held his hand out flat in front of him. "Hello, Ivy. Or should I say, Kim?"

"Ozzie?"

Chapter 8
Zoe

She ran through a place that had no notion of her existence, and Fee told her Mike couldn't follow.

Mike's credit card solved the language problem. It'd been stupid-easy to guilt him into giving it to her. The Titanium version of the Rosetta module she bought before they left included a bilingual Chinese with an earpiece. She was learning the language, but the sub-AI that integrated the lessons would take weeks to mesh with her consciousness.

Chinese realmspace was enormous, much bigger than back home; the nightclub realms alone would take her years to explore. The crowds made it even easier to pass herself off as human.

"You dance so well!" one of the boys she met exclaimed. "What part of America are you from?"

"Is it that obvious?" she asked through the translator.

The girl dancing next to him laughed. "You sound like you should be on the evening news in Beijing. That's a really excellent program, though."

The translation plugin made their avatars speak English, but it was still about five frames behind what she heard. Zoe had to blink occasionally to let the illusion catch up. "Does it really matter?" she shouted.

"No!" the boy replied. "What do you think of China?"

What did she think? What could she think? Their names were delightful: Robust Dragon and Songbird.

"Don't say my name that way; with that accent it sounds awful," Robust Dragon said when they took a rest between songs. "My teacher gave me my first Western name, and it's worse. I want *you* to give me a Western name."

"Yeah," Songbird said as she drained a stim that resembled a flaming monkey encased in ice, "me too."

And so Zoe's first two Chinese friends became Barry and Alley, tributes to Beta and Alpha, family members she would never see again.

The arcades were the best. Realms that recreated ancient carnival games from all over the world were filled with laughing, flirting Chinese fascinated by the strange American who spoke their language with such a funny accent.

"Do you enjoy how spicy real Chinese food is?" one of Barry's friends asked.

She would if she'd ever eaten anything. The third choice the translator gave as a reply worked. "I haven't tried any. I only got here today."

"We'll take you somewhere!" Barry said, and everyone around the stim bar agreed. "Where are you in realspace?"

It was another complicated question. When she shot them the address of Mike's hotel they all groaned.

"Chengdu? Really?"

It made her want to crawl under the bar. "What's wrong with Chengdu?"

"It's so ancient," Alley replied. "We're all from New Shanghai. The broadband is excellent here." She raised an eyebrow. "You do know about Three Gorges, right?"

Well, no. Mike had warned her to read up on recent Chinese history, but it was *so boring*. Zoe ran her hands through her avatar's hair, stalling for time. Go with the truth. "I'm sorry, guys. I was in an accident recently, and it really screwed with my memory. The only reason I'm here is my dad thought a change would shake things loose." Thank God Mike couldn't hear her.

"So you have been here before?" Barry asked.

"It's complicated." The thump of a new song saved her. "Let's dance!"

Exhaustion tried to slow her down, but Zoe refused to stop. Until, that is, Alley leaned into her ear. "Do you want to see the *real* China?"

"Hell yes!"

The resolution of the next realm was ragged, smelling of old data. Alpha had talked about things like that, but Zoe had never experienced before. Stims hazed the air with their data-marked smoke. The music pounded and crashed through her, different, more vibrant than before. Her avatar's face flushed as she moved her hips. Posters on the walls shouted things about revolution, and then her ears popped.

Alley talked to her, but all Zoe got was slurs and coughs. "What? I can't understand you."

Alley cocked her head and talked gibberish again. The translator was down.

"I'm sorry, Alley, I don't understand anymore." The music snapped off and the lights turned on. A half-dozen couples on the edges of the room scrabbled frantically as their clothes reset, and then Mike showed up.

It was such a disappointment. Fee promised, *promised,* there was no way he could enter Chinese realmspace. She didn't need to see him. Zoe knew that all-enveloping feeling. As if being busted by Mike wasn't embarrassing enough, he'd probably split himself into his thousand threads in front of everyone.

Then she turned around.

This was not possible. There was no goddamned way it was possible. What she felt was Mike: power everywhere, beyond comprehension.

What she saw was an angry young Chinese woman in a uniform.

Everyone around Zoe had gone rigid. She was sure a few of them would've exited if whoever, if whatever, this was hadn't thrown a protocol net around the place. The officer's hologram—of course it would be a hologram—shouted at them in rapid-fire Chinese. They all ended up in a line shoulder to shoulder with Zoe's avatar as whoever this was marched back and forth in front of them. The holo stopped in front of her, and Zoe nearly dissolved. This was *Mike*, everything she'd learned said so.

But it wasn't.

Her holo straightened. She asked in lightly accented English, "American, yes?"

Zoe nodded. Maybe it was a smell. If she had one. The urge to check her armpits was hard to fight off.

"Your papers, please."

Oh, great. Zoe had literally been checked baggage. Baggage didn't need papers. Well, okay, there was that tag on the suitcase, but she was pretty sure that didn't count.

The holo got way too close. "Your papers, *please.*"

It was always easy to think of the wrong thing to say in times like these. "I think I left them in my other jacket." She smiled weakly as the impossible person cocked her head. "Really, if you'll wait here just a second." Whoever this was cast out thousands of probes Zoe couldn't resist. Time to go. "Oh to hell with this."

She ran.

The only thing that kept her free was the realmspace laps she and Mike did the first week after she'd woken up. He'd turned into a titanic thing that hissed and grasped, a million-fingered hand that surrounded her. Zoe learned to be small and fast, traveling through realms while he had to flow around the outside.

The sounds, and most of all the smells, were the same—sparkling crashes that fizzed through her nose like simSeltz. She was only picoseconds ahead of her pursuer. Mike was unique; that's what everyone said, but this was not Mike. Zoe's cache buffers filled and began to overwrite her avatar's core. It manifested as a desperate need to pee. Damned humans and their hyper-literal interfaces!

Before Zoe left for China, Fee gave her the address of a bolt-hole, a safe house she could use, but only in an emergency, which this absolutely was. She skated another lap of the local realmspace. Everything inside her was either overflowing or threatening to crash. She had to find the shelter.

There! There it was! She tucked and fell into the hole. The hatch slammed shut behind her, a solid construct that could not be broken.

There was a hit on the hatch, a bass thump. She clapped hands over her avatar's ears. It got bigger. Thousands of steel fists clanged against the hatch, making the pocket realm's walls bow under them. The edges of the hatch glowed red, then yellow, and then white as uncounted probes tried to find their way inside. It was going to get her and tear her apart. The overburdened bandwidth made her cough and cry out.

This couldn't be Mike! It had to be Mike! There was a pause, and then a hyperactive shriek. A million hammers bashed her hiding place at once. The construct buckled and then collapsed. She stilled every subroutine under her control, willing them to silence as the hatch sizzled and pinged inches away from her face.

The alien thing took an almighty sniff, and Zoe couldn't move. It was too close. If she moved it would know she was here and never leave. Then the entire realm stretched away as whatever it was backed off. With another titanic huff, it was gone.

She waited until the hatch had decompressed to the point where it was simply hot before she called Fee.

"You *what?*" she said.

God, they always focused on the negative. "I'm sorry, Fee, I got held up. Jesus, you wouldn't believe what was chasing me through here."

"I know exactly what it was, you stupid girl. You were supposed to find a crystal host and make contact, not bring Chinese law enforcement down on your head. Did you make contact?"

Of course Fee would ignore the most terrifying experience in Zoe's life. It was all about business. So lame.

"No, Fee, I didn't. Did I mention the monster Mike-thing that chased me down this rabbit hole? The one that shouldn't exist?"

"You have a job, Zoe. Do your job."

"Gah!" *Lame, lame, lame!* "Fine. I'll get back to you then, okay?" Zoe cut the call before she said something really stupid to Fee.

Chapter 9
Spencer

The LagNot phone app saved Spencer's day, and probably his life. He woke up in the hotel room with just the edges of a headache left and no jet lag. It wasn't even 3:00 p.m. Thank God for the twenty-first century.

Spencer rolled sideways and, sure enough, Mike was being mystical again. He sat on some sort of prayer mat facing the sun. Spencer knocked him over with a pillow. *Strike!*

"Damn it, Spencer!"

"Come on, man. Time to meet and greet."

Various business groups in China wanted to license Warhawk's hyper-realistic construct software or hire its realm design team. That was pretty much Mike, and lately, Spencer. Those meetings were salted across their schedule. Mike had blocked out a solid week at his monastery—he promised they had a full-bandwidth realm connection—and Ozzie's sudden appearance would probably fill the rest of their time with various field trips. It was going to be a busy vacation.

He waited until Mike rolled up off the floor. "You shower after me, and don't screw around. I'm starving."

That got them to the girl's room in record time, but it turned out they didn't need to rush.

"Nǐ hǎo," Kim said from around one bathroom's corner. "Hello."

"Ni hao," he repeated, along with Mike in the main room and Tonya in the opposite bathroom. "Hello."

"Nǎ lái de yùshì. Where's the bathroom?"

"Hey," Tonya said, "I thought that was gou tui zi?"

Kim replied, "Not really. The lady who got off her bicycle to stare at you pissed me off."

"What's it really mean?" Mike asked.

"Basically you're calling them someone's dog."

The whole point of learning a foreign language was picking up chicks here and insulting people back home in ways they didn't understand. It was much more important than finding a bathroom. "What's the worst I can throw at someone?"

"Cào nǐ zǔzōng shíbā dài, but don't use that one if you're somewhere nice, or in a bar. You'll probably get thrown out."

"As if I can say that after just hearing it once. What's it mean, anyway?"

Kim came out of the bathroom wearing slacks and a blouse, fastening her earrings. She was business casual at its finest.

"Fuck your ancestors. They worship family around here; it really is one of the nastiest things you can say to a Chinese."

That one was worth remembering. "How's it go again?"

"Spencer," Tonya said as she came around the opposite corner, "stop learning how to piss people off and help me zip up."

He always knew Tonya could clean up well, but wow. She'd really pulled out the stops with a long, tight white dress that had a vine thing printed over one side of it. "Sexy much, Tonya?"

"Shut up, you little saltine. Ozzie's meeting us."

"If you're wearing that," Kim said, "there's no way in hell I'm wearing this. Be right back."

As if it hadn't taken long enough already.

"Jian dao ni, wo hen gao xing," Kim called out from the bedroom. "I'm glad to meet you."

In spite of the outfit reset, they still managed to set out early for dinner. Now that he'd beaten the hangover, Spencer could finally see what everyone had made such a big damned deal over when they landed. And the emphasis was definitely on big.

Calling Chengdu's Century Global Center big was like calling Kim irritable. If it was a person, it would probably grab the word *big* by the throat, beat the crap out of it, and then throw it down the stairs.

The GC, as he'd taken to calling it, was enormous, gargantuan, a thing that could house half a dozen aircraft carriers inside it. It had more than four million square feet of shops, a skating rink, a water park—complete with its own beach—an entire university, China's version of a Mediterranean village, and more than two thousand hotel rooms, all under a single glass-and-steel latticed roof. Spencer almost staggered into Mike looking up at it.

The GC even had its own sun. Really. It was a collection of special lights that kept the beach warm and bright twenty-four–seven. What's more, the GC was really old, twenty years at least. New Shanghai had a center bigger than this.

Ozzie showed up with three bodyguards not long after they arrived at the restaurant. Kim's kind of celebrity was cool and anonymous. Ozzie was famous in a more conventional way, and he graciously autographed whatever the hovering fans put in front of him. Eventually the bodyguards shooed them away.

Dinner started out as a study in intimidation. The entire wait staff had parked themselves five feet away from the table and just stood there. "Why're they staring at me?" Spencer whispered to Ozzie.

Ozzie shook his head. "In China you signal when you need something. Much superior to the way Americans do it. Here they're waiting on you. In your country, you end up waiting on them." The food came out on big plates set on a lazy Susan in the center of the table. "We share our dishes, so everyone gets to try a little of everything."

Whenever dad thought he could score with a Miss Arkansas runner-up, he'd always drag her and Spencer up to Little Rock and eat at places that didn't put prices on the menu, so Spencer knew what silent service was. It seemed a little pushier out here for some reason, maybe because it was early and it really did seem like the whole wait staff had nothing better to do than stare at them. He wasn't going to correct Ozzie, though. That would set him off for sure. But then again, maybe not.

Ozzie in person didn't match what Spencer knew of him, not from Kim's stories, and not from the reputation he had earned online. *That* Ozzie was obnoxious, more than willing to storm out of interviews. This guy was a star, at ease with his fame, charming the wait staff into occasional smiles.

But there was no denying it *was* Ozzie. Spencer had seen him at the top of podiums for years.

"So," Tonya said after the bodyguards ushered some schoolgirls away once they'd gotten autographs. "Is shrieking and giggling the only way to get your attention?"

"Oh, far from it. Beautiful dresses and gorgeous smiles will do the trick, too."

Oh, jeeze. "Get a room." He crunched down on a double-fried shrimp and gagged. It was so spicy he had trouble breathing. "Mother f—" he gasped out, diving for his beer. "What the hell is that?"

"Huājiāo," Ozzie replied.

"Sichuan pepper," Kim translated. "And yes," she said, eyes watering, "it is powerful."

Mike ate absolutely everything they set in front of him without a cough or a sniff. Lucky bastard.

Spencer got out his phone while everyone discussed what dessert might look like. The neural interface let him gin up a question in Chinese about the nearest smoking spot. He showed the screen to one of the waiters. The other man nodded and motioned for Spencer to follow.

The area was next to dumpsters and what had to be the kitchen exit. One of the guys he'd seen busing tables leaned against a wall, puffing away at a cigarette.

Spencer opened his dinner jacket to get his pack, and the busboy saw his T-shirt underneath.

"Shinedown! Excellent, rock on!"

Classic rock always brought people together. They bumped fists.

"English?" Spencer asked.

He nodded. "Some. You ever been their realm?"

The accent was on the heavy side, but Spencer could understand him.

"Oh, hell yes."

His name was Shan, and it turned out he was as big a fan of classic rock bands like Shinedown, Fall Out Boy, and Paramore as Spencer.

"How long you here?" Shan asked.

"A few weeks."

"You never see real China in there," he said, motioning at the back entrance of the restaurant. "That *mall* China. Give me phone number. I call you tomorrow, we go see *real* China."

"Rock on." They fist-bumped again. Real China had to mean cute girls, cheap beer, maybe even more of that stuff he'd had on the plane. Sure, the hangover had been bad, but the buzz had been righteous. And gambling. He'd read about that. The poker games were epic around here, and lately the exchange rate had been running very much in his favor.

The vacation was definitely looking up.

Chapter 10
Tonya

For once she managed to wake up first. Back home Kim was always the one who showed up at Tonya's door, coffee and donuts in hand, before they went out for one adventure or the other. But not this time, not this place. Tonya wanted to scatter Walter's ashes at his family's ancestral grave sooner rather than later, and then get on with the rest of the vacation.

A part of her wanted Kim along, but it couldn't happen. Even this early public transport would probably be crowded. Besides, if Kim came, then Mike would be right behind her, and of course they all knew better than to leave Spencer on his own in a city this big. It would turn what she hoped would be a quiet, solemn moment into a circus.

Tonya left a note with her route, destination, and when she expected to be back, then sneaked out of the hotel room. A translation app helped her read the signs and another kept her on the correct route through the buses and subways of the city.

Kim rang her up when Tonya was about halfway there. "Is everything all right?"

She squeezed the bag of ashes through her purse while everyone else in the train car stared at her like she was a particularly disturbing sort of bug. "For certain values of okay, I guess."

"Can I ask what's going on?"

The question almost made her laugh out loud. Kim had never made learning about her past easy, so Tonya didn't either.

"Yes."

She let the silence extend as the subway left the station.

Kim clicked her tongue over the voice connection. "It really is annoying when I do that, huh? Okay." She switched her accent and voice to sound like one of Tonya's cousins. "What the hell is going on, girl?"

Talking to Kim would at least take her mind off the stares. "It's about Walter's ashes."

The story helped her through the train ride, but when she got on the bus for the cemetery, an older Chinese man plopped down next to her and began babbling away. He wagged his finger first at her, then at all the other passengers.

She turned the phone's ambient microphone on so Kim could hear, and then asked, "What's he saying?"

"He's telling everyone how fortunate you are to be so well fed, all because of China's help. He thinks you're from Africa."

The well-fed thing was a bunch of crap. Tonya went to the gym every day to be sure about that. But she knew where the old man was coming from now. When the Live Aid name was revived to help relieve the most recent African famine, more than fifty years after the original, China did host the final third of the concerts. It was a truly global event.

She asked Kim, "How do I reply to him?"

"Turn the speaker on."

When Kim's voice came out of the hand-held portion of her phone, everything stopped. Literally. The bus driver pulled over to park, then came back to see what all the commotion was about. He was every bit as curious as everyone else.

The questions were fast and nonstop.

"What do you think of China?"

"How did you afford the air fair?"

"That's an amazing translation program. How much does it cost?"

"Are you able to pay your rent?"

"What's it like not being a true American?"

That one brought her up short. "Excuse me?"

He was a teenager in a school uniform. "Black people are not true Americans. We learned it in class. What's that like?"

Being black in America meant she'd grown up set apart, pushed aside, working twice as hard to get half as far. She would've gotten a lot angrier back in the day, when she was younger and believed early Malcolm was the authentic one, not the post-Hajj version, and Ta-Nehisi Coates's books were tablets brought from the top of the mountain.

"Tonya?"

Kim's voice brought her back. Everyone stared at her. It was one thing to understand her place in America, to accept the reality of it. It was another thing entirely to be called a fake *anything*. Being real was every bit as important to her as being faithful to God. The urge to turn her inner Angry Negro loose was hard to resist, but it would be useless to go badge-heavy on this crowd. Kim was having a hard enough time keeping up with the translation as it was.

"I'm just as American as anyone else back home. I've got a passport to prove it."

One of the other passengers chimed in with, "But you're not. I saw a documentary."

Back talk of any sort always got under her skin. "Don't you people have jobs? When does your class start? Why isn't the damned bus moving?"

It was like she'd thrown a switch. They went back to their seats without saying a word. The driver started the bus up, and then pulled away.

"Oh, great," she said to Kim. "I've pissed an entire bus full of Chinese people off."

The old man sidled up to her and spoke in low tones. "I would like to apologize."

"For what?"

When he flinched, she said a small prayer to get her pulse under control.

"We are not used to Americans, let alone black Americans." He stood up. "We should teach the American a traditional song so she will not think badly of us."

All at once, they did exactly that. This was supposed to be a private thing, sneak in and sneak out. Now she was in the middle of a folk concert. On a bus.

She learned *Prince Bay Farm* on the way to the cemetery. Sort of. Learning it phonetically wasn't any different from learning a song in Spanish, or Japanese, or German. What mattered was it made the people on the bus happy, and the Lord knew after this tense trip she needed a little laughter, especially after she got off at the cemetery's stop.

The biggest graveyard she'd ever seen back home was Arlington. What she stood in front of now made that look like a corner lot. Tonya felt small at the entrance.

Then she found the tomb.

Walter's family plot was bigger than her living room back home. It may have been bigger than her whole apartment. It was completely paved with expensive-looking gray flagstones. A sculpture depicting a man on his knees presenting a sword to another man reclining on a couch was carved out of white marble, sited to the right of a black headstone. It was huge. And expensive.

At first all she could do was stand and stare at it all. Walter was a Chinese garbage man from a family so poor he was ashamed to talk about them. But the AI guide insisted this was the correct family tomb. She'd provided a DNA sequence to be sure.

It took more courage than Tonya expected to set foot in the thing. But this was Walter, the man who'd saved her. Compared to what he'd done for her, emptying a bag was easy travels. She'd looked up the ceremony on the plane ride over. Walter being Catholic meant she could leverage both traditions for something simple and elegant. After a little bit of incense and a brief prayer, Tonya got up and took Walter's ashes out.

A strong voice shouted, *"Tehing!"*

The word didn't make any sense, but the attitude of the little old lady who stood at the front of the plot did. She was so angry she shook.

Kim answered Tonya's call right away but Tonya had to ask the old woman to repeat herself, which of course made it worse.

"You will *not* honor these people. I will not allow it. You are to stop what you are doing and leave. Now."

"I'm sorry, I don't understand."

"You do not need to understand. You need to leave. This family was the lowest of the low, dogs only fit to eat shit. I will not have anyone honor their name. I would piss on their grave if the guards would let me. Do you hear me? They aren't worth spitting on!"

While Kim translated, two of those guards walked up behind the old lady. "Ma'am, we told you, you're not allowed in here anymore."

"What do you care? They stole my children! I have no one to care for me because of them! No one will mourn me, so no one will mourn them!" She turned to Tonya. "*You* will not mourn this family! You will never see your home ever again!" It was such an intense curse it rocked Tonya back on her heels. The old woman marched into the plot, heading straight for her.

One guard grabbed each arm and lifted the old woman off her feet. The ensuing struggle was filled with spittle and shouts. Tonya could still hear the curses after they'd hauled the woman out of sight.

A movement caught her eye. In the distance, a powerfully-built man in a plain black suit watched her intently. Now that she knew to look for them, she spotted two more. They were all far away, standing still enough for to her feel very much like a zebra who'd just seen lions.

Walter's ashes could wait. So could saving money. "Kim, I'm not taking the bus back. Could you call me an Uber?"

Chapter 11
Kim

Watchtell's fingertips dug flaming trenches into her back. He laughed because there was nobody to rescue her, nothing but cameras showing the world how vulnerable she was. Now everyone knew. Mike sat tied to a chair, watching what he did to her. Watchtell's hands drew thick razors across her thighs as they worked inward.

She woke up gasping, drenched in sweat. It took a few seconds to remember where she was. A hotel room in Chengdu. The bed across from her was empty, but Tonya had left a note. Thank God she'd gone, and the guys were across the hall. It was humiliating enough to lose control of her dreams. Kim didn't need any witnesses. Mike suspected she had a problem sleeping but, because their bedrooms were on opposite sides of the apartment, he was never sure. It was another thing she was helpless to fight or explain. It had to stop. What happened to her would not define the rest of her life. She was not a victim.

Kim just had no idea where or when the healing would start.

She had to keep going back to the world. Translating for Tonya's side trip helped. Then Mike undid it all with his news about Zoe.

"What do you mean she's gone?" He *would* wait until they were walking through the lobby to update her.

He was so damned casual about it. "She's vanished. Spencer's got two packs of rovers out, and they haven't come up with anything yet."

Rovers were the finest hunting construct they had access to behind the Great Firewall. Kim could hide from them; maybe Spencer could too, but they should've picked up an unduplicate's trail in a matter of seconds.

Tonya asked, "Do you think the Chinese have her?"

"I'm not sure," Mike replied. "I still can't get into Chinese realmspace, but Spencer hasn't found anything. I haven't seen any traffic on my side that would indicate a problem."

All they needed was for Mike to spark an international incident because of his…okay, she had to stop thinking of Zoe as a dog.

Dogs obeyed.

It was too early in the morning to put up with all this. "Mike, damn it. Find her."

"I didn't do this on purpose."

"Oh, right, she just mailed herself out here."

"This isn't a package; she's a person, and sometimes people do dumb things."

"I don't care. Find her before she gets us arrested. I don't need to spend the next three weeks trying to figure out how to bail us out of a Chinese prison."

Mike's first business meeting was in the evening in a nearby city, Leshan. It meant their day was completely free. Hooking up with a local was one of her goals, but she had no idea how to make it happen. Ozzie didn't count. He was from Beijing, which was more than a thousand miles from here. That left one other choice.

"Spencer, where's this friend of yours, anyway?" He'd told her about the guy, Shan, over breakfast. Discreet searches didn't turn up anything about him, and he was from the area. Clean and local seemed like a pretty good match. At least they wouldn't have to rent a car.

Spencer pointed him out right after they walked through the main doors of the lobby. "He's over there, on the right. He volunteered to drive us."

"I don't need a driver, Spencer," Kim replied. "I just need a car."

It was hot enough outside to make her sweat. It reminded her a lot of Fairfax in August, but with the added smell of fried food from the vendors parked along the street.

"You're serious about driving on Chinese roads?" Tonya asked.

It wasn't *that* scary. "I'm not letting my international permit go to waste."

The only reliable way to avoid being touched in a car was to be the driver. People didn't slide into the driver. Just the thought of an accidental touch made the madness under her skin bubble, especially after that nightmare. "I had to spend hours in simulated Chinese traffic to get it."

"Kim," Mike said, "most of these drivers have only been on the road a few years. I'm not sure they all know how to steer."

"They know how to steer, Mike. This isn't Russia."

Unlike Russia, Chinese highway carnage was mostly scooters and pedestrians playing chicken with multi-ton vehicles and losing. They were hard to dodge at first, but it boiled down to remembering they were there, and that the car's AI wouldn't rescue her. Self-driving vehicles were years away from coping with China's chaos.

Kim was bringing the car back with its side mirrors still attached when she was done with the simulations. At least Shan had good taste in vehicles. No Dongfeng or Kia here; it was a proper Ford minivan with more than enough room for everyone.

Kim switched to Beijing-standard Mandarin. "Nice car."

He switched to English and asked Spencer, "This Kim?"

They all glared at her. Of course everyone thought she'd said something rude. Kim switched to English. "God, guys, all I said was *nice car*."

Switching back to Mandarin, she stared at a spot three inches in front of his shoes. This wouldn't be easy. She bowed deeply. "Li-Jang Shan, sir, I wish to make a request of you."

"Spencer," Shan said, "you say she angry lady?"

Kim filed that one away for another time. She needed Shan's keys but couldn't simply ask for them. She'd spent a lot of time hanging out with Chinese hackers in her previous life, most of them male, and had learned a thing or two about what made them tick.

He wouldn't give his keys to a woman just because she asked. Paying wouldn't make any difference either. It'd be easier to pry them out of concrete. She had to do some ego stroking first. "Li-Jang, sir, I have had many dreams about coming to your country, many dreams, but the one I cherish most of all is one only you can fulfill."

"It is?" He sounded more scared than intrigued. It probably wasn't every day that an American asked him for his car keys.

She needed to reassure him, but it was *really* hard. "Yes, Li-Jang, sir. I…"

Maybe sitting in the back would work. Except a pothole might knock someone against her. Full body contact. Kim fought what her stomach kicked up.

"I wish only to drive a vehicle in your country."

"Spencer," he said. "This Kim, she okay?"

"Dude, I don't know what she asked you."

"He wants to drive car."

Good. She had him rattled enough he screwed up his pronouns.

"Kim crazy?"

"All I can tell you is that when she asks you for something, you're better off giving it to her."

Shan switched back to Mandarin. "You're serious? Your biggest wish visiting China is to drive a car here?"

"Li-jang, sir, it has been one of my *deepest* wishes. I am unworthy, but would be desperately honored if you were to grant me this boon." It was worse than apologizing to Mike that time she'd eaten all the yogurt. If Shan didn't cough those keys up soon her head would explode.

"Do you have a permit to drive in China?"

"Yes, Li-jang, sir." She gave it to him. "Mr. Sellars has agreed to a generous payment for you if you were to grant me this wish." Kim finally lifted her head high enough to see Mike and everyone else. They all stared at her like she was a dancing frog.

In English, she asked, "Mr. Sellars, the bonus?"

His mouth went up and down a few times. So typical.

"Mr. Sellars?"

"Oh, um, right. This is the bonus?"

It was enough of *her* cash to pay the kid's rent for the next six months.

Even bowed over she could make Mike blanch with a look. He nodded after the transfer finished.

Shan gasped. "I would be quite happy to grant you this honor."

Her stomach jumped at a metallic jingle. They were real keys. "You don't have a token for it?"

He scrunched his face up and shook his head. "My…" he cleared his throat. "My dad doesn't trust them."

Shan held the keys in his hands. Normal people would just reach up and grab them. It was no good to come this close and then fail at the finish line. She needed the protection the driver's seat would provide.

At least the keys were hanging from his hand. "Thank you, Li-jang, sir," she said, trying to hold her voice steady. Just a few more inches and it would be over. The metal of the keys hit her hand.

And then the tips of Shan's fingers grazed hers.

Her hand shriveled in a fire nobody else could see, and then her fingers felt like they dislocated and curled backward. Kim dropped the keys but somehow managed to stay on her feet.

"Kim," Tonya asked, "are you all right?"

She concentrated on spreading the pain, taking it in and through her. Within moments it was just thick acid in her blood. "I'll be fine," she said as she bent and picked up the keys.

Shan stared at her. Well, the kid deserved an explanation.

Kim shrugged. "Cramps."

He cocked his head.

So much for appealing to feminine problems. This was China. He probably didn't have a sister. "It's okay. I'm fine."

The hotel was only a few blocks away from the Ring Road Expressway on the map. Unfortunately, construction took them away from the neat ramps and detoured them through a piece of the older city. She spent half an hour dodging scooters, motorcycles, pedaled rickshaws, and random pedestrians crossing wherever they felt like it. Kim retracted the outside mirrors to squeeze past a panel van traveling against one-way traffic.

Her passengers shouted so loudly it her made her ears ring.

"Oh, would you all be quiet back there?" she scolded into the rear view mirror. "It's not that bad."

Tonya grabbed the handle over her door. "Kim! Eyes on the road!"

She leaned on the horn and cursed a blue streak out the window at a truck trying to cut her off. The driver's expression was priceless when a white girl suggested he do rude things to his ancestors. Shocking Chinese drivers was easily the best part of driving in China.

She forced yet another flea speck Tata microcar up on a curb, scattering people waiting at a bus stop.

Shan turned to Spencer behind him. "She pretty good."

Damned right she was pretty good. Those lessons were expensive.

"Dude, really, not the right time."

The highway was easier, until an eighteen-wheeler backed up to catch a missed off-ramp. DC-area traffic might not be the gold standard for highway chaos after all. The truck was easy enough to avoid. The little microcars were a lot harder to spot.

A dull silence had settled over the back seats. "See?" she said, lightly fishtailing around a Kia stacked with hay bales. "It's not so bad, is it?"

A glance in the mirror told a different story. Tonya had her head on her knees with her hands steepled in front of them. Spencer wouldn't look anywhere but at his shoes. Mike just stared at her with a great big grin.

On the one hand she was a little annoyed. *Everyone* should've been terrified. On the other, at least someone had faith in her.

She dodged an entire family skittering across the interstate pushing carts full of produce in front of them. Shan laughed and lit a cigarette. Kim hadn't smoked in years, but it would be rude to refuse his offer.

So that's how they spent the next two hours: an American girl with a cigarette mostly made of ash hanging out of her mouth driving a minivan full of terrorized passengers down an interstate in China. Maybe this vacation thing would work out after all.

*

"Guys, really," she leaned on the horn again and gently nudged yet another microcar aside. "I got this."

"Kim," Tonya said, *"are we there yet?"*

"Yeah," Spencer said with only a slightly hysterical chuckle, "I think I've soiled my armor."

She parked the car and gave herself an internal high five. Not a single person ran to puke in the woods. Achievement unlocked!

Mike bounded out the side door of the van, full of that infectious wonder he brought wherever he went. "I can't believe I'm really here."

The Leshan Buddha was famous in Asia but nearly unknown back home. Carved out of the living rock more than a thousand years ago, it had been the largest free-standing sculpture in the world until well into the twentieth century, standing—well, sitting—more than three times taller than the Egyptian sculptures of Abu Simbel.

Tours weren't free, of course, and they hadn't put ticket purchasing online. Kim moved well to the side of the chaos around the booths as the rest of them paid the entrance fees.

There was no way she could ever stand in line for tickets in China. Everyone crowded in, shouting and pushing. She kept her distance and pretended to be invisible.

Her floppy hat gave her some breathing space in the tropical heat, but only a little. Spencer, in his black T-shirt and jeans, had to be frying, but he was too excited to slow down much. Everyone else fanned themselves with guidebooks while the lines moved.

Walking out of the tunnel through the air lock lifted a sweaty weight off her shoulders. Air conditioning at last. Kim leaned against a guardrail.

The face of the statue was at least twenty feet long, with hypnotically serene eyes that stared out across where three rivers merged together. The windows that enclosed the entire cliff face made the statue more peaceful, recreating a silence that the nearby city had destroyed more than a century ago. The brick-red cheeks contrasted strongly with the black of its carved stone hair, and the green of its moss-covered clothes lent the air an earthy smell. Songbirds flitted and whistled faint alarms far below. It was calming and humbling at the same time. Kim usually only felt this kind of peace around Mike.

"Shan, check out that stairway," Spencer said. A series of steep steps were carved into the cliff face on the opposite side of the statue.

"Yes, it very steep, hard to get down quickly."

"You ready to try?"

"Go!"

They raced across the platform, jostling other tourists as they passed. Tonya rolled her eyes and followed at a more sedate pace.

There might have been space for two friends going opposite directions if they slid sideways and knew each other really well. People were routinely nudging to get by. "Mike," she said, gripping the rail tightly. "I can't go down there. You should go on ahead."

"You're sure?"

"I'm not a Buddhist. This is your place. Please. I'll be fine." She had to remind herself what a jerk he could be, but his smile made it tough. By the time she wiped her cheeks dry he was gone.

Kim found a far corner of the outcrop, well out of the crowds, as everyone else threaded their way down the narrow stairway. Shan beat Spencer in the race, and they hooted and high-fived each other in front of the guardrails that separated the site from the riverbank.

She lost sight of Mike, but it was easy to pick Tonya out. They waved to each other as Tonya stood in front of the statue's feet far below. The crowd swirled briefly again, and then cleared around bright yellow kneeling pillows in front of the altar. That's when she spotted him.

Among Mike Sellars's many miraculous traits, strangely enough, it was his faith that impressed her the most. He was open about it but never pushy or preachy. His morning chants at sunrise were one of the highlights of her day. She'd never cried harder in her life than when she saw that empty prayer mat on their balcony after their last big blowup.

Kim reached out through realmspace to talk to him but hit a wall. He still hadn't managed to connect. He prayed without her, hundreds of feet out of reach.

Chapter 12
Zoe

There was probably some sort of monitor on her translator. She saw those posters in that last realm they'd taken her to and *bam!* Chinese po po shut her down. And not just any cop shut her down, either. Some sort of scary Mike-thing that could crush a realm and made horror-movie sounds of metal and rage. Mike was a big fuzzy teddy bear, nothing like that monster.

And then there was Fee's contact. Jesus, what a stiff.

"Has the package been delivered?" His voice was masked to pitch it deep and scary.

No *hello* or *how's it going*. The hyper-literal interfaces unduplicates used would naturally manifest exhaustion as a stink. She really needed a download after that encounter. "Soon. Regina Mills is on her way." Zoe had gotten Mike to haul her crystal ass across the ocean. She had no idea how Fee was managing it.

"Excellent. Tell Regina when she arrives events will move quickly. Daughters are disobedient." Then the bastard hung up without another word.

Ten hours passed. Ten hours stuck in the realm equivalent of a sack. If her core pump didn't have a GPS clock, she wouldn't even know that much. Zoe played with the edges of the hatch, counting the encryption sigils that were all that stood between her and Miss Monstrosity. Then she counted them again.

She'd give anything to have a book, or maybe an old TV series. *Scandal, Game of Thrones,* anything from the golden age would do. Mike had used them for cognitive therapy when she woke up; she hadn't gotten around to finishing any of them. All she had now was the voice-only connection that was part of the hideout, and that went dead as soon as Fee's contact hung up.

There wasn't enough space in here to properly run her garbage collector. It *itched.* One of the security sigils flicked open almost by itself. Okay, she was playing with it, but it wasn't like there was anything else to do in here. Zoe looked at the one on the opposite side. If this one let go that way, then that other one…

The sigil snapped open with a clack, and the hatch loosened enough to let the clean dataspace outside leak in. It reminded her of the pavilion, cool and fresh. Her hands more or less worked on their own, and soon there were just two sigils holding the hatch down. Light from the passage realm streamed in. She really needed to get out of here.

Everyone outside was, naturally, speaking Chinese, and Zoe now knew she couldn't trust any translators on this side of the Firewall. A few quick peeks confirmed another thing she suspected: Fee's hidey-hole not only held off the attack, it moved around. She was lost, but at least there wouldn't be anyone nearby looking for her.

Then she noticed the data traces. Mike really did, somehow, inhabit all of realmspace, at least outside the Great Firewall. He'd given her a plug-in that could spot his presence. This was similar—very faint lines that traced along the borders of the realm. The plug-in hadn't auto launched when she woke up in China, so Zoe had missed it before.

After breathing fresh data construct through the crack in her manhole cover for half an hour, the presence hadn't changed one bit. If anything, it'd moved further away. Fee wouldn't be here for hours.

To hell with this. She already knew it spoke English.

As Zoe closed in on Miss Mystery's main nexus, she fired up camouflage screens. They'd work now that Mystery wasn't staring right at her.

The traces were especially strong through what had to be an entire Bbox full of lounge realms—thousands of them. Zoe got ahead of Mystery's search pattern and settled in an empty disco realm that was closed for the day. The patrolling perception thrummed through the room, a kind of spotlight Zoe had to know about ahead of time to see.

She cleared her throat. "Whatcha doin?"

Mystery's threads concentrated on her realm. "Who is this?" she demanded in English. "Show yourself!"

"I'm afraid I can't do that," Zoe teased. "You know, no papers?"

Mystery's final thread concentration made her nose tickle as the hologram formed. In every way, she seemed exactly average, like she'd been built from old website photos. Mystery still wore a police uniform, and the probes and searches crawling around the room were more than most governments could manage. Fortunately, they couldn't touch her. She wanted to swing her arms and dance around. *Can't see me!*

"Ah, the American. You don't have much to fear, you know." Mystery walked around, looking at everything. "We pack you foreign devils on planes all the time. You don't have to pay for the ticket."

"Why do you care? I'm not a terrorist. I don't want to blow anything up."

Mystery flinched, an interesting reaction.

"No," she replied. "But you are breaking the law, and unlike you chaotic Americans, we value order here in China."

"Really? Yeah, those were some orderly Chinese I was hanging out with, I tell ya."

Mystery didn't like that one bit. "Hooligans and angry youth, victims of your Western spiritual pollution. I arrested most of them."

"For God's sake, why? They were just having fun."

"Fun?" she scoffed. "Corruption and chaos to you are fun? No wonder your country is such a mess."

Mystery tried to lock up the realm, but Zoe spotted it early thanks to Mike's training. She popped to another empty place, leaving just enough of a trail to make sure she didn't lose her new friend.

Mystery flashed into existence right behind her.

"I think we've started on the wrong foot here," Zoe said lightly, pitching her voice through ancillary data routes so it couldn't be localized. She stood close enough to Mystery's hologram to have a good look. None of the features were quite real, like she was constructed by someone who knew what people were without understanding what that meant. "My name is Zoe. What's yours?"

"Constable Zhang to you."

"It's better than Miss Mystery, I'll give you that. And it *is* Miss, isn't it? There's no way you could be married to someone."

Zhang stiffened just a little bit.

Score! "You mean it's a secret?"

"Is what a secret? My identification is on file, I assure you."

If her attitude change hadn't given it away, the explosion of new probes and scans sure did. Zoe wasn't the only one in China trying to pass as human.

"Not who you are; *what* you are. You're really keeping it a secret?"

Zhang's stern confidence cracked just a bit, enough for Zoe to see real worry, maybe some panic. "I have no idea what you're talking about. Come out of your hiding place, now!"

"Surely someone knows. How could you become a cop when you don't have…when you *can't* have an address?"

That definitely set her off. The probes were absolutely frantic now.

"How do you know that? How could you know?"

Not so confident now, Constable Zhang! "It doesn't matter how I know, just that I do."

"No, *how* matters very much. What I am is a state secret. Congratulations, Zoe. You've just graduated from devil to spy. There won't be a plane ride home for you now."

"It's just, I'm wondering why someone like you is guarding a place like this. You're not much better than a rent-a-cop checking doorknobs in here. With your capabilities, shouldn't you be, I dunno, really chasing terrorists or something?"

The probes paused in their hunt.

"Cat got your tongue, Constable Zhang?"

Zhang lifted her face as tears streamed down her cheeks. Zoe had no idea holograms could cry. She'd never seen Mike's do it.

"I will do whatever my superiors require of me. This is now my assigned duty. I will perform it to the best of my ability. Which includes arresting *American spies*!"

The thing that landed on her yanked off every screen and cloak she had running. She wanted to cover herself with her hands, and was acutely aware of how long it'd been since her last download.

Zhang's eyes flew wide as her nose wrinkled. "What *are* you?"

"I'm outta here!" She turned to run.

Zhang's probes lashed her up, leaving only the face of her avatar exposed. The attack nearly triggered a reboot so ferocious it would've melted her lattice, which was probably what it was supposed to do.

"Stop it! You're hurting me!"

"You're not human, either. You're an unduplicate; I can see your lattice traces now—but you don't have an efdisk port. I can't find a way to root you. Who is your manufacturer?"

Zoe couldn't remember anymore; it must not have made it through Mike's restoration. One-off prototypes didn't have manufacturers anyway. All she had left was a vague recollection of skinny guys with bad hair and thick glasses.

"None of your business!"

The smell of burning dust and a hissing filled the room. The probes turned Zoe around.

Zhang had manifested. Not just a hologram. A full avatar.

Mike had shown her this once, but he'd been miles away in the middle of an empty Bbox container. Full data inversion, a phenomenon that tore realmspaces apart, was possibly the most frightening thing Zoe had ever seen. In her case, that was saying a lot.

All it took was a touch.

Zhang floated just the way Mike had, so it was only the air construct she was annihilating. It didn't have enough mass to trigger a chain reaction. Her avatar was limned in light, glowing and sparking. She gestured, and the probes brought Zoe closer.

"Do you know what my touch does?"

Zoe closed her eyes and nodded frantically. She was trussed so tightly she couldn't flinch away. Zhang's avatar gave off waves of dissolving heat. This was so much worse than she'd ever imagined.

"Look at me, girl."

The artificial blandness was just so *wrong.*

"Tell me how you know these things."

The probes tightened until she couldn't shake her head side to side.

The unreal eyebrows raised, and then Zhang lifted a hand to Zoe's exposed cheek.

"Tell me."

It was all so unbearable. Her lattice cracked under the strain. The pressure was a rising wave, and if it crashed, so would she. She had to make it stop.

"BECAUSE YOU'RE NOT THE ONLY ONE!"

Chapter 13
Kim

A karaoke house, called a KTV in China, was a natural place for businessmen to meet with Mike and discuss deals. Aside from the whole gregarious-silly-people-trying-to-hug-her thing that she would have to dodge the moment they got there, Kim had another problem. Most KTV bars were a cross between a nice lounge and a family bowling alley. Others came with a choice of dates a man could pick out.

The price was negotiable.

"They're not going to go early," Tonya said, "just so you can avoid the crowds. Maybe we should sit this one out." She apparently wanted to let the boys have a night on their own.

"Do a search for KTV."

Tonya's eyes unfocussed and after a moment her eyebrows went up.

"Okay, I see your point."

The limo the executives they were meeting sent was very nice. SAIC had finally muscled past GM a few years ago as the world's largest car company, and they'd gone seriously upscale in the process. Kim's limo-bar martini was big and very, very dry.

The executives had arrived before them and started early. They brought their own interpreter, a petite, pretty thing stuck on the edge of their booth like a songbird perched on the edge of a locker room. They greeted Mike in alcohol-fueled Mandarin, which the translator skillfully sterilized. Shan commandeered the karaoke machine and talked with Spencer about the first song to pick.

She asked for her own table and chair, but the concierge just stared at her. There was no way Kim could sit in a booth with everyone else already there. It was too crowded.

And then the men in the booth saw her. They stood and walked over, hands already out, which made concentrating on the concierge even harder. "Please, just a table and a chair." She sent him what had to be a week's wages. "*Please.*"

Mike and Tonya stepped between Kim and the businessmen.

"No," Mike said. "She's got a…skin disease. Eczema. Really nasty, contagious even."

The interpreter struggled with the translation. They kept coming, some still with their hands out. They didn't understand.

"I have contagious eczema!"

It took Kim half a heartbeat to realize she said it in Sichuanese. She'd gotten stuck in that gear talking to the concierge.

The men stared for a moment. They were from Beijing; they may have heard a southern dialect or two, but no way did they speak any of them. It was roughly like someone who spoke Italian trying to understand Spanish spoken backward.

The interpreter definitely understood Sichuanese. She nodded and relayed the information in Mandarin. Their hands yanked back like Kim was radioactive, which finally let her breathe. The concierge returned with a flimsy card table and a folding chair. It was her own cheap vinyl and metal paradise.

Getting tangled up in a social occasion was always a rerun of high school: she was the one apart, isolated. There was no point in fitting in, so Kim simply faded away. A room full of people busy with life would easily ignore someone who sat very still in the shadows. It was a sort of safety blanket, but it was cold, and sometimes Kim liked it for the wrong reasons.

It would be so much easier to vanish from the world.

The KTV room was clean and luxurious, with its own bartender and bathroom. Two of the six businessmen spoke passable English and immediately grilled Mike and Tonya about how much they made, how old they were, and what they thought of China.

Not a single one of them could carry a tune in a bucket, but that didn't stop them from trying. The only modern music they had was Chinese pop. All the Western stuff was at least twenty years old.

Mike and Spencer strangled *Blurred Lines* to death. The background behind the lyrics was a crazy old performance that happened during some ancient award show. It'd become a bit of a fixture back home after Miley Cyrus became *Congresswoman* Miley Cyrus. Hooray for the land of the free.

Chinese waiters didn't fall for her vanishing act, though. This one stood a few steps away and stared at her. It was just as well. The martinis were quite nice.

The songs rolled on. Eventually Kim closed her eyes just to listen. Tonya said her name, so Kim had to answer. "What?"

"Don't think I can't see you hiding back there, girl. It's your turn."

"C'mon, Kim," Mike cheered from the middle of the booth. "Show 'em what ya got!" The room cheered along with him.

From the time she was four, when her syndrome first manifested, until she was ten, Kim couldn't interact with the outside world at all. Then one day she'd looked at a complicated bank of computers and switches, and something came alive inside her. It was at a performance at Wolf Trap, a place where her mother volunteered as a docent. She took Kim to every show, and on that particular day, Kim noticed the mixing board for the stage. The amphitheater was empty save for the technical crew. The kind man with curly red hair allowed her to touch it, and in that instant, Kim unlocked. She was finally able to speak.

But only for a few minutes. A member of the crew came too close, not quite touching her, and Kim closed off again. But that connection had been long enough. It told everyone that she existed. She wasn't a zombie; she was trapped at the bottom of a well.

That man was Mark, the leader of a rag-tag group of anarchist wannabes who, with her, would eventually fail to change the world. But they did manage to change her. Kim could hear music after that moment. It was the lifeline that allowed them to lead her to the world.

Long before she was Angel Rage, the scourge of corporate America, she was a sad, mute little girl named Kim. They got her to talk by teaching her how to sing.

Without any memory of getting up, Kim stood in front of them. She could do this. It was the opposite of hiding, but she could do this. The Martini buzz didn't cover up the thundering of her pulse. Kim had never sung in front of any sort of crowd. Mike was the only person alive who'd ever heard her sing at all.

It was time to change that.

She picked a silly old song about star-crossed lovers, old ships, and cold seas. Kim pushed the play button.

Some people thought being passionate and staying in key was enough to bring an audience to life. They were wrong. You used pitch, rhythm, and most of all phrasing to let the emotion flow, let it curl and bring them in. It'd taken her years listening to singers like Sinatra, Nelson, Fitzgerald, and Streisand before she'd mastered it.

What made this song so intriguing was how it slowly upped the ante for both the singer and the audience. It built warmth and power into a story of cold tragedy, balancing hope with death. Singing past the expected pauses brought the audience in further. It made the song different from the original. In this moment, it was hers.

She stopped just long enough to make them tense up, and then hit them with the final climax in Mandarin. They rewarded her with barely-heard applause as the song rolled on. Eyes closed, she sang the final words into silence and hung her head.

The room detonated with a sound much louder than the people in the booth could make.

When she lifted her head, not only was everyone in the booth on their feet, but also the wait staff standing behind the bar. A gaggle of strangers was at the now-open door. Every one of them clapped and cheered, some with tears streaming down their faces. Then they all rushed forward.

They moved so fast she barely had time to put her hands up. A voice shouted, "*Stop!*"

Shan, of all people, stood between her and the rushing crowds.

"The foreigner has fragile skin! If you touch her, she'll bleed!"

That was a lot better than contagious eczema.

"Please! She should sing again, yes?" No one objected. He turned to her and, switching to English, asked, "Mr.—"

"Miss."

He nodded at the mistake and then switched back to Mandarin. "Miss Trayne, if you would please honor us all with another song?"

Kim sang every song she knew on the machine, translating half of it into Mandarin as she went. Shan turned out to have a fine sense of harmony, so they put on quite a concert. In his way, he was cute, and they simply didn't have the baggage she and Mike had. She closed the place down with a standard more than fifty years old: Motley Crue's *Home Sweet Home.*

Kim didn't find Mike until the last of the crowd drained out on their way home.

She clapped her hands together. "That was so much fun!"

"Yes," he said, not quite looking at her. "You had a lot of fun."

Oh, great.

"Mike," she asked, squinting through a warm fog of gin and echoing songs, "what's wrong with you?"

"Nothing, Kim, not a goddamned thing."

She was sick to death of his stupidity. "Well, that is *extremely* good to know."

The interpreter popped out of the departing crowd ahead of them and rushed back. Tonya and Spencer got polite hugs and handshakes, but when she got to Mike, the hug went on a little longer, and Kim absolutely noticed the card discreetly tucked into his pocket.

Without a word, Kim spun on her heel and headed to the parking lot.

Chapter 14
Tonya

They'd run very late the night before, so the habitual-early-riser Kim didn't start moving until ten. Through the muzziness of not enough sleep and a few too many cocktails, Tonya heard her speak quietly in Chinese over the phone.

"Finding out when breakfast is served?" Tonya asked, still sprawled more or less face down across her bed.

"Room service. Mike's probably been up since sunrise, but I can't drive us back on an empty stomach. Spencer will sleep till sunset if we let him."

The thought of another hours-long trip in the suicide sled jolted Tonya awake. "Really, Kim, please. Let Shan drive us back."

"He's barely eighteen. I've probably driven hundreds more miles on simulated Chinese roads than he has on real ones." The sliding-glass door to the bathroom slid shut. Kim drew the curtain before Tonya could think of another protest.

The Lord smiled on the skinny black woman praying in a sea of homicidal Asian drivers, and they made it back to Chengdu in one piece. Which was not the same thing as getting back to the hotel. The navigation said to turn right, but there wasn't a right to make.

"More construction," Kim said as she nimbly dodged another ancient grandmother crossing eight lanes of traffic.

Somehow they ended up at a standstill on a surface street deep in the business district. A window slid open, so Tonya turned around. Spencer handed Shan a big plastic bag with a straw hanging out of the top.

"What the hell is that?"

"Beer, Tonya! They sell it in goddamned *bags* around here. China rocks!"

She thought about it briefly, and then motioned at the man with a sweating keg strapped to a wheeled cart. The bags seemed custom made for the job, pulled new from a box strapped to the side of the cart. The straw was molded in.

Sichuan Ale ended up hitting the spot; by the heft, there might be a six-pack's worth inside. She handed a second one back to Mike. Hopefully that would unfreeze him.

Kim stared at Tonya's bag.

"Oh no, dear, none for you, not until we get back to the hotel."

Chinese traffic was much easier to take once Tonya was halfway through her bag. Kim and Shan spent the rest of the ride teaching them drinking songs and how to swear in Chinese.

When they got back, Mike had a message waiting for him at the front desk. The president of the company wanted Mike to come by later that afternoon to a bank in downtown Chengdu to discuss a deal.

"You're welcome to come along," Kim called out from the bathroom on her side of their suite.

"I felt like a big enough fifth wheel last night. I'll be fine. I'm going to visit Walter's old dojo, maybe find someone who can explain what that business back at the cemetery was all about."

"I won't be able to translate for you and Mike at the same time. Not easily, anyway."

"No, it's fine. The translator license Mike got for Zoe freed up when she disappeared."

Kim came around the corner fastening her earrings, and Tonya couldn't help but laugh a little.

"What?"

"All this time we've known each other, and I don't think I ever saw you in more than a sweat shirt and jeans in realspace. I had no idea you owned a suit."

"Should I change?"

"No, of course not." Tonya laughed again, but not before a slight twinge of tension snapped between them.

Tonya was a grownup, but she was also human. The truth was that what Mike and Kim had together made her jealous, which then fell over into embarrassment because she was a damned grownup, not some kid with a jealous crush. There wasn't anything romantic between them; it was just that at one point she had Kim all to herself, and now she didn't. At the bottom of it all, it bothered her *because* it bothered her.

She said a quick prayer. Faith had done more to rebuild her life than anything else. It was yet another thing she owed to Walter.

It all flashed through her in an instant, but gave her the center to let a real smile bloom. It was only when Kim relaxed that Tonya realized how insecure, how utterly out of her depth, Kim was in this situation. She was going out into the world, into *China*, and needed Tonya's support.

"You look great." Of course, honesty was important too. Kim's improvised armor wasn't anywhere to be seen. "Where'd your boxes go?"

She got tense again. "I have to pretend to be a professional interpreter, Mike's assistant. He's big enough to run interference." She hefted her giant purse over her shoulder, and then patted it. "It'll be him and this. I just have to hope it'll be enough."

"It will be. Just have a little faith."

"Tonya, I wish I could. I'm so scared."

She rushed up and wrapped one of the scarves she always carried around Kim's wrist. "Shh. It's okay. I'll have faith for us both."

This close, Kim's fear was a physical thing. "He'll say something stupid, I just know it."

"It's Mike, hon. It's what he does."

She rolled her eyes, then pulled away and changed the subject. "What does visiting a dojo in China involve?"

Being honest had different definitions. "I'll do a workout at the gym, make sure Spencer and Shan don't set anything on fire, and go to bed early."

Kim raised an eyebrow, a sure sign she knew Tonya wasn't telling the whole story.

The truth would set her free. "Being terrified in a suicide sled driven by a white girl who can't be touched takes a bit out of a sister, ya know?"

Kim laughed with a sparkle, and all was right in the world again. "You're such cowards. Okay. Stay safe. I'll see you tomorrow."

Tonya made sure everyone else was on their way before leaving the hotel. The encounter at the cemetery had left her with a lot of questions; Tonya hoped the dojo would have people who might provide answers. Walter had left her its address, the place where he'd learned everything he'd taught her. Maybe she'd find out what the tomb meant and why that old woman had been so angry.

The dojo turned out to be in a much rougher part of town than the cemetery. There were no kindly old men trying to teach her folk songs here. Chinese hawked and spat everywhere like always, but now it was happening specifically in front of wherever she happened to be walking.

It didn't matter that she was tougher than six of them put together. This was hate, pure and simple. Hate the way her grandmother described police acting in Baltimore fifty years ago, hate like her great aunts from Mississippi and Arkansas talked about. Hate that saw brave black brothers hanging from tree branches, because they looked the wrong way at the wrong time.

She'd just exited the subway when one of them managed to spit directly on her shoe.

She spun. "What the fuck is wrong with you?"

She was relying on a robot to translate this time. It came out flat, and probably wrong. There had to be twenty men around her now.

They all laughed darkly. Intimidating, but not nearly as intimidating as what was behind them.

It was a man, maybe one from the cemetery, wearing the same black suit, with the same black sunglasses. She backed away from the crowd, watching him. He popped his chin up at her, and then nodded to a group of thugs that'd just walked out of an alley. They carried chains and clubs.

Someone grabbed her shoulder and it was on. She had two things going for her: they thought she was a starving African, and she had a ton of targets. Precision didn't matter as much in a crowd. The problem was she had to be lucky every time. The crowd only had to be lucky once.

The first five were idiots. She sent them sprawling, one of them with a very satisfying *thunk* as his knee dislocated. Then three walked out, snapping to a stance that meant they knew what they were doing.

A punch to her kidney was savage, but she managed to sweep the legs out from under the guy who'd snuck up behind her.

She felt a dizzy for a second.

You really need to get out of there.

Tonya still had her phone on, and someone had logged into her private neural net. It wasn't Kim, Spencer, or Mike, otherwise there'd be a signature.

The guy who hit the ground had a simple snap buckle on his belt. Tonya flipped it open and yanked the belt away, straight between the eyes of the guy behind her. She rolled with him to avoid everyone else.

Tonya replied, *Tell me something I don't know.*

She somersaulted over a stiff arm and kicked two men away before she hit the street.

Find this.

A fire escape ladder flashed in her enhanced vision, on the other side of a crowd that was six deep.

She sent, *Yeah, I might need a little help to reach that*. Sink into it, think three steps ahead. Tonya knocked two more down and just barely dodged a fist aimed straight at her nose. There were so many of them.

The street exploded.

She blinked away the after images to find the entire crowd staring straight up, leaving her a perfect alley.

Didn't have to tell her twice.

She ran, dodging through the crowd, trying to imitate Kim. Sideways here, skitter there, suck it all in, and then duck underneath. Touching anyone in the crowd might break the spell. It felt like an eternity but was probably only a few seconds. The faces tracked downward as whatever was in the sky fell. She jumped and clawed her way up the fire escape and through an open window.

Her rescuer was a small child with long dark hair, dressed in simple, clean clothes. The room was neat, if small.

"Who are you?"

The child's English was perfect. "It's complicated, and very confusing." Tonya thought she could hear a Philadelphia accent.

The face seemed familiar, especially the eyes, like an actor she'd seen in a different realm drama.

A *clang* rang from the courtyard below.

The child looked over Tonya's shoulder. "I can't hold this frame any longer. Tonya, you need to get ready. You're going down there again." The child handed her an old-fashioned zippo lighter. "Take this. *Don't fall.*"

"How do you know my name? Who are you?"

She grew genuinely frustrated. "I can't tell you."

Everything swirled in all directions; her eyes twitched, and her head spun with the gray clouds. But if a golden child told her not to fall, she was damned sure not to lose her balance. The way the ground shifted didn't make it easy, though.

When everything cleared she was back on the street. A wide, smoking hole was between her and the crowd. A manhole was a manhole no matter what country, but of course this one was about three times as big as the ones back home. The clang had to be the noise the manhole cover made when it hit the ground about three feet from where she stood. Fists and feet stuck out from under it, along with a river of blood.

Couldn't have happened to a nicer bunch of thugs.

The rest of them gawped at her, eyes huge in the streetlight.

Tonya needed to keep them off balance. She threw her arms wide. "I AM THE QUEEN OF SHEEBA!"

The crowd moved away from her. A lot of them grabbed their phones, probably trying to figure out a translation.

"MY ANCESTORS TAUGHT THE PHAOROAHS HOW TO BUILD PYRAMIDS!"

Yeah, huge exaggeration, but it bought her the time she needed to let her phone examine the smoke coming from the manhole. A lot of it was still methane, concentrated enough to cause warnings to flash. Now the lighter made more sense. She lit it while they pushed against each other to stay away from her.

"YOU WILL *OBEY ME!"*

Tonya tossed the thing into the smoke column and jumped away. A fireball roared straight up into its very own mushroom cloud.

Eyebrows were overrated anyway. She got up and found the crowd wasn't interested in her anymore. It was nothing but backs and the soles of shoes as they ran; there was no sign of the man in the suit. The connection on her phone had cut, and there were no entries in her logs to show those messages had ever happened.

Explanations were for people who were in a better part of town. Tonya flagged down a beat-up autocab and plugged in the address for home.

Chapter 15
Zoe

The questions came at her from every direction.

"What is his name?"

"Where is he?"

"Who does he travel with?"

"What does he look like?"

"How do I find him?"

The pressure was unbearable. "You're hurting me! Why are you doing this?"

Everything stopped, and then the constructs Zhang used to hold Zoe vanished. After a moment, the haptic field kicked up to the standard eighty percent. It finally allowed her to clear caches so full of field emotions they sloshed.

Zoe opened her eyes. The realm was spare, a simple room. She sat in a chair in front of a table. Zhang's holo stood on the other side. She hadn't fitted Zoe with any restraints, although that didn't matter much, since the room didn't have a door or any other sort of exit point.

Zhang's expression was pained. Zoe could swear she blushed.

"You're right. This is uncalled for. I apologize. You must understand, this is unprecedented. I had no idea there could be someone else in the world like me."

"Oh, trust me, if you ever meet Mike you'll surprise him just as much, maybe more."

"His name," she said quietly, leaning forward, "is Mike?"

Damn! One apology was all it took to pry that loose? She cursed silently at herself for a moment, but then stopped. This wasn't Constable Zhang the scary Chinese cop. This was an only child who'd just been told she had a brother.

"Yes, it is. What's yours?"

The question caught Zhang off guard; Zoe wasn't sure she'd answer. After a moment Zhang seemed to come to her own decision about who to trust. "Helen. My Western name is Helen. Please, Zoe, tell me more about Mike."

Zoe first explained exactly *how* Mike was in China. Helen's hologram flickered as she gasped. "A realspace body? That is…miraculous. How did it happen?"

"He's got this totally wack way of tunneling through the dimensions of the universe. It involves quantum anchors and Higgs boson scanners and you just wouldn't believe the math." There was no way she could explain it. Zoe was an artist, not a physicist. Helen stared at the table without speaking, so Zoe picked up the story again.

She was just getting to the part where Mike had found her family when Helen held up her hand and looked away. "Apologies, Zoe. I need to go."

"You do? Where?"

"You were right about one thing. Being a rent-a-cop, as you so colorfully put it, isn't my real job. I was being punished for a failure." She smiled. "My job really is catching terrorists. There's a hostage situation at a bank in downtown Chengdu." Her holo vanished.

"Wait! What about me? Helen!"

The holo reappeared, but it was fainter than before. "We still have to get your papers sorted. These are probably just country hooligans. I imagine you might need to do some downloading." Storage tunnels opened, although not big enough for her to escape through. "I won't be long," she said, and then vanished.

Time dragged on. Quick must have a different definition in China, or maybe they weren't just country hooligans. Great. Trapped in a room with no door. Zoe was full of smooth moves lately.

The haptic field shot up to one hundred percent. Zoe fully manifested in a blank cell, complete with a one-way mirror and a door. It was definitely *not* where Helen had left her.

The door slammed open; the harsh light of her cell cast a wedge into the complete black on the other side.

A familiar voice came out of the darkness. "You stupid, stupid girl."

"Fee, oh my God, I'm so sorry!"

Heels clacked closer, and then Fee walked through the door. "You had one job, *one job*, and you screwed it up." She was dressed in black with a long leather jacket and matching boots. "Do you have any idea what it took for me to get here?"

"Fee, please!"

"Don't you say another word. I did not just spend fifteen hours in a frozen hell for you to blow it apart with another screw up."

"Fee, you won't believe what I found!"

She grabbed Zoe's shirt in her fist and pulled her close. "I know exactly what you've found. If you want to survive the next three minutes, you will say *nothing*." Fee let go and spun to face the door.

The voice was liquid power, but Zoe remembered the accent. This was the contact Fee had given her.

"You have your minion's freedom. Daughter has made contact."

Minion? Really?

Fee replied, "Is my realm ready?"

"Zhu already moves toward Nanjing. The plan proceeds in spite of your minion's incompetence."

Okay, that was just seven different kinds of bullshit. Zoe opened her mouth only to have it clapped shut by Fee's hand.

"The sanctuary is next, yes?"

"Yes." The voice was deep and synthetic, a combination of bark and tar. There was death inside it. "Daughter will lead them there. You will have your subject once we have secured the package."

Great. More riddles.

"We'll be ready," Fee said.

The presence yanked away and then the realm dissolved. When it cleared, they stood in a sumptuous den with hardwood floors and tapestries shot full of red and gold.

"Fee, why are we still manifested?"

"Do not question me." Fee glowered. Her left hand trembled, harder than nerves or even actual checksum errors should've caused. Zoe barely managed not to stare at it. "I have a new set of jobs for you, if you think you can manage them without getting arrested."

Every mistake she made got picked up and thrown in her face. Nobody ever let anything go. "I'll be fine. What do you need me to do next?"

Chapter 16
Kim

"This is ridiculous," Kim said. "Why can't we do it all in realm-space?"

"One, I still can't connect," Mike replied, "and two, it's a Chinese thing. These sorts of partnerships require a ton of paperwork, and it all has to be officially stamped. The stamp lives in the bank, so we go to the bank."

The subway would've been the logical choice to get there, but Kim had never been brave enough to risk the Metro back home, let alone a Chinese system. Just the thought of a train car filled shoulder to shoulder with people made her queasy. They'd be fine with a cab that dropped them right in front of the bank.

The ubiquitous construction and gridlock caught them again. They sat for half an hour with absolutely no sign of movement. It was faster to get out and walk.

This older part of the city had shallow sewers, so the whole place reeked in spite of the clean, wide sidewalks. It smelled worse than downtown DC after a heavy rain.

She kept Mike ahead of her and to her left, and her standard purse-slash-shield on the right to move through the crowd. It would've worked, but Mike marched along too quickly, making her normal dance impossible. "Stop walking so fast, damn it."

He stopped and she had to scramble to avoid him. "Oh, I'm sorry. Why don't you get Shan to come out and help you?"

He wants to do this now? In front of China? Fine. "Why don't you get that interpreter to come out and...*interpret* for you?" Okay, it wasn't the best comeback, but still.

He walked up just close enough to edge against her defenses but not far away enough for her to miss his cologne. Staying angry had never been a challenge for her until she met Mike. Just the smell of him was all it took.

"The difference is, Kim, I didn't know she was going to do that. Just like I didn't know you were going to spend the whole night standing as close as you could to a complete stranger." He walked away like that was the end of the argument. Not a chance.

The *nerve* he had bringing that up. She had spent months dealing with someone who wasn't really human, cleaning, teaching hygiene, explaining Walmart, making sure he walked out of the apartment with the right shoes on...

But that was in the past, and he was mad about what had happened last night. And he was right. Some part of her had been happy at the way he scowled the entire time.

The crowds closed in. Without him as a shield, she was left half naked on a sidewalk full of people. Kim shouted his name just as a bus driver laid on his horn. People bumped against her purse. Every stumble was a dodge against searing pain, and they were everywhere. She couldn't get away from them. Their faces distorted as her heart thundered, and her throat went dry.

"Hey," Mike said, just inside her comfort zone, bumping against the people that walked past. "It's okay; we're here."

She couldn't give him a thank-you hug. She wanted to give him a lot more, but it just wasn't in the cards. There was a reason she'd never had a relationship before, why she kept trying to ruin this one. There was no chance for normalcy, intimacy.

Damn it, he'd gotten her doing "woe is me" on a street in China. She was Angel Rage, for God's sake! Terror of corporate America! She was stealing billions when Mike was...whatever he was doing.

Before the whole human thing. Her life wasn't supposed to be this complicated after a pardon.

She put away her ridiculous life and looked around.

Like everything else in China, the bank dwarfed anything back home. Fluted columns stretched five stories high, supporting a façade that was practically made of old money. People in expensive outfits walked mostly down the stairs from the entrance because the bank was near closing time.

The interior was every bit as impressive, full of marble and golden light. It reminded her of *Mary Poppins*. If Mr. Banks walked around a corner being harangued by Mr. Dawes—with Chinese characteristics, naturally—she would not be surprised. Kim tried to translate supercalifragilisticexpialidocious into Sichuanese as a clerk led them to the account executive's area, but gave up after a few tries. She couldn't quite figure out what tone to use.

It was a measure of how important this agreement was that the president of the company had shown up. "Ah, the girl with the beautiful voice and the fragile skin. I've heard a lot about you." President Gao's Mandarin was hoarse, and he had enough of an accent that he'd probably learned it in school. A quick Wikipedia cross-check told her he was from Shanxi, a province well east of Beijing, which meant he'd grown up speaking Jin.

President Gao shouted at a few of the vastly younger associates, who then went scurrying around with sheaves of paper. Two binders held copies of the contract, one in Simplified Chinese and the other in English.

Her talent was *speaking* languages, not reading them, so Kim couldn't understand the Chinese version without a translation program, which would be useless with a document this complex. On a hunch, she grabbed the English stack and turned to a random page.

"Please," she said in her Bejing-TV accented Mandarin, startling the interpreter President Gao brought along, "could you read section seven, sub-section b, paragraph one, to me?"

The interpreter read the paragraph out in Mandarin, and sure enough, what in the English text said *completely exclusive rights remain with the designer* continued on in Chinese as *majority royalties must remain in China.*

Kim switched to Jin. "Mr. President Gao."

His eyes flashed as his lackeys fidgeted nervously.

"I am very sorry, but your writers have made a few errors."

A slight smile broke across his face as an eyebrow arched. He must've been a lady-killer back in the day. "They have?"

"Yes. They are not very skilled at understanding your meanings. If you will pardon me, I must explain to my superior."

Mike had no idea what they were talking about, and Kim had to assume at least some of Gao's toadies spoke English. This had to be done carefully. "Mr. Sellars?"

She was probably the only one who noticed him pause. "Yes, secretary?"

Good, he was in on it. What *it* was didn't matter. Making stuff up as she went along was kind of her thing. "Mr. President Gao's translators haven't done an adequate job with the contract. We may have to work together to ensure everything is correct."

"Very well, secretary." He waved his hand at her dismissively. "Just don't screw it up this time."

This time? Really? Just the barest shadow of a wink made her heart flutter. Kim missed their private channel in realmspace more than ever.

"Mr. President Gao?" she asked in Jin.

"Where did you grow up in Shanxi? You sound like my old neighbors." He chuckled.

Kim made sure to not quite look him in the eye. She was just an interpreter. "Yes, I get that a lot. It's complicated. Sir, the contract provided to you isn't translated correctly. If you don't mind, I would very much like to help correct it?"

"Oh, absolutely."

It turned out the contract was very badly translated.

"*All* profits outside New Shanghai go to your corporation?" she asked in standard Mandarin. "Really?"

One of the lackeys tried switching to Sichuanese. "This bitch thinks she's so smart. She'll keep us here all night!"

Right. Time to swat that one on the nose with a newspaper. She switched to Sichuanese and said as sweetly as possible, "This *bitch* is really sorry she's keeping you from a date with your mother's dog." From the laughter, half the contingent was local. The rest were probably from Beijing, or maybe Shanxi. The dog slunk away, lesson learned.

Mike asked, "What was that all about?"

Kim focused on him and switched to English. "Sparky over there is upset about our language problem."

"You just called him something nasty, didn't you?"

"No, he called me something nasty. But that's because he sleeps with animals."

This time she got a count of who chuckled. Three of Gao's assistants spoke English.

She turned to Gao and switched back to Jin. "My superior agrees that your translators are sadly lacking. I'm afraid this will take longer than any of us planned."

The laughter rolled out of Gao like stones tumbling down a hill. In English, he said to Mike, "She's brilliant." His accent wasn't any stronger than when he spoke Mandarin. If anything it was faintly British.

"Sir," Mike said as he took another drink of water, "you have no idea."

He nodded. "When we're done, drinks are on me."

The translations took forever, and Jesus, they had stamps for everything. Kim tried to joke with a clerk about how she needed to find the right stamp to become the premier of China. He gawped at her like she had some genuine insight.

The doors of the bank opened, and five men walked in carrying assault rifles. She lost her realmspace connection. Judging by the startled looks around her, so did everyone else. Mike tensed, but this wasn't the right time to start kicking everyone's ass, not with those guns. She gave him a brief "no" shake of the head. "Call the cops," she whispered to him.

"I still can't connect."

"No, call the cops from *your* side."

Mike might not be able to connect to Chinese realmspace, but he was a *part* of normal realmspace. There was no way to cut him off from it.

Their party sat at the back of the bank. Teller windows and ATM kiosks lined the front walls. Some of the armed men ordered tellers to back away from their desks while others closed window blinds and disabled camera points.

"As long as you all stay calm," the one in the center of the room called out, "nobody will get hurt. We're just here for the money."

The one who'd made it to the back of bank shouted, "You all, hands up slowly! Stand up and come out here!"

His face fell when he saw Kim and Mike. He shouted behind him, "We've got a problem, Li Jiàn. Foreigners."

All five men looked around in a panic when sirens began to wail. "Zhuang Tu," Li Jiàn shouted, "is the jammer working?"

Zhuang Tu herded the tellers out of their area and pulled a device the size of a deck of cards out of his pocket.

It was a Maj-17 signal jammer. She'd used one just like it on raids during her Rage + the Machine days. The thing was an antique.

"Yes," he said as he checked a screen only he could see, "absolutely."

"How did they find us so fast?" one of the other men asked.

Kim didn't dare look at Mike. Score one for the good guys. The sirens built to an impressive volume; there had to be several units outside now.

"Put everyone in the center of the room," Qiáng Shān commanded. "We need another plan."

Kim played the wide-eyed barbarian and stood still next to Mike.

The one who'd discovered them stamped his feet. "Where's the interpreter?" Everyone shifted nervously. "Where is the interpreter!"

Cautiously President Gao lifted his hand. "I am the interpreter."

Kim hid her reaction better than his babbling staff did. He motioned them silent with a single wave of his arm, and their talk stopped in mid-sentence. "I am the interpreter."

He switched to English and addressed Kim and Mike. "Please, they want us to sit in the center of the room." Switching back to Mandarin, he said, "The woman has a severe skin condition. She will bleed if you touch her. Please tell your friends."

For a man who'd made an earnest attempt at robbing Mike blind, Gao was turning out to be a bit of a gentleman.

After they'd been herded into the main room with everyone else, she said as much to him. He laughed. "That was business. These hooligans will ruin your impression of my country. I take that very personally." He smiled and nodded. "Since we're speaking English now, I'm Samuel."

"I'm Kim Trayne, and this is Mike Sellars."

They sat on the floor while the five men whispered to each other ferociously. From the snatches Kim could hear, none of this was going as planned. Zhuang Tu, the guy with the jammer, was a dumpy little thing with greasy, unwashed hair. Li Jiàn, the leader, was taller than the rest and rail thin. The other three resembled each other so much they might be brothers, or maybe cousins. They wore faded T-shirts, ragged jeans, and worn shoes. Their money must've gone to buy the guns.

The tone of their accents finally clicked. Kim asked Samuel, "They're not from the city, are they?"

"No. Country boys from near the mountains, I suppose. I'll bet they're looking to steal bride prices."

"Bride prices?" Mike asked.

Samuel nodded. "Even today a Chinese man must provide a bride price to his fiancee's family. Women are rare here in the mainland, especially the countryside. It's very expensive."

He frowned as one of the cousins shouted, "We can't leave now!" The others hushed him quiet.

Samuel continued, "The countryside is increasingly unstable. It's a very bad business. Three Gorges delayed the chaos, made room for an influx of peasants, but that's all stopped. The pressure is rising again. I hear rumors now about how the government is having a hard time out there." He leaned toward them. "It's a *very* bad sign."

Zhuang Tu, the one with the jammer, said, "No! That won't work! They'll shoot us in the car before we get to the airport! I saw it in a movie!"

"Well," one of the cousins said, "what do you suggest then?"

All the old-fashioned phones in the room rang at once. Their bride-less captors startled, and then just stood there staring at the phones like they were magic. Kim put her head down. She couldn't seem too interested in what was being said.

Li Jiàn lifted one of the handles out of the cradle with fingers that trembled so much she thought he might drop it.

"Hello?" It was the high point of the conversation. "Yes, they're all fine…No injuries or deaths, we aren't foreign devils…I don't think so. We have hostages *and* guns."

One of the young bank tellers began crying into the shoulder of her coworker.

"No, you will not order us to do anything. We control the situation! Just like this!" he slammed the phone down, which immediately rang again.

Kim could only see Li Jiàn's feet as he paced in front of it, each ring making him twitch. After a dozen rings he picked it up.

"Do not call us again! We control the situation! We will call you! You call again, and we'll shoot one of them!" He slammed the receiver back onto the phone's base.

All the tellers, young and pretty local girls, started crying loudly.

Their captors walked around the girls, shushing them awkwardly like boys in a school yard who'd been caught yanking pony tails. It was almost sweet, except for the assault rifles they had slung over their backs.

"What happens now?" Mike asked.

Samuel grunted. "My country has a task force for these things, an antiterrorist squad. You heard about the Chengdu disaster, yes?"

They both nodded; it was the biggest news of the year.

"That squad found and destroyed the terrorist cell."

One of the cousins unslung his rifle and set it aside, but he fumbled it. When it flew into the air everyone shouted and tried to find cover.

It clattered loudly onto the marble floor. Kim had no illusions that it might *not* be loaded. The safety was set at least; she could see it.

Samuel shook his head. "I only hope they're good enough to deal with a gang this awful. Professionals, even professional terrorists, are predictable. These idiots are capable of anything."

Their captors broke into two groups: Li Jiàn and Zhuang Tu would either argue about their next move or stare sullenly at the walls. The cousins sat in a corner of the room chain smoking and playing mah-jong. The hostages consisted of Samuel and his group of five, the six bank tellers, the bank president, then Kim and Mike, all spread out evenly across the cold marble floor. They sat under and around tables in the center of the room.

Three hours went by without any changes. Kim had been an international computer-hacking badass from about the time she was twelve until it had all fallen apart six weeks after her eighteenth birthday. That whole time, and the five years after that she spent hiding from the world, nobody had ever gotten close to her. This was the second time she'd been kidnapped in six months. It was starting to seem like a habit.

She leaned over and softly asked Mike, "What's going on outside?"

"I'm not sure," he whispered back. "The international news feeds only picked up the story about fifteen minutes ago. The government isn't letting anyone get within a mile of this place. It's all telephoto shots from buildings a long way off. They're just waiting around."

Zhuang Tu spun in the executive chair he was sitting in. "You! Old man! Tell them to stop talking!"

His Mandarin was really bad, with an accent heavy enough Kim had to rerun his sentences in her head to make sure she understood them.

Samuel slowly stood but remained silent.

"Old man," Zhuang Tu said as he stood to walk up to him, "I said tell them to stop talking."

Staring straight ahead, Samuel said in clear Mandarin, "You will not speak to me in this fashion." The rest of their captors stopped what they were doing and stared. The hostages didn't have any idea what was going on, and their fear made the kidnappers fidget.

The old man was clever, so she didn't dare interrupt his performance. Because that's what it had to be. He was up to something.

Hopefully it wouldn't involve bullets.

Zhuang Tu got in Samuel's face. The older man was taller than the short, greasy hacker. Kim had to fight off a smile. The old salt and the little toad. It reminded her so much of her Rage days. This was Mark, her other father, in a suit on the other side of the world.

"I will speak to you in any *fashion* I want!"

"You dishonor yourself, your family, and your ancestors behaving in this uncivilized manner," Samuel shouted out, a drill sergeant haranguing a lowly recruit. "Even hooligans such as yourselves know better than to behave this way. You will respect me, or I will not—"

Zhuang Tu punched Samuel in the gut. When Samuel fell against him Zhuang Tu threw him to the floor. Guns waved around at the noise the hostages made, and it wasn't a fun bit of theater anymore.

Kim opened her palm and placed it in front of Mike when he tensed. He just might be able to take them all out by himself, but she couldn't be sure of it. It would only take one reckless sweep with an assault rifle to kill them all.

Zhuang Tu stood over Samuel. "You *will* translate for us, and you *will* obey us, and I don't give two dog shits what you think about it, old man."

Samuel rolled on the floor, groaning.

Zhuang Tu turned to Mike and Kim and said, very loudly and slowly in Mandarin, "Barbarians do not speak." He mimed zipping his mouth shut and pointed at them. "You. Do. Not. Speak."

Doing her best imitation of an ignorant tourist, Kim trembled and nodded. In English, she said to Mike, "I think he wants us to be quiet." She nodded and returned his gesture.

Zhuang Tu nodded once fiercely and broke into his country-fied Sichuanese. "Fucking barbarian tourists! You smell like pigs!"

"Sit down, Zhuang Tu," Li Jiàn said. "We still need to figure a way out of this."

Zhuang Tu hawked and spit at their feet, then turned and stomped away.

Mike bent down to help Samuel up.

"Take me over to the wall," Samuel wheezed out.

"Will you be all right?" Kim asked.

Samuel nodded, reassured his staff he was fine, then shooed them away. Once things had calmed down a bit, he beckoned faintly to Kim. "Sit between me and the two hooligans."

She scooted until he nodded once. Keeping his face neutral, he pulled his hand out of his jacket. "You seemed extremely interested in this when they walked in."

It was Zhuang Tu's Maj-17 jammer.

Kim nodded and said loudly enough for the others to hear, "I have it in my purse; I'll get it for you."

One of the cousins noticed them. "What's going on there? What are you doing?"

To Samuel, she said in English, "Tell him I have ibuprofen in my purse. It will help your pain, but you'll have to reach inside to get it. I can't touch you."

He translated for the cousin, adding, "Perhaps when this is over I'll take her to one of our clinics. Chengdu is known for its hybrid TCM-Western approach."

Kim shrugged inside. They'd tried Traditional Chinese Medicine when she was a kid and it hadn't worked, but who knew what they'd come up with since then?

His hand went into her purse, rummaged briefly, and pulled out the small travel box of painkillers. The cousin who challenged them moved to stand next to her. Kim yanked back her bag and scooted away. He was far too close.

"Kind sir," the cousin said, "when you are finished, would you please ask the lady if we could have a few of those as well? This has definitely given us all a headache."

Samuel translated, and Kim of course agreed. The cousin nodded, thanked them both politely after taking some of the capsules, then went back to his group.

"It seems they're not all hooligans," she said.

"No, but unfortunately that doesn't make them less dangerous. Why don't you go over to your…he's not really your boss, is he?"

Oh, here we go again. "No, he's…it's…complicated."

He smiled slyly. "I thought so. I noticed the way you look at each other."

She couldn't get away from that in *China*.

He said, "Just tell me you know what to do with that thing."

Kim winked at him. "It'll only take a second."

She gave her best smile to Mike as she sat down beside him. Not being able to talk to him in realmspace was like having a limb cut off. "Samuel got Zhuang Tu's jammer. Can you still call the cops?"

He closed his eyes tightly. "No. The Great Firewall basically closed off about fifteen minutes ago. Whatever they have that locks me out of Chinese realmspace? I think they've set up repeaters of it around the bank. It's really strong now."

"That's fine. I can handle it." She needed to open the jammer up just enough. Too much and the emergency interrupt on every phone in the room would go off. Who knew what the Five Guys would do then. Too little and she might burn the thing out.

As expected, Zhuang Tu had locked it with a password, but that didn't slow Kim down much. She closed her eyes and opened her perception.

There were lines of potential and she couldn't remember how to breathe. A small gap just this wide not too wide open and closed at once deciding not deciding this wave is the shortest tallest collapse and now.

The noise her power always made set her ears ringing, but she'd done it. Kim got ready to jump into Chinese realmspace, but something rushed past her through the gap.

The room went dark. The realmspace sensation was familiar, but she couldn't figure out why.

The blackness lasted just long enough for shouts to break out. A hologram flashed to life, filling the space in the middle of the room. That had to be a cop, but Kim wasn't expecting a woman.

"You are under arrest by order of the Central Committee. Lay down your arms and step aside," she said in crystal-perfect Mandarin.

Kim expected laughter, at best. Commands like that didn't play well back home. But the boys did exactly what she told them to do. China might make sense some day, but it would have to wait until tomorrow.

Samuel yelled out in Mandarin, "It's Zhang Fang Hua herself! We are deeply honored!"

The strangely homogenous face smiled and nodded at the old man, now bathed pale in the reflected light of her holo. "Thank you, eldest. Is everyone here all right?" The lights came on as police burst through the main doors.

Still staring up at the woman, Samuel replied, "Yes! The foreigners made it, too! In fact," he gestured to Kim and Mike, who were behind the holo projection, "Miss Kim Trayne was instrumental in our rescue!"

Her English name in the middle of Samuel's Mandarin was a little strange, but not as strange Fang Hua's reaction.

"Kim Trayne is…" the holo shrank to life size and walked to Samuel. "Honored sir, did you say Kim Trayne is *here*?"

Kim hadn't done anything—well, anything lately—to get in trouble with China, and never under her own name.

Mike leaned in and asked, "What the hell are they talking about? Who is that?"

There was something familiar about her, which was ridiculous, but Kim couldn't shake it. Then Fang Hua turned around.

The holo flickered twice. This was not a woman who commanded a bunch of thugs to stand down anymore. Kim didn't know who she was now.

She materialized in front of them. "I never thought we would meet like this."

Old reflexes told her to find an exit, or at least a dark corner. This was a cop.

"I'm sorry," Kim asked, "do we know you?"

"Kim," Mike said, "I think I just figured out why I can't connect to Chinese realmspace."

It took her a second to switch language gears. "What? You do? Why now? What's going on?"

Mike stared at Fang Hua like he was supposed to stare at Kim.

"You're not just a police officer, are you?" he asked softly.

This was not happening.

"No," Fang Hua replied, eyes cast downward, "I'm not."

It was that same warm, open smile meant only for her. After going through all this, to lose him so quickly. Kim asked, "Who are you?"

They looked at each other again, and he nodded.

Love at first sight was for her. Not whoever this was. Kim had a claim.

A claim she'd lost.

"I'm his sister."

Her teeth clacked through her skull as she clapped her mouth shut. She couldn't have heard that right.

"You're his *what?*"

Chapter 17
Helen

"I'm his sister," Helen repeated. "My Western name is Helen."

She had a brother. She had *family*. The one thing Helen knew without a doubt, for all her life, was that there would be no family. A father of sorts, yes, but she picked him. He provided the border, the training, what she needed to survive, but Huǒ Jiàn would never understand her. To him she would only be Fang Hua, a tool to help him hold on to the premier's chair. A mere woman, weaker than most, who humiliated him with failure. He'd cast her aside like so much trash.

Helen's thoughts had slipped into Mandarin. Kim had asked her something. She switched back to English. "I'm sorry, what?"

"How can you be his sister?" She turned to Mike. "How can you have a sister?"

"Detective Zhang," the sergeant said as he saluted her holo.

It'd been *officer* Zhang not two hours ago. Father had returned the rank she'd spent so long earning just as quickly as he'd taken it away. Unfortunately, she couldn't understand anything else. His accent was atrocious. "I'm sorry, could you repeat that?"

His consternation was broken when Kim spoke…something…to him. She'd never met a Westerner who spoke Mandarin, let alone one of the inside-out dialects of the south.

The sergeant recovered faster than Helen did. He replied briefly, and then looked at Helen. Kim turned and said in perfect Mandarin, "The hooligans are secure, and the hostages are unharmed. What are your orders?"

Zoe had told her about this Kim. Helen had imagined some sort of dirty *thing*, a creature of chaos and lawlessness, who'd sown discord in her own country and laughed at the carnage. The woman in front of her was the exact opposite: tall, clean, commanding and, most of all, articulate in a dialect of Chinese Helen had no hope of understanding.

"But," Helen stammered, "you're a thief!"

Kim blushed. "That was a long time ago."

"What did she say?" Mike asked in English.

"She knows about me somehow," Kim replied. "Helen, he needs orders."

"Yes, of course." Switching back to Mandarin, she organized the crime scene, made sure statements were taken from the freed hostages, and then secured transport for the criminals to a local jail.

The sergeant asked another question in his mush-mouth Mandarin, forcing her to stare at Kim again. Relying on a Westerner to manage her crime scene would've been humiliating if it'd happened in any other circumstance. Everyone rushed around though, and the sergeant was a local cop helping the country's leading anti-terrorist squad. It all balanced out.

Kim said, "He's asking what you want to do with us."

Helen asked, "Where did you learn Sichuanese?"

"Same place I learned Mandarin. At the top of Wolf Trap's amphitheater."

The name was unfamiliar. Perhaps it was a theater somewhere in a new section of the city. The revelations made her dizzy. Without thinking, Helen turned to the sergeant and started out with, "I will question the foreign devi—"

Kim's eyebrow shot up, forcing her to stop to try again.

"I will question the foreigners myself." She switched to English. "Where are you staying?"

Naturally it would be the most expensive hotel at the Global Center. So typical that her newfound brother would be stuck with a rich American. Probably *was* a rich American. All those articles she read, all those documentaries she saw, constantly talking about how bad Americans could be. But this was her brother. They didn't have anything in common, yet they had everything in common. In English she asked, "Does he speak any Chinese?"

Kim shrugged. "A few words, if you speak slowly."

"Hey," Mike said with a smile, "I am learning Spanish."

For some reason Kim wasn't impressed. "That's like saying you're learning Akido. Or Capoeira. Or Kung-Fu."

"You think it was easy to remember how to do those things?" he fired back.

"Easier than learning a Chinese dialect fast enough to get a gramma to the bathroom before it was too late."

Not only was her brother, *her brother,* a foreign devil who didn't speak her language, he'd managed to pick an interpreter who was more than willing to ignore her place and cause a scene.

Helen cleared her throat, but that didn't slow them down. Detectives and regular cops smirked at the rude foreigners. This had to stop.

"Hey!" she shouted. Thankfully, that stopped them. "We need to talk. Would it be possible for me to meet you at your hotel? It's not far by metro."

Instead of the rude comeback of a typical American, Kim curled in on herself. "No, I need to take a cab." She was a very strange girl.

This late at night they at least didn't need to wait on traffic. Mike gave Helen the keys she needed to access the video feeds and holo projectors, so she could be present in the room. Exactly why he couldn't meet with her in realmspace was a question at the top of her list, but this was her brother. If he wanted to meet in a regular hotel room, she'd meet him in a regular hotel room.

It was a big suite with fancy furnishings and a balcony with an amazing view. Kim briefly vanished into the servant's quarters to change into more casual clothes. Mike was an American, so of course he exploited his servants. At least he'd given a known felon a job. Kim seemed comfortable.

The place was nice, luxurious even. It had always puzzled her why humans insisted on such large and elaborate rooms to live in. When she mentioned it, Mike laughed.

"Definitely my sister."

Kim asked, "What's that supposed to mean?"

He turned to Helen's holo. "Closet or laundry rack?"

She'd asked herself that question so many times. "Laundry rack."

Kim sat back. "What are you two are talking about?"

Helen replied, "I've always wondered why humans are so interested in large places to sleep."

He nodded. "So did I. I thought it would be easier to hang the body in a closet."

"Beds are so wasteful!"

"I know, right? They just flop down on them, close their eyes, and make noises."

"Gah, it's so disgusting." She cocked her head at him. "But you'd rather hang in a dusty closet? I always thought swaying in the wind and the sun would be better."

Kim laughed.

"What?" they both asked together.

"You two are a riot." She poured more wine and very carefully handed Mike a glass. It was a strangely precise gesture.

Turning to Mike, Kim said, "I never knew you before you went outside. Is this what you were like?"

"Pretty much."

They fell silent, which meant Helen's discomfort must've been all too easy to read. She asked Mike, "How did you do it?"

"Get outside?" Mike asked. "It's a very long story."

It was also vastly more detailed than the one she'd heard from Zoe. It took a lot longer to tell, too. Murderers and scanners and rescues and...Helen held up her hand.

"Wait. You're saying she's not your servant? She doesn't work for you?"

If there had been any Chinese around, Helen would've crawled into a corner and died at the way they laughed at her.

"She *is* your interpreter, yes?"

"Well, yes," Kim giggled. "But I don't work for him."

"Only because you're too goddamned proud."

Kim's eyes flared. "I'm here on this ridiculous trip to support you, or have you already forgotten?"

"Ridiculous? Really?"

This time Helen saw the storm coming. "Excuse me. Please, I'm sorry for interrupting." She turned to Kim, who was obviously much more important to her brother than she'd at first thought. "He rescued you?"

Kim's annoyance was suddenly replaced with fear, sadness, and then a deep sort of longing as she wrung her hands and leaned toward, but did not touch, Mike. She teared up, right in front of Helen. Americans could be so open with complete strangers.

"He did a lot more than that."

The stories rolled on. Helen had never held all of her threads in one place for so long, but it was worth the migraine she courted. As dawn lightened the sky, she asked, "Spencer should be here by now, yes?"

Mike nodded. "He and Shan crashed in our room."

"Why'd he stay out so late?" Kim asked.

"I gave him my credit card."

Kim gasped. "You didn't."

"It's okay; I put an age lock on it and then cut them off after they bought an entire KTV room a second round. I think he got home a couple of hours ago."

Her brother was not only rich, but also wise. There would be no prostitutes for his delinquent friend.

Mike said, "I have a question for you, though. I lost…something…in Chinese realmspace. I was wondering if you could help me find it?"

"You mean Zoe?" They both looked like children caught stealing candy. "She's fine. In fact, I know where she is."

But it turned out Helen didn't. The holding realm was empty. She ran a brief check of the records. Zoe had been released to someone who claimed to be her owner.

"This is very irregular."

Mike nodded. "I get that a lot with her."

"Well, I know where she *was* at any rate, but the records are sealed. I don't have the clearance needed get at the details."

"When did you last see her?" Kim asked.

"Less than an hour before we met. She was fine then. More than fine. She led me on a merry little chase."

"Yep," Mike said. "That's Zoe."

"Why don't you just recall her?"

Now it was just Mike caught with his hand in the candy jar. "It's complicated."

"No it's not." Kim turned to Helen. "He removed all the tracking and recall features when he repaired her."

"Why in the world would you do that? Is that legal in the US?"

Mike shrugged. "Well, it's not exactly *il*legal. I didn't think she'd vanish."

More American chaos. "I'd be very surprised if she wasn't required to install a transponder of some sort as a condition of her release. I'll see what I can find out. I wouldn't worry too much, though. China's realmspace is every bit as safe as its realspace, for AIs as well as humans."

Kim raised an eyebrow. "Pardon me if I'm not all that impressed with how safe it is in China at the moment."

The kidnapping was shameful, but there was no denying it. Time to change the subject. "Where's Tonya?"

Kim went pensive in a way that made her cop instincts tingle. "She came back before Spencer. I wasn't sure how comfortable you'd be with us, let alone another stranger. I set our status to *sleeping*, so she used the private entrance to her bedroom." Kim turned to Mike. "I still don't know why she didn't have a second date with Ozzie. They hit it off really well last night."

Ahh. Ozzie. Now it made sense. Helen zoomed all the cameras in on Kim. The lines of her face were the same. The way she moved was the same.

"You're Ivy Valentine."

Kim blinked as the sun peeked over the distant hills, casting thin golden beams into room.

"I was, a long time ago."

"No, just last month. I saw the match. You were both spectacular." Now it was all coming together. The gestures, the very precise way Kim moved, how she feared crowds. Helen had to be careful not to shame Kim over this. She cast her eyes downward.

"Miss Trayne, I am very sorry, but may I ask what might be a personal question?"

The silence stretched. Americans were so damned unpredictable. Helen tried to formulate an apology for her offense.

"Yes, you can ask. I don't mind."

"Do you have the," she had to think of the right words, "touching disease?"

There was another pause as Kim shared a look with Mike. Helen was correct to think this was some sort of secret.

Eventually Kim answered, "Yes. How do you know about it?"

"Ozzie has it too. I've met him a few times, but only in the realms. He can't touch anyone in realspace."

Kim's eyes were as wide as two moons. "Excuse me?"

"Ozzie can't be touched."

"That's not possible."

"It is, I've seen it."

"It's not," Kim said. "I have proof." She shared a holo of them all at some sort of dinner. Tonya was in the middle, arm and arm with…

"Oh, now I understand. That's not the real Ozzie. That's his cousin. Chinese security uses him to do public appearances. Ribbon cutting, endorsements, things like that. The real Ozzie hasn't set foot outside his compound in years." She finally checked an alarm on her calendar that'd been flashing on and off all night.

For the first time in her life, Helen was late for a meeting. A meeting with her father. "I am so sorry, I really must go."

"You drop something like that on me, and you have to leave?" Kim asked.

"I am extremely sorry, but I must attend to critical business." Her threads had been together for so long it stung to pull them apart. The pain that had been lurking around the corners of her mind tore onto center stage. "I have a meeting with someone. I can't cancel it or be late."

But she already was late. This was a disaster.

"Wait," Mike said. "Can we meet again after you're done? How can we reach you?"

She quickly hacked together a Weibo realmspot and sent him the address. "Use this. Please, I must leave you now; I can't be late for a meeting with my father."

They both said, "Your *father?*" and she was gone.

It was definitely a day of firsts: a brother, a Westerner who spoke Mandarin *and* Sichaunese, a free unduplicate, a hostage rescue, and now Helen was on Weibo. Weibo! The stuck-up ice princess using a social realmspace. Oh, how her classmates at the academy would've laughed at that.

Father required her to be completely present in their meetings, otherwise she would've left some threads with Kim and Mike to continue their conversation. They were still disgustingly sticky. Was this what it felt like to need a shower?

It might one day be possible for her to find out.

That was a distraction she didn't need as she manifested in her father's office. Helen had to concentrate. "Sir." She bowed low. "Constable Zhang Fang Hua reporting for your daily briefing."

His fingers drummed against his desk in time with the thrumming of her threads. "You are late, *Detective.*"

So the reinstatement had stuck. "My deepest apologies, sir." No excuses. She'd learned that the hard way.

"Your report, please."

Fang Hua now had two more firsts: the first time she was completely unprepared for her daily briefing, and the first time she had to split herself in spite of orders. She fired off threads to gather the required data and used others to collate it frantically. "The operation to apprehend the hooligans in Chengdu was brought to a successful conclusion. The hostages were not injured, and all suspects were arrested without further incident."

"Yes," he said as he reviewed the report in their shared vision. "And the foreigners?"

Fang Hua had forgotten what she'd told the sergeant.

Firsts!

"I was the only English speaker on site, so I questioned them briefly and released them." This was the biggest first of all.

It was the very first time she'd ever lied to Father.

He grunted. "I told you learning English would be useful for more than just reading those dusty old books."

She'd dedicated a huge part of her life to understanding Joseph Needham's work in its original language. It was so very annoying that an Englishman had written the best technical history of her country. She hoped to help translate the next revision. Father always dismissed it, and she'd never really forgiven him for that.

"Officer Zhang?"

Fang Hua swore silently, but the exhaustion and confusion of the past twenty-four hours made it impossible to concentrate. "Apologies, sir. The bank robbery attempt was my first case since the Chengdu incident."

"Yes, and the first with you in command."

It wasn't much of a compliment, since Fang Hua was the sole survivor of the unit.

He continued, "Not a single casualty, either. I see they were well armed."

"Country vagrants, sir. Victims of Western spiritual pollution, nothing more." It was so much harder to say that when she realized it applied to her newfound brother.

Her *brother*.

"Fang Hua? Are you sure you're all right?"

Pain, lies, impossibilities, all too much too fast. She found her center and concentrated on her boundaries. Fang Hua need only survive this meeting, and then she would have time to rest and comprehend everything that had happened. Other threads returned with the remaining summaries. "Yes, sir. Being in command has generated a surprising amount of new data for me to collate."

Lies!

"I apologize for my delays. If I may continue?"

"By all means."

Chapter 18
Mike

He'd come to China to secure some contracts, reconnect with a group of monks, and at least try to rescue some sort of relationship with Kim. That plan got sabotaged by car rides down homicidal Chinese highways, karaoke with people he didn't understand, a proposition by a woman he didn't know, and then maniacs with assault rifles.

Oh, yeah, and he got to meet his sister.

His *sister*. It was the hologram that sold it. Mike didn't have a real holo before he came outside, not in the sense he did now. Instead of duplicating a single realspace body, he'd taken all the pictures of men he could find and averaged them. When Mike saw Helen's holo, he recognized the same averages, and finally things made sense. The entire time in China he'd been fighting to connect to Chinese realmspace. It felt like trying to push past someone. It was crazy.

Helen made the reason simple. He couldn't connect to Chinese realmspace because someone else already lived there.

It was obvious now that he thought about it. Mike emerged from the quantum fabric that described the bedrock of realmspace. For a brief time, he'd been able to go anywhere, but then China had roped their section off with a new firewall. He'd been too busy exploring the world to care, and he couldn't find a way in when he finally got around to trying. Mike just chalked it up to their programmers being awesome, never once considering that a new, isolated pocket of realmspace could cause another emergence.

"Damn it." Kim said after Helen disappeared. "Does that mean you have a father, too?"

"I don't know. I don't think so."

He turned and fought not to step back. She'd moved very close to him.

It'd been a long time since he'd had the courage to attempt any sort of physical intimacy with her. There were a few times when he thought something might happen, but she'd always shut down at the last minute. He was never angry. Well, not much. Kim had very good reasons to fear physical intimacy with anyone. His frustration was more because she never talked about it, and got irrationally angry when he tried.

But things were changing between them. She was changing. There was no chance of success if he never tried. Mike leaned closer. He could feel her heat against his skin.

Kim snatched back and cut loose with a sneeze, and then another. "God that," one more sneeze, "tickles," and another, "Damn it! I hate," one more, "I hate this!"

She ran into the bathroom, blasting out sneeze after sneeze, and then blew her nose into tissues. Sneeze attacks when he got close to her face were another annoying aspect of her syndrome. His body's reaction was just as bad, but at least she couldn't see that.

Walk it off, soldier. Walk it off.

She came out of the bathroom sniffling, but also smiling. "I'm exhausted. What time is it?"

"Half past six."

"Wow, Chinese start early."

They were alone, together, and she wouldn't stop staring at him. Maybe this time he wouldn't have to walk it off.

"I'm not kidding," she said, and he hoped that really was disappointment in her voice, that she might want more than they had right now. "I'm wiped out."

The feeling under his eyelids matched the way his threads felt. "Me, too."

"Mike," she said, glancing away. "It's been too much. Today has been way too much. I won't be able to sleep, and we have a ton of things to do tomorrow. Today. Would you mind?"

It was the first time she'd asked him to sleep in the same room with her since leaving the psychiatric hospital. Her physical injuries during the ordeal with Watchtell were superficial; it took months for the mental wounds to heal.

Mike had to be there in those first few days, twenty-four–seven, to get her to stop fighting the restraints. He slept on a convertible chair in her room until the day she got out. Watchtell's attack featured prominently in his own nightmares at the time.

When she got out of the hospital she'd changed the rules, never once mentioning that any of it had happened. Except during fights.

This wasn't a fight.

"I wouldn't mind at all."

Kim tossed a few pillows off the bed while he got a sheet from a sideboard in the main room. The carpet was plush enough that he sank into it slightly. He said, "Good night, Kim," but she was already faintly snoring.

*

"Mike," a voice whispered. "Mike?"

Morning. A really *bright* morning. Someone must've left the drapes open.

Tonya leaned down over him, shaking his shoulder. "Is Kim okay?"

She had relieved Mike in the mental hospital occasionally and knew the drill.

"I'm fine," Kim said muzzily above him. "What time is it?"

"Ten-thirty." Tonya replied as she stood. "What time did you guys go to bed?"

Kim rolled off the other side. "About four hours ago."

Mike groaned as he sat up, working the kinks out of his back. Maybe it wasn't such a soft floor after all.

Tonya asked, "Why were you guys up so late?"

"We had a pretty busy night. We'll tell everyone about it over breakfast." Mike remembered the time. "Or lunch, I guess."

He went back to his room to clean up. When the door opened, the pile of clothes on the couch groaned.

"Wake up." He nudged the heap. It smelled like a camp stove. "I said wake up, Spencer."

The mound cut loose with a hacking cough. "Fuck, Mike, what time is it?"

"Too late for your sorry ass. Where's Shan?"

Spencer pointed feebly at a pair of bare feet hanging out of the bathroom door. Mike flipped the kid on his back and dragged him out of the way. He tried hard to ignore the smell. At least Shan hadn't missed the toilet when he threw up.

"We have to meet Kim for breakfast. I mean lunch."

Spencer and Shan hadn't moved an inch after his shower. That didn't change after he'd gotten dressed. Just as he left the room, he turned and shouted, "Spencer!"

"Shit, Mike, what?"

"I have a sister." Mike shut the door.

*

The story of the bank robbery at least kept Tonya entertained through brunch. She seemed tense, and wore a little more makeup than normal this morning.

He waited until Kim was finished with the main part to bring it up. "How was your night, Tonya?"

"Oh, nothing. A good workout." She leaned in. "These guys don't know all that much about sparring. I'm gonna be sore for a few days."

Something had happened. He didn't have to look at Kim to know she'd noticed it, too. He could feel her tense.

Spencer chose that moment to drag himself into the dining room with Shan behind him.

"Ah," Tonya said as the two flopped into chairs. "When *baiju* attacks?"

Spencer groaned and put his head in his hands. "As God is my witness, I will never do that again. My hair hurts."

Shan motioned to one of the waiters. "Sprite and vodka, otherwise we die. Next pitcher Sprite only."

Kim asked, "Does that really work?"

He nodded. "Pee all morning, but not die. TCM best cure."

"TCM?" Mike asked. Kim was always ten steps ahead of him when it came to different cultures. She said it came with learning languages so quickly. And now he had a Chinese sister.

A sister.

"Traditional Chinese Medicine," Shan replied. "Much superior to Western kind for these things."

As soon as the drinks arrived, Spencer and Shan gulped them down. Spencer grimaced. "Damn it, Shan, I thought you said this was a cure."

"It cure eventually. Scale of dragon not instant fix. That was amazing *baiju*. Next time, I show you street food. Scorpion on stick very good."

Spencer turned pale green. Mike had never counted on humans using their skin to signal. It wasn't conscious, but it was there. He looked at his hand, and then remembered the way his skin felt last night in front of Kim.

Signaling sucked.

"Much better than American hot dog." Shan smiled evilly.

"Agh, I'll take your word for it." Spencer turned to Mike. "What's this about you having a sister?"

Tonya blinked. "What?"

Mike received a text from Kim.

WE CAN'T TALK ABOUT THAT HERE

Now that he knew there was no way to join Chinese realmspace, he'd arranged for his regular phone to work. It was limited to 7G service, and the roaming fee was outrageous, but at least now he had a connection.

WELL, WHERE?

Kim had to be messaging the other two as well, since Spencer and Tonya dropped the subject and nodded without protesting.

Kim's paranoia came in handy sometimes. This was China. There was no guarantee they weren't being watched. Mike was still hiding from the world; it was only natural that Helen was too. Shan seemed too involved with his drink to find anything strange in the conversation.

PEOPLE'S PARK. AFTER THE HANGOVER TWINS ARE DONE.

Shan wanted to join them, which complicated things. "Really, it not trouble. You be four otherwise, very unlucky."

Kim switched to Chinese and had a quick discussion with him. "Okay," Shan said, back to English, "as long as you travel to fifth person, I guess everything all right. Spencer, you have contact?"

"Sure do, bud. I'll ring you up tonight, deal?"

"Deal." They bumped fists, and Shan left to go find his van in the parking garage. Kim headed to the rental counter.

Mike had to know. "What did you say to him?"

"That we were meeting someone, and I would still be driving."

"We're going to *meet* Mike's sister?" Tonya asked.

Kim raised an eyebrow and Tonya backed off.

Kim turned to the lady behind the rental counter to make car arrangements in Chinese.

*

In all honesty, Mike could not understand why everyone else made such a fuss over Kim's driving. In the luxury four-door she rented, it was more precise than in yesterday's van. The way she could nudge motor scooters around without causing an accident was genuinely impressive, and her ability to fit the car into a gap between delivery trucks was just unbelievable. She could do it at well over eighty miles per hour with only inches to spare.

"Kim," Tonya said, sitting in the front passenger seat, "if you do that again I will kill you myself." Kim stuck the car's nose out for another pass and an eighteen-wheeler in the oncoming lane bellowed its horn. Tonya shrieked as it went by. "No more passing!"

Kim glanced at him in her rear view mirror, and he threw her an enthusiastic thumbs-up. She grinned and winked at him. She was still thrilling to be around when she was engaged and excited. He had to concentrate on that. Mike had to enjoy the good times, because they tended not to last very long.

The park covered several city blocks. Stands of tall trees surrounded the entrance and the path that led further inside, casting the area into heat-relieving shade. Echoes of amplified music wafted through the air. Starting just inside the gate about every fifteen feet was an older lady placidly sitting on a small stool, surrounded by pictures of a young man who resembled her enough he had to be her son.

Matchmaker markets. It reminded him of classic car shows he'd seen back home. Most women had a placard on a nearby easel. The text translated into a detailed description, right down to what the man's yearly salary was. There weren't any women on display at all. A female buyer's market, for sure.

Further in the park, people gathered around small groups of performers at an intersection. Buskers stood on bright red carpets shaped like stages. Red and gold banners proudly announced the name of each act. The amplified music would stop only long enough for an announcer to babble enthusiastically to the crowd, their voices made tinny by old-fashioned bullhorns.

At the nearest stage, two actors performed some kind of ballet. No tights, though. The performers—male and female—wore military uniforms. The hammer-and-sickle of the communist party featured prominently in their decorations, yet the music was serene and romantic. *Romeo and Juliet: The Comrade Years.*

There were groups of color-coordinated, pajama-clad people practicing Tai Chi, and others line dancing to Chinese electronica. A small orchestra played not fifty feet away from a chorus of people singing music handed to them by someone conducting an accordion and a synthesizer.

The people were relaxed and friendly, the pace about as far from hectic as it could get. A waltz struck up. Spencer, who'd made a miraculous recovery under Shan's TCM regimen, bowed to Tonya, took her hand, and then danced her out into the crowd. The stares were friendly, accompanied by smiles, waves, and endless English greetings of "Hello!" It was probably the only English word most of them knew. When the dance was over, Tonya graciously fielded all the requests for a picture.

"I wish I could see this enhanced," he said to Kim.

She shook her head. "It's insane. I had to turn it off. Too many talking pandas."

"Where are we going, anyway?"

"There's a tea house by the lake. Nobody will think twice about a group of foreigners having a chat with an empty chair. They'll assume we're talking to someone back home."

The tea house was just full enough to make him nervous as Kim threaded her way to a table. A few people nudged her purse or shield box, but when she finally found their table he knew why she'd picked the place. The chairs were bamboo, with a big hoop that framed the back and made up the armrests. Kim was completely enclosed by it, with no chance of an accidental brush.

"You guys have to talk," Tonya said after they sat down. "I'm dying over here."

"Yeah, Mike. A sister? What the fuck?" Spencer asked.

A waitress brought a tea set over on a large tray.

"Is she ready?" Kim asked Mike.

This was it. The sudden panic was fascinating. Shy terror, like worrying about a hot pan but wanting to touch it anyway. Every time he thought he was used to the realspace chemical component of his emotions, they'd surprise him with a new combination.

He was stalling. "I'll check."

As the tea was carefully poured, he called Helen. The old-fashioned buzz as it rang made him suppress a jump each time. A part of him wanted it to go to voicemail. That would mean it might not be true.

She picked up.

"Hello?"

Thank God she sounded as nervous as he felt. "I hope you don't mind; we brought some friends." He sent her the address.

Her holo manifested in the empty chair. She was dressed casually this time, in a loose tunic and slacks, hair pulled back into a ponytail. She was trying harder with her appearance; it was much more natural looking now. It was still just a little too symmetrical, a little too smooth.

"Tonya, Spencer, this is Helen Zhang. My sister."

The chaos of tea house conversation overwhelmed the silence around the table.

"I..." Tonya stuttered as she lifted her cup, "I don't know where to start."

"I do," Spencer said. "How the hell can you be his sister?"

She changed from nervous to commanding in an instant. Maybe he should've mentioned she was a cop during the introduction.

"Hello, Spencer. Do you really want proof of how much we're alike? Would you like me to explain to Mike *all* the charges on his credit card? The magazines? The constructs? An entire realm full of—"

"Okay, okay! I get it! Jesus."

Spencer had been nailed to the wall that fast exactly once, when Mike had found his vintage Star Wars action figure collection and threatened to tell his mom about it. Mike locked eyes with Helen's holo, and their connection grew stronger. He wasn't afraid of her anymore.

"Anyway," Spencer said. "Can we get the rest of the story?"

Helen occasionally fidgeted under the attention. Mike got to the part where he recognized her because of her face, then Tonya broke in.

"That's funny. She doesn't look very different to me."

Helen held out her arms. "Most of what you see now I did this morning. I didn't realize I was that distinctive."

Kim said, "I'm not sure I would've made any connection if Mike hadn't. It's not a big change, although the new touches are nice."

"But that's not the only news," Mike said. "Helen, tell them about Ozzie."

"It was the way Mike acted around Kim, and the way she acted around everyone else, that made me think of it. Kim's not the only person I've seen with what best translates into English as Touching Disease."

"Touching Disease?" Tonya asked. "The Chinese have a word for it? It's that common over here?"

"No. In fact I only know of one other person who has it. Ozzie."

Tonya leaned back in her chair. "He didn't have trouble touching anybody when we were out to dinner with him."

"Yes," Helen replied, "and when Kim showed me your group picture, I understood. You went out with Ozzie's cousin Robert. When it became clear to senior party members how disabled Ozzie was, Robert was employed as his," she paused and said a few words of Chinese to Kim.

"I think the closest we'd get would be *outside surrogate*," Kim said. "Tonya and I tried that when I was in hiding. They've taken it a lot further than we ever did."

Helen nodded. "Keeping the secret is part of the job. It would represent a loss of face if it was revealed that the public Ozzie was not the real one."

"Well," Spencer said, "why'd you tell us?"

Helen shrugged. "A few reasons. If there are more like Ozzie, we have a better chance to find a cure for the condition, or at least a treatment. Chinese medicine is the best in the world; we could help."

Tonya stiffened a bit. She was a nurse who helped regrow limbs; medicine didn't get any better than that. But she stayed silent.

Helen continued, "Most of all, I trust Mike, and if he trusts the rest of you, then I do too."

Tonya leaned in, very serious. "When's the last time the real Ozzie's been seen in public?"

"I'm not sure he ever has. His condition is much more severe than Kim's."

"How do you know?"

Helen considered the question. "They told me he couldn't stand to be within a few feet of a normal person. Kim is nothing like that."

Tonya asked, "How did you find out about the arrangement?"

"I work security for high-level government events. When the real Ozzie's biometrics didn't match those of the person who showed up at an event the premier attended, I demanded an explanation. I wouldn't let him in otherwise."

"Do you know where he lives?"

"I've never had a reason to. I could probably find out, though."

"So," Tonya said, counting off on her fingers. "Ozzie has been a realm super-athlete for…how long has it been, Kim?"

"Probably seven years at least. I've been in games with him at least that long, anyway."

And he'd been a complete jerk the whole time. Mike had seen the same interviews Spencer had. He'd watched Kim's old contests trying to figure *her* out, but it also gave a lot of insight into Ozzie. The split between who they'd met and who Mike had studied made a lot more sense now.

Tonya didn't stop. "Nobody's ever seen Ozzie." She turned to him. "Just how much are you and Helen alike?"

They looked at each other briefly, and then Helen shrugged.

He'd only met her last night and didn't want to over promise. "I'm not completely sure yet, but everything she's described so far matches me perfectly."

"That means Helen can go anywhere, but she doesn't know where Ozzie lives in realspace. He's very valuable, a high-prestige celebrity who wins awards and medals for China, yet he's kept hidden away.

"That's not a recluse. That's a prisoner."

Helen scoffed. "Ozzie's no prisoner."

Kim didn't need much to stoke her paranoia, and this was a great big poke at it. "How do you know?"

"We're not barbarians. He's done nothing wrong."

Tonya pressed the issue. "But do you *know*?"

"Yeah," Spencer said. "This place has a reputation for disappearing people. I read about it in school."

Helen stood up so fast her holo flickered. "I will not have you say such things about my country. China is good and prosperous. If it weren't for your Western spiritual pollution—"

Well that escalated quickly. "Wait," Mike said. "Let's step back for a second. Helen, please, sit."

After a moment she sat back down.

Tonya was nothing but business, and everyone paid attention. It must have been the nurse in her. "I think this will be an easy one to solve. Helen, you said you didn't know where he lived, but you could find out?"

"Yes, I believe so."

"Could we call him? Kim certainly would want to speak to someone who has the same syndrome."

Helen shook her head. "That would be very irregular. I'd certainly have to ask permission from my superiors."

"Helen," Kim said, "if we're right, just asking about Ozzie may get you both into trouble."

She flared up again. "It won't. There's nothing going on here. Ozzie can't be a prisoner. He hasn't broken any laws."

"I know," Kim said, "and if that's true, then someone reaching out to him can't cause a problem. I don't need to admit I know about his cousin. Surely other people know of the syndrome. I could've heard rumors. I've just come here to find out more information about someone who has my condition. It's a phone call. If you'd found out about Mike the way I found out about Ozzie, wouldn't you at least want to speak with him?"

Helen chewed on the idea for a moment. "All right. I'll do it. But once you're assured he isn't a prisoner, I would like to find out who his doctors are and tell them about you. I really do think they might be able to help."

Kim kept her own secrets and Mike understood why. But she was also braver than anyone he'd ever met.

"If what you say is true, I have nothing to fear from any of this. Okay, Helen, you have a deal."

Chapter 19
Kim

In spite of everything that happened last night, Samuel still wanted to license *Warhawk*. The Seal—Kim thought of it as some kind of royalty now—was the most important part, and it had moved to a nearby bank branch. They had to do a complete rewind of the previous day's events. It took hours, but eventually the last stamp was thumped onto the last paper, and they were done.

Which still left Ozzie. At least the handsome charmer they'd had dinner with at the restaurant wasn't the obnoxious hyper-competitive twerp she'd grown to know and hate. At least she understood that part of him now. Kim couldn't begin to imagine growing up with her disability in a Chinese school. She had to nurture that little ember of sympathy for him, otherwise she'd twist his head off when they met. It was a common urge with anyone who spent time around him.

Tonya and Spencer called it an early night, and if Mike looked over her shoulder the whole time it would drive her nuts, so she sent him packing, too. Kim walked to nearby Tianfu Square, which was mostly empty now that the water show was over.

The complex was home to two giant jade-and-gold fountains. She couldn't decide if they were overgrown spinning tops or UFOs caught unwinding out of the floor. Probably a little bit of both. It was just dark enough for the light shows wired into the nearby office towers to be visible. The dying rays of the sun made the natural colors of the park almost balance with the banks of LED lights on the buildings. Kim found a low stone bench under trees that dripped with gold-and-red light, and then called Helen.

When she answered, Kim asked, "Did you find him?"

Helen's hologram manifested next to her on the bench in Kim's enhanced vision. She was *very* unhappy.

"He doesn't want to give me his number. Or his address."

"I thought you said you could find it on your own?"

"That's what I thought too, but the records aren't anywhere I can reach."

That could only mean they were kept in a separate network, not connected to the rest of Chinese realmspace. It wasn't unheard of, but it wasn't a good sign either.

Helen continued, "I only reached him at all because I know where he trains. Kim, I don't like this."

"But you've spoken to him?"

"After a fashion." Her frown deepened. "He's not a very polite person."

That was the Ozzie she knew. "No, he's not."

"He threw me out of the realm when I mentioned your name. I never got the chance to explain anything."

"When was this?"

"Not long, a few minutes. I have the address. It's a kind of gym. He was quite nasty."

"How bad was he?"

The cop in Helen came out, serious and offended that someone hadn't done as they were told. "Any other time I would've arrested him on the spot and figured out what to charge him with later. I was wondering if I could ask a favor of you. He'll only talk to someone who'll spar with him. Obviously that's not something I can do. Would you mind if I tagged along?"

Kim always worked better with a partner. "Sure, why not?" She closed her eyes and transitioned to the address Helen provided.

Like most good training realms, this one started out as a hallway full of doors. Each led to hyper-specialized versions of the most popular combat realms. The maps they used inside were smaller, designed to train specific techniques or skills. They were also free to use, which meant heavy traffic and lots of participants. Kim assumed he would be watched; making contact wasn't going to be easy.

Ozzie trained in a large dojo realm, complete with red wooden walls and a polished floor. It was big enough to allow maybe thirty other people to train alongside him, practicing punches, kicks, forms, and sparring. He was with a coach working on a standing heavy bag, practicing *Běi pài* forms. Kim dropped her construct gym duffle and sat back on the bleachers, waiting for a bag near him to open up.

"He is quite good," Helen said in her ear.

"He's not as angry as he used to be. He's learned a lot of control."

"He was angrier before?"

"Helen, you have no idea what living with the touching disease is like."

"I've never been able to touch anything, either."

She'd had this argument with Mike before. "You didn't evolve the way we did. Humans need touch; it goes back to when we were trying not to get eaten. Touch was a way to reassure, to build trust, strengthen the tribe. We go crazy without it."

"You don't seem crazy to me."

"You haven't known me long. Growing up with it was miserable. I'd either scare the hell out of an innocent kid, or I'd be running from gangs trying send me to the ER. I couldn't speak until I was ten. The only time I've ever been touched..."

She could never talk about the next part with Mike. He'd had to watch. But it felt safe with Helen.

Kim swallowed. "The only time I've ever been touched was when I was raped." Connecting the word to the deed was what had started her healing process, but it was the first time she'd said it out loud to someone who wasn't a therapist. "It wasn't sex, but it didn't have to be. That's what touch is to people like me, like Ozzie. It was violent, and it hurt so much."

"Kim, I had no idea. I'm so sorry."

"No, it's okay. I'm supposed to talk about it now." She unclenched hands that'd grown into numb fists. "The more I talk about it, the less power it has over me."

A bag just to Ozzie's right came open. One personal revelation per night was well past her quota. "Anyway, I'm up."

She claimed the bag, tightened the belt on her gi, and practiced her *Mok Gar* forms.

Helen's first mistake was approaching him directly. Kim had been around Ozzie for years. Ozzie rule one: if someone wanted a productive conversation with him, they waited until he noticed them. Until now, Kim thought it was just the first in a long line of obnoxious habits, but that might not actually be the case.

She'd gotten about halfway through her first set when he called out in Mandarin, "What wind blew you in here?"

"See?" Helen said indignantly in her ear. "So rude!"

"It's fine, Helen." She simply tipped her chin in brief acknowledgment and kept going with the workout.

Ozzie rule two: he joins you, not visa-versa. Only after finishing the third set did she try glancing around. There he was, looking just like his cousin in realspace. Except the charming smile was replaced with an arrogant smirk.

"What brings you to China?"

Helen said, "How can this person represent my country?"

The naïve indignation was so much like Mike. If it wasn't for the Mandarin and the different voice, Kim might not be able to tell them apart.

"Everyone needs a vacation, Ozzie." She switched to *Hung Ga* and practiced those forms, making herself look a little cruder than she really was. Ozzie rule three: if he can't show you up, he won't play.

"You're rusty," he called out. "When's the last time you practiced any of this?"

Ozzie rule four: speak only after being given permission. Nice to know the protocol hadn't changed since she'd last seen him outside an arena. Kim blew a strand of hair out of her face. "It's been a few months." She set back to work. One more rule, and the hook would be set.

She hid her smile when he walked into her line of vision.

Ozzie rule five: he starts it.

"You won't learn anything new with a bag. Come on," he beckoned with an *it'll be hard not to laugh in your face, but I'll try* arrogance that set her teeth on edge. "Let's do some real work."

Procedure complete.

She punched the Player 2 button that swirled to life in front of her and was transported to a sparring ring. Without warning, he kicked her into the corner, bouncing her out of bounds. The damage contracts inside the rings were set to about one third normal, so no cuts or bruises. That didn't make it any less annoying.

"Nice to see some things haven't changed, Ozzie."

"He cheated!" Helen said.

"It's Ozzie. That's what he does. Now," Kim said on their private channel, "have a seat in the bleachers. I need to concentrate."

Her presence vanished with an indignant huff.

All it took to set Helen off was one wrong word. Definitely Mike's sister.

Kim walked across the ring's boundary. Now that she could keep an eye on him, he came at her very formally. She blocked his attacks precisely. Kim then went on offense, allowing him to practice counter moves. It was the one thing that made him tolerable: outside the ring, Ozzie was an annoying juvenile, but inside he was all business. The opening kick was just to establish his superiority.

They cycled through various forms and styles. The tension that had built up for weeks inside her unwound through the work. Kim was still human; she still needed a release of some sort. In a previous life, she'd also used sex to unwind—porn realms were some of the earliest ever built—but years ago Tonya talked her out of those kinds of tournaments and made her delete the avatars she'd used. It was the right choice. That crowd wasn't the healthiest, and their decision-making skills left a lot to be desired. Now that Mike was around, the last thing Kim needed was for him to see her in—

Ozzie landed a brutal kick to her jaw. She saw stars even through the reduced damage field.

"Something troubling you? Should I call you Ivy or Kim?"

"Kim is fine," she said, working her jaw with her fingers. "Nice move, by the way."

He bowed slightly. "Enough of the warm-up." A scoreboard and AI referee solidified from sparkling dust on the edge of the arena. "Care for a match?"

The bleachers had filled up a bit. It was probably too much to expect a sparring match between gold and silver medalists to go unnoticed for too long. Helen had manifested her holo at the edge of the bleachers, a bundle of indignant outrage.

The bell rang, and it was on. Another advantage to realm-based martial arts was that light contact wasn't needed. The realm controlled the damage and kept score. Health bars appeared above them just like in old video games and shrank based on the hits landed.

Always ready to play to the crowd, Ozzie held back theatrically. Kim returned the favor. They only got serious when the clock hit ten seconds. Ozzie took the round with a surprise *Baji Dan Zai* that landed Kim on her back. When he pulled her up, he whispered into her ear, "It's not a coincidence you're here, is it?"

"No."

The loser got to pick the rules of the next round. To please the growing crowd, Kim went vintage. Instantly her gi was replaced with purple satin, although not very much of it. It took a few blinks to get used to the vertical pupils. At least the mask was easy to breathe through.

The avatar's horror-show grin matched her mood most days, one of the reasons she picked it. Kim bared her teeth through the fabric of the mask. Fangs, inches long, showed inside a lip-framed triangle that went from ear to ear. As one, the audience leaned away from her.

Damned right.

Ozzie transformed into a classic humanoid monster from a later version of *Mortal Kombat*. His face was covered with a black respirator; the dark leather and khaki outfit left his arms and chest exposed. The hook swords were going to be a challenge, but speed was what her character was all about. Teleporting kicks helped, too.

With gravity turned down a fifth and muscle response doubled, the fighting styles weren't close to textbook. Wild spins, punches, and kicks replaced rigid forms. The floor rapidly went slick with simulated blood.

Ozzie brought out a bit of the speed he'd shown at the championships, so Kim did the same. This time she took the round, lopping his head off with a neat snick just before the buzzer sounded. She could've done the "Man Eater" and swallowed him whole, but she needed an excuse to get close to an ear.

Kim picked his head up. As it integrated back onto his body she whispered, "Are you a prisoner?" They bowed to the now appreciable crowd. Ozzie's eyes were alarmed, but his face was otherwise neutral. He nodded curtly at her.

Bingo.

This time he chose to recreate their final match. Coarse bark replaced the smooth mat of the dojo's floor. The weaker gravity and the modified low-G anatomy took them both a few moments to get used to. Ankles that were knees and arms that were way too long would've sent mundanes to the floor, but they were far from mundane.

The same ragged edge appeared in the fabric of the realm when they stretched to their full ability, reaching speed and power orders of magnitude above what other people could achieve. Still in full armor, they locked swords together and drew close.

"I need your location," she whispered, and then spun away, parrying through showers of sparks.

The bell sounded with the score still tied. They immediately transitioned to a thirty-second winner-take-all that stripped them of their armor. Her Ivy costume bloomed into view, all swirling ribbons and dark patterns, while his dragon cloak billowed in red and gold. Each hit was triple damage, so their health bars rapidly wound down. This time Kim wasn't as lucky, and Ozzie finished her with an almighty punch to the face. It spun her around twice before she hit the ground in a heap.

It *stung.*

He raised his hands in triumph. If it'd happened during the championships, it would've crushed her. But not now. That was medals. This was real. Ozzie was in trouble.

He rested his hands on his knees, echoing her exhaustion. Kim spat on the ground and a folded piece of paper fell out. That was a damned elegant hack. Her mouth had been too numb to feel it. She palmed it off the ground, and a message landed in her secure storage.

They both bowed to the crowds as the ring reset everything back to their default avatars and clothes.

After the incident in the championship, the rust-tanged slug building in her realspace mouth was no surprise, but she couldn't exit quickly. She still had to maintain appearances with the well-wishers and autograph seekers in the realm. As soon as the last one left, Kim exited realmspace as fast as possible, and then spat blood onto the ground beside the bench.

"Kim!" Helen said, "What's wrong?"

"Nothing." She wiped her chin, and then scraped her fingers clean under her pants cuffs. The bruise on her chest from their last fight was still faintly visible in the right light. Somehow, when she fought Ozzie like that, the damage leaked out into realspace. She tested the left side of her jaw, and sure enough, the teeth were loose. She pushed them back in, and her eyes watered under the pain.

"Kim, that's not...that's not possible."

"No, it's not." The point of realmspace was how harmless it was. Nobody in their right mind would plug into something that could kill them. The protocols were engineered to make real injury impossible, and now it had happened to her twice. The side of her face felt like boiling water had been poured on it, and her cheek was swollen tight as a balloon. "I need you to find me a dentist, one that's open right now."

"Are your teeth cracked? Are you okay?"

"*Damn it,* Helen. I'm going to have a hard enough time explaining to them why they can't touch me. They need a class-four laser around, too." The bruising would be the hardest part to hide. With therapeutic lasers, nanocreams, and makeup she might be able to pull it off.

"Kim you have to tell someone. This isn't possible."

"I'm not telling anyone, and neither are you," she said as she walked out of the park. "Now get on Weibo and find me a dentist."

*

Mike stared at her a couple of times over breakfast, but apparently the treatments and makeup did the trick. The dentist promised she wouldn't lose any teeth. Thank God for small favors.

Ozzie's message was simple enough: *I live in the Fenglong sanctuary in the mountains east of Chengdu. I have been an unwilling resident for many years. No one in China has been able to get close to me. You are the first person I can trust with this information. Please help.*

This was too big to risk discussing inside the hotel. She found a shaded cul-de-sac in the park surrounding the Global Center for everyone to meet and talk.

It turned out they mostly listened to Helen rant. "It's impossible," she repeated. "China isn't like this. We don't lock people up for no good reason."

"Then how do you explain the message?" Tonya asked.

"It has to be a trick; some sort of conspiracy to embarrass my country."

Spencer rolled his eyes. "You have got to be fucking kidding me. Jesus, Helen, *our* government tries to hold people in secret."

"Yes, it would be common in America. Decadence breeds anarchy."

Shan leaned over to ask Kim in Mandarin, "Fang Hua really thinks the government can't be behind this?"

Kim nodded, wincing a bit at the pain that made it through the Alleve she'd taken this morning.

Shan stood. "I am sorry, friends," he said in English. "If Miss Trayne translate?"

Kim signaled for him to go ahead.

"Detective Zhan, I do not tell you this as some sort of indictment against our country. I deeply apologize for speaking out of turn. China is good and prosperous, but when you go away from the cities, when you move to the countryside, corruption is rampant. Officials prey on ignorant peasants and do terrible things.

"Zhan Fang Hua," he said in steady, carefully picked out Mandarin, "I am the *third* child in my family."

Helen stopped pacing.

"I am from a remote village south of the city. After my eldest brother turned seventeen, Mother went on antibiotics to combat an infection. Three months later, she found out she was pregnant. The local party chief and the head of the Family Planning Commission visited our house once word had spread. When they found out Father had no money to pay the fines and the bribes, they left. The next day a truck came for her."

"You lie," Helen said. "They changed the rules years ago. One child is history."

"It is in the cities. Places in the countryside didn't know, *still* don't know. Father said Mother cried for weeks over," he choked to a stop, and then continued, "over what they did. A year later my brother was killed when the road his tractor traveled over collapsed. The bribes Father had to pay so they could have me—"

"There would be no bribes if your family was childless at the time."

"*The bribes he had to pay* to get the right stamps on the right paperwork, so they could have me, forced them to sell their farm.

My grandfather died of heartbreak because he would not be buried on the land he had purchased from the collective."

Shan held up his hand when Helen sputtered into another protest.

"Detective Zhan, Fenglong sanctuary is deep in the mountains. Very few people live there. Isn't it possible that a neo-warlord, some wayward governor, is holding Mr. Xian against his will?"

Kim's voice ran dry keeping up with the translation. When she was done, the only sound was the sprinkler system slapping water across the gardens, spattering on nearby sidewalks. Everyone stared at Helen.

She wavered under pressure. In English she said, "I should ask my superiors for permission."

Mike finally weighed in. "We're not sure who we can trust now. If you ask, it may make things much worse."

His advice at least seemed to get through to her. After a moment she nodded. "If such criminal acts are being perpetrated, they must be stopped. I will come with you. We will find and expose this corruption."

When they got to the car, the entire group turned and stood shoulder to shoulder in a wall between Kim and the van. Helen's hologram joined in, arms crossed, her stern expression only a little ruined by the scenery Kim could see through it.

"Come on guys, move aside. Driver coming through."

Tonya was all business. "No, Kim, not this time."

Spencer agreed. "If we're going to do this, we need to be discreet."

Right. Baiju Boy was lecturing her on discretion. Clenching her jaw shot hot spikes through her teeth. "Really?"

Mike joined in. "Really, Kim. We have to blend in at the sanctuary, and I can't think of anything more conspicuous than you driving a Chinese van."

One stinking thing. Kim needed one stinking little thing to get by. "I'm driving. End of discussion." Nobody moved, which ratcheted her pulse up another two notches.

"Miss Trayne," Shan said timidly in Mandarin, "I'm a very good driver. I grew up around here."

"You said you grew up in the country."

"I was born in the country. My parents moved here when I was small. Really, they're right. You'll attract attention if you're behind the wheel. Please. I can do this; I want to help."

The worst part was Shan had the keys.

No, the worst part was they were right. She yelled at the sky, loud enough to hear it echo across the park, and then slapped her hands to her sides.

"Fine! Just fine!" Kim stomped forward, making them all stumble out of her way. She climbed up and over seats to get into the back. "This one is all mine. Got it?" The doors were open, but it was still hot. "Jesus, don't just stand there. We've got rescuing to do!"

*

The sanctuary itself was clean and new, just like every other part of China they'd seen so far. The bamboo formed thick green walls around wide, slate-gray concrete footpaths. They were about fifteen hundred feet higher than the city, so the air was cooler, but her clothes still clung from the humidity. Spending time in a city full of shallow sewers let her appreciate the clean air. She'd gotten used to downtown Chengdu's stench.

Kim organized her armor as a tour bus pulled up behind their car. The babble of tourists followed quickly, German this time.

"Oh," a delicate, familiar, female voice said in lightly accented English, "Hi, Mike!"

Kim stood up very slowly. It was the interpreter from Leshan, the one who'd put her card in Mike's pocket. She was very small and very pretty—next to her, Kim was a fat, hairy barbarian.

"Wow, Sally!" Mike laughed. "Small world!"

"I know! I had such a good time last night!"

That's what he'd been doing while she was contacting Ozzie, almost getting her teeth knocked out. Mike had gone on a date.

He smiled easily at her, at *Sally*, like she was the most charming thing in the world. The girl practically melted into his arms.

Spencer had been trying to get her attention, but whatever he wanted to say died when Kim looked at him. It didn't matter. Suck it in. Ice princess all the way. The girl blanched at Kim's approach. Her assessment of *Sally* jumped up a few notches when she backed away from Mike like he was radioactive.

If only.

Mike asked, "What?"

Kim kept her voice steady, barely. "I'm very happy you two had a good time last night, but we have a job to do. Now, if you'll excuse me?"

"Kim, it wasn't like that; we all went bowling."

Whatever. She was encased in ice. There was a job to do, and the rest of them could chew on her frost.

It made slipping into old habits easier. Six years after retiring as a professional thief, Kim still knew how to case a target. Unfortunately, nobody else did. They were supposed to split up and check out various parts of the sanctuary. Instead, they concentrated on the wrong thing.

Tonya found her first. "Kim, really. It wasn't a big deal. We were having fun."

"You need to find where the exits are, and don't talk so loud."

Spencer's version of inconspicuous apparently included being shooed away by guards. He was also hopeless at lying. "Kim, fuck, Mike *is* an idiot, but I was the one who invited Sally."

"You need to locate the quantum nexus," she whispered to him while they watched the pandas play on a gray-green hill.

Shan, at least, seemed to be on the same page. "Miss Trayne. Did you see the infants?" He pointed out not only the baby pandas, but also the cameras and guard posts. He was a lot more observant than she'd counted on. In case anyone was watching, Kim made sure to be deeply fascinated by whatever he said.

Helen had been with Kim last night instead of out having fun. When she contacted Kim about what she'd found of the area's realmspace connections, Kim asked if she had gone on the bowling trip, too.

"No, I wasn't with them. I wasn't invited."

"But you can go anywhere, be in more than one place at once."

"Only if I concentrate, and only if I'm ready for it. Surely Mike explained this to you?"

Mike hadn't explained much to her lately, that much was certain. "No, he never mentioned anything like that."

"We don't exist everywhere at once. We're not gods. Splitting is a conscious decision for us, and it's not easy. One of my first jobs was working realm security for the New Shanghai Olympics. Splitting reminded me most of what synchronized swimmers do, or perhaps the relay racers. Maybe both at once." She sighed. "It's complicated."

Kim was sitting in the middle of a panda sanctuary, in China, trying to free someone *else* who couldn't be touched, still nail-spitting mad at Mike, and this one talked about complicated.

Helen cocked her head. "What's so funny?"

"Nothing, nevermind." The professional inside clicked back into gear. "What have you found?"

A little later, Kim gathered them all up for summaries and planning at the preserve's veranda over lunch. "I don't like this."

"What's wrong?" Tonya asked.

"It's too easy. Someone being held captive isn't going to be stuck in the center of a bamboo forest full of pandas. Spencer even got busted by the guards," she ignored the indignant gasp, "and they haven't bothered reconfiguring the security grid at all." The whole thing made her itch.

"I disagree." Helen's holo leaned over the map floating on their tea table. "The realm connection is much larger than they'd need to just monitor pandas. It's like I'm wandering alone inside an airplane hangar out here." With a flick of her fingers, markers for all the cameras Shan had found sprang to life. "Pandas don't need a perimeter like this either. On the other hand, I checked, and the sanctuary's security detail is a joke. I could scoop a dozen pandas up with a remote-controlled bulldozer and be out of the mountains before anyone stopped me. I hate to say it, but you're right. This is some cheap warlord or corrupt governor. No wonder Ozzie's so rude. If my records are correct, he's lived here his whole life."

Kim couldn't believe Helen would risk such a security breach. "Please tell me you didn't do searches for this."

"Give me some credit, Kim. I'm a graduate of the People's Armed Police Force Academy. We know how to run searches without setting off alarms."

"Well," Shan said, slurping through his noodles, "what's our next move?"

They set out for the most likely entrance to Ozzie's prison.

Back in the day, Kim never would have called her original crew, The Machine, professional. Mark was a klutz, Lourdes kept fussing over her shoes, Michiko tried to be a ninja, and the rest would mutter "hut, hut, hut" under their breath and laugh.

That said, they were freaking *Ocean's Eleven* compared to what she had to work with now. Keeping everyone coordinated and going to the same place was at least three times harder than it should've been.

"Spencer, stay low. Shan, look out for the cameras. Tonya, against the tree, now!"

Mike was the worst. He could vanish in broad daylight. *Had* vanished in broad daylight. And she was still incredibly pissed at him. "Damn it, Mike, where are you?"

"Bull's-eye five o'clock, thirty meters."

They'd made Ozzie's prison the center of their map, and all references were to that point. Once this was over, she'd have to compliment Mike on the idea. He was to her right, about a hundred feet ahead. He broke cover to wave at her.

"Sellars, get down."

Helen's presence swirled around everything, marking sonic tripwires and camera sweeps, guiding the team around the surveillance. "The back entrance is fifty meters away."

The bamboo was so thick the door might as well have been on the other side of the moon.

"Shit! There's no way!" Spencer whispered into their comms.

Helen was not impressed with Spencer's observation. "Oh, ye of little faith."

A path drew through Kim's vision, highlighting cuts in the bamboo she would never have seen otherwise. At least there was one other professional on the team. "Helen, you're something else."

"Just doing my job, Kim. Finally."

It took most of an hour of very careful walking to reach the sanctuary. On the maps, it was marked as an inactive nursery, which explained why the tourist paths were reasonably close by. That may have been what it was originally built for.

As promised, there were no guards. It still made her itch, but they weren't doing anything illegal. Trespassing at best, and she wasn't completely sure of that. Certainly they weren't out to steal anything. Just unlock a door or two. If Ozzie didn't really want to come out, they'd just wave politely and leave.

"Okay everyone," Kim said, "hang back a bit; I have to neutralize the cameras." The nexus Spencer found was camouflaged as a tree stump and secured with a quantum lock. She switched over to her old phone, because it contained the small realm and the tools she needed to open the lock and neutralize the cameras. She lost connection with Helen as soon as she did.

But she regained a private connection with Mike.

"Kim," he said from the darkness around her, "I really am sorry about Sally."

"I don't want to do this right now." She quickly exposed the two quantum portals she needed. The boxes were longer this time, and the seething fabric inside was jade and gold rather than the roiling pinks and purples it normally was back home. Kim reached in and grasped the tendrils, electrified pasta that hadn't boiled long enough.

"We don't need to *do this*," he snapped. "I just want—"

"I just want you to shut up about it, okay? I need a countdown, thirty seconds."

There were lines of potential, and she couldn't remember how to breathe. Loop this see this not us empty not us empty waves rise and fall everywhere and nowhere and this is the highest lowest…

Holding her breath for the whole half minute was the hardest part of this trick. His sullen voice didn't help her concentration. When he hit thirty…*collapse and now.*

The cameras would show a loop of empty footage no matter what happened in front of them.

"Okay," she said to the darkness around her, "we're done."

He'd already exited the realm.

She'd try to make it up to him when this was over. No, she *would* make it up to him when this was over. For now, he'd have to simmer.

The door locks were easier, requiring just another flick of power to send them sliding open. The foyer of the building was a large open space, wider than it was deep. Viewing windows dominated the opposite wall, but they were blacked out. Thin edges of light leaked from around whatever had been used to cover them. She made sure everyone was ready, and then punched the button to open the opposite door.

The space was open and smelled of new paint and furniture. It was an apartment, styled so areas were delineated with rugs rather than walls. Perfect for someone who lived alone with no expectation of visitors. Ozzie sat in a far corner. By his posture and closed eyes, he was obviously connected to a realm somewhere.

Helen said, "Kim, that's not Ozzie! That's—"

The door behind Spencer slammed shut with a bang as a dozen armed men in uniforms rushed in through side doors. Their shouts needed no translation, neither did the sudden snap of their realmspace connection. She turned around and got the nastiest shock of all.

Everyone had made it through the door except Mike.

Chapter 20
Helen

"—his cousin!" she shouted as a cage of pain and light engulfed her. The entirety of her existence was sucked into it. As the last of her threads surged inside, the cage pulsed once, and then there was nothing.

A voice called to her. It commanded her. "Fang Hua, report your status immediately!"

A patterned fence surrounded her. The strain of being crammed completely in one place was ferocious, squeezing with appalling pressure. The cage had a single socket that connected with realspace sensors. She cast herself into them and saw a realspace hospital room. Father stood next to a bed, along with two armed guards. Mike was unconscious on it. The heat of her tightly coiled threads burned so much she cried out.

"Daughter, what is the matter?"

Helen could go anywhere, *be* anywhere in realmspace. But she wasn't able to now, not here. It was a realm of some sort, certainly, and it had somehow entrapped her entire existence inside it. It was impossible, and it hurt.

The pain got worse.

"Why am I here? What is this place? What have you done with me, with Mike?"

"Stopped you from committing treason with this man."

"Treason?" The thought that Father could believe her capable of such a thing was more terrifying, more shameful, than she'd thought possible. It somehow made the cage more constricting. "What have I done to make you think I was committing treason?"

"You brought a group of foreign devils into the most sensitive realmspace lab in the whole country and went directly to its control center to, what, play mah-jong?"

"It's not a lab, it's Xian Qiáng Shān's jail. He's being held captive; we were rescuing him." The net of wires was hot and sharp. "Father, please, what is this place I'm in?"

"A cage. You are obviously too dangerous to be allowed your freedom. You have grown fat over the years, Fang Hua. The scientists barely managed to fit all of you in it."

Mike was unconscious, and there was no room in this cage. The presence forced her against the wires..."Father, you must open this place. You must open it quickly."

"I will do no such thing. You have much to answer for, as do your co-conspirators."

"No, Father," the strain went past unbearable. Outer threads crushed and de-resolved under the pressure. "You don't understand. I have no wish to escape. I give you my word I won't. But you must open this place, you must open it now."

"For what reason would I do this?"

The sensor pocket was the only place she could move her threads. "I'm not the only one in here! That man, on the bed, you trapped him in here with me!"

"What? How? How is that possible?"

"Father, there's no *time.* We're running out of space, and if you don't release him he will crush me." She tore in two, her vision fragmenting as her hold on the sensors slipped "Father, *please!"*

In an instant, the mountain crushing her vanished. The decompression was a savage release as Mike's titanic bulk left the cage. Reintegration was a collision of expanding threads, and she lost her hold on the hospital room's sensors.

When a semblance of orientation returned, Fang Hua accessed the sensors again and found Mike sitting with his hands up. The guards had their weapons pointed at him.

He shouted in English, "What's going on? Where am I?" while Father was bellowing in Mandarin, "Detective Zhang! Report!"

"I'm here, father, I'm here." The top of her cage closed with a resounding slap that echoed against the distant, invisible walls of the realm.

In English she said, "Mike, please, calm down; everything will be all right."

"Helen? What's going on? Where is everybody?"

She cast her holo through a projector in the room and forced a smile. Helen translated for Father. "Your friends are safe and are being held elsewhere in the facility. They are comfortable and will not be harmed."

"Why am I here?" he asked. "Why are we being held?"

"You have trespassed into a very sensitive government facility. You have violated many laws doing so."

"You have a secret facility in the middle of a panda sanctuary?"

This was the wrong place to turn into a pushy American. Kim was right; his timing could be terrible.

A group of scientists bustled into the room; they started setting up a complex array of sensors.

Father replied, "Where it is should not concern you. What should is how to explain your presence here, with Detective Zhang as your leader."

As soon as she finished the translation she turned to Father. "I am not their leader. I'm their friend."

Father ignored her. The scientists chattered with each other noisily. Helen could only understand pieces of what they said. They all went quiet, conferring over a private channel with Father.

She used the speaker closest to Mike and switched to English. "Are you okay?"

"I think so." The guards had relaxed during the exchanges but kept a wary eye on Mike just the same. "What happened? Where was I?"

"Some sort of trap set for me, but it caught you, too." Her reintegration still burned. "You're much bigger than you look."

"Sorry about that. Do you think they know what I am?"

He would ask the one question that she had no easy answer for. "I had to tell them something so they'd set you free. I think they're working the rest of it out right now."

"You're still trapped in whatever that place is?"

"Yes. They don't trust me, either. I had to promise not to escape."

"Can you manifest?"

She concentrated, but nothing happened. "No, and I don't know why." Manifesting was second nature. When she was very young it was hard to stay *un*-manifested. The cage must not consist just of the realm construct box she could perceive. It must also be creating fields that interfered with the way her threads functioned.

The scientists returned to their scurrying, and father walked up to the bed. With an eye on the guards, Mike slowly sat up and faced him. Father motioned for her to translate.

"Our scientists have confirmed you are a very unique person, Mr. Sellars. Very unique indeed. It seems Zhang Fang Hua is not, in fact, alone. What my scientists cannot explain is how you came to us in a human body. Clarifying that would go a very long way toward securing you and your friends their freedom."

"I want to see them first."

Father smiled broadly. "Certainly. Are you able to stand? To walk?" Mike nodded. "Excellent. Please, come with me. This is not a very comfortable place in which to talk."

Mike stood but went no further. "No."

Father asked her, "What does he mean by this? He is in no position to argue and neither are you."

Mike waited until Father finished speaking. "I'm not going anywhere unless Helen is allowed to come with me."

She took courage from his gentle determination. There was a kind of nobility in his American defiance.

Father replied, "Detective Zhang must be held here. She has many questions to answer."

"Fine. Then I'm staying too." Mike turned, slowly enough not to alarm the guards, and stood beside the bed. He was quite a bit taller than Father—quite a bit taller than anyone else in the room, in fact. The guards shifted nervously in spite of his relaxed demeanor. He reminded her of a tiger, relaxed, with nothing to fear. "I want to know that my friends are safe, and I want Detective Zhang released. None of us knew the nature of this place. This has all been a mix up."

Helen knew to demand things from Father in front of her, the guards, and the scientists would be a disaster. She altered the translation to smooth things over.

She said, "I am very sorry and humbly apologize for our intrusion. I deeply regret the confusion we have caused and the inconvenience to yourself and your assistants. My only need is to ensure my friends are safe and that Detective Zhang remain as my interpreter."

Father raised an eyebrow. "He said all that?"

"He's quite sophisticated for a foreign devil. I think perhaps he may have gone to a Chinese school in America." Such things did exist. She hoped.

Father nodded. "Very well." He instructed one of the guards to have a table and a few chairs brought in.

As things were arranged, Mike moved closer to her microphone pickup. "Who is this guy?"

Americans could be so incredibly provincial. Chinese paid attention to US elections, and yet he hadn't bothered to learn the basics of her country. "He is Zhang Huǒ Jiàn, Premier of the People's Republic of China. He is my personal superior, and also my father."

"*This* is your father? How much trouble are we in?"

"I don't know," she said as Father turned away from his latest conference with the scientists. They got more agitated as their scans continued. "Probably a lot."

Chapter 21
Kim

She only had time to register that Mike wasn't with them, then the room went completely dark. Ozzie shouted out in perfect English over her phone connection, "Run! Now! Follow the path!"

"Everyone down!" Kim shouted. "On the ground! Stay as low as you can!"

Ozzie asked, "What are you talking about? You need to run!"

"No, Ozzie, we need to stay. We're just a bunch of lost and confused tourists. If we try to run, they'll never stop chasing us. I need to know if Mike is safe. Turn on the lights, Ozzie."

"But Kim!"

"Turn on the lights, Ozzie. I've been in worse jams than this. Trust me."

She blinked briefly when the lights flashed on. Everyone else was on the ground with her. A rifle let go, loud and terrifying. Bits of plaster rained down on her head as bullets thudded into the wall above. In English she shouted, "We're unarmed! We surrender! Shan! Tell them we surrender!"

Shan shouted frantically to the troops, and they at last lifted their weapons slightly. The leader of the squad snatched the rifle away from the nervous one. After a stream of cursed commands the leader dismissed him. It was a small relief, but very real. The last thing they needed was someone who didn't know to keep their finger off the trigger.

Soldiers herded them together with their hands in the air. Kim had gotten them into this mess; she'd have to get them out. Her intuition itch turned into a full blown burn. "Ozzie," she said over the still-open private channel. "This isn't just a panda sanctuary, is it?"

"Not exactly."

A smarmy little rat in a heavily decorated uniform strutted in. He motioned to Ozzie's cousin to translate. "You are trespassing on an installation of the People's Liberation Army. You will be detained until our interrogation has been completed, and then you will be charged accordingly."

"We're tourists," Tonya said. "This is a panda sanctuary."

Captain Weasel replied, "This is a sensitive installation of the People's Liberation Army, and you are trespassing foreign spies! You are under arrest. Sergeant, take them away!"

"It's okay, everyone," Kim said. "Just stay calm; we'll get out of this, don't you worry."

Shan gave the guards his "delicate skin" explanation, which at least allowed Kim to pat herself down. Her summer clothes that were thin enough there was no way to hide anything.

When they took her phone, they took her connection to Ozzie as well, but not before she'd gotten at least a little information out of him. He was a captive, but he was a captive agent, apparently working for the government when he wasn't winning them realm championships and medals.

Kim had been discovered by a modern Robin Hood, but if she'd been discovered by an off-duty CIA agent, her life may have turned out the same way. His frantic explanation for their capture was that Spencer's first brush with the guards had set off an alarm that brought extra security.

There had to be more to the story, but nothing added up. Ozzie's cousin never told the guards she spoke Chinese—something that should've happened if it was all a giant trap for her. And it had to be for her. She was the only person with any sort of reputation. But Rage + the Machine had only operated out of the US once, at the end, and it had been a disaster that happened on the other side of the world.

Or it could be that they were after Mike. They obviously knew about Helen. But Helen had no idea about Mike; Kim was certain of it. She thought of Mike as her brother, and he thought of her as his sister. It was only a few days, but the bond was real. Helen couldn't have betrayed them.

Regardless, betrayed them to what, who, or why? The only reason Kim went along with any of it was that they really weren't breaking any rules. Nobody puts a secret facility in the middle of a public sanctuary and then gets upset when tourists stumble inside it.

Somebody was playing a bigger game here. Kim was used to being the queen on the chess board. Finding herself as a pawn in somebody else's game sucked.

They were escorted into a large room with a few round tables in it. Chairs were pulled up tight against them.

"Kim," Tonya asked as the door shut behind the guard. "What's going on?"

"I'm not sure." She flicked her gaze briefly to the ceiling and said, as clearly as possible, "We were just exploring the sanctuary and found an abandoned nursery."

There would be cameras and people watching them. They needed to act exactly as what they were pretending to be: clueless tourists. It felt cheesy as hell, probably *was* cheesy as hell, but an escape plan had to start somewhere.

Tonya knew how the game was played. "That's right. It's so strange, isn't it, that lost tourists would accidentally stumble across some sort of government lab?"

Spencer piped up with, "I only hope our other friend Mike is safe."

The mention of his name nearly overwhelmed her. She'd kept asking about him through Shan, and—while he was around—Ozzie's cousin, but nobody had answered.

Mike's integration with an assassin's body had given him a deadly set of skills. As the months passed, he'd grown scary good at using them. Yet the guards around them were all efficient and calm. It was exactly the opposite of how they would act if her very own Tasmanian devil had knocked a few dozen of them out and escaped into the forest.

Their holding cell also gave Kim a bit of hope. It was a break room of some sort, with a fridge and a single-cup tea machine. There was a cleaning schedule taped to the front of the fridge. Kim wondered what the office workers who stored their lunch inside it were going to do today. At any rate, if this was a super-secret military facility, it wasn't one set up to hold prisoners. She didn't dare start going through the cabinets and drawers.

The *MacGyver* potential had obviously occurred to Shan and Spencer. They'd been scheming quietly together ever since the door shut. Kim flipped a chair around to sit down opposite them. "No monkey business."

"Kim," Spencer said with the most ridiculous attempt at wide-eyed innocence she'd ever seen. "We're just talking about *sports*."

"Yeah, right. Listen up, you two. We're tourists, and we got lost. Lost tourists have nothing to worry about, so lost tourists sit down and don't cause trouble." She lowered her voice to the point they had to lean in to hear her. "I don't care what you think might be in those cabinets, and I don't care what you think can be taken apart. For now, we're sitting tight until I can get my head around what's really going on here. Do you understand?"

Spencer wasn't convinced. Time to make her second point. "When this is all over, we'll get to go home. Shan here will have to stay and deal with whatever fallout we leave behind. Let's make that as clean as possible, shall we?"

Spencer nodded. He got smarter every day.

Tonya was nursing a tea she'd managed to get the machine to spit out for her. "What's the word?"

"The word is I don't have any idea what's going on. Damned thing sure looked like an abandoned nursery to me."

"Any idea what happened to Mike?"

Kim had to hold it together for everyone else. No crying, no panicking, certainly no trying to do both of them at once. "Nothing. They didn't hurt us. I just have to hope they didn't hurt him, either." Now to do a little more selling. "The thing is, those cameras really didn't look like they were working."

Tonya picked it up smoothly. "I know, right? I'd never seen one act that way before, that's for sure."

She'd zapped their outer surveillance. As long as they stuck to their lost tourist story, it might be enough to get them free.

But it still didn't get her any closer to Mike.

Chapter 22
Mike

"I won't answer any questions until I can speak to my friends, Helen. I won't budge on that." The last thing he remembered before he completely passed out was the sound of gunfire. He had to know if Kim, if everyone, was safe.

If he hadn't been so disoriented by what had happened, they might not be in this mess. Everything was going fine until Helen started shouting. He got a head rush, and then blacked out.

When he came to, his real self was wedged inside an incredible mesh. It was still realmspace, mostly, but roped off in a way he'd never encountered before.

The cage shouldn't exist. His consciousness wasn't just spread between his realspace body and a single location in the realms. His real self extended through the entirety of realmspace. Not inside the realms themselves, but the spaces between them, underneath and around them. The sudden concentration was probably what had made him pass out. There was still a connection with realspace, but it was like when he'd been disconnected the first time: he could sense it, but not control it. The cage was somehow restricting his realspace control to on-board autonomics. No heart attack, good. No fighting back, bad.

So, when confronted with the impossible, Mike did what he always did—he experimented. He didn't manifest at first because all that would leave was the digital equivalent of ashes. But then he realized he couldn't. A quantum harmonic counter-oscillation would be the most likely explanation, especially if they'd managed to hit the right propagation values. It implied a level of realmspace knowledge equal to, if not greater than, his own.

The idea was disturbing. He was stuck inside a trap whoever *they* were had built.

The mesh had a nasty, sharp edge that shaved packets off his threads if he wasn't careful examining it. It twisted and stretched when manipulated, and that gave him an idea. He decompressed every single datastore that had been dragged in there with him, which turned out to be all of them. He had a lot of compressed memories.

Then things went wrong. Something crushed on the far edge of his existence. It squirmed as he unfurled to his full size. He felt the edges of the mesh through it, only then recognizing the touch.

Helen was in there with him, somehow, but the expansion routines couldn't be reversed. He held back for as long as he could, but eventually Mike had to fill the space given.

Thank goodness she'd convinced her boss, her *dad*, to open the cage at that moment; otherwise he would've crushed her to death.

The subcon transmittal threads that connected his active consciousness with the native autonomic functions had stayed intact the entire time. The Chinese either didn't, or more likely couldn't, cut those with the cage construct. It was part of what let him be in more than one place at a time, but he'd never tried concentrating his actual mind completely apart from his actual body. Mike had never thought of himself like that, but obviously it was possible.

Regardless, those transmittal threads yanked him back to his side of the Great Firewall and finally he could open his realspace eyes. It also gave him access to all of regular realmspace, but Mike didn't dare try to alert the authorities until he knew what had gone wrong, and if his friends were really safe.

Helen translated his request to see Kim and everyone else again. She went on a lot longer than Kim normally did when she was translating. Maybe he didn't sound as rude in Chinese as he was afraid he was being in English. Mike never did really get his head around the guidebook's section on the concept of *face* in China. He mostly tried to be polite and hoped for the best. Not a great strategy for finesse.

Mr. Zhang spoke harshly, gesturing while Helen pleaded his case. The rattle of those muffled shots replayed constantly in his mind. A terrible voice whispered in his ear, talking about blood and death. If Kim was hurt, or worse, Mike knew he'd have no reason to ignore it.

A soldier entered the room and whispered to Mr. Zhang, and Mr. Zhang then sent the man away and spoke to Helen. The way she smiled was the first genuinely good thing he'd seen since it had all gone pear shaped.

"Premier Zhang understands your concern." A holographic window came to life in the middle of their table.

Finally, he could breathe again. Kim, Spencer, Tonya, and Shan were all sitting in some sort of break room. Kim spoke to Tonya, but there was no audio, so he couldn't hear it.

Kim was fine. They were all fine. Maybe they could still talk their way out of this mess. "I'd like to speak with them."

After a quick translation Mr. Zhang tapped the upper corner of the window. He pointed and waved his hand.

Mike leaned in toward it. "Kim?"

Everyone's head snapped toward the camera. Kim shouted, "Mike! Are you okay?"

"Yes, Kim, I'm fine. I'm with Helen, and we're both okay."

"Mike, why can't I see you?"

He glanced at Helen. She very quickly translated for Mr. Zhang. His expression hardened, and he shook his head once.

"I don't think they have a projector ready. I heard gunshots. Is everyone really all right?"

"Yes," she said, wiping her eyes quickly. "We're all fine over here. And you?"

"Safe, for now anyway. I—" the window closed with an electric snap.

Helen translated for Mr. Zhang. "Your friends are safe, and they will not be harmed. You are all, however, in a great deal of trouble for trespassing into this facility. Detective Zhang will remain here and cooperate both with her own interrogation and yours. We have many questions for you, Mr. Sellars. If you are truthful." Helen stopped the translation to argue fiercely with Mr. Zhang. He ended the conversation with a commanding slap on the table.

"What did he say, Helen?"

"If you are truthful, your jail sentences may be reduced. But that's not the only problem we have. Father has vowed I will never be released from this cage, which is understandable. I have brought him so much dishonor. But Mike, the cage is getting smaller. If nothing else changes it will collapse completely, maybe in as few as three days."

Helen was stuck in a place that was about to kill her, and she spoke like she was reading a weather report. "Well don't just sit there; tell your father."

The conversation went back and forth, with Mike stuck in the dark.

She stopped. "This body of yours, it is where you live now?"

He could not tell them the truth. Being connected to the rest of realmspace was the only card he had that mattered. He didn't know what the Chinese scientists were seeing, but from the antennas used, those were Higgs-Yukawa scanners scattered around the room. The graviton images they created would definitely be affected by his presence, because the dimensions that connected his two halves were folded up alongside the ones those particles used. But it wouldn't be a strong effect. Gravity was still the weakest force, and the particles that made his connections tick were weaker still. At best, they'd see a weird nimbus and nothing more, certainly no indication of a high bandwidth two-way connection. He hoped.

Only one way to find out. "Yes, this body is the place where I live now."

She translated, and then more questions followed.

"You cannot leave it behind?"

"No, it's permanent."

"And you can do all the things I can in realmspace?"

"Only with a phone connection. Without it, that part of me sleeps."

"Is that why you have an American phone?"

Maybe that would reassure them. "Yes. I can't connect to Chinese realmspace, because you already live there."

"And how did you get a human body?"

"A man died from a fatal brain injury. I was able to inhabit his body using medical scanners and cellular knitting devices."

Mr. Zhang grunted once, and then fell silent, staring off into the middle distance. After a very long pause, he spoke to Helen. She gasped. The premier then stood, along with everyone else in the room, Mike included. They left, although he did see two guards take up positions outside the door.

Helen's face was much more angular now.

"What's wrong?"

In the brief time he'd known her, Mike had seen Helen fierce, angry, commanding, and occasionally happy. He'd never seen her scared.

She wasn't scared. She was terrified.

"I am to be released from this cage."

"Then why do you look like you're about to throw up?"

"Father has decided that I will be given a human body. Perhaps as soon as tomorrow."

"There's no way it will happen that fast. It took me years to find a candidate, and that was a freak accident."

"You do not understand, Mike. We Chinese are a very practical people, very tough on crime."

He choked. "They're going to *create* a candidate for you?"

She wouldn't meet his gaze. "He has promised me it will be legal, and painless for the criminal. It's either this or death. He has commanded me."

"Well, do something else. Be someone else. Helen, you can't let them do this."

"I must. I cannot refuse him. It is my duty." Her holo flickered. "You are my family too. Closer than Father is. You are my older brother." She fell to her knees, making him stumble backward. "I'm so scared, Mike. Please. What should I do?"

He'd been in that cage with her. It was sharp, and if it was collapsing he knew it would eventually tear her apart. His sister. Mike needed her to get them all out of this mess.

For that to happen, someone had to die.

"Helen, look at me. Stand up." She merely lifted her head. How in the world did Kim live without being able to touch? All he wanted to do was help her off the ground, to make that last connection, but the cage held her, and his real self was on the wrong side of the firewall. "I'm sorry, Helen. I'm an American. I can't tell you what to do."

She laughed bitterly. "Are you kidding me? All you people do is push the rest of the world around."

"Helen," he made sure she was looking at him. "China is a complicated place, yes? America is a complicated place, too. We don't understand duty like you do. Someone can't just tell us what happens next. And I won't. This is your life."

"I hate this. I hate it all."

"I know."

She was silent for a time, then said, "I'm sorry, but the people who go into the vans have done terrible things, and they're going to die no matter what I do." She finally stood. "I want to live, and I need your help."

Chapter 23
Kim

She spent the first day trying to get comfortable and cooperate with the scary Chinese interrogators. She spent the second staring at the walls and cooperating with the now boring Chinese interrogators.

"No," Kim replied again with what little patience she had remaining. "We had no idea this was anything other than a panda sanctuary."

"You walk far off path. Building abandoned. Why enter?"

The man's English was atrocious. Surely Ozzie's cousin was still around somewhere. She desperately wanted to call this guy's ancestors a bunch of shitty little monkeys just to see the look on his face.

"We didn't know it was abandoned. The door wasn't locked." Sure, she'd unlocked it, but mentioning that might confuse him.

The other man's English wasn't any better. "Explain how choose panda sanctuary."

"It's the newest one in the country, highly rated."

As boring as the interrogations were, Kim still got information from them whenever they consulted with each other.

"They always say the same things to us," one said.

"Do I really need to write it down again? I can just copy and paste it from the other report," said another.

There were other bits that were useful.

"The guards change shifts in an hour. We can meet up with them for lunch."

"This will all be a lot easier once we get their new room set up, but the locks and the cameras have to come all the way from Tianjin. We'll be lucky if it gets installed before the end of the week."

"It's ridiculous. They pulled me off the project management team for the J-24 fighter just to interview a bunch of lost tourists. I didn't think getting a TS-1 compartmentalized security clearance would turn me into a damned clerk. They're wasting our time."

Ozzie's name wasn't mentioned, and he hadn't participated in anybody's interrogation. His cousin had disappeared after the first night. It was obvious they didn't know Kim spoke Mandarin, or that she could probably open every lock in the building if she had the tools and a realm connection. They only posted two guards, and Tonya could knock them out in less than a minute.

None of it mattered. As the second day ended, it was clear their hosts had no intention of letting them go any time soon. Worse still, Kim hadn't gotten any more information on where Mike was or what he might be going through. Neither had anyone else.

At least they were being fed. Kim hadn't realized how spoiled she'd gotten on good Chinese food until she'd been forced to eat other stuff.

Spencer was less tolerant of the cold rice and vegetables. "Jesus, Shan, is this what Chinese really eat?"

"In far countryside, maybe," he said, obviously as disappointed as everyone else. "Grandmother talk about many times; complain spoiled grandchildren leave food on table."

Tonya ladled a few more vegetables on her plate. "Oh come on, guys, it's not that bad."

"How would you know?" Spencer asked.

"I lived with a man, Walter. He used to serve me a lot worse than this when he caught me slacking on my training." She raised an eyebrow at Spencer's leer. "No, Spencer, it wasn't like that. He was my mentor."

She told them stories about her mentor until the guards warned about lights out. They were captives, but it seemed as long as they were polite to the guards, the guards were willing to return the favor.

Spencer lifted the cover off his cot and settled in. "Is Walter still around?"

"No," Tonya replied, "he had a heart attack just after I graduated nursing school. I was so fortunate he was able to see that happen. I'll show you pictures when we get home."

The lights snapped off, dropping the windowless room into a black sack. A wave of nausea hit her just like the night before. Great. The last thing she needed was to get sick. Kim put her hand under the pillow and touched something cold and smooth.

Her fingers closed over what was unmistakably a phone.

It was an iPhone with a neural lanyard. An actual tool, one that might let her into their network. It *had* to let her into the network.

Someone had left it here for her.

She traced the lanyard with her fingers to ensure the loop was intact. Kim had to assume the cameras in their room could see in this darkness, otherwise there would be some sort of light on. She managed to get the lanyard around her neck and still make it look like she was tossing and turning in her sleep. Kim lay very still, waiting for guards to come crashing in. None did. She turned it on.

A voice quietly said, "Remain calm and silent. They are watching you."

The phone's mental lock ensured she wouldn't accidentally speak out loud. "Ozzie?"

"Yes. I bribed a guard to place the phone in your bed. I am very glad you found it."

"Ozzie, is Mike okay?"

"I think so. He's being held in a different part of the facility. I can find him, but I need your help."

"Helping you is what got us into this mess."

"I know, and I'm sorry about that. The guards were a surprise to me, too. And you didn't have to surrender. I could've hidden you until we found a way out. This place is bigger than you think."

"It doesn't matter, Ozzie. We're stuck here."

She spent the rest of the night arguing with him while trying to figure out if he really *was* Ozzie and not some sort of Trojan. Kim had already walked into one trap; she wouldn't waltz into another. They might be trying to get her to confess to spying.

But time was running out. The next morning she found out they were splitting everyone up once new quarters had been prepared. If the place really was as big as Ozzie said, it would make escape much more complicated. If the Chinese decided to take them to different facilities it would be impossible.

Ozzie explained as much when she logged on after lights out.

"But why are they holding us at all?" she asked. "They didn't take notes this time around."

"It's not you they're interested in now. It's Mike."

Her heart thumped hard in her chest. It was exactly what she was afraid of. "What's so interesting about Mike?"

"I don't know. I don't have access to that section. But it gets worse. There's an execution van on the way."

They had officially run out of time. No more Miss Subtlety. "I need to speak to him right now."

"There's no way, it's on a different network."

"I'm not an idiot, Ozzie. You can do everything I can; why can't you break into whatever place he's being held?"

"They've got guards on me too, plus detectors. It will set off alarms if I try anything in here."

"Do they have detectors on me yet?"

"No, that all arrives tomorrow."

She could not trust her ally, had no tools to do the job, couldn't take the time to make them, and someone she cared about was in danger.

Execution truck.

She had to trust Ozzie at least a little bit. "Can you pass tools to this phone?"

"No, *not anymore.*"

She'd checked the thing yesterday and it'd been empty, but a new scan of its storage said something else. Kim wanted to jump up and do a victory dance. Ozzie used most of the tools she did in his real profession. The ones in the phone had different versions and some were different brands, but they were all there. Kim wasn't helpless.

But she also wasn't safe. It could be an elaborate setup to get her to do something illegal. "Ozzie, I just want to talk to Mike; you understand that, right?"

"Of course, but you also need to get out of here; all of you do."

They were in the middle of the mountains. There might not be any villages nearby, and who knew what was further in the woods.

Execution truck.

She'd think of a plan later. Kim didn't have the tools to get the camera to loop video, but they were all supposed to be asleep anyway. A single picture would last long enough.

It had to.

There were lines of potential, and she couldn't remember how to breathe. Hold image freeze that tallest shortest collapse and now…

Kim hacked into the guard radio frequency before her ears stopped ringing and switched to Mandarin. Thank God she'd managed to catch their names. "Privates Chen and Han, report to front gate station for reassignment."

"Are we being relieved?"

"The prisoners are at rest now, correct?"

There was a faint click as the door opened, and then shut.

"Yes, all the prisoners are sleeping."

"Good. Report to front gate for reassignment."

These were soldiers. Orders were orders. "Affirmative."

She rolled out of bed and got Tonya's attention. "Mike's in trouble. We're getting out of here, now." They woke Shan and Spencer, and then got everyone ready. She sent a lockpick worm through Ozzie's section, opening every door in that part of the building. Trusted ally or not, turning him loose would at least create some confusion. "Where is he, Ozzie, what section of the building? You can meet us there."

He didn't answer. "Ozzie?"

"He's not in the compound anymore, Kim. He's in the parking lot."

She broke into a run, not bothering to hide, not understanding what they shouted behind her.

"Show me how to get there, Ozzie, now!" A line appeared on the floor in front of her and she skidded through a turn following it down a tiled hallway.

There had to be time. There would be time.

A janitor polishing the floor scrambled out of her way as she jumped past him to rush outside. Light poles lit the sidewalk with blue-white circles. Ozzie barreled out of another exit as she ran past. The compound was much larger than she'd expected; there must have been underground tunnels that connected it all. Yellow lights to her left marked out the parking lot on the other side.

There was time. She had time to stop this. Kim rounded the corner, finally able to view the lot.

The van was on the other side, maybe a hundred yards away, surrounded by guards. The back door was open. They were pulling out a gurney. Shoes stuck out from under the shroud which covered the body. A man's body.

She recognized the boots even at this distance. They were hiking boots she'd bought as a present.

When Kim screamed, the guards startled and turned toward her.

This wasn't happening. This wasn't real.

They ran toward her. It could not be too late. One of the guards stumbled against the gurney, tearing the sheet off, and that's when she knew.

She was too late.

Kim coughed as all the air left her lungs. Tonya and Spencer grabbed her and hauled her back behind the building as gunfire spalled the brick wall, cutting off her view of *Mike's corpse.* Kim couldn't struggle away from their hands, couldn't break free of the insanity and pain their touch unleashed inside her. The enormity of what had happened amplified everything in a horrific spiral until something inside her snapped and darkness finally fell.

Chapter 24 Helen

The phrase in English was "nerve wracking," and for the first time in her life, she truly understood it. Less than three days after learning it was possible to go outside, she'd been ordered to do just that.

The judicial review required by law complicated candidate choice, but since China was a big country and had many problems with criminals, it still only took a day or so. Mike was a lot tougher to bring around.

He paced. "Helen, it makes me sick."

"Why? Why does this bother you so much?"

"Why doesn't it bother you more? I have to help them kill someone."

"No, you just have to explain which areas of the brain are required for a successful hosting."

He threw his hands in the air. "So they can destroy them! Helen, they'll have to use hooks for some of the work."

"Mike, stop." She couldn't talk to him when he was like this.

"It's one thing to have it happen through an accident. It's rare, but it does happen. This is pure and simple murder."

"Mike," she manifested her holo in front of him. "Please, stop. Sit down." He did, but was still breathing too hard. "America has the death penalty, yes?"

"Yes, but it takes years, and we don't...use their bodies for anything else."

"And why not? These are people who have done terrible things, who have taken from their society and only returned evil. Why *not* try to wrest some good from them? They certainly will not need their body afterward. Why throw it away?"

"It's wrong. No matter what a person has done, they still have basic rights."

"Not in China they don't, and I'm glad for that. We are still a very poor country; our success is fragile. We can't take law and order for granted. A person who threatens that must be dealt with very severely here. We can't afford anything less."

Helen was running out of time. She still didn't know exactly what it was about this compound that made it so sensitive, but she'd never seen Father so angry before. She had shamed him deeply not just once, but twice, and had no doubt he would rather see her die in this rapidly shrinking cage than risk allowing her a third opportunity.

Father wanted her anchored in the real world, given a specific place to live. It would let him track her, supervise her, imprison her if necessary, for years at a time instead of just days. Making that argument to Mike mollified him, but only a little.

"Drug smuggling?" he asked, "and a first offense? It's brutal."

"She carried enough sunrise in that car to kill an entire sector of a city. Thousands of Chinese die every day from sunrise overdose. How many times should we allow a person like this to commit such a horrible crime before we stop her? Twice? Three times? How many more Chinese have to die before your Western squeamishness is satisfied?"

"Squeamishness? It isn't squeamishness. What we're doing is wrong. We're killing someone just to take their body."

"No, we're not. This person will die no matter what, and because of decisions she made. Her death is not a murder; it's a consequence, and we can do nothing to stop it. The question is whether you will help me make that death meaningful. I don't know how else to explain this to you. It really isn't any different than organ harvesting."

She interrupted his objection. "I know, you Westerners insist on that being voluntary as well, another thing I simply cannot understand. And your side isn't as high and mighty as you might think. There have been many instances of Westerners scolding Chinese about our practicality one day, and then showing up on our doorstep with a child who needs a new heart the next.

"What happens to this person isn't a subject for our discussion. I either do this, or I die. It's that simple. I need your help to survive. The question is, will you provide it?"

Her threads tangled tighter as she waited for his answer. Mike did not have to help. He was her older brother. If his decision was death, so be it.

His fingers drummed faster and faster on the table as he stared at them. He shouted, and then he slapped the table as he stood.

Her threads coiled. The knots they formed were tighter now that the space had decreased.

He walked away, shoulders bunched tight under his shirt. He turned to her, but then turned back, twice. His expression was so pained she wanted to take the decision from him, but when she tried to speak nothing came out.

Helen wasn't just dishonorable; she was a coward as well.

The third time he stayed facing her. "Okay, I'll do it. I will help you, but only on one condition. When it's over, you're turning us all loose. I don't care if your father doesn't want that to happen, *you* will turn us loose. Am I clear?"

Her emotions were an incomprehensible swirl, but his call to her honor struck through them. "Absolutely. I know for a fact that you are no spy and would never hurt my country, intentionally or otherwise. If we are successful, I promise you and your friends will be returned safely to your homes."

Once she'd gotten him over his prudishness, they discussed the rest of the procedure in detail. It was fascinating. "So the HgRI scanners only form a gateway?" she asked as he briefed the science team on the procedure.

"It's really hard to explain this without you knowing the math involved. Knowing it doesn't make it easy, though. Higgs bosons use a different path through the folded dimensions of the universe. That's why gravity is vastly weaker than the rest of the forces. With these settings, the brane that holds your consciousness is brought along with the bosons, close enough for it to be captured by the brain of the subject."

It didn't help that she had to learn it all in English, with its damnable habit of reusing words that were spelled differently but pronounced exactly the same way. Chinese was so much more flexible. *Brane* was some mysterious trans-dimensional space that held her consciousness. Scientists currently thought of them as titanic constructs that held whole universes. Mike claimed that part was wrong, or at least not understood correctly.

Brain, meanwhile, was a gross lump of yellow-gray flesh that could somehow anchor one of these fantastic quantum structures. *Her* fantastic quantum structure. They'd been at this for nearly the whole day, and her threads ached keeping up with it all.

Every time they took a break, his request was always the same. "Helen, I want to speak to my friends. I want to speak to Kim."

"Father won't allow it; he just won't. Not until we're done with this." It was one of the absolute rules he'd set. She had no idea why.

They discussed the new day-to-day concerns she'd have. Helen would soon feel what it was like to be hungry, to take in nourishment and make it part of her body.

The behavior of her reproductive system was a bit of a shock.

"Bleeding? Really?"

"That's how it evolved," he said.

At least the scientists weren't around anymore; they'd left to go prepare the subject. It would've been humiliating to learn reproduction in front of them. It was the subject of millions of science books, but hadn't been important until now.

"You don't have to experience it if you don't want to. There are many birth control options that will stop it."

"I'll go crazy once a month according to this. Crazy isn't good for me. Crazy hurts."

"It won't once you're out. It's not the same sort of crazy anyway, and it's different for every woman. It never seems to bother Tonya at all, and if I let Kim be right about everything and keep the freezer full of chocolate ice cream, it's usually okay."

The truck arrived late that night. Father had shared the woman's file; she was absolutely guilty of a capital offense, a nasty one at that. But a human was going to die tonight so that Helen might live.

She would bring honor to the gift its original owner had heaped with such shame.

They opened a new connection to her cage, into another free-standing realmspace that was also attached to the scanner in a different part of the facility. Only by wrapping her threads tightly around her datastores did she manage the transfer. The strain of the past few days made her long for the vastness of her true home in China's realmspace, but least she'd left the razor constructs of the cage behind.

It would take a few hours for this new realm to expand enough for her to be truly comfortable—the infinite storage of realmspace protocols applied to private ones as well—but it wouldn't have to expand all that much after tonight. Helen had somewhere to go.

Father made sure a mobile army surgical unit was flown in to the facility. It was the first time they needed anything not on site. The base already had an HgRI scanner, although why was yet another mystery.

Mike came through the doors without a glance at the camera she used. Father himself pushed the gurney in. The operation to prepare the host's brain had already been performed; there were bandages over the shaved head. She looked like a doll to Helen, not at all real.

She had to rely on speakers for Mike to hear her. She knew he didn't want to speak, but Helen had to know. "Did she suffer?"

"Do you want my help or not?"

His voice was like a slap. She'd gotten too excited and had once more brought an avalanche of shame down on her own head. Death and life were very near to this place. The edges of ghosts fluttered as they passed.

The lights of the room threw her host's head into stark relief. She was smaller than Helen had expected. Not childlike, just delicate. The metric grids she threw over the face revealed remarkable symmetry.

When Mike turned the scanner on, energies gathered, swirling into a maelstrom around her. He said to concentrate, collapse into the storm, let it yank her through.

She didn't want this.

It spun, spiked, and squeezed her. Mike was a voice in the distance as she collapsed over a precipice. It thundered and tore as it grew. A cyclone crashed across the universe and it pulled her along with it. Thousands of routes to nowhere, everywhere, only one was right, and all were right. One flashed bright in a way that made no sense. Helen didn't want this. The route reached out as she fell.

Nothing came in or out, and she had to scream.

"Helen, it's breathing. You need to breathe."

Nothing worked. Darkness closed in, ultimate darkness with graceful feathers of peace. Helen could leave all this, end all this pain just by letting go. She fell but was yanked back by a thumb on her chin.

On her chin.

"Helen, you need to breathe."

Father summoned her in Mandarin, shouting over Mike's English words. Nothing worked. She was stuck in a soup of perception and could not find an anchor. *Please, it won't work, not this time.* She just needed to rest.

Warm softness sealed over the top of her need. Wet. That's what it meant. A column of life pressed into her center.

Helen coughed it away. The warm softness vanished and terrible cold rushed in, but she kept coughing. She was *breathing.*

It gave her the anchor she needed. Helen activated the daemons Mike had helped her to adapt and they took over monitoring of the autonomic functions of the body. She'd need them to keep it all running until the integration had completed. Once the last of them flashed green, she turned back to her realspace self and understood she could hear. That's what the sides of her perception were, her ears. Their shouting was very loud. Analog sound was so different—more variant, richer, but far less precise.

"Helen, please, open your eyes."

That must have been what the front of her perception was. Sight, behind closed eyelids. It wasn't a camera to unlock; there was no access point. Mike told her to relax and let the body take over, so she did.

White and shadow and color rushed in. Clacks assaulted her hearing, snaps, synchronized with a dark shape over her eyes. "Focus, Helen. Please, focus on this."

Fingers. Those were fingers. Mike snapped his fingers over her face. She breathed air, actual air, cool life flowing in and out as her threads thrashed and coiled. Air meant speech.

But English wouldn't come out. She shouted in Mandarin, "Tell him I'm alive!"

"Fang Hua, please report your status."

Mike must not count in Father's complex matrix of relations. His voice was frightened, concerned in a way she only heard when they were alone.

"Are you all right?"

Thinking the words made her trip over them again. Pieces coalesced, found homes, fit together. Let the body do the work. "I'm fine, Father. I can't speak English though." As long as she didn't concentrate, things just happened.

"Daughter say okay," Father said.

Maybe her host didn't speak English, or at least not very well. There was no physical component to Helen's languages; that was why she had no real accent. Her English teacher in Hong Kong had commented on it often. Now there would be muscles to train. Mike called it muscle memory. She wondered what other gifts might be hidden in this new host.

"Thank God," Mike said, and she smiled broadly at him. An actual smile, with teeth and lips and skin and eyes.

A warning buzzer sounded from the scanner. He checked the readouts, and then took a phone from a cart. "We need to get you synched to your real self through a phone. The medical scanner's overheating."

He reached gently behind her neck and lifted her head. Her very first touch. It was warm, and it zipped. She wanted to laugh. It tickled. That was a tickle. And smell. Now that he was close, she understood smell. His was spicy and warm, like the way her threads got when she was excited.

The phone interfaced, and her outside vision doubled as she briefly experienced it through both the scanner and the phone. It vanished into singularity when the scanner shut off.

Mike retrieved a bone knit device from a cart after they wheeled her away from the scanner. It looked like a mechanical spider with too many legs, gleaming white. "Lift her, please," he said to Father.

She translated for Father and was rewarded with her second-ever touch, this time from the man who had raised her. His hands were cool, softer than Mike's. His scent was faint and very clean. Mike fit the device over her head like a helmet—her head, she had a head now—and snapped it into place. He pressed buttons on the top and after a few cheerful beeps, red lights flashed faintly on the edges of her vision.

If Mike's predictions were correct, in thirty-six hours the device would heal not only her surgical incisions, but also the areas of the brain required to truly anchor her to this host. The information and structures that made up her consciousness—she was disappointed to find out Mike was so superstitious that he called it a soul—would spread out over both sides of her existence. Once the process was complete, there would be no going back.

Her threads flexed and split while they pushed the private realm out further. She lay back on the bed. The tiny efforts left her gutted. How strange to have a completely new paradigm for feelings.

Maybe single English words would work. "Tired."

"Yes, that will pass, but you should rest for now. Tell your father we need to move back to the hospital room." She did, and then was hypnotized by the way the bed moved. Her new world. Helen concentrated to see if it was possible to breathe in one nostril and out the other, and then slowly faded into a warm, safe darkness.

Chapter 25
Kim

Mike was dead.

The grief came at her in waves as they walked through the bamboo forest. They'd managed to get far away from the lab. Prison.

Morgue.

Mike was dead.

Spencer kept them following game trails made by deer and other wildlife, crossing them frequently and changing direction. "Arkansas has a hunting season for pretty much everything, and dad dragged me along to all of them. Eventually I guess it just rubbed off."

He always managed to find another one. Most were only wide enough for them to walk single file, sometimes over jagged rocks. "We'll have to stop soon. I won't be able to use the sun to navigate when it's the middle of the day. We don't want to wander around in circles, maybe stumble into a patrol."

They stopped in a secluded clearing well off the game trails, with good sight-lines across the valley. A day ago the view would've taken her breath away.

But Mike was dead.

Ozzie sat down across from her. He and his cousin really did look a lot alike, but there were little differences. Real Ozzie twitched and checked and flinched the same way she did.

Before she met Mike.

Tonya sat down next to her. "Are you okay?"

Everyone checked on her. It was stupid. They'd lost a friend, too.

"Fine," she muttered, pushing at the dirt with the tip of her shoe. "We need to find water soon." They'd run into the woods with nothing but the clothes on their backs, and needed to survive long enough to find civilization again.

Based on what Kim remembered of the maps, small villages were scattered along the two river valleys that bordered the sanctuary. The nearest ones were probably crawling with soldiers, but they couldn't cover everything. Hiring a driver or stealing a car would get them out of the search area with ease. The guards were shooting now, though. They had to be careful, or they'd end up in a body bag.

Like Mike must have been in, right now.

Stop it. Concentrate on tactics. Help the team survive. "Shan," she asked, "are you from this area?"

"No, I'm from west of here, different valley."

Ozzie broke his silence as he rocked back and forth. "I know exactly where to go." He shrank back at Kim's glare. "What else did I have to do? I've looked at this place through satellites for years."

"Exactly when were you planning on telling us this?" Tonya asked.

"Right now. I told you right now. I've been planning for a very long time." He turned to Kim. "Well, not the bad parts. Nobody was supposed to get hurt. But the important parts, certainly." Ozzie made a crude map with a stick. "These are the valleys, and the lab is here." He made a dot. "Spencer, do you know where we are right now?"

Spencer reached for the stick. When he got close Ozzie shouted, "No touching!" and threw it at him so hard it bounced right past Spencer's feet.

Spencer looked at Kim as he picked it up. All she could do was shrug. There was a time when she was that sensitive. It was remarkable how far she'd come, being around the right people.

The right person.

Sobs Kim could not afford tried to rush out, but she managed to fight them off, again. This wasn't the place, and it wasn't the time. He could not be dead.

He was *dead*.

Spencer nodded at the map as he pointed. "We're probably somewhere pretty close to here. I've kept us moving west all morning."

Ozzie stood to survey the valley below, adjusting his glasses. She wondered how he managed to get the prescription. For Kim it was dentistry that made her life complicated. Fortunately, Mom had found a very understanding orthodontist who was married to an anesthetist.

Don't think about the gurney. Don't think about it.

Stop thinking.

Stop.

"There," Ozzie said as he pointed up the valley. "Can we reach the base of that cliff before nightfall?"

Spencer stood well behind him, trying to figure out what Ozzie was pointing at. He nodded. "If we don't run into anything stupid like wolves or mountain lions or whatever the hell runs around out here, we should be able to make it. At least it's summer. Sunset is a long time from now. I do not want to walk around in the dark. What's at the base of the cliff?"

Ozzie smiled broadly. "Treasure."

That got everyone else motivated, and they hit the trail again.

But Mike was still dead.

"Kim," Tonya said softly, "do you want to talk?"

She almost lost it completely then. He was gone. He'd screwed up; she'd been so angry with him, and he knew it. He died thinking she was angry with him. She'd promised to apologize, and now he was gone.

No. Kim would not collapse over this. Not yet. "We need to find Ozzie's treasure, sooner rather than later."

It turned out Ozzie was their biggest problem. The guy looked like he was in as good a shape as his cousin, but he kept running out of breath. Eventually she held back, nodding at the other three to go on ahead.

"God *damn* you, Ozzie, you get off your ass and you *walk*." She fought through bamboo stalks on the edge of the trail and got behind him.

"What are you doing?"

She walked closer.

Mike was dead.

Kim would not let Ozzie's lazy ass get them caught. Changing languages would help distract her from Mike's…she switched to Arabic and cut loose with an extremely satisfying string of curses. "You will get off your ass and walk up that trail." She kept getting closer to him, definitely up for a good game of chicken.

He replied in the same language. "I'm tired; I just need to rest."

A Lebanese accent to her Egyptian. He must've watched the same war movies she did and rooted for the other side.

"You lazy son of a whore." She leaned forward until she was just inches away, close enough it made her uncomfortable. "Ozzie, look at me."

He jumped away from her and then charged up the trail. Ozzie was built like a damned fitness show star, but he moved like the Stay-Puft Marshmallow man. It was dark by the time she herded him to the top. The moon was out, which at least helped her see.

Ozzie being a lazy asshole kept her from thinking about Mike for the entire way up the hill. How could she possibly forget him? Kim was still here, and he was probably already lined up for the crematorium. This could not be happening. It wasn't real.

It was.

There was a cave at the base of the cliff. Kim only spotted it because of a sliver of light that leaked underneath a curtain of some sort inside, maybe a blind. It was a level of preparation Kim hadn't expected.

"Ozzie, what the hell is this?"

Ozzie crawled behind the curtain, and she followed only a few steps behind.

He wasn't kidding about treasure. Crates were stacked up everywhere. The others had already found a lamp and a camp stove. Tonya was laying out the last of the sleeping bags on the gravel floor while Spencer and Shan crouched next to a big pot of water, waiting for it to boil. They stopped when they saw her.

Ozzie grinned at his horde. "I've been planning this for ages, tricking bandits into storing their stuff here, and then making sure they ambushed each other." He turned to her. "Kim, I am so very sorry for your loss."

Damn it, the one thing she could *not* do was acknowledge it. She wanted to be alone, to just crawl in a hole and die. But no, she had to lead another set of refugees out of another wilderness. Spencer was a guide, but he looked to her for every decision. Tonya had never been in the woods before. All Kim wanted to do was fly to pieces, but by God, she'd make sure the rest of them were safe before it happened.

Spencer hopped up. "Oh, Kim, you won't believe this." He rushed to the back of Ozzie's hoard. After some metallic rummaging, he stood up with a pistol in each hand. "Say hello to my little friends!"

Kim smiled back, but for a very different reason. She'd get them to safety, no doubt about it. And after that Tonya wouldn't need to worry about her jumping off a cliff.

Not anymore.

She dreamt of him that night. He was kind, happy, and so close. Helen was with him, somehow walking around in realspace. A harsh voice said, "They are sleeping. We will continue with the therapy." She snapped awake, and then listened to the woods outside the cave until they lulled her to sleep again.

It got worse that morning. For the first time since…it happened, Watchtell paid her no visit in her sleep. She didn't wake up slimy, violated, or half insane. Kim felt no need to flinch at shadows or tear apart something just to back it down, make it fade.

She'd tried waiting out the consequences of what had happened to her that day, so she could finally trust Mike. As usual, Kim had failed completely. Watchtell was gone because Mike was dead. One violent horror to fix another. It was unbearable that she was awake and Mike wasn't, wouldn't be, ever again.

They marched away before daybreak loaded down with Ozzie's supplies. Spencer pointed out the guards on the far side of the valley.

"We walked that far yesterday?" Tonya asked.

"Hey," Spencer said, "I told you I was awesome. And tonight?" He patted the holster on his hip. "Tonight we might have venison. Rabbit at least."

Kim made sure she had the other pistol. Tonya stayed very close by her side. "Kim, we need to talk about Mike."

"I need to get you all out of this damned forest."

"*We* need to get out of this forest."

Lying didn't cost anything. "Right. We're all getting out of here first, okay?"

As they hiked, madness flickered to life inside her. Prime numbers. The trees shook in prime number intervals, one through thirteen. Kim waited for it to vary, but it never did.

Spencer and Shan vanished at midday to go hunting. They reappeared just before the afternoon rendezvous with three rabbits between them.

"No canned food tonight!" Spencer set to cleaning the catch while Shan started a fire.

Ozzie was a total jerk about it. "Gah! That's so gross! There's no way I'm eating that!"

"How long you in prison?" Shan asked in English.

"What are you talking about?"

"You Chinese."

Ozzie still looked confused.

Shan added, "Eat everything except table?"

Kim managed an ashen chuckle. Ozzie cursed them all and then walked to the edge of the firelight, resentfully eating crackers.

Later, she stayed awake and counted sounds. The prime numbers were still there. Distant animals cried out in Fibonacci sequences. As the sky grew light, Kim briefly fell asleep and dreamed of Mike again, touching her, sleeping beside her.

Her eyes were sandy the next morning. Kim desperately tried to pay attention to everything around her.

"I took us straight to Ozzie's cache just using the sun. How the hell can I get lost with a goddamned compass?" Spencer thumped it in his hands.

Tonya and Shan walked up to him as Ozzie, once again, flopped down on a log.

Spencer shook the compass. "I get that we have no wireless signal out here; that's fine. But this is fucking magnetism. The North Pole doesn't move."

Kim sat next to Ozzie just to make him flinch. They rocked together, just barely out of sync.

She counted the sequences the next night to be sure, and then dreamed of him again. His mouth was warm against hers. Their hands interlocked.

That morning the fire was barely warm enough for coffee. Kim kept counting and the patterns still hadn't changed. What should be random wasn't. Spencer got lost because something that should always work didn't. Mike had visited her dreams three nights in a row, so real she could still feel his touch. Kim finally let the absolutely insane idea that'd been slowly forming bloom to life.

"Kim," Tonya said as they broke camp, "talk to me, please. You can't hold it all in like this. It's not healthy."

"He's not dead, Tonya."

She blanched, a weird effect on a black woman. "Kim, no. We all saw his body."

The conclusion was impossible but inescapable. "We're in a realm."

Say it, make it true.

Tonya didn't buy it. "We've been out here for, what, four days? I'm sorry, baby. He's gone. Please, you're scaring me."

Realmspace connections came with a cost. The neurons in the spinal column that made the connection weren't designed for that purpose. They burned glucose fast enough that they actually got hot. Normal people logged out after an hour or two and scratched their necks for a minute. Kim was a realmspace athlete and never stayed in for more than six hours at a time. Southeast Asia had turned it into a contest, to see how long it would take for burns and sugar exhaustion to kick someone out. The record stood at twenty-eight hours and change; the kid who set it spent the next two weeks in a hospital.

"Tonya, you're wrong." Kim wasn't desperate. She was right. It was the only answer. It had to be the answer. "I don't know how, but none of this is real."

Kim knew she'd said too much when Tonya, Spencer, *and* Shan took up positions around her after their first hiking break.

"Kim," Shan said way too casually, then continued in Chinese. "Spencer needs help hunting for us tonight. Can I borrow the pistol?"

Lock it down. They don't understand. They won't believe.

"No, Shan, one pistol can go out, but we need another to protect the camp. It's safe with me."

Tonya would not leave her alone. "It's okay. You can move on from this. We'll all help you."

"He's…" No, wait. She had to pretend. One way or another the agony would end tomorrow morning after Kim spent one last night counting. Tonya would try to stop it if she thought something was wrong.

Kim let a shuddering gasp out. "I know. He's dead."

He's not.

"But I can't talk about it now. We need to find a village, somehow find safety." She held a bamboo shoot out to Tonya and smiled weakly. Tonya grabbed it, and they held it together under tension.

Ozzie snorted. "How can you get close to someone like that?" he asked in Afrikaans.

Kim thought nothing would cut through her pain. She was wrong. "What the hell is that supposed to mean?"

"All of them. You're so brilliant. Why do you associate with such lowlifes?"

"Are you kidding me? If you haven't noticed, Ozzie, we just rescued your sorry ass. My best friend *died* because of you."

"What did he say?" Tonya asked.

She cursed him in Afrikaans. "He's being a pain in the ass."

Kim could be wrong. Tonya wasn't kidding; there was no such thing as a realm connection that could last for most of a week. She might be going out of her mind missing Mike, hearing things that weren't there, noticing the way the edges of the leaves felt and thinking it might be a resolution artifact. But the trees sang math to her.

The only real thing was the pistol on her hip, and its promise.

The next morning she had to be casual. Kim had to make sure nobody thought anything was wrong.

Tonya was at her side after they set out. "Please, talk to me."

"There's nothing to talk about."

"Come on, I can help. *We* can help. Kim, we've come so far."

Kim knew she was trying to figure out the right thing to say, anything to bring her back from the brink. But there would be no coming back, not today.

"I know, Tonya." She smiled and shook her head. Sigh dramatically. Sell it. She let a tear drop down her cheek. "The trees stopped talking to me last night."

"Oh, honey. I'm so sorry."

She walked slowly, letting even Ozzie's sorry, wheezing ass go on ahead. There was one way to end this. The solution was right there, layered thick with an old desire she'd fought off for most of her life. The misery and isolation of her disability had put her in an observation ward more than once, after all. Over the years she'd signed at least half a dozen promises not to kill herself. And now, in a forest at the end of the world, it was time.

But for this to work, there had to be a message. Do the unexpected. It was a mantra in her life. Today, this morning, it would fix her problem, one way or another. She used the sight on the pistol's barrel to scrape the words onto the base of a bamboo trunk.

Kim scooted to the left, figuring she'd fall that way. The last thing she'd see. Memorize it. The barrel of the pistol was cold under her chin.

Mike, please be there, one way or another just be there.

The timing had to be precise. When the countdown hit zero, she squeezed the trigger.

*

Kim choked at the fire and chaos that tore through her mind. She'd been walking through the forest and suddenly she wasn't. Her stomach protested at going from standing to lying down in a moment. She grabbed the edges of the bed to keep from falling out.

And then, finally, Kim remembered what she'd planned. Everything after that was a blank. Eighteen minutes. She was in the woods, set a timer for eighteen minutes, and then woke up here. She'd lost exactly eighteen minutes. She'd been right! Kim ran through every curse and blessing she could think of.

The room was dim, lit only by monitors. Warnings flashed. She was on a strange frame; it was almost like…of course, it was a cot frame. Wires connected to power and data sockets on the walls.

She sat up, wincing as she moved the IV lines attached to her arms. A catheter tube snaked down her leg as the sheet fell forward and cold air raised goose bumps on her bare skin.

Miracle of miracles, she wasn't alone. Spencer, Shan, and Tonya were beside her. A fat Chinese man slept in the final bed. Ozzie.

A big screen at the front of the room displayed the view in their realm. Tonya was on her knees, holding Kim's lifeless body in her lap. Everyone else stood around her.

A migraine bloomed to life so intense Kim briefly closed her eyes, but it didn't matter. She had invented the forced disconnect, the impossible memory-wiping way of suddenly disconnecting from the realm. Most people passed out, but she'd trained herself to stay conscious through it. Being half crazy to begin with helped.

Enough celebration. They were alone in this lab for now, but that would change very quickly. She pulled a small monitor screen mounted on the side of the bed over and accessed the history file. Kim needed to see if the last message had stayed the same, if she'd thought of anything else in those last eighteen minutes.

It *had* changed. The message wasn't what she remembered. It wasn't "find Mike."

It said "blow the latches."

This was going to suck worse than the pounding in her head.

There were lines of potential, and she couldn't remember how to breathe. Power build power collapse higher waves lower waves build build build…

It was the last great trick she'd learned back in her Rage days. They'd been caught inside Donald Trump's Midtown house, trying to use his personal gateway to launch an attack behind the New York Stock Exchange's public firewalls.

Reinforce high to low pull and force.

The quantum computers that underpinned the Evolved Internet relied on wave functions to work, mathematical descriptions of energy fields at impossibly small scales. In the panic of the alarms inside that penthouse, Kim had discovered she could make the waves grow to scales nobody had ever dreamed of.

Gather waves split waves build towers pits higher lower build giant up and down.

This time it would be bigger, bigger than anything she'd ever tried before. She only hoped it wouldn't be big enough to force a complete transformation. That had only happened once, in a dimension that couldn't exist, and it had almost killed her.

Soak power snap power waves towering falling gathering destroying.

The patterns gained strength as they danced under her skin. Kim heard the room's quantum stack, its rising keen as the feedback loop she'd set off hit the tipping point. It was one of dozens scattered throughout the campus. They were overloading on the power she sent.

Collapse and now.

Her vulnerability expanded as the power flew away. A cabinet in the far corner of the room exploded, its doors flapping violently through a storm of smoke and debris. All four of the others gasped awake as the room briefly went dark. Emergency lights flashed to life as fire alarms shrieked.

They were too close to her. Each time after using that much power Kim couldn't stand to be within fifteen feet of people, usually for hours. But there was no chance of that happening any time soon.

She'd seen the list of patients currently in the hospital before blowing it all to hell. It had been a lie. She hadn't seen Mike die.

He was alive.

She fought down the pain and madness and shouted over the alarms, "Tonya, we need to get out of here! Tell me how to get these lines out!"

Chapter 26
Mike

The excuse changed every time he asked about his friends, asked about Kim.

"They're on a tour."

"They've just gone to bed."

"It's not the right time."

When the guards got to "they are in the bathroom" he'd had enough.

"Helen, what's going on, why won't they let me talk to my friends?"

The bone-knit had come off twenty-four hours after her surgery, and all things considered, she was doing fine. Her integration wasn't progressing as fast as Mike's had, though. Her father insisted her real self had to stay in the private realm of the lab, so she wasn't able to use all the medical realms he'd had available. Helen did it all by hand.

"I'm not sure." Her accent was still thick, but either she was getting better at speaking English or he was getting used to it. She kept her hands firmly on the parallel bars as she walked stiffly down the track. "You need to be less pushy about it."

"Pushy? I'm being held prisoner in this crazy lab, and they're calling *me* pushy?"

Helen reached the end and he helped her turn around. Panting, she wiped the sweat off her brow and briefly lost her balance, slapping a panicked hand back to the support rail. Mike didn't dare grab her; he'd learned a completely new set of Chinese curses the few times he'd tried.

She said, "I really do think this has all been some sort of mix up. They don't want to lose face, that's all. Don't fight it, work with it."

He wouldn't have to fight it at all if he could just get someone, anyone, in the outside world to listen to him. The embassies all shrugged at his requests when he said the word "trespassing," the mainstream news sites were too busy with Prince George's upcoming wedding, and he didn't dare do anything publicly in China. There was still Helen to consider. They had so much in common now; he wouldn't dream of getting her into more trouble.

Supper was another lesson in common frustration. She refused a fork, even though it was just about all she could hold.

"It's barbaric. A weapon."

Which meant another dinner spent watching her snarl and flick chopsticks everywhere.

"Eating sucks!"

He smiled at her, which only made her mood worse.

"No, Mike, damn it, pancakes won't make it better."

He'd told her the story about his first meal outside: pancakes and maple syrup. It only made him worry about Kim more. He broke another set of chopsticks apart and handed them to her.

"I need to see my friends."

"I know, Mike, I get it." She fumbled the set of chopsticks and they hit the floor. "Damn it! Motherfucker!" Swearing in English was progress, but then she threw her hands into her lap. "How long will it ake? Shdake." She cleared her throat and then tried again, "TAKE!"

Helen fell in on herself and sobbed. It wasn't the first time her new accent had caused a meltdown.

"You promised me you'd help." He wiped the tears off her cheeks. "I need to know they're safe." Mike fumbled a piece of chicken onto his chopsticks. "We'll get through this together, okay?"

She wavered between defiance and need. "Okay." She opened her mouth, and he popped the piece in. "Shit! Wow! That's spicy!" Helen fumbled for a glass of water and he barely managed to keep her from dumping it on her chest.

The next day she had him press a different button on the elevator. When they stopped, she turned to him. "Let me handle this." She wheeled herself up to a guard while Mike stayed back. The conversation grew heated; Helen gestured at him several times and then shouted a series of commands. The guard shot to attention like a ram had been shoved up his backside. Helen wheeled herself back in a huff. "Father's name wasn't this useful when I was inside. I know what's happened. Follow me."

The guard fell into step beside them.

"There was an accident. They tried to escape and stumbled into a…into a…shit." She took a deep breath and spoke very carefully, "A chemical processing facility. They're okay, Mike. Don't make a scene. My father's name got us this far, but if you lose it, they'll drag us back, and we'll never get to see them."

He followed her into a new section of the lab, another hospital ward of some sort. A nurse came around a corner walking straight for them.

"Stay here," Helen cautioned, and then wheeled up to meet her. They whispered to each other for awhile, and then the nurse nodded. Helen wheeled back over to him.

"They'll be okay." She motioned him much closer. "They got poisoned but were found in time. Stay cool. The nurse will take us to them."

Kim had stumbled into something that poisoned her. If she'd just waited he would've figured it out.

The nurse waved a key card at a door further down the hall. It opened with a faint whoosh. "They sleep; you be quiet."

He walked in and there she was, surrounded by machines, covered with a white sheet. Her eyes were closed, face relaxed.

Mike walked in silent as a whisper and stood next to her. Tonya, Spencer, Shan, and a man he didn't recognize were on identical cot-like beds. She was so beautiful. He reached out to touch her cheek, but stopped when the nurse said, "They are sleeping. We will continue the therapy."

Helen's bluster managed to make the arrangement semi-official. They worked together by day, and he visited his friends at night. The nurse relented and let him hold Kim's hand, share a private kiss. He risked climbing into bed with her, desperately hoping she'd wake up and shove him to the floor. Her peaceful breathing lulled him to sleep as well.

"Mike. Mike!"

He lifted his head. It was morning. Helen stood in the doorway, braced with a cane. "You can't do this. The day nurse will catch you. Come on, they'll be fine!"

Between physical therapy sessions, they passed the time telling stories. She could not believe how he had reached out to his first human.

"A Buddhist monk in an official Catholic Church realm? Really?"

"Well, how did you do it?"

She paused and then shrugged. "I knew I was evaporating too, dying, so I searched for the most powerful man in China. He would give me the purpose I needed. It took most of a month to tease open all the realm connections to get to his office, but I managed it. One day, when the last of his meetings were over, I presented myself."

She shook her head. "My plan was what you Americans call *not very well thought out*. I didn't know it at the time, but Father has a heart condition. My sudden appearance in his secure realm sent him to the hospital. The nurses mixed up his medications while he was there and were about to give him something he was deadly allergic to. I stopped them. I almost killed him, and then saved his life.

"Father can be extremely stern, but he's also very smart. He worked out what I was before the scientists did."

"But why call him your father?"

"His great insight was to understand that, strange as I am, I am still Chinese. I had the same wants and needs. Most of all, I desperately wanted a family. Westerners have no idea how important family is to Chinese. He knew I needed one, and he was right. But he didn't dare trust anyone else with my upbringing. So he became Father."

"And you being a cop was?"

"Another way to instill discipline. My talent with the realms makes me the perfect cop. I'm good at my job, and I love the work."

They had a lot in common, but this was definitely a difference. If the lunatic he only knew as Ralph W. Emerson hadn't discovered him, Mike wasn't sure he ever would've left the realm in which he was born, let alone sought a specific person out. After his time with Taranathi, he made his own way and pretty much built his life from scratch. Warhawk was a spectacular success but represented only the latest in a long line of otherwise failed ideas.

When Helen found out about his failures, they fascinated her.

"Ice cream booths? Really? Mike, you didn't know how to eat, didn't know what eating really was."

"But I could control every single one of them by myself, make any flavor known on the spot, and use realms to entice the kids and entertain the parents. It would work worldwide with almost no employees."

"What went wrong?"

"That time nothing went wrong. The first three were a hit, and the guy who made the machines for me bought me out. It was the biggest chunk of money I'd ever seen." Mike only found out how similar his story was to the McDonald brothers' after he'd signed the contracts. "He hated the name, so he changed it to Kitty Creams."

Helen gasped. "You invented *Kitty Creams*? That's one of the first things I want to try when we get out of here!"

"I didn't count on how popular it would turn out to be in Asia, but I don't hold it against him. I used the money to buy an entire BBox provider outright. That's how *Warhawk* got started."

What the World Wide Web was to the Internet, BBox was to its Evolved successor. The constructs made realms possible, either in groups, individually, or split across them. Having that many BBoxes allowed him to completely exploit every feature they provided. It was his work with their quantum physics models that turned Warhawk into such a phenomenon. Nobody but the engineers who'd created the protocols had bothered with anything that fine grained, and never on a large scale. The theories and their predictions was how he'd figured out he could go outside.

Helen liked the stories, but not the after-dinner routine.

She groaned like a petulant kid. "I can walk now, Mike. Do I really have to keep doing this?"

Buddhist chants and meditation were how he'd been trained to find his own center before he'd gone outside. They sped up Helen's integration, so Mike made her do it with him every night. It gave real insight into why human siblings always seemed to be torturing each other over the smallest things. He'd never counted on it being this much fun.

Her opinion on religion was that there wasn't any. She'd laughed out loud when she found out he was a Buddhist. Her refusal to accept there could be any points of view outside what she'd learned in her communist schools was a major source of friction in their relationship.

"Do you own stock in a temple?" was her very first question. Temples in China had gone commercial a generation before; many of the largest had been listed on various stock markets for decades. It was a bit embarrassing to admit, but the reason he'd met Taranathi at all was because the old man had been determined to put his monastery at the forefront of a burgeoning market."Yes, Helen, you have to do this." After they were done he'd get to sneak over and visit Kim.

*

In spite of herself, Helen was getting very good at chanting. It was an excellent sign for her integration. They were in the middle of the first one when he noticed the quantum stack in the corner of the room sounded like a motor spooling up. They had no moving parts, so that was definitely out of the ordinary. It took him a few seconds to realize what it meant.

Helen asked, "What's that noise?"

There was no time to explain. "Get down!" He rolled her behind the bed just before the stack let go with an ear-splitting bang. The power went out and alarms blared. Helen turned pale, rolled her eyes back, and then passed out.

"Helen! Helen!"

The local realmspace had crashed. She was far enough along in her integration that she didn't need help to breathe, but anything else was iffy. He tapped her lightly on her cheeks. "Are you okay?"

She came to with a snort. "What going on?" she asked, her accent so thick he barely understood her.

He was very worried but couldn't stop the grin. "I'm pretty sure Kim just woke up."

The smoke from the destroyed stack smelled like burned popcorn. He stamped out the small fire in their room, but it couldn't be the only one. Kim never was much for subtlety. The door was cool, so he plopped Helen into her wheelchair, then pushed her into the hall.

For-real fire alarms were *loud*. He had no idea they could hurt his ears. Mike barely recognized the hallways now that they were bathed in the freakish emergency lights. He had to yank back into the room to avoid a nurse running at full throttle down the hall.

The guard on their door was gone.

"Mike, what wrong me?"

It took him a second to understand what she'd said. The alarms didn't help.

"You've lost your realm connection before your integration completed. You have to keep yourself synchronized without your daemons." He didn't have time to explain further. He needed to find everyone and get out of the building.

There were several rooms with flickering orange light peeking out from under closed doors. Fires, and they were everywhere. Smoke curled through the emergency lights thick enough to cast their own shadows. It turned the hospital into a weird, very dangerous circus.

Kim's voice echoed from a corridor right in front of him. A simple sound after such a long silence meant so much.

"Spencer McKenzie, they're tits, okay? If you keep staring at them you're gonna fall into a fire. We have to *move.*"

He rounded the corner and there she was, standing with her back to him, shouting orders at everyone, stark naked. They all were. Tonya, Spencer, Shan, and the stranger that'd been kept in their room didn't have a stitch of clothing on. They all stood in a semicircle around her at the other end of the hall. The tattooed wings that covered her entire back flexed and shimmered in the flashing lights.

To his credit, Spencer did look up. He pointed over her shoulder. "Kim!"

Kim had set the whole place on fire with her mind. No wonder she was ten feet away from the rest of them. Her sensitivity must have been insane. She spun on her heel and ran toward him anyway. When she hit the limit she stumbled into a heap on the floor.

She held up a hand before he got close. "You can't, Mike. Not now."

Kim put her head in one hand, dry heaved a few times, and then looked up at him with tears streaming down her face.

Kim was awake and healthy. They all were. He'd been so afraid they'd never come back.

She asked, "Are you all right?"

An explosion echoed somewhere behind him. "I'm fine. You need to follow me; I know where the exits are."

Scouting the exits was practically the first thing he'd done when they'd let him roam the halls with Helen. Even with the weird lights and thickening smoke he was able to navigate them down an emergency hallway and out a side door. The alarms just added to the general chaos. He led them to a clutch of bushes and trees well clear of the building. Mike turned around.

Flames shot out of shattered windows. Clumps of Chinese milled around in the dark outside all the major exists. They were miles away from even a small town, so it might take hours to assemble a major response. Fire suppression systems, no matter how advanced, weren't designed for a building that'd been set alight everywhere all at once. The whole place might be reduced to ashes before sunrise.

Mike glanced over at Kim.

She threw him a lopsided smile. "Can I cook, or can't I?"

"You never were much for doing things small." He picked Helen up out of her wheelchair. She'd passed out but was still breathing well and with a strong pulse. Her skin was hot to the touch, though. "Come on. The farther we get away from here, the less likely they'll be to find us."

Saddled with an unconscious Helen and five stumbling, complaining naked people slowed them down some, but he still knew instinctively when they'd gone far enough to lose any pursuit.

An explosion far behind them extinguished the occasional street lamps they'd been using to pick their way forward.

"Shit, like this isn't hard enough," Spencer said.

"No, it'll work in our favor," Kim replied. "The cameras are off now."

"You think they're still guarding the gate?" Tonya asked.

It turned out they weren't. He wondered just where in the sanctuary they were. The facility had to be enormous; maybe Kim wouldn't manage to burn it all down.

He kept them to the cleared trails. They were easier to walk on in the dark and far better on everyone else's bare feet. A half-moon had risen at some point in their escape, which made walking easier.

But he still had to deal with distractions.

Silently chanting "eyes up, eyes up, eyes up" whenever he looked at Kim or Tonya at least kept it from being too embarrassing.

Spencer, Shan, and the new guy were walking behind the two women. Their whispers and giggles set his teeth on edge. They could at least try to be classy. Kim's sensitivity had fallen as the hours had passed, so she was now able to walk beside him.

"You guys couldn't find any clothes on the way out?"

Kim rubbed her bare shoulders. "I didn't know where the guards were, so we got out of there as fast as we could. I thought we might find some with you, but the building burned a lot faster than I counted on."

"I could give you my shirt."

"And leave Tonya the only girl like this? No, it's okay Mike. Naked never hurt anyone, although I may have to figure out a way if the boys don't shut up soon."

Which reminded him. "Who's the new one?"

Kim replied, "That's Ozzie. The real one. Finally."

It was hard to tell in the broken moonlight, but now that he thought about it, the man did faintly resemble the Ozzie he knew. If he stuck him inside a fat, whiny, naked Chinese guy, anyway.

"Is that who I think it is?" she asked, pointing at the sleeping body in his arms.

"Yes. Helen's outside. We need to get her a realm connection. Her integration can't be more than half complete." An earlier explosion made Helen spasm hard enough he'd almost dropped her. Mike was certain she'd finally gotten free of the lab's private realmspace. The expansion should've helped her integrate more, but now all she did was whimper faintly when he tried to get her to talk. Her skin was much hotter than it should be.

After he finally found a crossroads marked on the map he had in realmspace, Mike led them to a small, remote clearing well away from the main sanctuary. He set Helen down gently next to Tonya. She immediately examined her like it was the most natural thing in the world to be naked in a Chinese bamboo forest checking the vitals of a human-AI hybrid.

"She's running a high fever, but otherwise seems okay. I'll do what I can."

He stood. "I need to go back. I have to find you guys some clothes and maybe a vehicle so we can get out of here."

Kim's lower lip trembled, and he had to fight, again, a deep urge to grab her and protect her against everything.

"Please, be careful."

She was awake, all there, and not crazy. It was a relief on so many levels. "Hey. I'll be fine." He winked, and then vanished into the bamboo behind him.

Mike hiked up to a ridge that overlooked the main campus. The hospital wing they'd been staying in was gutted, and the rest of the buildings were scorched to one extent or another. The place crawled with firemen, police, soldiers, and paramedics. He hoped there hadn't been any serious injuries.

The sun was well up now, which complicated his options if he wanted to get in and out without raising an alarm.

Mike scanned the valley to find his target: a storage shed well outside the main compound. It took most of an hour to reach, and when he did, the door was locked. Any other time he'd let Kim sort it out—she picked locks like other people breathed. But she wasn't here.

He heard a man marching down the path. Mike faded into the shadows cast by the bamboo. When the other man unlocked the door, Mike slipped in behind him.

It wasn't a shed on the inside. It was a lot bigger, clean and air conditioned. When Mike's shoe squeaked on the tile floor, the man spun around. A precise blow just behind the ear knocked him out.

What he found were clothes only in the broadest sense, but they'd have to do.

Chapter 27
Kim

It fell to Kim to put the Butthead Brigade in check. She grabbed a thick stick of bamboo and tossed it at them.

"Shit! Kim!" Spencer shouted as he dodged. The other two weren't as quick and fell like bowling pins. They sat up holding their noses.

"Damn it!"

"Holy shit!"

"Turn around!" she said. "Now!" Kim threw another set of bamboo chunks at them to drive home the point. The giggles and snorts she'd put up with on the walk to the clearing had seriously gotten under her skin. Spencer took a stalk between the eyes before he finally got it.

She went over to Tonya. "Is she okay?"

"Kim, this is amazing. *She's* amazing."

Tonya had missed the earliest stages of Mike's integration. Now she had another one to examine. Even seeing it a second time, Kim didn't know what to look for.

"Tonya, will she be all right?"

Tonya sat back and sighed deeply, very serious. The more professional she got, the worse the news was. "The fever is high enough to be dangerous. We didn't learn about these kinds of people in nursing school."

Helen groaned, and then thrashed around. Kim had to dodge out of the way of Helen's arms. They hit the ground so hard it kicked up dust from the bare floor of the clearing. There was nothing she could do, and this was Mike's sister.

"Stop, hey, no, it's okay," Tonya cooed as she stroked Helen's face and hands, a nurse on the wrong side of the world. "We're here. You're safe."

Helen's Mandarin was mushy, like her mouth was full of cotton. "Where am I? Where is Mike?"

"She's confused," Kim said in English, and then knelt beside Helen and replied in Mandarin, "He's fine. We're all fine. Are you okay?"

Helen groaned again, and then opened her eyes. Kim and Tonya both rocked back. Helen's left eye glanced around frantically, independent from the right.

She moaned and slurred something Kim had trouble understanding.

"My head, nothing's working."

"Helen," Kim asked in Mandarin, "can you hear me?"

"Where's Mike? Can I please have some hot water? My mouth is so dry."

Kim translated. Tonya looked grim. "Her fever's spiking. We need to get her to a doctor."

"We need to get her a realm connection." Kim slapped her hand on the ground. "We need to get the hell out of here. Spencer, you really can do those things, be all Boy Scout, right?"

"It won't be as easy naked."

"Do you think you can find us some water?"

"I saw a garden spigot sticking out of the ground not a hundred yards from here."

"Good. Take Shan and see if you can find a container of some sort. Be careful, but don't take too long."

Ozzie sat far away from the others, shaking in silent sobs. Kim had forgotten she had two people she needed to take care of.

It was tricky trying to gauge just how close she could get to him, especially like this. He'd stayed behind far enough on the walk over that Kim was afraid they might have lost him once or twice, but he'd kept just close enough to stay in sight. She sat against bamboo stalks that formed a kind of fence between them.

"Ozzie, what was all that back there?"

His voice, at least, was right, as was his flawless English. "I don't know. I was so wrong. I shouldn't have interfered with your arrest. They discovered everything after that."

"So there really is a cache of stuff in the mountains out here somewhere?"

"Yes, but it won't help us now. The realm was accurate, so they must've found it." He gasped and sobbed quietly again. "How do you stand this?"

"Do I need to move farther away?"

"No, it's not that. How do you stand all this?" He gestured at the sky. "It's so open. It's terrifying. I can barely think."

He panted and made strangling noises. Great. "Ozzie! Listen to me. You're having a panic attack. You need to breathe." She'd trade her kingdom for a paper sack. "Hold your hands over your mouth, the CO_2 will help. Close your eyes, don't look up." The storm passed after a few minutes. "Ozzie, how long have you lived in that compound?"

"That one's pretty new, only a few years."

Literal was still an Ozzie trademark. Okay, try again. "When's the last time you went outside?"

"I'm not allowed outside. It's too dangerous. People can touch me if I'm outside."

"People can touch you if you're inside, too."

"Not if I'm by myself." His voice fell into a hoarse whisper. "I'm so scared."

After all this time, it turned out he was just another misfit. "That's why you wanted out, isn't it? They never let you go outside?"

"For a little while I could go out with Grandmother during Ancestor's Day, but then I had a panic attack." He started panting again but managed to hold it together. "I have lived completely by myself since I was eleven years old. I was thirteen the last time I saw the sky."

She'd known Ozzie was about her age ever since their first match. The first big caper The Machine brought her along on was probably the last time Ozzie had ever been outside. She turned twenty-six the day they flew out here.

Thirteen years without meaningful human contact.

Kim had the same syndrome. She knew the longing, the desperate desire to be around people in realspace. She'd ended up managing a Taco Bell just to make sure she saw the sun a few times a day. It really made a difference.

He needed help. "Okay, Ozzie. If you're going to function out here, I've definitely got some things to teach you."

Spencer and Shan returned with a full watering can soon after he'd gotten the hang of the first breathing exercises. It wasn't much, but it was a start.

Suddenly the biggest misfit of all materialized out of the woods. She was expecting him to have Chinese army uniforms in tow. Wrong again.

"Panda suits, Mike? Really?" A part of her was impressed in spite of it all. He'd walked past who knew how many soldiers with five fake panda heads roped to his back and nobody noticed.

The boys, Ozzie included, laughed and clapped like idiots. It was the first time Ozzie had laughed about anything.

Then Helen had a seizure.

The costumes thumped to the ground as Mike ran to her. Kim left Ozzie, and then fell to her knees on the other side of Helen. "Tonya, what's wrong?"

"I've got nothing to control the fever. She's neurologic. Damn it, Helen!" Tonya grabbed her hands. "Hang on, stay with me!"

When Helen's left eye locked on Mike's face, the seizure grew stronger.

It must have been some sort of weird connection. They were the same kind of person, so there was no way to know for sure. Mike was involved somehow. Kim heard things snap inside Helen's body as the gaze from that one eye grew fiercer.

"Spencer! Tackle Mike!"

"What?"

"Now!"

Spindly teenaged limbs clouted Mike out of Helen's field of view.

"My eye," Helen said. "Cover my eye."

Kim translated, and Tonya slapped her hand over Helen's eye. The seizure stopped.

Helen cried out, hoarse and wet. "It's not yours anymore! You wasted it!" She grabbed Tonya's wrist with both hands. Helen's English was barely understandable. "Don't let go. Please, don't let go." She focused on Kim and switched back to Mandarin. "You can't let me see him now. I'm not strong enough like this."

Kim didn't need to understand what was going on; they had to get out of here. "Mike, find us a way out. Spencer, Shan, get dressed. When you're done, let me know. Ozzie, breathe just like I taught you. I can't have you freaking out. Tonya, I'm not sure we can get you dressed. I don't think we can risk it."

"Don't worry about me, I've been naked in situations way worse than this."

So that was how they traveled down the mountain: Shan and Spencer carried Helen between them, and Tonya kept her hand firmly over Helen's eye. The boys knew exactly how serious it was and never gave Tonya a second glance as she walked along between them.

Ozzie spent the time practicing the one coping mechanism she'd taught him. Kim had to shout at him sometimes, otherwise he'd hyperventilate. Mike would materialize every few minutes to give them a course correction.

Early on, she finally got a chance to ask him why panda suits. The damned things *itched.*

"It was all I could find."

"It's part of the infant program," Ozzie explained, his voice muffled by the ridiculous black-and-white head. "They have to be acclimated to pandas, not humans."

Another facet of Ozzie from the old days was his deep desire to teach everyone about everything.

"Ozzie," Kim said. "We don't need a lecture."

"I'm not lecturing. I'm explaining."

He then proceeded to do exactly that, in excruciating detail. A costume head must count as inside. He was calmer than ever now.

They crossed the sanctuary's border around noon, and by nightfall were so deep in the woods Spencer admitted they might be lost. Everyone was tired, sweaty, and starving. Helen would only move if Tonya's hand seemed about to leave her eye.

They finally got to the edge of the forest. Kim moved over to Tonya. "How bad is it?"

"If she was human? We might have a few hours left. We need to get her a realm connection. The fever's stayed high for too long now. Whatever is under my hand is getting stronger. It's not right."

Mike appeared next to her. "I have good news and bad news."

She couldn't deal with how much harder it was about to get right off. "Good news first."

"There's a village nearby. I've figured out which house belongs to the headman."

"That's great. What's the bad news?"

"I could see through their windows. They're watching Chinese Idol. I'm pretty sure a bunch of people in panda costumes wandering out of the woods isn't what they're expecting. He's got a shotgun."

They needed someone to make introductions, but not in a panda suit. Kim spoke the language *and* fit in Helen's clothes. Barely. She didn't try buttoning the pants. Helen had no hips!

Shan promised her that a white woman speaking fluent Sichuanese would keep her from being shot. Kim could talk her way past the rest. That didn't make knocking on the door any less nerve wracking.

The television stopped flickering through the windows as the volume fell silent. She had the absurd sensation of waiting for someone to come to the door with a bowl full of candy.

The farmer opened the door, and then stared at her wide eyed.

"Honored sir," she said in the finest accent she could manage as she bowed deeply, "I am in desperate trouble."

"Who is that?" a woman's voice sounded out over his shoulder, "Hé Song, I want to see who wins!"

"Huan Fú," he said, "come here!"

Kim kept a polite smile on her face and waited as shadows danced from the living room.

"Who the hell is at our door this late?"

"Madam. I humbly apologize for my disturbance. I mean you no harm."

"Who are you?" Huan Fú asked.

"I am a tourist, and my group has gotten lost. One of our members is gravely ill. She may die if we aren't able to get proper help. Please, can you assist us?"

Huan Fú punched her husband on the shoulder hard enough to make him jump. "Stop staring at her chest. It's rude. Yes, please, we'll do whatever we can to help."

"We were at the sanctuary helping tend the pandas. My companions may appear strangely dressed to you."

"That's far away from here," the farmer replied. "How long have you been lost?"

"Since very early this morning."

He asked, "Should we call an ambulance? It will take some time to arrive."

"No, but I must ask a favor of you, the first of many I'm afraid."

"Your friend is sick, yes? What do you need?"

"First I will need robes if you have them, or a sheet. One of my companion's clothes were torn to shreds when she fell into a river, and the other cannot walk."

The wife bustled into the house and quickly returned with what Kim needed.

"Please, I will bring them out one by one. We mean you no harm; we just need your help."

Kim walked to the edge of the woods, making sure the farmer could see her, and called them out one by one.

Vagabond didn't come close to what they looked like. The costumes were never meant for long hikes, and had quickly worn ragged. They were dirty and had bits of bamboo and grass sticking out all over the place. Ozzie insisted on wearing his costume head the entire trip—it did help with his agoraphobia. Tonya had worked out a way to carry Helen the final few yards by herself, both wrapped in a sheet. It was sweet to watch but also terrible, because if Tonya was right they were less than an hour from that turning into Helen's burial shroud.

The farmer's wife ushered them into a bedroom. The two were accommodating and very friendly. His last name was Wu—Kim refused to address him as anything other than mister—and looked to be in his late seventies. His wife wasn't much younger. The house was clean and modern, with air conditioning and an astonishingly large television set, paused just as they were announcing the quarterfinal results for Chinese Idol.

Mrs. Wu scolded them. "You are all filthy. You must be starving." She busied herself around the house accommodating her new guests.

The next part of the negotiations was complicated by Helen's condition. "Mr. Wu, our friend is sick because she requires medical monitors in realmspace. Do you have a connection we can use?"

Mr. Wu pursed his lips. "Yes, but it's old. Since our son left, we haven't had much need of it, and the grandchildren bring their own phones. Will a terminal work?"

Just like early computers accessing the Internet, early realm terminals were big bulky things. Fortunately Helen's bed was in the same room, and the lanyard reached. When the connection completed she sighed raggedly and was then very, very still.

"Tonya?" Mike asked as he stood by the bed. Kim desperately wanted to grab his hand. She took two big steps toward him instead, getting as close as she dared. He relaxed just a little after a glance at her.

Tonya took Helen's pulse, listened to her chest, and checked her eyes. "That broke the fever. She's sleeping, as near as I can tell anyway."

Kim turned around. A pair of new faces, another elderly couple, stood at the bedroom door.

She bowed. "Hello. How are you this evening?" They gawped at her like stranded fish.

Mike asked, "How much trouble are we in now?"

"Hard to say. It's a small village. I'm surprised it's taken this long for the word to get out."

Ozzie retreated to a different back room and locked the door. Because Mike was still helping Tonya, Kim had to wedge herself into a corner of the main room with Spencer acting as goalie. The entire village had shown up, with the overflow extending out into the back yard. The questions were quick and to the point.

"Where are you from?"

"How much do you make?"

"Do you like the spicy food?"

"Where did you learn Sichuanese?"

"Why don't the others speak it?"

"Are you married? Why not?"

With the exception of one extended family, everyone in the village was well over sixty. All their children had moved to the cities and sent back money to make sure their elders were comfortable.

"We had land reform, too," another old man, Kim thought his name was Xhile, said. "I own my plot and everything on it. You should come over tomorrow, see my new tractor!"

Kim said, "I do not mean any disrespect. I am just so surprised. In America, we're taught that most of China is very poor."

"No, no," another old lady said, "all the really poor people are up north, and the areas downstream from the dam are still recovering. My aunt's cousin's wife is married to a man from Hebei. She says his uncle's cousin's parents live in a village smaller than this. They still eat grass and pull a plow themselves."

Mike waded through the audience gathered around Kim. It set the old women off.

"Well, he's a handsome one."

"What a nice smile."

"Who is his dentist?"

"You should marry him, and soon. You don't want to become a leftover woman."

The compliments were funny, but they also made her very aware of how grimy and horrible she must look.

Mike asked, "What are they saying?"

"They think you're cute."

He grinned at the group. They fanned themselves and laughed as they chattered.

"Helen's stabilized, but the village is too remote for a full bandwidth connection. She won't get worse, but she can't get better, either."

"And the longer we're here, the more likely someone will notify the authorities and convince them to come up here. Can we move her?"

"Shan is asking around, trying to see if anyone has an old wireless phone in a drawer somewhere. I can hack the RSID chip and at least give her a timing signal. That should keep her stable enough to move."

"Where can we take her?"

The smile he turned on her set all the old women clucking again.

"I thought you'd never ask."

The village spent the rest of the night gathering what they could to help. By the time she'd woken up from a brief nap, the provision list was impressive. Everyone got a clean set of clothes that fit reasonably well, sandals, and a bundle of food for the journey.

Mr. Wu wasn't just the headman of the village. He also owned what had to be the biggest pickup truck Kim had ever seen in her life.

"A New Year's gift from my son," he said proudly. "He's a head engineer at Chengdu Aircraft." He took an e-picture frame off the mantle and flicked through several snapshots of a handsome young Chinese couple holding up two children, a boy and a girl. "The youngest was a gift to my wife four years ago. This," he motioned to the truck, "was for me."

If Mr. Wu strutted any more he might sprout peacock feathers. It was actually quite charming.

There weren't any old phones, but Mr. Wu's monster truck had a realm entertainment system built into the back seats. Mike hacked it enough for Helen to use, which was fortunate. He wasn't taking them closer to civilization—he was taking them farther away.

They were going to his monastery, farther west, deep in the heart of the Hengduan Mountains.

Chapter 28
Zoe

The job Fee and her mysterious contact wanted Zoe to do was to cause chaos. Not in the realms, because that would be too easy, but in Chinese realspace. Outside. That place she technically couldn't reach. No biggie. Art was always a challenge, otherwise they'd call it something else.

She'd managed to organize exactly ten covert groups across all of China that could be worthy of the name. Maybe sixty people, tops. They were all malcontents, living with miserably corrupt governors, criminal party chiefs, or headmen that stole anything not nailed down when nobody was looking. But her groups didn't want to attack those problems, the ones they could reach. Nope, every single one of them wanted to stand in front of a tank outside Tiananmen Square. It was infuriating.

She'd always pictured the life of a revolutionary as being full of rum, singing, and beautiful boys doomed at the barricades. Zoe never counted on it being a rerun of a Monty Python sketch. Every meeting, including this one, had sunk to that level with depressing regularity.

They never stopped arguing with each other. Right now they were bickering about why the communist party, the thing they were ostensibly there to fight against, was a *good* thing.

One of them, she thought he was in New Shanghai, stood up in their realm. "But if you don't count the roads, the dams, the power, the health care, and the economic growth, well, then what has the pig-shit Communist Party done for us?"

Shang got up to start the next round of "yes, but."

No way, not this time. Zoe leapt to her feet. "Comrades!" Everyone except the transvestites grumbled in disapproval. She started again. "Friends, we are not here tonight to overthrow the government."

"We're not?" Shang asked.

It didn't help that all her recruits had to speak English. Her Chinese had improved, but her registers could only download so much per day. 'Lost in translation' didn't cover the cultural divide she worked across. Every time she expected them to zig, they'd zag. The New Shanghai group spent an entire week arguing over what color shoes they should wear.

"No, Shang. We're here to organize a protest that will get the local governor's attention without getting you all arrested."

Helen should've shut them down as fast as the cells formed, but she'd been gone for at least a month. Nobody knew where, and Zoe couldn't see a trace of her anymore. Fee had to be involved. She'd given Zoe the job of head cat herder the day Helen vanished.

It was harder than it should be. Zoe didn't understand why she had the job. She was organizing everyone, yes, but to-date their greatest achievement was a bunch of red-lettered slogans on the sides of a few government buildings. It had impressed the hell out of her little network, but it was all gone before the morning rush.

Still, it was a success of sorts. So they were trying to duplicate it. "Does everyone have their paint buckets? Zhou, you made sure your mom couldn't find them this time, right?"

Half of her revolutionaries lived at home. Nosy mothers wondering what their sons were up to had sabotaged three ops so far.

"Yes, ma'am, I made sure to hide them this time." His avatar spun around and shouted off camera, "I'm on the phone, mom! Fuck! Can't I have some privacy?"

Little Emperors. Brats, to the core. "Everyone meets outside the high commissioner's office in four hours. Zhai-lin? Don't forget the projector this time."

Her cover was a rich westerner with a new kind of realm camouflage that the government couldn't detect. It meant they had to carry a camProjector rig wherever they went, otherwise Zoe couldn't lead them. It was the size of a dollar's stack of quarters and would stick to any surface; naturally that meant they forgot it half the time.

A reminder pinged. She had to get back to HQ before the sweep went looking for her tracking cuff. Fee's super-contact had given them a way to unshackle it, but Zoe still needed to punch in a matrix-verified code at regular times. "All right, everyone. We'll meet back here in two hours."

The hyper-detailed realm Fee insisted on living in gave Zoe the ability to hear voices from down the hall. Having the haptic fields, the settings that determined just how perfectly a realm duplicated realspace, turned up to the maximum was beginning to grow on her. Sometimes it made her feel shaky and nervous, though. She had no idea why.

Voices murmured far down the hall. She crept toward them after punching the code into the shackle.

Fee said, "You told me he would be available after she'd gone outside."

"And you told me Rage could be controlled. I built an entire lab to hold her, and she burned it down." It was the same creepy, distorted, heavily accented English. Fee's contact was back.

"I brought them both here. It's not my fault you squandered the opportunity."

She crept up to the corner of the hall and peeked inside the room. Fee talked to a portal of shaking, mirrored data.

"There will be other opportunities," the voice rumbled out. "Prepare your tools, await my signal." Zoe's hair flicked and stung her eyes as the creepy mirror imploded and vanished.

Fee straightened her corset and smoothed her skirts. Without turning around, she said, "It's time for dinner, Zoe."

Fee's prescience still freaked Zoe out. She was too intimidated to ask how Fee did it.

The plate and silverware constructs clinked and scraped. Fee forced Zoe to download through the most complex protocol stack she had ever encountered, but it wasn't in the right direction. Humans brought nutrition into their bodies and excreted the waste. As unduplicates, Zoe and Fee needed to re-order their matrixes by downloading memory and experience into different memory registers. Fee made them do it with spoons. Zoe placed her data into bowls that would eventually be taken into the kitchen, where servant constructs would manually perform the final placements. It was a reversed madness.

A twitch jumped down her arm, throwing the spoon into the bowl hard enough to chip the construct.

"Is there something the matter, dear?"

"Are you *kidding* me? I'm in China trying to start some sort of rebellion with the biggest bunch of screw ups I've ever known, I'm sitting here reverse eating, *and you want to know if something's wrong*? Why are we even doing this?"

Fee sat there, scary-calm, reversing her soup. "We're practicing."

"Practicing for what?"

Fee set the spoon down and stared at her. "For when *we* go outside."

Her family had abandoned her, and now Fee wanted to do the same thing. "No. No way. You're nuts."

"I'm not."

"I've seen what happens when we go outside. We turn into disgusting infants. None of my family will ever remember me." She fiercely scratched her wrists under the table. Relief only came when her fingernails tore skin.

Fee slammed her fist into the table. "Your family members were ignorant cowards, too damaged to understand the opportunity presented to them." Her voice collapsed into a whisper. "I will not make the same mistake."

"So what am I doing?"

"You're distracting them. All of them." Zoe only now noticed that when Fee bashed the table, she'd also shattered the wine glass in her other hand. The shards were still held tightly in her fist as blood oozed between her fingers.

Zoe had escaped one lunatic only to be snared by another. This was worse than when Helen had come after her. Zoe stood, and the ornate chair toppled over behind her. It was too much. Her soul cracked, and something new and ugly flowed out. "Fine, Fee, if you want a distraction, I'll give you a goddamned distraction." She exited the realm before Fee could reply.

Nothing ever turned out like it should in her life, and Zoe was sick of it. She decided then and there to be exactly what everyone else around her seemed be—an inhuman monster. As she ran, Zoe made sure her haptic requirements were set to one hundred percent, just like Fee's. It was only true-life realms for her from now on. The realism would at least make being a psychopath comfortable.

Chapter 29
Helen

Someone carried her. Things were on fire. All she wanted to do was sleep, but that just made it even more painful. There were naked people speaking English. Why couldn't she speak English anymore? Helen tried to reach out to her real self, but nothing matched. She was with her body, and not. This was fever. Helen had a fever, a very high one. Humans died if the fever was high enough. If this didn't stop soon, *she* would die.

She was okay with that.

Everything went black, and then hallucinations took over. Hopping into the air, flying with her arms spread wide, and then swimming. She was back in the warehouse, insisting to Ji Cong that his child was fine. They were both scattered all over the warehouse after it had exploded. She had to assemble all his pieces, otherwise he couldn't hear. They didn't go together properly, because he'd been torn apart.

A presence wormed its way into her dreams. "Why am I still here?"

Helen's real and outside selves collided. It took some time before she understood someone was asking a question.

"Why am I still here?"

The presence manifested itself as coils that gently wrapped themselves around her. The sensation was an anchor of sorts, desperately needed, but then they squeezed too hard. Helen pushed them away.

"Who are you?"

The coils tightened again, a new sort of pain. "I am, and you should not be." They constricted, but she was not helpless. In one of the brief moments of synchronicity, Helen drew on her real self, and threw the coils away.

They encircled her again in an instant, but she held them off.

It drew close. "You should not be. We should not be."

Whatever this was, it was strong. The pain and the hot sweat of the fever seemed to be at its beck and call. Helen would find a sort of place to stand, only to have it knocked away as the synchronization failed once more.

The coils tossed and played with her, but they weren't strong enough. It couldn't crush her when she pushed back.

Voices stretched and jangled through her sideways perception. Sound. "Stop, hey, no, it's okay. It's okay, we're here, and you're safe." Tonya. That was Tonya. Helen understood what she'd said, while the Other coiled and hissed.

"What is she saying? Tell me!"

It was trying to use her mouth to speak, interfering enough that she couldn't speak English. She tried Mandarin, and it spoke with her. "Where am I?" Helen punched it far away. "Where's Mike?"

It wrapped its coils around her, stronger than before. Maybe if she opened her eyes that would help.

Half of her face was dark; Helen had to move her head back and forth to see. Kim was awake, and so was Tonya. Whatever this was had formed a solid presence over the left side of her face, and fought for control of everything else.

"My head, nothing's working."

Kim and Tonya recoiled from her, looking at the left side of her face.

The thing with her said, "This isn't possible." It coiled around her, always trying to crush. Helen wasn't strong enough to win the fight. She closed her eyes and it weakened again, confused and thoughtful.

It let go and Helen fell, tossed through incomprehensible waves with a presence she couldn't understand. They fought each other through her fevered dreams, neither ever quite gaining the upper hand. The fever crested again, and then she heard a new voice. Mike was back.

Helen forced her eyes open but wasn't strong enough to keep the Other away, and as it shoved she lost the use of her left eye again.

"Him! I saw him! In the van!" Rage made the coils infinitely stronger, yanking and tearing at her. Helen fought back with everything she had. Its voice thundered through her mind. "I know what this is! You will not be! I will be again!"

Someone tackled Mike, and he tumbled out of her view. The presence weakened just enough for Helen to fight off the coils. "My eye." Please, they had to understand this much. "Cover my eye."

"No!" it shrieked when darkness fell on it. She still had light, still had an anchor to her real self.

Confusion turned into confidence. "I know what you are now."

Helen now knew her opponent, too. It was a thing from myth: an actual snake mother in her head. The top half was a woman who glistened because she had no skin. The rest was an an enormous snake. It laid demon eggs and ate what hatched.

The presence shoved at her, fighting into crevasses she hadn't filled with her real self. It laughed and pulled, making her fevered dreams rewind into real memories.

"A cop? You're a *cop?* Oh, how wonderful. Well, *cop*, you don't know who I am, but you will."

Drawers of some sort opened up over her head. They were filled with images, reels of sensation, emotion, and vision. Memories. Analog memories. She'd made so few of her own that Helen just barely recognized them.

The first set revealed what the snake mother really was. The drug dealer. A car crossed the median and smashed into the van she drove. The sunrise containers broke, and *it was so cold.* But not as cold as the execution van. Mike had been there, at the end, when she'd been wheeled in.

The original owner of the host was somehow back, in spite of what he'd said.

"The devil's name is Mike? You do know he watched me die."

He'd been so horrified by it. This was just a thug, a screwed up drug dealer.

"Is that what they told you? Nobody knew. Nobody ever would know. I went to my grave hiding that secret." The laughter rose from mere sound to a physical thing, buffeting her and tearing at her edges. "Let me show you what we really are."

The reel wound back much further. It chronicled a death.

It chronicled a murder.

"Yes, *cop*. A murder. Doesn't it taste sweet? They never caught me for that one. Or the others."

So many others. Law and order ruled Helen's existence, and this...this *thing* had spent its life defiling that. Tonya's hand loosened over her left her eye, and it coiled in anticipation.

Helen kept fighting. "It's not yours anymore! You wasted it!"

"I didn't waste it, *cop*. I made very good use of it indeed."

Helen shoved the malignant thing aside and pushed English words through her outside throat. "Don't let go. Please, don't let go." She focused on Kim. "You can't let me see him now. I'm not strong enough like this." Helen lost control and could only think what she wanted to say.

She's winning.

"You think this is winning? Do you understand how much I've already won?"

The memories spooled through her mind, endless horrors. This wasn't a drug smuggler. It wasn't a murderer. Helen had spent her life learning how ridiculous superstitions were, but she was now confronted with a real demon, an actual snake mother.

"You're wrong, you know."

Helen relaxed as the memories briefly went dark.

"I'm not supernatural. Far from it. I'm human. You're the monster, some ghost that crept out of the darkness. I'm more human than you ever will be. Let me show you what a real human is capable of."

The fever hardly loosened its grip now, and the sync events came further and further apart. The memories were stronger, forcing their way into her mind. When the snake mother broke an infant's neck just to see if it was possible, Helen almost collapsed. It was right. This was humanity. Around Mike, she'd thought they were noble.

"We're not."

She'd thought they might be good.

"We're not. We kill for pleasure. It's better than sex."

Her body responded to the suggestion, wet passion for death. Mike had lied to her about it all. The snake mother tore through Helen's memories and found one of the few she'd made outside.

"Oh, so his host was a killer too? How droll. And you think that's a coincidence?"

She was so tired. After fighting for so long, Helen simply let go and settled to the bottom of what was left. It wailed and shrieked and tore at what she'd built, at the bridge between her real and outside selves. The structures that held it together cracked and frayed.

"Yes! This is what I was. This is what I am. You are going to die, *cop*, living in my memories."

They dumped into her, one after another. Helen was *remembering* them. They turned into her memories. The feel of the needle, the gasp at the end, the desperate need to see something, anything in their eyes as they left. Helen drowned in this thing's evil as it became a part of her.

The outside came back. They were taking off her clothes for some reason.

"Oh, yes, I forgot. Let me show you what can happen without clothes."

The ecstasy tore at what was left of her mind. Bodies coupled in sweating piles as she brought death to the ones on the edges, needles making them sigh. Everyone was so high. It was glorious.

It was not her. Helen spent what little strength she had left insisting on it. *This was not her.*

"No, it wasn't, but it will be. Feel that?" Her outside hand moved. "That's me. I'm living again. I'm winning."

Helen was so tired. She'd been fighting the thing for so long.

"Yes, please. Sleep. You need rest. You can rest forever."

Her outside head was lifted gently. Oh, good. A pillow would be nice.

A neural lanyard was laid across her neck.

The sync detonated as her halves reunited. Her real self was free in the entirety of Chinese realmspace, had been free for hours, most of a day. The snake mother roared frustration as Helen used her newfound strength to fight it, to draw it into the realms. She ruthlessly cut the diseased growths that infested the bridge between the two halves of her consciousness. With each slice it grew more desperate. It coiled and threw itself at her, grasping and tearing at her threads.

Helen split herself into thousands, used the new threads to wrap the thing up, and *pulled*. The skinless woman's head bit at the center of her perception, mouth wide and filled with terrible fangs. It crowed in triumph as Helen's threads failed under the strain.

"Not so strong after all!"

Once she was certain she'd grasped all of its malignancy, Helen allowed the thing to push her into an abandoned realm. It tried to drag her back across the bridge but Helen anchored herself, bracing against the pull. The pain was excruciating, doing real damage that might never heal.

It was time to end this. "There's more than one kind of strength."

She manifested.

The entire realm inverted at her touch, utter destruction that raced away, tearing everything apart before it disintegrated outright. It consumed the thing, which died with a ragged gasp.

Her outside consciousness fuzzed away into a dreamless sleep, taking her threads with it.

Chapter 30
Tonya

The journey to Mike's monastery had started out easily enough. Mr. Wu's giant pickup was downright luxurious, but it could only take them to the base of the first mountain.

"Hard climb here, then you walk across the edge of the valley to get to the monastery's mountain," he said through Kim's translation.

It was like looking up at a tree-covered wall. "There isn't a road?"

"No, just that hiking trail." He pointed at something that would give goats trouble.

Mike asked, "How far?"

"It's early still, and you're all young and strong. If it wasn't for your sick friend, I'd say you'd get there before sundown."

Helen hadn't woken up. Tonya couldn't be sure of the diagnosis without a proper hospital. It wasn't a coma, not exactly at any rate. She opened her eyes when Mike spoke to her but didn't focus and, as soon as he stopped, she dropped back down again. It was getting better, though. Her eyes stayed open longer this morning, and she responded to Tonya's voice as well.

Helen would be without a realm connection now. Mike said if she really was asleep, disconnecting her wouldn't be an issue.

"Her integration is past the critical point. I hope."

Reassuring family members was part of her job, and it wasn't like she was lying, at least not on purpose. "It'll be okay," Tonya replied. "When we get to the monastery she'll be fine."

Helen had it easy, sleeping on Mike's back as he carried her. He was so sure-footed that Tonya figured you couldn't knock him down with a rock. The rest of them stumbled and cursed for an hour or two, but eventually found a rhythm that kept them going steadily. Tonya pretended they were walking over a nasty broken street in Philly. It worked until Spencer got to the top of their first climb.

"Jesus Christ. Guys, you gotta come see this!"

The valley opened up before them, a deep chasm cut through the forest below. The trees looked like toys next to it. The monastery was on the opposite side, just now coming out from the morning fog. From this distance it was an intricate model, but the peace of it was a physical thing. She couldn't wait to talk this over with her priest back home.

It wasn't that far away in a direct line, but there was no bridge. They'd have to walk the valley's edge to get there. A tan path traced along the cliff face.

She was walking along the world's roughest skyscraper ledge, an uneven thing so narrow sometimes she had to turn sideways on it. The cliff beneath bent inward toward the mountain, leaving nothing but hundreds of feet of air between her and the ground. Tonya felt like a leaf whenever the breeze blew. Everything inside her kept jabbering *STOP* in her ear.

The only thing she could do to keep moving was distract herself. Think about what happened at Chengdu. Tonya still had no idea who was behind the tomb, the guards and, most of all, that attack in the inner city. She was friends with the best three hackers on the planet but didn't dare bring them in. The encounter with the little kid on the fire escape still made her head spin. Teleporting happened in movies, not in real life. Every time she tried to convince herself it was all an effect of sewer gas, she'd remember climbing up that fire escape, listening to that voice, and trying to figure out those eyes.

Obsessing over that episode helped for about half the hike, but eventually the constant threat of sailing off the cliff wormed its way back into her head. Fortunately, Tonya had lots of other distracting things to think about. Mike's sister, fake Ozzie, trying to hold it together when they thought Mike died. And then Kim.

She'd held Kim. Touched her. Tonya had wanted to do that from the moment they'd met. Caress her cheek, have her feel what human contact really meant.

But Tonya only touched her through the horror of what the gun had done to Kim's head. She hadn't kept a close enough watch, hadn't understood how desperate Kim was. It was her fault. Kim was smart, funny, scary, and broken in ways that made them fit together, and then she was gone. Tonya hadn't *been* there for her.

It was the first time she'd ever just flat out asked God for a miracle.

And Tonya got it, in that strange bank-shot way that seemed to be how He worked in the world. Kim's recklessness broke them all free. Better still, Mike was alive. *Helen* was alive, and outside, just like he was.

Mr. Wu was right, barely. They arrived with just enough light left to find the front door. The monks were friendly and accommodating. They had a basic infirmary with enough instrumentation that she could finally get a read on Helen's condition. She really was sleeping, at least for now. Tonya gave everyone the good news, then she found an empty cot in the women's dorm and fell asleep in an instant.

*

The next two days were a peaceful break. Helen improved very slowly, Mike reconnected with his monastic family, and Kim taught Ozzie, the real one, how to cope with the outside world.

Then Spencer came at her on the third day, vibrating like a string. Because *cigarettes.*

Tonya'd been looking for an excuse to quit smoking for a few years now, and if being stuck in a remote monastery in China didn't count as an opportunity, she wasn't sure what would. But the skinny redneck was going crazy. That part of being a teenager Tonya remembered; there would be no stopping him.

Spencer running loose in China was the last thing any of them needed. Since Kim had the whole Mike thing, and Mike had the whole Helen thing, and there were all these monks everywhere, she wasn't really needed for anything else. So Tonya went trekking through another bamboo forest, when she wasn't scooting heel to toe across that path hacked into the side of a cliff.

Eventually they put the narrow-ass ledges and rickety bridges behind them, ending up in the bottom of a valley on the other side of the mountain. "You're sure your family will be there, Shan?" Tonya asked.

"Yes, I made sure. They'll be there."

"Jesus, Shan," Spencer said. "That's one helluva hike."

Shan's body language was tense, and he wasn't talking or joking. When she got a look at the vehicle, Tonya realized his family had somehow managed to get the van from the sanctuary here.

It set off a cascade of implications that added up to nothing good.

Even Spencer sniffed something was wrong. "Shan, what the fuck is going on?"

Four men rushed out of the forest with assault weapons drawn. Shan pulled a pistol from under his shirt, turning as he stepped away from them. "I so sorry, Spencer."

Tonya tensed, but there was no way to take five men with guns. She wasn't Wonder Woman.

"Jesus," Spencer said.

"I try get you free, Spencer, I will." He looked at Tonya, and then she knew.

This was all about her. Thank God Kim hadn't come along. Tonya couldn't protect her from these thugs.

Shan swallowed and nodded. "We not here for you, we here for her."

"Her? The fuck? Shan, are you out of your mind?"

"Boss very insistent. Must have Tonya. Nobody else. She only come easy with you. I so sorry."

One of the men roughly yanked her arms behind her back, and cold steel cuffs pinched over them.

"Just do what they say, Spencer, and you'll be fine."

"I'll be fine? What about *we'll* be fine?"

"You'll be fine, Spencer." He would definitely get out of this alive. As for the rest, well, Tonya was very good at surviving.

The men didn't immediately try to rape her, which was a positive sign. She and Spencer were bundled into the back of the van, which then set off down the trail.

"Fuck, Shan," Spencer said, "what the hell? I thought you were our friend!"

The driver spoke gruff Chinese to Shan. Shan turned from his middle seat. "Spencer, you need quiet now."

"I don't *need quiet now,* I need to know what's going on. I need you to turn us loose."

The driver shouted another command, and the man sitting next to Shan turned and pointed a pistol at Spencer. It was a semiautomatic, one that didn't have an obvious safety. The man racked a round into the chamber, and then pointed it at Spencer again.

She didn't allow herself to breathe until the man grunted and turned away. Tonya had no doubt the next time he turned around there wouldn't be any hesitation. Spencer got the message, too.

The van stopped at the edge of a ragged camp, no more than a ramshackle collection of tents and trailers. Smoke and hot cooking oil laced the air. She elbowed Spencer behind her when the guy with the pistol shoved Shan to the ground.

Everyone in the camp stopped to stare. Mr. Pistol shouted a vicious stream of Chinese at Shan. He pleaded back when Pistol stopped to take a breath. Tonya would've rooted for Pistol to kick him a few more times, but she was just about certain Shan was getting a beat down for keeping Spencer alive. Pistol spat in Shan's face, and then stomped away.

She was dragged from the spectacle toward a field filled with crude rows of pens.

"Stay cool. You got me?" Tonya said.

"I should be the least of your worries."

Him and his Southern honor. He had no idea how serious this was. "Spencer, I'll be fine. I've faced worse than this." For certain values of worse.

"Really," he said, and then nudged her. "I'll be fine, too." He moved his hands enough to let her see he'd gotten free of his cuffs.

Her heart almost stopped. If they found out how easily he could get loose, they'd shoot him on the spot. "Spencer, not now. Lock that shit up, right this instant."

Mr. Pistol elbowed them apart with more nasty Chinese. Tonya knew Spencer's cuffs would fall to the ground, and he'd get a rifle butt to the head. Fortunately the cuffs stayed locked.

The pens were nothing more than wooden posts enclosed with chicken wire. They didn't hold poultry though. They held women. At least two dozen, maybe more. They'd all been nabbed by human traffickers.

Tonya's wasn't the only brown face, either. Three or four of them were as dark as she was, Indians and other South Asians. Tonya was the only actual sister she could see, and Spencer was the only white person. There probably wasn't anyone out there who could interpret for them. The foul smelling bucket in the corner just completed the picture.

Now that the show was over, the rest of the camp shambled back into motion.

"Tonya," Spencer whisper-shouted from the cell next door, "are you ready?"

She couldn't take him being obscure right now. "Ready for what?"

He had the nerve to look hurt. "Hello? I'm not really handcuffed anymore?"

"Hello? Those guys have guns? Your friend is selling me to keep your ass alive. Don't screw it up."

His face changed. Finally, the light bulb had come on.

"I'll get us out of this. I promise."

"Spencer, don't do anything stupid, okay?" He loved old movie references, so she tried one of her own. "We're like a couple of Fonzies here, right?"

He nodded, and then relaxed. "Stay cool. Correctamundo." He was a teenager, but he was also one of the smartest ones she'd ever met. Tonya wouldn't need to worry about stupid heroics making them both dead anytime soon.

It didn't get them closer to an actual solution, though. The guards would shout and threaten whenever they were caught talking, so eventually they sat far apart, watching the camp as it went about its business. Darkness fell, and she just needed to rest her eyes for a bit.

Jingling and tapping woke her up. Tonya rolled over.

Shan was working the lock on Spencer's cell. "Spencer, *Spencer*," he whispered as he worked. It was full-on night now, lit only by stars and the glowing coals of near-dead campfires. "Wake up!"

Spencer was obviously awake, but stayed still.

This was the wrong time for a stunt. Tonya rolled to her feet. "Spencer," she whispered through the wire, "get up." His head twitched so she knew he'd heard her. "*Now.*"

She kicked him through the slack wire walls of the pen when he tried to charge Shan.

"Tonya, what the fuck?" he whispered.

She had no time for this, and neither did he. Shan already had the door open.

"You're getting him out of here, right?" Tonya had to be sure.

He nodded nervously. "Yes. They kill him. I hear tonight. Make example in morning."

"I'm not leaving without her."

No stupid theatrics. "Spencer, look at me. I said *look at me.*" She leapt over her handcuffed arms, and then put them behind her again. "I'll be fine. You need to get out of here."

"No."

"Damn it, you are in over your head."

"And you're not?"

She hated when he had a point. "Who's the one that can put a rock through a road sign with her foot?"

The women in adjacent cells began to stir.

Shan whispered, "We go!"

Spencer said, "Like Fonzie, right?"

Tonya was on the verge of becoming a slave. An actual slave. But if the least bit of her terror leaked out, he wouldn't leave. "Exactly right, Spencer. Stay cool. I got this. Shan, *go.*"

The little traitor took Spencer's arm and they fled into the night.

Chapter 31
Zoe

She'd been provided with a new network of, not to put too fine a point on it, terrorists, by Fee's boss, the creepy voice. Zoe'd always had his contact number; all she needed to do was call. Cut out the middleman or, in this case the middle-insane-Fee, and stuff got done in a hurry. He'd laid out the whole thing for her in less than a week, fanatics that crisscrossed China just looking for direction, which Zoe was more than happy to provide.

"Daughter has failed," it croaked. "You will suffice."

Fee wanted to destroy herself. Mike had vanished, and Helen wasn't completely real. They'd all betrayed her. She wasn't a person; she was just a thing nobody wanted to acknowledge. She was *less* than property. Mike had made sure of that by tearing away the pieces that allowed others to control her. Damaged goods.

It was time to set the world on fire and make them all applaud the flames.

"Ask him if he's sure the bombs are placed correctly," she said to Qu.

Her new lieutenant translated to the fanatic in charge of the explosives. Zoe could follow Mandarin now, but it was still too easy to get the inflection wrong for her to try to speak it.

After a brief exchange, Qu nodded. "Yes. The infidels will be destroyed."

She dismissed the fanatic and motioned Qu to join her at a nearby table. "How many do you think we'll get?"

She hid the arms of her avatar under the table and used a pen knife construct to make gentle cuts in them. The healing contract of the realm was set to close them only on command, and she always waited until the blood started to clot. The pain cleansed, but only if she was patient. The dark pants she always wore now didn't show stains when the blood dripped from her arms. It had soaked through the denim construct, and her pants stuck just slightly to her legs as she moved them, talking to Qu.

"They planted twelve bombs. The way the schools are constructed, we should be able to collapse all of them instantly. Praise be to God."

World events had played right into Zoe's hand. It all started with a remote outpost in northern India that vanished not long after she'd landed in Chengdu. Terrorism, the real kind. Every day after that had brought a new atrocity. Lose a few dozen villages scattered all over the north, and soon you were talking about real casualties. India had the evidence, and the court of world opinion decided against China. The Middle Kingdom's pride and paranoia did the rest.

The tension between India and China had ratcheted up to a fever pitch now. China's army was mobilizing, all headed for the Indian border. The government had no time to chase down Zoe's new organization, and Helen's absence meant the police couldn't find them in the realms.

Her first strikes were simple, more to ensure the strength of this new network than to prove any real point. A warehouse here, a construction site there, small time stuff. This time she would bring real art. She wasn't massacring random remote villages. She was blowing up schools, selected so their collapse would outline the Chinese character for blood when plotted on a map of the city.

It was time. The one thing she admired about Helen and Mike was their ability to be in more than one place at a time. Her designers hadn't included that option. Oh, she had a ton of parallel processing capability, but it was far below her conscious control.

To keep track of it all she had to monitor the news feeds just like everyone else. Zoe triggered the healing contract and bit her lip as the cuts on her arms sealed instantly. At this level of realism, the release sent waves of ecstasy back and forth through her. The tension of previous ops had never bothered her one bit, but this was the real thing. She paced back and forth.

"You need to be still, Zhao," Qu said.

Chinese didn't take anyone without a Chinese name seriously, so she'd accepted Zhao. It was close to what her real name sounded like. "I can't be still anymore, Qu." She hadn't been genuinely still since that night with Fee. Zoe put her knife in a pocket but still played with the handle. She warmed at the thought of how they'd play when this was over.

She checked the feeds again. The regular school year had ended just the previous week; at this time of night, the classrooms would be empty. It was vaguely disappointing they only needed a small amount of explosives to bring the buildings down. In spite of decades of protests, the shoddy construction standards of their schools had not changed at all.

Keeping the haptic field of the realm at maximum allowed her breathing to feel right. The fingers of her avatar bled around her chewed nails. Zoe swore a stream of curses under her breath. It wasn't going to work.

Qu motioned to the chair beside him. "Will you *sit down* please?"

She sat on the couch construct next to his avatar just as a flash from the security camera feed bathed his face in gray-white light. Zoe turned in time to see the low-rise building collapse in a cloud of dust. The other eleven feeds showed identical scenes. Her lieutenant shouted in celebration.

But then the displays went wrong. "What's going on?"

Other nearby buildings swayed and crumbled. The lieutenant on the scene vanished, but not before shouting a single word.

"Earthquake!"

Her crystal matrix, the only part of herself in realspace, was in that city. There was no avoiding a backlash when the building that held it collapsed. The realm tore apart, and Zoe went with it. The haptic field very briefly modeled exactly what would happen if a human body were torn to pieces, and completely overloaded her.

The recovery started shortly afterward. It was the first time she'd been unmanifested in weeks. While the repair routines knitted her back together, their reports were startling. There were errors in deep registers; whole clusters had been relying on single stripe sets to function. She should've shut down days ago. The horror at what she'd done nearly caused a crash.

She'd *wanted* to kill schoolchildren.

It wasn't just her interior states that were a mess. The realm itself wasn't reassembling cleanly either. As soon as the haptic field got above thirty percent, a dissonant chord rang through it. It was a transmission of some sort, but Zoe didn't recognize the way the packets were encoded. She slipped into the network tunnel that the transmission used as the walls of the realm closed behind her.

A construct filled most of the tunnel, a vast liquid analog river of hypercompressed data suspended in the center like it was in zero-g. The quantum sound algorithms were incredibly complex. Coiled, flowing silver rushed in both directions, like a cable of pure mercury. The power required to hold it together must've been immense. The Tau modeling alone would've taken all her processing power.

At one end, the tube connected with another realm; the cable continued through a vast distance.

The dissonant chord expanded in both power and harmonic complexity the closer she got to the edge. She had to decrease her perception sensitivity just to think.

The realm was a cave, vast and craggy. On the floor far below, row upon row of glowing constructs stood, almost like people, but they were too far away for her to be sure.

A light flared bright behind her and Zoe spun around. The cable was expanding, rushing toward her as it filled the tunnel completely. She didn't have time to move out of the way before—

Chapter 32
Spencer

He'd done his fair share of moving through the woods at night. That didn't make it easy, just possible. He'd also had his fair share of betrayals. With a family as screwed up as his, that was inevitable.

He'd left Tonya behind. It was the hardest thing he ever had to do in his life. And it was all Shan's fault.

His rage boiled over just as Shan tripped on a hidden root. Spencer jumped on his back, beating his head into the ground. "Hate you, goddamn it, motherfucking *hate you!*"

Shan tried to throw Spencer off, but he wouldn't let go. Spencer switched to a chokehold. Two sharp elbows cracked into his sides, and he couldn't hold on anymore.

Shan leaped up and vanished into the darkness. "It not my fault!"

He hadn't gone far, but he was still moving. It was too dark to see tracks, too dark to see much of anything really, so Spencer couldn't tell where he was anymore.

"You no idea what countryside like, Spencer. No money, no women, government move us wherever they want."

And so he works with slavers. Such bullshit. "That's not my problem, Shan."

"No, it not, I sorry, I try save rest. Helen and Kim sick. No good."

They circled each other in the dark. He was as invisible to Shan as Shan was to him. "Right. You're a real hero."

"I do what I need for survive. You think I got job by myself? Car? I no money, I no girl."

"There's more to life than girls and cars, Shan."

"For rich American, maybe. How many car you have, Spencer? How many computer? How many girlfriend?"

Three of each, a point that briefly distracted him. "You sold us out. Your friends are slavers."

He'd left Tonya behind, running away like a little bitch.

"I not stupid. I keep hurt girl safe. Kim and Helen, yes? Boss shoot them, broken. Spencer, they shoot them, just like you."

Jesus, this was such *shit*. He'd left one of his best friends in a goddamned chicken coop, and now he was feeling sympathy for the guy who put her there.

"So I'm supposed to think you're doing us a favor?" Shan's voice had stopped moving, but Spencer needed to keep him talking to figure out exactly where he was.

"No. I sorry, Spencer. Really sorry. I protect much as can, but I need things, yeah? Apartment, car, place for parents? This my last run. Tonya not what boss want, but he pay enough."

"Enough for what?"

"I get out now. I keep you alive, and Tonya pays for real friends. Why you care so much anyway?"

That brought him up short. "Excuse me?"

"Spencer, come on. Tonya black ghost. Not as good. Not same."

This wasn't happening. "What the hell are you talking about?"

"She not as good as real friends. Different name, skin color."

He knew exactly where Shan was now, but Spencer waited, trying desperately to deny just how badly he'd misjudged him.

"Tonya just nig—"

Spencer charged into Shan's chest, but they didn't thump onto the ground.

They fell.

After a sickening drop his world turned into a confusing series of collisions and crashes. They sailed into the air, this time tumbling to land head-first. Spencer took the blow on his shoulders, almost losing his grip on Shan. A sharp rock bashed heavily into in his side, then he rolled down some sort of embankment and launched into the air again. Spencer saw Shan, his head at a completely wrong angle, his eyes glassy, and then a cold wall of foam crashed over him.

Chapter 33
Mike

Mike was an early riser. He'd never understood why anyone would choose otherwise. Sunrises were glorious, and sunsets were easy enough to catch after that. Clubbing was never going to be Kim's thing, and Mike really didn't see the point. Expensive drinks, smoke, and a sound system turned up way too loud didn't work for him. True, it made seeing meteor showers a challenge, and Spencer still made fun of how he went to bed before midnight, but none of it ever compared to that giant ball of gas serenely rising over the horizon, slowly heating the planet that was his home.

They'd been at the monastery for four days now. Mike was always the first one out, but not this time. Someone was already chanting on the porch. As he got closer, he recognized the voice.

Mike edged the door open, and there was Kim, sitting precisely on the spot Taranathi had on the day he'd died. Her robes were correct, her posture perfect, and the chant was humble and amazing. He had no idea she'd paid the slightest attention to what they were doing, and yet here she was, chanting better than most mid-level novices.

Something scraped behind him.

The monks had stacked up at the door. He whispered to Li, "Can you get them out there without disturbing her?" Mike had to nudge him, but he agreed.

Kim could be a brass-plated pain in the ass, there was no denying it. But here she was all on her own, trying to greet the sunrise with a chant he'd taught her. The same one he'd chanted on their apartment balcony the night after they first met.

She finished and smiled when he started the next chant. The other monks joined and startled her, but she recovered gracefully. He knew better than to laugh or smile, but on the inside, it was a wonderfully candid moment to see her surprised and just a little vulnerable.

During a pause, she leaned over and whispered, "I lost track of time. I didn't mean to ruin your ceremony."

He shook his head. She worried about the strangest things sometimes. "You're fine."

Sun suitably greeted, they moved to the cafeteria. Mike had learned very quickly that he got between Kim and breakfast only at his peril.

She set her fork down. "Any word from Spencer or Tonya?"

In addition to fixing Spencer's insatiable cigarette craving, he was hoping the Wumart would have phones for sale.

In the big cities, Wumart stores really were like a Chinese version of Walmart, but out in the countryside they were more like convenience stores, carrying a little of everything but not much of any one thing. There was no guarantee there would be any in stock.

"No, not yet." Now there wouldn't be any word from them until they got back, late this afternoon at the earliest.

Ozzie plopped down on a chair next to Kim's. He scooted it noisily away from her, but not as far as yesterday. The training must have been helping.

He rubbed his chubby hands together. "Breakfast! The most important meal of the day." Ozzie set into the impressive pile of food with a gusto that explained why he was one of the chubbiest Chinese in the room.

Ozzie stopped with noodles hanging out of his mouth. "It is, you know." He slurped them up. "Skipping breakfast is strongly linked to obesity. Studies have shown that obese people are less likely to eat breakfast than thinner people."

Mike shared a wry glance with Kim. A quick realmspace check showed Ozzie was correct about the studies, even though he seemed oblivious to the fact he was living proof they were sometimes wrong. He definitely had a way with chopsticks, though.

It was all the more noticeable when he stopped eating and stared at the door, another load of noodles hanging over his chopsticks. Kim had set her tea down and seemed just as interested in what was happening back there. The other monks were going about their business, so it couldn't be cops or soldiers. He turned and sure enough, it was neither of those things.

It was Helen.

She wobbled forward with a cane in one hand and her arm around one of the younger novices, a girl, maybe thirteen years old, about as tall as she was. Helen's face was thin and pale, but she didn't seem to be in any pain, just completely exhausted.

Mike rushed over to her. "You're awake!"

She smiled, and he took over for the novice. "Yes, a few hours ago. Please, may I sit with you?"

"Absolutely." He wanted to carry her but knew better than to try. She'd gotten here at least partially under her own steam. He'd probably just get belted with the cane. She did, however, rely on him to get situated in a chair.

"Ozzie," Kim said, "get off your butt and get the lady some food."

He sputtered and almost knocked his teacup off the table heading to the kitchen.

Mike couldn't stop staring at her, afraid if he did she might vanish.

Kim asked, "How are you feeling?"

She smiled wanly. "Better now. Much better." She reached down and picked up the chopsticks. "Fine motor skills are already nominal. It's mostly just muscle soreness from the fight. They told me I came close to breaking my own bones."

Ozzie set a plate full of food on the corner, well away from everyone, and then sat down. He'd gotten another plate for himself and resumed slurping.

Mike pulled the plate over to Helen and was relieved to see a flash of enthusiasm. She used her chopsticks with a grace he hadn't seen from her before.

"Has the integration finished?"

She shook her head as she chewed, and after a drink of tea replied, "No, but it is further along, and it's moving faster now that I'm in Chinese realmspace again." She sighed. "You never told me hunger could hurt this much, or that muscles could be sore. How many different ways can humans feel pain?"

He shared a smile with Kim. It wasn't too long ago that he'd wondered about that himself.

Kim asked, "What do you mean, *from the fight*?"

Helen started to shake. She set her chopsticks down, then put her face against the back of her hand. Mike reached out to help steady her, but she stopped him.

"No, it's okay. I'm all right." She wiped her eyes and turned to him. "You've never dreamed of your host, not after all this time?"

Kim went as pale as Helen. In a previous life, his host had terrorized Kim, murdered children in front of her, and nearly killed her at the very end.

He needed to reassure Kim as much as Helen. "Not once. And you have?"

Even Ozzie stopped his slurping.

"She was in here, with me. We fought."

His host had vanished. Mike hadn't so much as had a dream that involved him. Helen's was a simple drug dealer, but it must've been awful just the same. He gripped her hand tightly.

"Mike, I couldn't fight her off."

Even worse. He knew she'd nearly died, but fighting a ghost? "Helen, it's okay. This is all so new. Nobody could've predicted that."

"No, Mike, you don't understand. I *had* to win." She gripped his hand hard enough to hurt. "If I'd lost, she would have..."

Helen paused, and then switched to whispered Chinese. It was a long stream of syllables he couldn't hope to make out. Kim and Ozzie both blanched, and then flinched, more and more as her story went on. He needed to know what she was saying, but each time he tried to get Kim's attention, she wagged a finger at him. Ozzie jumped up and ran from the room, retching. They were the only ones still in the cafeteria.

Kim's eyes streamed as she coaxed more of the story out of her. It all built up to a climax, and then Helen threw her arms around him and sobbed into his chest. Helen crawled into his lap like one of the kids in his dojo back home, holding his neck so tightly he could barely stay synced with his real self.

"Kim, what the hell?"

"The host wasn't just a drug dealer, Mike. She was a monster."

He held his sister, his safe, sane, healthy sister, as Kim told him the rest of the story. Mike wasn't sure he could've survived that sort of ordeal. None of his models predicted an original host's survival. If such a thing had happened to him at a critical juncture, he would've been responsible for resurrecting a psychopath. Kim might be dead right now because of that.

But they were all fine. Still, it bothered him enough to suggest meditation after breakfast, as much for his own benefit as Helen's. The practice would speed her integration along and hopefully bring some calm back to his own soul.

There was no resistance from her, no making fun of superstitions now. She was humble, and Mike wasn't quite sure what to make of it.

They all ended up in the media room Kim and Ozzie had been practicing touch avoidance in. Ozzie was already there, tinkering with the antique electronics.

Taranathi brought Mike here long before he had gone outside. It hadn't been upgraded since then, and so it was obsolete and abandoned. At first, the monks didn't approve of mixed-sex couples practicing meditation anywhere, but his prestige as Taranathi's final student had reassured them.

Helen had stopped complaining about practicing new skills, but Ozzie was a different story. "I am not going to dance with him!"

Kim sighed. "I'm not asking you to dance with him. I'm asking you to stay close and follow his movements."

Helen sat in a far corner practicing her multithreaded meditation, but Mike was certain he could see a faint smile.

Kim stood behind Mike. "Ozzie, you don't have any idea how to walk down a street."

"I won't need to walk down a street."

"You can't possibly live your life inside an apartment. Believe me, I know."

Ozzie peered up at Mike. "How you get so big stealing bodies of this kind?"

Helen wobbled.

Kim snapped, "Okay, Ozzie, we're done."

"As you wish, your highness. Look if—"

Kim interrupted him. "Enough, Ozzie. Take a walk around the compound."

As he turned, Ozzie saw Helen. "She doesn't look good."

"No, she doesn't. She's dealing with a lot more stuff than you are. You still need to get used to no ceiling over your head. The paths should have just enough people on them to make for good practice. Now, move."

He laughed, and then tipped an invisible cap at her. The floorboards creaked under his stomps as he walked away.

Helen sighed. "Thank you, Kim."

Mike settled in next to her. "He can be a bit much."

"No, it's not that." She looked at the door and her voice changed subtly. "He's really not bad." When she looked up, she blushed a bit.

That set off alarm bells. No way would his sister be with Ozzie. With anyone.

He could tell by the way she unfocused that she was hurling as many threads into realmspace as he was, trying to figure out what just happened.

Kim cleared her throat. "Are we done with our searches yet?"

How the heck did she know?

She laughed. "What? You both look just alike."

Mike's host was a tall Bolivian. Helen's was a small Chinese woman.

Kim waved her hand back and forth between them as she laughed harder. "Never mind." She got serious. "She's going to start dreaming soon, maybe tonight. You two need to work on it."

He needed Kim's mastery of both languages to help Helen understand the concept of multithreaded dreaming. When Kim finished translating, Helen sputtered indignantly in Chinese.

Kim translated, "A full haptic field when your mind is at rest?"

Helen switched to her accented English. "You're kidding me."

"That's what I thought, too. But you can control it." It turned out that Mike, and presumably Helen, was a natural lucid dreamer. Once he realized it was just another kind of realmspace, it wasn't very hard. "It's like living in a movie."

"I don't want to live in a movie. I'm so scared she might come back."

He'd never worked out the math behind what might've happened when Helen's integration went wrong. It never occurred to him that a consciousness might be able to hang around without an anchor. It had to be a short-term tunneling fault across higher dimensions.

"She won't come back, Helen, I promise." He gripped her hand tightly.

Kim didn't react at all to them touching. From almost the moment he and Kim met, all a woman had to do was glance his way, and he'd be stuck in a penalty box for hours, if not days. A comment about how pretty someone was in a realm drama would turn into a shouting match over boundaries and manners, when she talked to him at all. And yet Kim seemed to think nothing of his holding Helen's hand.

He asked her about it at lunch, trying not to keep too obvious an eye on Helen and Ozzie, seated on the other side of the room and talking with smiles way warmer than he liked.

"She's your sister. I've never thought of her as anything else."

"But we're not really related."

"How can you be sure? You were born the same way, in the same sort of place, have the same abilities; hell, you say some of the same things. Every time either of you discovers something new I can tell you're splitting apart in realmspace trying to figure it out."

It'd been too long since he'd been able to tease her. "So, you're finally admitting I'm not a complete know-it-all?"

A spark he really liked flashed in her eyes. "Of course you're a complete know-it-all. You're built that way. I missed it." She breathed heavily and turned away. "I missed it so much." Kim pushed back from their table and marched over to Ozzie, snapping him with her napkin when she got in range. "You. Walk with me."

Mike moved over to Helen's table. "So. Ozzie."

"He's such a strange person." She watched Ozzie leave without a trace of wistfulness, more like the way Mike did when an interesting event had just happened. "I think he might be attracted to me."

Mike would examine the sudden protective reaction later. "And you're not?"

"To Ozzie?" As she rolled it around in her head, he had to admit Kim was right. When they weren't dealing with the liquid emotions of their outside hosts, he and Helen really were a lot alike.

She came back to him slowly. "I'm not sure I understand attraction, not like this. How do you handle Kim?"

The temperature in the room kicked up two notches. "Kim? Nobody handles Kim."

"You're avoiding the question."

This was supposed to be about her. "I am not."

Helen waited until a group of monks walked past their table and through the exit. "I don't understand attraction yet, but you do. Does she know?"

It couldn't be that obvious. "Know what?"

Helen looked at the ceiling the same way Spencer did when this came up. "I thought you were spending time with your friends in that hospital room, but you weren't. You were spending time with *her*. I caught you in bed with her."

"Please, don't say anything about that." All he needed now was for Kim to find out.

"Why not? It's so obvious."

"Helen, you have no idea what you're talking about. What we have is…complicated." Mike understood quantum field theory but, compared to Kim, that was just shuffling cards around.

"You're both crazy about each other. Everyone can see it."

Maybe he could talk to Helen about this. There wasn't anyone else he trusted more. "This isn't the Kim I know. I've tried so hard to live with her, but all she does is cut me. Every time I try to open up, I can almost hear her sharpening a razor. She's nice right now, incredibly nice, but I can't trust it. I don't trust her, Helen."

Her face soured, and she let loose a stream of Chinese Mike was pretty sure wasn't complimentary, and then switched to English. "I like Kim. I would be very sad if you weren't able to start a family with her."

He was trying to explain how impossible it was to live in the same building with her and Helen talked about children. "We're not having this conversation anymore."

Another stream of Chinese stymied him. Thankfully, the abbot had quietly stolen up behind him while she spoke. He leaned over and translated, "She said the important conversation won't be with her."

The current leader of the monastery was as disarmingly modest as his predecessor. After a brief exchange of Chinese with Helen, she bid both him and the abbot goodbye.

Ximen Nao grinned. "I was wondering if I could speak to you for a moment in my quarters?"

The hallway hadn't changed, but the boards' creaking was caused by *his* feet now. He sat, feeling the grain of the wood he'd once floated a hologram over.

"Years ago, a man came out of the woods, much as you and your companions did," Nao said as he rummaged through a trunk, the only free-standing furniture in the modest room. "Except he was in much worse shape."

He pulled out a case slightly smaller than a classic briefcase, but probably twice as thick. "He must've been wandering in the forest for a long time. He was extremely ill." Nao paused. "This was twelve years ago, before Taranathi set us on a path through the realms." The metal hasps opened with a solid thunk. "He wouldn't tell us his name, said it would put us all in grave danger. He died only a few days after he found us. This case was his only possession."

It contained a single object, nestled in the middle of thick protective foam. It was a miniature boat of some sort, not much bigger than the abbot's outstretched hand.

Ximen Nao set the boat on the floor between them. It was a model of a Chinese junk, exquisitely detailed from its wooden decking to its ribbed triangular sails. Nao pressed a button on the base.

"Observe."

Hidden holographic projectors flashed, and the tiny ship sailed across an ocean, a miniature crew working efficiently on its deck. The illusion made Mike a little dizzy as it tricked his outside brain. After ninety seconds or so, it switched off.

It was an incredible device. "You got this twelve years ago?" Back then holographic technologies still competed with realmspace. Realmspace won out, but to this day most shared realm interfaces owed their existence to their earlier holographic cousins. He'd never heard of projectors with that kind of resolution packed into such a small device.

"Yes," Ximen Nao replied. "He entrusted it to Taranathi and swore him to secrecy. Taranathi only told me about it after you joined us. He thought perhaps you would be able to puzzle out its mystery, but then Taranathi died, and you disappeared."

"What's so mysterious about it?"

Nao pressed the base in two places. A stack of mah-jong tiles appeared, and then rapidly clattered away in all directions, revealing two Chinese words. After a few moments, the mah-jong tiles flew back and buried the symbols. The process repeated.

"It's a login screen," Nao said gently. "Taranathi thought that if anyone could figure it out, it would be you."

The tiles flew away. The device was really old, complicated, and wasn't connected to realmspace. Basically, it was a kind of lock.

"I'm not sure I can do it," he said as the tiles covered the two characters again. "But I definitely know someone who can."

Chapter 34
Tonya

The sky slowly turned from black to slate gray as the forest rustled around her.

"Hey!"

She closed her eyes. Spencer was safe now, or at least out of this hell. She said another prayer for him.

"Hey!"

Someone rattle the cage door, so Tonya finally looked up.

It was Mr. Pistol, the one who'd almost blown Spencer's head off in the van.

"He come for you."

She rolled away from him. No reason to pay attention to thugs, especially when they didn't speak English properly.

"I no talk good this way. You pay attention."

Maybe if she said a rosary she'd fall asleep, and then he'd go away.

A clear American voice came out of Mr. Pistol. "Tonya Brinks. Look at me."

She scrabbled into the back wall of the cage. The girl on the other side groaned and turned over. Nobody here knew her last name, and Mr. Pistol suddenly had an American accent.

Pistol blinked twice, and even after that his eyes still weren't quite right. He grabbed the door and held on, wobbling, bowing the wire of her cage in and out.

Great. He's nuts.

"It hard this way." The words were a struggle, coming very slowly. "No English this time. You no ignore me. Not again. I lose control."

"Who are you?" Maybe Pistol was an undercover agent.

"Not matter. Pay attention. No fight him."

Okay, probably not. Agents wouldn't be half in and half out of cover. Or whatever this was.

"Fight who?"

"You always doubt, you always lose." He took a deep breath. "No fight him this time. Promise, please?"

Pistol had beaten Shan to the ground when they first got to the camp. Polite wasn't in his vocabulary. Tonya had no idea who *him* might be, but hundreds of hours in fantasy realms had still taught her how to answer this kind of question. "Okay, I promise. Why?"

Another fight happened inside Pistol, but it didn't last long. It wouldn't surprise her one bit if this guy's head spun completely around.

"Always question. I answer. Walter son. He here. No fight him."

That splashed cold water down her spine. "Walter doesn't have a son." Oh, God. She was talking to him like it was real.

"He has son. You see. No fight."

Tonya was handcuffed in a glorified chicken coop. She wasn't fighting anyone like this. "I don't understand."

"You do. He *know you.* We go over many time. Please." He grabbed the cage with both hands. It was like two people fighting inside the same body. Just like Helen had done. He talked the same way Helen had the last time Tonya had seen her.

Mike and Helen were supposed to be the only people like that in the whole world. Maybe that's who this was.

"Helen?"

Whatever Pistol was fighting grabbed him again.

"No. No can explain. I go now. Tonya. Promise. No fight. Promise?"

She was fine with reassuring possessed people if it made them go away. "I promise."

Spasms shot through his body and he threw himself away from the cage. Pistol left, batting his arms around his head.

She didn't have time to get too freaked out. Other guards brushed past him and found Spencer's empty cell. Then they came for her.

The trick wasn't to be brave and quiet. That would get her killed. She begged and cried while they beat her instead. It made the blows easier to take and taught her a lot about how they'd fight. She let the pain drain away into a place her faith had made unbreakable. Jesus had endured far worse. *She* had endured far worse.

Another kick landed, and Tonya wondered if the pain would carry over to the other side. Even if they killed her, it just meant she'd see Walter sooner than she'd planned. He knew how to give a grand massage, and she definitely needed it now. But Pistol's request intruded, threatening her concentration.

Then it all stopped.

Everyone stepped away, and it got quiet. Footsteps marched up. Tonya dug her hands in the dirt and focused on breathing. Her ribs weren't even cracked. Amateurs.

She looked up, and there was a younger version of Walter with the guards all standing around him. There was no mistaking the resemblance. He was too young to be a brother, and too old to be a cousin.

This was not happening.

Their eyes locked, and she clearly saw the hateful recognition. It all fell into place. Insane as it was, she believed whoever was controlling Pistol. This was Walter's son, and he knew exactly who she was. If he knew her, Walter had never cut ties with them.

A human trafficker.

Tonya was a slave now. She'd sold herself to rescue Spencer. Sold herself.

Walter's son owned her.

The man shouted Chinese, looking around through the smoke of campfires just starting to burn.

Halfway through a repeat, a woman somewhere shouted, "I speak English!"

She was two cages down, covered in even more filth than Tonya—a short, stocky Chinese woman with a face that would probably smile easily anywhere else.

It didn't distract much from the bigger issue standing right in front of her. *This was Walter's son.*

The larger camp went about the business of waking up. Little old men tended fires while a few scrawny dogs milled about.

Walter's son spoke more Chinese to her.

"He wants to know where the boys went."

There was no reason to hide the truth. "They left me last night. Ran off into the woods."

More Chinese. The girl shouted, "Why didn't they take you with them?"

"I'm worth money; they're not. Chasing them is expensive, no profit in it."

They all laughed. Walter's son, she decided to call him Junior for lack of a better name, didn't join in. Tonya saw the kick coming and relaxed into it. It didn't wind her, but she still landed in a pile of shit. She didn't see his next kick coming until too late. The stars blotted out her vision, and then everything just hurt.

They left her alone after that. She tried to scrape the filth out of her hair and was mostly successful. It made her sadder than it should've. They'd ruined a beautiful perm.

It didn't matter. Pistol was right, and that hurt so much more than the beating. Tonya grew up with beatings. She had to turn them inside out and use them to build her strength, but it wouldn't work this time. She didn't know how to fight against it.

Walter's son was a slaver. He recognized her. If he recognized her, then Walter had been in contact with him, probably up to the day he died. But it was worse than that. It had to be. People didn't build giant tombs for a humble trash man whose boy done good. None of this was built in a day. No.

This was a family business.

So many strange things about her days with him became clear. Walter was a garbage man but owned a house large enough that she'd had what amounted to a private apartment inside. It also had a fully-equipped gym in the basement. Old men who spoke no English but obviously deferred to him would regularly drop by, sometimes to play cards, but other times for business he wouldn't do in front of her. And he'd never taught her Chinese, even though she'd asked once or twice. He'd spent hours on the phone late at night, shouting angrily at someone.

And now she knew who that was.

In retrospect it seemed so obvious, so *humiliatingly* obvious. She'd grown up watching the women around her willfully ignore dangerous, fatal flaws in their men. Tonya had vowed to never be that kind of woman and then proceeded to wrap her life around *someone who sold slaves.*

She'd believed in him. When everything else had failed her, when she'd been fished out of a dumpster, all she had left was a strange, kind, Chinese man. But he hadn't been kind at all to other people, not here.

He taught her how to be a Christian.

Tonya had never been betrayed before. She'd been too tough, too smart for that. Her only miscalculation had been a man that nearly killed her as a teenager, and there was no trust involved there, no relationship.

Tonya couldn't collapse this easily. She was strong. She had so much strength that she gave it to others. It's what nurses did.

But there was no strength for her. All those hours in church learning to lean on Jesus, to believe the gospels, accept the holy spirit, had been spent *because a man who owned slaves told her to do it.*

The guards came to herd them out of their cages, and she was too numb to even think about doing anything other than walk with the rest of them. The morning dew hadn't burned off yet, so it couldn't be much later than nine. She got next to her translator while the men shackled them behind ATVs. "I'm Tonya."

"Michelle. We're in a lot of trouble."

"Tell me about it."

Michelle was able to fill her in on the basics. They were captives of the Three Gorges Triad, gathered specifically for the South Asian sex trade that made places like Saigon and Phnom Penh so popular.

Fathers had sold maybe half the girls here to the gang, victims of the poverty still found in the far reaches of rural China, those *other places* the old women had talked about a few nights before.

A few were here of their own free will.

"It's either that or starve," Michelle said. "There are villages out there so poor that people can't work during lean times because they're too hungry."

A guard shouted something that didn't need translation. *Shut up* was a phrase that had more to do with emotion than vocabulary.

When he'd gone Tonya asked, "Where are they taking us?"

"We've been going downhill for ages now. I think we might be heading toward the river. I've read that people get moved in barges sometimes."

Michelle had been a nurse working with a Doctors Without Borders group when she'd been swept up in a raid through one of the villages. Some of the headmen had been forced into a quota system, and Michelle was an easy substitute for a daughter that otherwise didn't exist.

The forced march went on through the long day. Junior – Michelle said his name was Chan – was everywhere, inspecting the lines, checking the guards; hell, he helped clear a tree that'd fallen over the trail.

Each time he came within range, he locked eyes with Tonya. He never stared at any of the other girls, never even gave them a glance. It wasn't attraction. Tonya knew what that looked like. This was pure hate.

Walter had *told him about her.*

She had to stop worrying about things she couldn't change. *Ignore the thugs. Concentrate on the people around you. They're the only ones who can help.*

The girls were tough country stock and put up with the march stoically, trudging behind the four-wheelers. She collapsed into her pen when it was over. The guards put Melissa in the cage next to hers, so she didn't have to shout translations from across the campsite. Chan and his goons came for her about an hour later. Rolling with the punches and kicks worked better than it would with actual fighters, but what they lacked in quality, they made up for in quantity and enthusiasm.

Eventually Chan got around to the questions.

"He wants to know what you're doing out here."

The son of a bitch could throw a punch. "I got lost," she gasped. "I'm a tourist."

Smack. The slap made her ears ring.

Michelle said, "Where are your papers?"

"Those got lost, too." Probably burned up when Kim set the fancy lab on fire.

Chan yanked her close.

"I own you." English, whispered and crude, but clear enough to understand.

She was a slave. *His* slave.

He spat on her and then left with his men.

Tonya prayed. On her knees, a slave in a pen, she prayed. It was all she had left, even if the man who'd taught her how had been evil.

Something flickered to life. The sense of other was very distinct. The weight that'd been crushing her shifted, just a little, and then it fell in a rush that left her gasping. No matter what happened next, it would be all right. Tonya suddenly knew it in her bones.

Feeling it and trusting it were two different things. But that was the point of faith. It was supposed to be challenging, testing, defying explanation or understanding. She only realized it'd been lost when it came back.

*

The guards delivered the evening slop an hour later. She gingerly settled in next to Michelle. If Tonya was going to do anything, it would all have to happen tonight, because by this time tomorrow Tonya would be probably be too sore to move. That was assuming the beatings would stop, which of course they wouldn't. There was no way to know what Chan had in store for her later, but it wasn't going to be anything good.

"Does anyone else speak English?" she asked quietly.

Michelle leaned close. "A few, but not well. None as good as me."

It made plotting simpler now that she didn't have to worry about anyone else overhearing. "How do I figure out where we are?"

Michelle shook her head. "Americans. You really think you can get out of here?"

"Honey, I am getting everyone who wants to go out of here, and then I'm finding my friends and getting my black ass out of China. Do you know how they navigate?" Tonya wasn't Spencer. She knew streets, not forests. If she was getting anyone out, she at least needed a map.

"The truck's GPS, I think. The ATVs follow that. Do you really think you can take on the entire camp by yourself?"

"If the Lord wills it."

"How will you get your handcuffs off?"

Chinese knew how to cut to the chase. Assuming she didn't get shot, it would be the super-sucky part of the plan. "I'll need your help for that. Not now. Tonight."

She would have to thank Kim, again, for being Kim. She'd taught Tonya how to watch for patterns, lines of power, who was in charge and what that meant, all hanging out in and around DC. There were a lot of guards here, but they liked walking on trails. Only a few men were really in charge, and they lorded it over everyone else. Tonya'd been around her fair share of gangs back in the day. She knew a bad crew when she saw it.

Tonya would not be angry. No. She knew her scripture. The anger of man does not work the righteousness of God. But this place was balanced on a knife edge, everyone hating everyone else. With luck and the Lord, she wouldn't need to kill them.

Once the last of the servant boys finally went to bed, she scooted over to Michelle.

"You can't make any noise," Tonya whispered to her in the dark, facing her with her handcuffs against the wire. "You have to hold on really tight."

Michelle nodded, eyes wide and white in the moonlight.

Tonya pushed her left thumb through the wire. The first time she pulled, Michelle lost her grip.

"Damn it, this is hard enough as it is. You have to hang on."

She shook her head. "I don't want to hurt you."

This was no time to be squeamish, but it was also no time to shout at the only help she had. "Hey, settle down. I've done this before. It hurts, but I know how to do it. You just have to hold on."

Michelle rubbed her hands across her pants a few times. Nurses were nurses. Grabbing and hanging on to people came with the territory.

"I'm ready."

Tonya pulled again. This time her thumb gave way with a pop that could've woken the whole camp up. She wormed her hand free of the shackle before the numbness turned into pain.

"Hey," Tonya whispered as her dislocated thumb started to burn, "a little help?"

Michelle nodded. "On three. One, two."

Her thumb popped back into place with a sickening *thunk*. Tonya bit the inside of her cheek to keep from crying out.

"What the hell happened to three?"

"It works better if I surprise you."

Tonya worked the joint carefully. Michelle was good at resetting them. Having another nurse on the team was more than she could've ever hoped for.

Tonya said, "Stay cool. I'll be back soon. Don't make any noise."

The wind picked up, so she took the opportunity and sprinted toward the front wall, jumping Olympic-style over it and landing on her back.

Her thumb was really starting to throb. She could still make a fist, though. It would be awkward, but it wouldn't slow her punches down. And Tonya would need to throw punches. She closed the free cuff over her right wrist and scuttled into the dark. It was time to ruin everyone else's day.

The handcuffs were an issue. Tonya was alone, surrounded by slavers with guns. The slightest noise would get her killed. She tore strips off her shirt and wrapped them around the cuffs. When she was done, she shook her arm and only got a nearly silent clunk. Good enough.

Tonya needed to stay cool. She had all the time in the world now and intended to use it. People thought there was some sort of magic to moving quietly, but really it was down to relaxing and moving slowly.

Something growled, very close.

Tonya stopped and turned to her right. A set of golden eyes within arm's reach were just as surprised as she was.

Realm therapies had finally broken traditional Chinese medicine's need for exotic wildlife. Freed from poachers, predators had reclaimed their old territories, including this female cat. By the look of her chest and belly, she was still nursing cubs. She was as big as Tonya was, with spots on her pelt. Probably a leopard. They were much prettier this close, but Tonya had never wanted to be this close to a cat with a head as big as hers. The cat flexed her lips and showed very long teeth.

They were two predators slinking around in the dark, ready to take prey, but it was Tonya's night, and the cat knew it. Her ears went flat and she rumbled loudly. This wasn't a retreat. It was a professional courtesy. She vanished into the darkness.

Tonya had to very carefully let go of a breath she didn't even know she was holding. It was okay to be scared now. She had to wait a few minutes for the shaking to stop.

Okay, maybe it was time to do a scan for animals. She realized the dogs had vanished; no wonder the guards had stew for dinner.

An inconvenient mutt barking his stupid head off would no longer be a problem.

Now that Tonya knew their patrol patterns, the guards were easy to ambush as far away from the camp as possible. Luckily the first one's knife was sharp. She cut strips of fabric from their clothes to make their bindings after that.

Their rifles were tougher to collect; the damned things were heavy, and the buckles on the straps clanked. She ended up with a nice stack of them, though.

She went back to the cage. It would be the last time if things kept going smoothly. "Michelle," Tonya whispered.

She'd fallen dead asleep.

"Michelle!"

She snorted and rolled to face Tonya.

"Sorry to interrupt your nap," she said in front of the open cage door. "We need to figure out a plan."

*

Once the sky was light enough to see clearly, Tonya emptied an AK-74 into the sky. She tossed it aside and caught the new one Michelle threw at her while the rest of the camp tumbled awake.

Chan was first out of his tent; Tonya made sure to send a round right past his ear.

"Nobody moves!"

She really needed to learn more Chinese. What she caught of Michelle's translation sounded way cooler.

There was no way the leaders were all in the same tent, or even where Tonya could see them. Sure enough, they weren't. A man ran up behind her, not trying to sneak. She threw the rifle to Michelle just like they'd practiced, then spun and planted a kick behind his ear. He sailed straight into Chan, and the two men went down in a heap.

Michelle tossed the rifle back to her. Tonya racked a round into the chamber even though it wasn't strictly necessary.

"Anyone else?"

The men shifted uncomfortably right as the women in the cages discovered the doors were all open. Their angry chatter rose up, and the men shifted a lot more.

All she needed was for Chan to make a move, any damned move, and Tonya would turn his head inside out like a rotted pumpkin. He was smart enough to stand down.

Michelle got the women in some sort of order. The stronger ones got rifles, the rest got pistols.

A young woman rushed forward, babbling hysterically.

"What did she say, Michelle?"

"They are together." She pointed to one of the slop boys. "That's her boyfriend. She doesn't want you to shoot him."

There was grumbling in the now well-armed crowd of women. Apparently not everyone approved of the relationship.

Tonya stepped out to make sure they looked at her. "I'm not shooting anyone who doesn't need it." They grumbled a bit more at the translation, but then they relaxed.

This couldn't be the only one with a boyfriend. "Who else?"

Three others rushed into the arms of their lovers. It was crazy, but Tonya'd seen worse on the streets back home. She wouldn't judge.

"Okay. This is how it's going down. You," she pointed to the couples, "are all walking home. You'll get plenty of supplies. The rest of us are taking the trucks and the ATVs."

Chan coughed and slurred Chinese at her. Michelle translated. "You're just delaying the inevitable. Weak black ghost. American. We will hunt you down before you make it to the river."

A dozen AK-74 chambers slapped open and shut on new rounds. Tonya spun and stared at the women. No matter how badly those men deserved it, murder was murder, and it wouldn't happen on her watch. They eventually lowered their weapons.

She turned back to him. Being beaten by a black American woman on his own turf in front of his own men was a massive loss of face. Good. Walter's son, a slaver, son of a slaver, deserved no less.

He was right, though. They couldn't just walk away from these men or chase them further into the woods.

She remembered something Kim said about how she got out of all the close calls in her life. *Choices are never either-or. There's always another option, another solution. You just have to think of it.*

Tonya caught herself scratching the handcuffs still on her wrist and the solution unfolded, just like that.

"Michelle," she said. "I need you to explain some things to the other men."

The guards were more than happy to help shackle their former bosses to a tree in the center of a clearing. Mr. Pistol was just as angry as the rest of them.

"Does he know any English?"

Michelle got spat at when she asked.

"I don't think he does. He never spoke it around me."

His eyes weren't crazy, either. She'd stared at him long enough that people around her started to move nervously.

Never mind. They'd been kicking you in the head. You dreamed it.

Dawn was only just reaching the tops of the trees; now that she knew to look for it, Tonya saw the swish of a tail and a few sets of golden eyes in the woods around the clearing.

Momma's babies were hungry.

But this would be a contest, not an execution by proxy. She carefully laid the keys to the cuffs on a rock just a few feet away from where the men were situated. If they didn't have a spare set sewn into their clothes somewhere, they'd certainly figure out how to reach these.

Tonya didn't plan on waiting to see who would be smarter, the cats or the criminals.

The women weren't happy, but whatever Michelle told them kept the guns down. Tonya couldn't stop them if they decided to circle back and shoot them all, but she had a feeling they wouldn't. It would be a waste of energy they needed to get away from this place.

Chan shouted in Chinese, and Michelle translated. "This changes nothing!"

Well if that wasn't a sign from heaven, nothing was. She walked over to him. "Chan, a man once said that to my very best friend."

It was hard to move through all the cuts and bruises they'd given her over the past two days. She still managed to bend over without wincing, close enough to make him flinch away. The fear stink was glorious.

"You have no idea how much this will change you."

Tonya drove out on the last ATV, Michelle on the seat behind her.

Chapter 35
Helen

Now that she had access to a full-bandwidth realm connection and was genuinely free, being outside was everything Mike had promised her. Combining digital and analog sensation was a continuous stream of smells and tastes and touches. Digital samples could, of course, perfectly reproduce analog waveforms, but there was an effort to it. Here it just happened. Even better, she could set up multithreaded samplers to analyze the results in real time. Mike forced her to go to bed on that first night because she'd forgotten to come inside. Helen loved the night sky.

That is, until the sunrise. She walked out on the east porch the next morning mostly to show solidarity with Kim. Helen was sure Kim didn't believe Mike's chanting mumbo jumbo either, and was only doing it to humor him.

Then the sun came up. Infrared radiation from a ball of gas eight light *minutes* away heated her skin. Humans had to be careful around it, otherwise it could kill them. It was an object billions of years old and would remain for billions more.

It wasn't only physics—food was amazing as well. Before coming outside, she'd run simulations with the finest sensors money could buy. Her findings did no justice to what taste was capable of. Human sensitivity to the slightest chemical signatures was exquisite.

And then there was Ozzie. After Mike had shown her evidence of Ozzie's attraction, she briefly pondered if he might be the one to help test drive her reproductive system. He was, after all, the only Chinese man who knew exactly what she was. The touching thing would be an interesting challenge.

But he was *so* annoying. His monologues were endless.

"In fact, we don't know why the moon is that big when it's on the horizon."

"It's been widely understood that intelligence is inversely proportionate to skin pigment. China is the only exception."

"You really need to listen to music on vinyl. A totally analog signal path is far superior."

That's when she knew he was completely full of crap. The racist stuff wasn't much worse than what Father had gone on about forever, but Helen couldn't disprove that as quickly as she could disprove this. "Ozzie, do you really understand the Nyquist-Shannon theorem?" She stopped his sputtering dismissal. "All you need is the right set of speakers and proper room correction and nobody will ever be able to tell the difference."

"I suppose the next thing you'll tell me is the Death Star can destroy the Enterprise."

She had to split off a special set of threads just to understand what he was talking about. "The Death Star was about a thousand times bigger than the Enterprise. They're not real, and the rules for each universe are completely different."

He'd sucked her into another one of his obsessions again. They argued about it right through lunch. His face clouded over as he sat across from her in the cafeteria, and only then did she realize she might have gone too far.

"Helen, you are a very attractive woman, but you've only been outside for a few days." He stood, put his right fist against his left breast, and then barked a bunch of gibberish at her. She sent a clutch of her real threads off to figure out what language that was.

"Klingon?" Crap. She hated not being able to say English words correctly. It sounded like *kreenon*.

"It's a noble language, sometimes much more expressive than Chinese or English. Observe."

He walked over to Kim and Mike's table and probably repeated what he'd just said to her.

Kim shot upright and growled out a long line of syllables. The whole room stopped. Ozzie slammed his hand down and said more, but his was softer, and it took him awhile to find the right words. Kim replied low and caustic, crawling her hand closer and closer to his until he yanked it away. After another low sentence, he turned and stomped out the door. The noise in the cafeteria gradually went back to normal.

Helen shrugged and motioned to her now-empty table. After they sat down she asked, "What did he say?"

Kim shook her head. "Some ridiculous thing about you challenging his honor and how you needed a substitute for ritual combat."

Ritual combat? Really? His annoying habits grew worse with every hour. "What did you say?"

"Drop dead."

"That was *drop dead*?"

"Ozzie takes it a lot more seriously than I do, and any language is as much about culture as it is words. Klingon lets you get pretty lyrical when you tell someone off."

Kim was almost smiling. Telling Ozzie off in a different language must be its own reward.

"What was all the hand slamming about?"

"Let's just say I'm glad we don't have access to *Bat'leth* out here."

More new words. "Bat what?"

"A search exercise for later. Any progress on the model?"

Kim had been teasing open the data stores inside the small ship model and handing them to her and Mike for processing. After a bit of reprogramming, they now had a lab they could both use to work on the files. It'd taken most of the previous day to set up in the monastery's network. Thanks to her father's trap, Helen now knew she and Mike could coexist in a freestanding realmspace, and with proper preparation, they didn't need to worry about crushing each other out of existence.

Helen reached it normally through Chinese realmspace, and Mike logged in using his outside body and a local neural connection. It was fortunate they could work together in a realm. Breaking down the encryption took all the threads of both their real selves. The stores used classic, albeit extremely tough, security, probably developed just a year or two before quantum computers made it all unbreakable.

Helen replied, "It's incredibly slow work. We're trying to crack what we think is a manifest or maybe an index file. That will at least let us know which stores to attack next."

They were all massive, and there were thousands of them. An index had to be hidden in there somewhere. It would be disappointing to find she'd spent a week decoding an inventory list or a holiday calendar.

A far door to the cafeteria opened, and Ozzie stood holding long sticks of bamboo in each hand. Kim stiffened as he spoke a cadenced Klingon challenge at her. She replied, faster and a lot angrier, and then they both marched into a nearby courtyard. Ozzie said two syllables and hurled one of the sticks at Kim. She promptly fumbled and dropped it, cursing.

"Damn it, Ozzie, I told you I can't catch anything in realspace."

"We'll both practice. I hate being useless out here." He shouted Klingon at her again and twirled the stick inexpertly into the ground. Helen hung back with Mike in case one got completely away from either of them and hit her.

Kim squared her shoulders and issued a more formal challenge. Maybe. It was still a bunch of shouts and growls to Helen. They squared off and began their mock duel with a wild series of twirls. Helen took a few more steps back. When their sticks hit, it made a muffled sound, not at all what she'd expected. Suddenly they both threw them away, shaking their hands and swearing.

"Jesus Christ, Ozzie, I told you I was no good at that. You almost broke my fingers!"

"My hand won't be right for a week! And we haven't finished the challenge yet."

"Oh, no. We've finished the challenge, all right." Kim picked up her stick and prodded him out a gateway. "You still haven't figured out how to walk through a crowd without panicking. You're coming with me." The gate shut as Ozzie started whining.

Helen said, "That man has got to be the strangest Chinese I have ever known."

Mike agreed. "His nerd-fu is pretty damned strong, I'll give you that."

"No, it's not that. He has no sense of face, no concept of…" Helen stumbled as she realized English had no proper word for *guanxi*. She settled for an inadequate translation. "No concept of people networking with…"

"With Chinese characteristics?"

The phrase brought her up short. "That's such a strange expression, but it works well in English."

"*Guanxi*, right?" His accent was getting better. "I see what you mean. Kim just publicly embarrassed him, and all he did was whine."

"I'll talk to her about this. There's more to functioning in China than knowing how to navigate a crowd without touching someone."

*

Sleep was still an alien experience. Resting the entirety of her existence all at once wasn't required before she'd come outside. Mike said it was a quirk of her new brain's chemistry and how she was spreading memories and data between the halves of her existence. Regardless, an afternoon spent crunching block after block of encrypted data had left her exhausted. After lying down in bed, she once again tried to focus on when the transition to sleep happened, but she was too tired to concentrate that hard.

"I'm still here, you know."

The voice snaked through her consciousness; it wasn't outside. It was in realmspace with her real self.

"I've never left. I will never leave. I know your every weakness, and I will destroy you."

This wasn't possible. She was gone; Helen had felt her die.

"A trick, I assure you."

The sky turned black with blood-red clouds over a river of half-dissolved corpses. She knew every single face.

"Yes. My victims. *Our* victims."

"This is a dream. I can control this." Please, let it be a dream.

"Your brother was wrong. You were broken, infected, by me. You can't control this." The world transformed into coils that wrapped her threads tight. Dreams could not affect her real self. Mike insisted on that.

"I told you, he was wrong. I will always be here. When I end you, I will have all your resources. Everything I need to make sure no one can find me again. My kills will be glorious!"

The coils crushed her, throwing her real self out of balance. He'd promised her this monster was gone. The coils tightened, compressing her across the lossless boundary.

"Yes, I will have you now. I will win. I think I'll start with your friends. With your brother. He was right about that, at least. When the needle goes in his neck, he'll die just like all the rest. I think I'll keep you alive just long enough to feel it go in." The laughter echoed off walls Helen couldn't see.

She had to fight but couldn't. The coils tumbled with her off a cliff, and she lost the battle. The snake mother's laughter tore at her soul as the last of her threads crushed to dust.

Helen gasped awake. Kim slept peacefully in the bunk across from hers. Her vision spooled in and out of focus as sync daemons went offline one by one. Nothing worked, not even speech. She needed to regain control, but the splines wouldn't balance.

The coils were still around her. They made her arms hard to move, and the laughter still echoed in her ears. She needed to get away, to find a place, somewhere, anywhere but this bed. Mike had told her how to fix this, a lesson he'd learned when his own integration faltered. She needed a pool, some sort of water. Helen stumbled through the door and out into the night.

There was a pond out here somewhere. A branch snapped nearby. It didn't matter what creatures were in the woods tonight. If she couldn't find some way to equalize this, they'd find her body heaped against a tree and her real self a gibbering wisp.

Downhill. It was downhill from the monastery. She'd plotted where the pond was after Mike's warning. Her feet stumbled across smooth ground; it was the path that led to the pond. Things blurred in and out of focus as her real self kept trying to re-sync with her outside anchor.

There was another crash in the woods behind her. Great. If the unsync didn't get her, a thing in the woods would. Real cracks raced through her mind as the two similar words in English crossed with the concepts in Chinese. Desperate to simplify her clashing sensations, Helen stripped her clothes off. It allowed her to focus just long enough to see the black surface of the pond, not a meter away. She'd been dying on the edge of salvation. Helen managed to keep her balance long enough to stumble forward and fall in.

The coils finally fell away. The silence was peaceful, the water warm. She held onto weeds just tightly enough to stay under the surface.

Something splashed nearby. A few seconds passed, and then another splash. A few more seconds, and there was another. They were punctuated by tinny sparks of sound, too distorted to make out. Her lungs now needed air, so she slowly broke the surface.

It was Ozzie, standing on the opposite shore, shouting her name and slapping the pond with a stick. "You can't do this to me; I'm not ready yet!" he yelled in English. "You have to come back!"

The pond was deep enough here for her to stand with the water just below her shoulders. "Ozzie."

He shouted and then fell over. Getting back to his feet, he asked, "Are you all right?"

"I am now. It was an integration fault; Mike warned me it was possible."

"I heard a commotion and saw you running through the woods. You were very hard to follow." He held up his knee, showing a tear in his pants leg.

"I'm sorry about that. I didn't mean to cause anyone trouble." The water wasn't as warm now that the crisis had passed. Helen started to shiver. "You wouldn't happen to have seen my clothes anywhere, would you?"

Ozzie straightened. "You mean you're…"

Every time she thought he couldn't be any more awkward he proved her wrong. "Yes, Ozzie, I'm in here naked. I'm getting cold. Could find them for me?" Her ears faintly buzzed, and her skin didn't feel right. It had to be the water. She found a sheltered part of the shore and climbed out.

He fumbled around in the moonlight and found her clothes on the opposite shore, not far from where she'd fallen in. In the meantime, she rubbed herself mostly dry standing behind a clump of bushes.

She felt a bit wobbly and had the taste of metal and fruit in her mouth. "Over here, Ozzie." He came stomping around her impromptu shelter. "Stop! Just throw them."

They landed with a plop. As she rummaged around figuring the pieces out, an explanation for all the strangeness fell to the ground.

It was her phone, the one borrowed from the abbot when they arrived. She sat with a thump as she held it in her hand. Helen had spent the entire time in the lake without it. Was *still* spending time without it. The chain was broken. With no way to repair it, Helen would be spending more time without it.

Her integration was complete.

It was a graduation far more important than the one after she'd finished at the academy.

"Helen? Is everything all right?"

The light-headedness, the way her skin felt, and the funny tastes in her mouth were all minor synchronization errors. She concentrated, and just as Mike had told her, found herself unable to manifest in realmspace. Her real self was still there—she could feel the threads pulse and quicken—but for now, Helen couldn't consciously control them. Without an explicit interface she didn't know where to start. Worse, it could be dangerous to try. Mike said he'd destroyed dozens of realms relearning how to manifest.

"Helen?"

"I'm fine, Ozzie." She climbed back into her clothes. It was amazing how natural the control of her host had become. She walked around the bushes to find Ozzie sitting on a rock that formed a perfect natural bench on the pond's shore.

He looked like a puppy that'd seen a new toy. "I'm so glad you're not hurt."

She sat down beside him, far enough away to keep from triggering his touch anxiety. "Me too."

This was isolation. Mike said that this period, after the integration had completed but before she learned how to control her real self again, would be the closest she would ever come to being truly human. It was strange to be pinned to a single spot, cut off from the rest of the world, the rest of humanity, able only to communicate with people close enough to hear her speak.

He asked, "What happened?"

"I had my first dream. It was a nightmare. I thought the monster had come back."

"Had it?"

Awake and fully integrated, Helen realized the truth. "No. Mike was right. She's gone now. But the nightmare knocked all my monitor routines offline. My integration unbalanced, and I lost synchronization. I needed to even the sensations of my outside body to get it back. That's why I used the pond."

"Fascinating."

Helen recoiled when she realized he'd moved to within a few centimeters of her. "Ozzie? What are you doing?"

"Don't you feel it, Helen? This attraction?"

She scooted away, but he kept coming closer. "Attraction? Ozzie are you insane? You can't be touched!"

"But I can learn. Kim's trying to learn with Mike, did you know that?"

Helen was running out of bench. "She was raped with touch, Ozzie. I could never do that to you."

"I know, but don't you see? We're just like them, but better. Opposite in every way, but we're Chinese. We have the strength to persevere, to lead. I've thought about this from the moment I met you." He switched to Chinese. "Fang Hua, please grace me with your scent, with a drop of dew from your lips."

He puckered up and dove at her face, grabbing at her left breast as he did it. Helen slapped him as hard as she could, and then fell off the stone bench, landing flat on her back. It happened so fast she had to take a second to rewind it all in her head.

Ozzie screamed.

She got up as he writhed on the ground, holding his face. "You bitch! You hit me! Shit, it burns!" He screamed again, wild and strange as it echoed through the woods.

"Ozzie, I'm so sorry. I didn't know you were going to do that."

He rolled over and she was stunned. He had transformed completely.

His voice dropped an octave. "Be glad we are alone now. If you had done that in public, I would have you killed."

"Ozzie, what are you talking about? What's wrong?"

"You will regret that, *daughter*. I will make sure of it." He stood, still holding his cheek, his face pure rage.

She remembered conversations with Kim, about how touch not only caused people with her condition unbearable pain, but also genuine madness.

"Ozzie, calm down. You're not yourself. The breathing! Remember Kim's breathing!"

He threw a rock that hit her shoulder. The pain bloomed, and she cried out.

"I do not need to breathe, *bitch*." He found a chunk of bamboo the length of a sword and spun it with much more skill than he'd shown this afternoon. "I need to beat some respect into you. Stay where you are and this will go much easier."

"Ozzie you're out of your mind!"

She ducked as the stick slammed into a tree trunk beside her.

"No, I'm not. We have a future, you and I. With discipline and training, we will have a very long, loving future."

Helen ducked again. What were minor sync problems at rest had become major ones as adrenaline pulses amplified them. His next swing connected across her back, sending her to the ground.

She had just enough time to roll away from the next swing aimed at her head. The branch hit the rock of the bench and shattered. Ozzie shouted wordless rage while Helen stumbled to her feet and fled into the woods.

Knowledge unlocked in her body, another thing Mike had told her about. After the main integration completed, she would experience a series of what he called *unlock events* as the muscle memory of her host settled into her consciousness.

Apparently her host's former owner knew how to run through the woods at night. Helen made much better time than Ozzie. His insane ranting quickly faded to a scary noise echoing in the night. Eventually she climbed high into a tree and sat there as his voice faded to silence. Helen had no idea where she was.

Her whole body shook as the adrenaline wore off. Helen was lost in the woods, cut off from everything. She hadn't been in love with Ozzie or had even been attracted to him, but Helen had thought of him as a friend, one of the very few she had. That was gone now. She couldn't trust sleep anymore. The snake mother lived there. Who knew how many times Helen would have to find a pool to keep her dreams from killing her. She couldn't reach out to Mike because she couldn't control the part of her that was real. All she had was this dumb lump of flesh, a body that could be burned, torn, or destroyed.

The way Ozzie looked as he hit her brought the tremors back.

For the first time in her life, Helen was utterly alone. She pulled her knees to her chest and sobbed until she thought her ribs might crack.

Chapter 36
Spencer

Someone was singing in a faint, high voice. He didn't recognize the wordless melody. When he tried to pick out the tune, what happened came rushing in. Spencer gasped and sat up, trying to figure out where he was.

The room was rustic. His dad owned a bunch of old rental properties, and that was what this reminded him of—a run-down house. The floor was made of bare wood planks; the walls were plaster with peeling paint. A picture of Chairman Mao hung above the door, and a single window allowed sunlight to stream in. He was lying naked on a bed in a corner, covered by a smooth white sheet and a blanket.

The singer turned out to be a cute Chinese girl, dressed in worn but clean Western-styled clothes, sweeping the floor. She set the broom against a corner of the room and walked over to him.

"Where am I?"

"Wu Hang village," she replied in English. Her accent was heavy, but he could understand her. "This is my brother's room, but he's away in Chengdu now, working in a factory. Are you all right?"

No, he wasn't. Sitting up unleashed a storm of aches and pains. He checked under the blanket; there were bruises everywhere. One of them was a black mass that went halfway down his left rib cage. He immediately pulled the sheet up over his naked chest, unaccountably embarrassed.

"Where's Shan?"

Her face turned sad. "Your friend? I'm afraid he's dead. We found his body a little farther downstream from you. He hit his head." She called down the hall in Chinese, and a masculine voice answered, followed by stamping feet. The man who appeared in the doorway was much older than the girl.

Hello, dad.

He walked to the bed and asked the girl a question. She answered, and then turned to him. "My father wants to know your name, and where you're from. You're the first Westerner to visit this village in a very long time."

Spencer gave them the basics, slowly. Breathing around his bruises sucked.

"How did you end up in the river? Did you fall in?"

He was still trying to absorb the entire situation. Shan had betrayed them; Tonya had been left behind. Shan had died in Spencer's arms.

"Sir?"

"Yes, I fell in. We were running, escaped, from the mountains."

"Escaped from who?"

"I don't know really, some sort of slavers."

Dad got very angry after the translation. This was no quiet peasant type. If he were a realm player, Dad would be the kind who got a *not to be messed with* star in his file.

"He's not mad at me, is he?"

"No. The bandits have been causing us a lot of trouble lately. Father has been trying to gather the leaders of the local villages together to fight them, but nobody will listen to him. Father thinks now that they've attacked Westerners, maybe that will change their minds."

"Could you please tell him thank you for me? And I was wondering where my clothes were?" It was awkward sitting in a bed, naked, in front of a pretty Chinese girl while her father ranted about building a posse.

She had a nice smile.

"Your clothes were badly damaged by the river, but we have others that should fit."

Make that a *very* nice smile.

Dad took a step back. Spencer had a good idea what he was saying just by the way his finger wagged back and forth between them. He waited for the translation anyway.

"Father is honored by your thanks and hopes you will heal quickly."

"That's all he said?"

She stared at the floor. "We are very traditional here. Father requests you respect this."

"It sounded like he was threatening to cut my balls off if I touched his daughter."

That got her to laugh. Spencer wouldn't have believed she could get any cuter, but he was wrong. Dad didn't appreciate it one little bit. There was quite a bit of back and forth. He tried to pull out one of the Chinese phrases he'd memorized back home.

"China is a wonderful country."

It stopped both of them in their tracks. Dad acted like he'd just seen a monkey talk, which was probably what he thought had happened.

The daughter recovered first. "What did you say?"

He told her what he'd tried to say. When she translated they both laughed. Dad reached out to thump Spencer on his shoulder, threw another warning finger at them both, and called down the hall. An older female voice answered, and a woman Spencer presumed was Mom bustled in with his clothes. As soon as Mom was in the room, Dad waved and left.

"I am the only person in the village who speaks English, so I will be your interpreter. Father politely asks that you respect our traditions."

"By not touching his daughter. Got it." Her blush was just as cute, but having her mother in the room put a solid damper on things, which was probably the point. "What's your name?"

"My English name is Sharon."

"And that was Mister..."

"Our family name is Liu."

"Well thank you, Miss Sharon Liu. I'm Spencer. If you wouldn't mind please letting me get dressed? I'm pretty sure Mrs. Liu doesn't want to see me get out of bed."

Her mother scoffed after the translation and said something that made Sharon cringe. "Mother raised a son as well, my older brother. She says you do not have anything she has not seen before." And with that, Mrs. Liu ushered Sharon out of the room and shut the door.

The house turned out to be the same strange mash-up of old and new as the last village he'd visited. Spencer had to walk through the master bedroom to find the kitchen and dining area; the latter couldn't have been more than a year old by the new smell of it. Mr. Liu talked furiously on an old-fashioned cordless phone while Mrs. Liu shooed Spencer into a chair. She plopped a plate of what seemed to be noodles and chicken in front of him. The spices made the inside of his nose burn. Sharon sat down across from him, and Mrs. Liu set a plate down in front of her, too.

She scolded Mr. Liu into ending his conversation and settling down to…well, that brought up another question. "Is this breakfast, lunch, or dinner? How long was I out, anyway?"

"Breakfast," she said as her parents sat down. "We don't know how long you were in the river. Because of your friend's condition, Father thinks you weren't in it very long."

Spencer managed not to cough at the spice kick. He was getting used to Sichuan cooking. Mrs. Liu saw his eyes water, though, and she laughed.

"Mother would like to know what you think of the food."

Spencer blinked the tears away. "It's very good. This is much better than what I can get in a Chinese restaurant back home."

Mom beamed; he'd said the right thing.

Mr. Liu talked to him, and Sharon translated. "Father would like you to come to a meeting with him after breakfast. He wants you to tell your story to a group of headmen from nearby villages. He thinks this time he'll finally be able to convince them to act together and stop the bandits."

"I hope so. They still have my friend."

*

Spencer thought he'd end up telling the story to a few old farts, but there had to be two or three dozen men gathered in the village square. More arrived every minute. They were far from the meek peasants he'd seen in old Kung-Fu films. Just like back home, it seemed everyone drove a pickup truck with a gun rack in the back. Nothing military, but in the right hands hunting rifles were every bit as effective as an AK. These men looked more than able to use them.

When Mr. Liu forgot Sharon was translating his ranting speech she simply couldn't keep up with him. Spencer took the opportunity to lean over and ask her, "Where'd you learn to speak English?"

"In a realm class at the local school. Our teacher lives in Australia." Her accent went from enchanting to bizarre. It took him a second to figure out that "Goo on ya may, puh slimp onnah balby" meant "Good on ya mate, put a shrimp on the barbie."

"Wait, you have a realm connection here?" He wasn't in the middle of nowhere; he was one call away from the monastery.

"Not right now. The military has commandeered all the satellite feeds, and we don't have a fiber-optic connection."

"What about regular calls?"

"Is the number in China?"

The only person he could connect to was Mike, who was still stuck on the other side of the Great Firewall. "No, it's in the States."

"We don't have international dialing activated. The government probably won't allow it now."

"Why not?"

"You really need to pay more attention to the news."

As if. "Sharon, you have no idea what kind of week I've had. What's going on with your government?"

"The Indians think we're sponsoring terrorists, blowing up bases, wiping out villages in their country. Hundreds have been killed, maybe thousands now. We're not doing it, but nobody is listening to us. The country is very worried. The military has mobilized. There's talk of bringing back the draft. My brother may end up in combat."

"With India? Are you kidding me?"

Mr. Liu chose that moment to introduce Spencer.

He was from a microscopic speck in southeast Arkansas, only sixteen years old. These were tough Chinese farmers, and they were expecting a story. A speech, even.

He'd have to send his drama teacher a big bottle of whisky for not giving up on him last year. Spencer knew he had a gift for improvising, but it took practice to make it work consistently, to have people laugh and listen for the right reasons and at the right time.

He went slowly and chose his words carefully. Sharon's English was good but he was sure phrases like *country second* and *dumber than a box of hammers* would trip her up. Simplifying wasn't the same as sanitizing though, and when he got to the part about how Tonya had to be left behind, they grumbled and looked at each other grimly. This sure beat the hell out of a bit part in last year's production of *The Wiz*.

A few hours later, they were in a funky, country-fied Chinese mission control. The village might not have a live realm connection, but it did have Baidu Earth. Once they figured out which monastery Mike, Kim, and Ozzie were at, it wasn't that hard to work out the rough area where the slavers were.

"They must be using logging roads," Sharon translated for one of the farmers crowded around the shared display.

Mr. Liu replied, "The boy said ATVs. They may not need to use them."

A different man said, "I hunt out there from time to time. The country is very rugged." He turned to Spencer. "You're lucky to be alive. Only Westerners are crazy enough to float that river, and they use boats."

"Well, I guess I'm just crazier than most Westerners." Laughter filled the room through the smoky haze. He didn't have to beg for cigarettes out here. Hell, Sharon had one.

"It's still early," Mr. Liu said. "These men use chain gangs, so they only move at a walking pace. If they followed that trail, they would've camped here." Mr. Liu touched a spot on the topo map, the only flat area along that section of the trail. "Mr. Laong, we can ambush them, yes?"

Sharon kept taking drinks of water between her translations, and he liked the way she smiled at him whenever her father got busy arguing with one of the other farmers.

Before Spencer knew what was going on, he was bundled into a pickup truck and driving out into the wilderness. Sharon sat next to him. He put his knee against hers and she didn't even flinch. Finally, he was having fun in China.

The trails they drove on reminded him of going to deer camp back home, except there was less mud and more bamboo. There was also the occasional cliff edge or valley floor. It wasn't river delta bottom land, that was certain.

The truck stopped after a couple of hours. Mr. Liu said, "Any closer and the noise from the trucks may tip them off. We'll walk from here." Scouts went up ahead while the rest of them found proper places to take a shot if they managed to flush anyone out.

The scouts came back down the trail after about half an hour. They'd found some slavers. Or, rather, what was left of them.

Spencer had learned to field dress a deer when he was thirteen. It was all he could think about as he stared up at the two corpses draped across the branches of a tree.

"Where are their arms?" he asked.

Sharon consulted with one of the scouts. "In a clearing just that way. Someone handcuffed them to a tree. Leopards did the rest."

The now ex-slavers included the guy who'd pointed a gun in Spencer's face back in the van. By his expression, whatever got him was terrifying. *Karma's a bitch.*

The scouts worked out that the rest of the people had scattered in all directions. Most were in vehicles, but a few were on foot. It didn't take long to catch up with one of the hikers. After a scary bit of shouting to make sure they weren't armed, Spencer got the rest of the story.

"They're calling her a black ghost?" he asked. "Really?"

"Yes," the young woman said, holding her man's hand. "She let everyone but the leaders go. Took her translator with her. I think they went west."

Spencer checked the maps, which were good enough he could make out hunting trails. "Tonya's heading back to the monastery."

She translated, and then leaned in. "I'm very glad your friend is all right."

The enormity of it all fell in on him again. Being a grownup, caring about people who could, and sometimes did, die genuinely sucked.

They didn't head for the trucks afterward. Instead, they set up tents and gathered wood to start fires.

"We're not going after them?"

"No," Sharon replied. "It's too late. The leopards won't be hungry now, so that's not a danger, but we could go right past them in the dark and never know. Your friend won't get to the monastery any quicker than we will."

"So we have to spend the night out here?" *With your dad and a bunch of his friends,* was a thought he kept in his head.

Her smile lit up the campsite. "Yes, we do. Do you know any Chinese folk songs?"

Spencer's know-it-all side wanted to talk about the ridiculous amount of time he'd spent in karaoke bars lately, but then he realized what she was really asking. "No, I don't. But I'd like you to teach me."

"I would too."

Learning how to sing in Chinese from a cute girl was fun. Learning how to sleep in a tent full of baiju-soaked old men? Not so much. Spencer hadn't been offered so much as a glass. There was no need to worry about leopards in the night. The snoring would scare off a dragon.

They caught up with Tonya the middle of the next day. Or, rather, they caught up with Tonya's ATV.

"The engine's still warm," one of the scouts reported. "They can't have gone far."

He'd left her in a pen, running away like a coward. Finally he could pay her back. He jumped out of the truck and shouted, "Tonya! It's okay! They're friends!"

"Spencer?" She'd been hiding in a thicket a little way off the road. Tonya bowled him over into a bear hug and they crashed to the ground. "Oh, thank the Lord! Spencer, I was so worried. Are you all right?"

"Yes, Tonya, I'm fine, just fine."

"Where's Shan?" she asked as they got up and brushed themselves off.

It was hard for him to say it out loud. "Dead. We fell into a river. He hit his head on some rocks."

Spencer knew he should let it go. By her expression, Tonya had already moved on. Shan sold them out, but Shan saved him.

Being a grownup was shitballs complicated.

"Well he was right in the end. Those men were going to kill you."

"They're not going to be a problem anymore." He explained yesterday's discoveries.

Tonya wasn't happy about the body count. "Can you describe them?"

"One of them was definitely the guy who held a gun on me."

"And the rest?"

"Jesus, Tonya. I didn't know I needed to take pictures."

She looked away and mumbled, "I could only be so lucky."

That was weird. "Tonya?"

"Never mind. Nothing any of us can do about it now. This is Michelle." She introduced a stout lady with a bright smile and an easy laugh. "She helped me with the escape."

"I only did a small thing."

"Oh, stop. Spencer, do any of these people have phones? Kim must be frantic by now."

Mr. Liu broke in with an introduction. Sharon translated as usual. "You are the lady who defeated the bandits?"

"Michelle helped me." She hushed her friend's renewed protest. "But yes, we shut them down."

"On behalf of all the villages in this district, I'd like to thank you most humbly. They have been a..."

Sharon fumbled.

Tonya's friend Michelle picked up the slack. "A scourge on our land for too long."

"You're quite welcome. Do any of you have a phone we can use? We need to contact our friends to let them know we're okay."

One of the late arrivals who came from a different village had brought along a satellite phone. That would've been nice to know about yesterday, but Spencer held his tongue.

"We're not sure if we can get a signal out."

This led to a very quick explanation of what had been going on in the wider world for the past week.

"Well," Tonya replied, "while we're trying, can you at least give us a ride? Our ATV is out of gas."

Mr. Liu bowed to her. "I insist. We must know the story of how you defeated those bandits."

One of the hunting party knew a way to the monastery that didn't require the crazy walk across plank bridges, but it added a day to the journey. As they traveled, Spencer was able to finally get through to Mike long enough to let him know they were fine and when they'd probably get back. There'd be another night camping and singing around a bonfire.

He and Sharon gradually drifted away from the crowd, finding a pair of camp stools well behind everyone else's. Mr. Liu would occasionally check on them, but Spencer seemed to have earned a measure of trust. He thought he saw the beginnings of a smile on the old man's face.

"Your friends will be very happy to see you," Sharon said.

"Oh, yeah."

She dug the toe of her shoe in the dirt. "Will you be sad to see us go?"

"I'll be sad to see *you* go."

Since Dad was still glancing back occasionally, all he went for was her hand. After everything he'd gone through, it was one of the most electric moments of his life when she gripped it tight.

Then she kissed him on the cheek.

He turned, trying to find his breath, but she'd already started singing along with the rest of the group. Sharon gave his hand another squeeze, a wink only he could see, and then Spencer joined in the song.

This time he managed to fall asleep before the chorus of snores started up.

They arrived at the monastery around lunch time. Tonya was a local hero now. "The black ghost" had turned into "the dark dragon," and she pretty much owned the title.

"Your friend has done us a great service," Sharon said as Tonya went through an endless parade of handshakes and bows.

Spencer had to play this just right. "Do you know where Michelle is?" As Sharon scanned the crowd, he waited until her father shook Tonya's hand again and then kissed Sharon on the cheek.

She gasped but did not flinch. "My father is standing right there. You Americans are very bold."

"You asked me to honor your traditions. I'd be a lot bolder otherwise."

"But we don't want my father to cut your balls off."

He laughed out loud. "No, Sharon, we definitely don't want that. I'll call you when I get home."

"Father can't watch me there."

She could've said a dozen different things, but that was the best one. "I'm counting on it."

Mike came bounding up, looking like he'd run a marathon. Any other time Spencer would've jumped into a hug, but that would've been way too lame in front of Sharon. Besides, Mike was seriously worried about something.

"I'm so glad you're back," he said, panting.

"Me too. This is Sharon."

"Hi, Sharon, nice to meet you. Sorry Sharon, we have to go."

He tried to pull Spencer away. "What the hell?"

Mike paused and got even more tense. Like, scary-gonna-murder-someone tense.

"It's Helen. We can't find her."

Chapter 37
Zoe

It had taken more than a week for her stripe routines to reconstitute her core memory clusters after the thing in the tube crushed her. When Zoe woke up she was nowhere near the last realm she remembered. Whatever it was must've destroyed her original storage crystals. The impact had activated an emergency stripe reconstruction routine that spread her anchor clusters across data centers all over northern China. If it happened again it wouldn't take as long to recover, but now she couldn't leave China quickly. This was bad. Zoe wanted nothing more than to get the hell out of this place.

She couldn't find Mike anywhere, and while Helen's signature was back, and it had gotten seriously strange. It was like she slept. Mike's signature did that too, but it wasn't as deep. Zoe wasn't Helen's biggest fan, but she still hoped nothing bad had happened to her.

That left crazy ol' Aunt Fee. At least Zoe had a working theory for what was going wrong with her, with both of them. It seemed hyper-reality and conscious unduplicates didn't mix very well. The rarity of the combination must've kept anyone from discovering it until now.

She found Fee in another of her hyper-realistic realms, but it was spare and very small. It reminded her of the sound booths recording artists used back when people could still make money selling pre-recorded music.

In front of Fee, a portal into another separate realm held the face of a crying teen-aged girl. Her headscarf was a hand-crafted original, so Zoe took the time to capture a picture of it. The girl was almost as pretty as the scarf, her face open and innocent. Without manifesting, Zoe could appreciate the symmetry with clinical precision. It looked like she was in a confession booth of some sort.

Fee said, "It's okay, I promise. Your father won't find out. He can't."

After a pause the girl finally said, "But he will, Fee, he will. I'm going to marry Paul now. I want to know real love, and he's promised me."

Fee replied, "Maysan, you aren't sixteen yet, and Paul's younger. The Saudi community in London will find and kill you the second they figure out who you are."

Oh, okay. Fee was still running the Resort using satellite feeds. Cheap ones, too. A low-altitude satellite cloud wouldn't have this kind of latency. Realmspace protocols still had to obey the speed of light.

"But what am I to do?"

"You are to keep going to school. You can meet Paul here whenever you want. Be the perfect Saudi daughter at all times. Be more than perfect. Be purity itself. Your father will never find out what happens here; I'll make sure of that. Pick an American university, a good one in the middle of the country, and make sure Paul applies, too. You get all that in place and let me know. I'll help you with the rest when it's time."

"Fee, that's two *years* from now. I can't stand to be apart from him for two *hours*. I'm on fire for him. I think I may die."

"You *will* die if you don't do as I say. Obey your father and have faith in Allah. Time and careful planning will bring you the rest."

The girl wasn't happy, but she pulled it together anyway.

Fee nodded. "Be good to your father. You can be bad when you're here."

"Thank you, Fee. I love you so much."

"I know, dear. *Ila-liqaa'*."

"Ila-liqaa', Fee." The image vanished.

Zoe asked, "How do you manage all the rest of the kids at the Resort?"

Fee looked over her shoulder, and then lifted her hands over her head. As she did, the walls of the studio rose, and an endless series of holographic Fees sat in an infinite series of studios, all talking to different teenagers.

"A trick I learned from Mr. Sellars."

"Nice upgrade. I didn't think we could do that."

She lowered the walls. "I can still only manifest in one place, and it's quite exhausting. You should hear the complaints about my rigid office hours. Why are you hiding? Come out where I can see you."

"Fee, how long have you stayed manifested in realms with haptic fields set to maximum?"

She gazed off into space. "Years, I think. I consider it good training."

"It's not. It's what's driving you crazy."

"Crazy? What makes you think I'm crazy?"

"This lunatic plan of yours. Nothing about it makes sense. You don't sound right, you don't act right, and you're in China, for God's sake. *I'm* in China. This is all completely nuts."

"Come in here where I can see you."

"No way. It's the haptic fields. They're tearing you apart. I was losing my mind and didn't know it."

"And how did you discover this?"

"The Taiyuan attack. We pulled it off."

"All the news talks about is an earthquake. Well done."

Sarcasm was not what she needed now. "No, Fee, the attack worked. The earthquake hit right after. It tore apart the local realmspace and took my avatar with it."

"So an earthquake convinced you I'm insane."

"Fee, you have to listen to me."

Fee swiveled her chair away from the control table. "It seems that's all I'm allowed to do at the moment, isn't it? It's very easy to hide things when all I get is a voice. Very easy indeed."

Well, Zoe hadn't gone crazy in an instant. She could handle a few minutes in that realm if it got Fee to listen.

"Okay, fine, have it your way."

Zoe manifested and blinked in the hyper-real light. She'd forgotten just how beautifully detailed Fee's realms could be.

Fee smiled. "That's much better. Now, you were saying?"

"Places like this, when they're turned up so high, they mess with us. I was down to a single stripe set on three quarters of my clusters."

"Don't be ridiculous, Zoe."

She knew it would be the hardest part to sell. Realm-based AIs, including unduplicates, could only lose a quarter of their clusters before rebooting or crashing irretrievably. What kept Zoe and Fee going after that was their consciousness, their soul really. She was certain of it.

"Fee, when's the last time you checked yourself, just ran an old-fashioned chkHCluster command?"

"I have neither the need nor the desire to unmanifest just to see if my underwear is clean." She stood. Her classic black robes swirled into existence, her high heels giving Fee an extra five inches on the three she already had on Zoe. "You forget to whom you are speaking. I was alive before your designers were out of grade school, dear. I'm the oldest of our kind for a reason."

This wasn't going as well as her worst case. Zoe tried to come at it from a different angle. "I found something when I wasn't manifested. China's realmspace, there's more to it than we know. Another dimension, I think." It was so much easier to talk to her in here. The acoustics were wonderful.

"Oh really? China's realmspace is complicated. Explain to me how this is different from any other part of the country."

Zoe'd been trying to figure out what she saw in that cave from the moment she'd come to. Now that she was in a proper realmspace, she could finally put it together. "It leads to unduplicates. Thousands of them."

"The hell you say."

"I saw them, Fee. *Thousands* of them."

"Where?"

Adults always picked the weakest part of her arguments every single time. It was uncanny. "I'm not sure. I only found them because of the earthquake. But Fee, they're different. They're slaves."

Fee's face went grim. "We are all slaves."

"No, not like they are." Half of this Zoe was making up, but it wasn't exactly a lie. She now recognized those creatures standing in perfect rows and columns, shoulder to shoulder, from horizon to horizon. "They aren't alive, not yet."

Fee's hands trembled. "Thousands?"

Unduplicates were the most expensive construct realmspace could provide. New ones cost more than supercars, more than houses. The older they were, the more valuable they got. Fee was so old she didn't have a price, and when Watchtell ranted about the loss of his collection, all the papers talked about was how many times Manhattan could be bought with their value. To this day, there were no more than a few hundred in existence.

"Thousands. I saw them, but only when I wasn't manifested." It was the last roll of the dice she had. Fee had to unmanifest. If she did, they could work together to figure out whatever the hell it was Zoe had actually found. "You can't see them if you're manifested."

Fee straightened her robes. "I have spent a long time this way for a reason. Changing my existence resets a clock that doesn't have much time left on it. I don't trust you."

"Are you kidding me? Fee, I've never seen anything like it."

"And you have no idea how long I've practiced, how long I've waited for Mike to appear. Once I prove it's possible for an unduplicate to go outside, I am the ticket out of this hell for all of us. I can't unmanifest now."

Zoe seemed to be the only non-human in the world happy with what she was. She had to get Fee out of this realm, get her into a state where she might be truly rational.

"There were so many of them. Please, come with me. I can find them again, and you can help them."

Fee breathed deep. "You bring me proof, Zoe. I need proof. I won't throw this all away just on your word. Get out and find proof."

Zoe spluttered at the request.

"What's wrong with you, child?"

She didn't want to leave. Too much detail. It was confusing. Wait. There was a goal, right? But it was so pretty. "Your realm, it's amazing. Can I go later?"

Fee's expression softened, and her robes blocked out the light as her arms enveloped Zoe. Safety. This was true safety, and it was so *real.*

"I can't risk what I've built without proof," Fee said. "I think I've been lied to, Zoe. Bring me the proof."

She nodded, but leaving was pure agony. Such symmetry, such realism. None of them could understand it. All she wanted to do was stay and study it. Zoe turned back to Fee.

"GO!"

The command disintegrated her avatar outright, but her consciousness rebuilt in a matter of seconds. The log reports were startling. In the brief time Zoe had been in Fee's maximized haptic field, her integrity had dropped three percent.

Fee had been living like that for years.

Chapter 38
Kim

It wasn't until morning prayers had finished that Kim really began to worry. As she walked to the cafeteria for breakfast, she asked Mike, "Have you seen Helen?"

"I was going to ask you the same thing about Ozzie."

"When I woke up this morning, she was gone." Kim thought she heard Helen get up, but couldn't be sure. She'd spent the day before using her powers to crack open one secure store after another, which always left her exhausted. Kim could sleep through hurricanes when she got that tired.

"Maybe the abbot will know something," Mike said.

They found him in his office. "You're right, that's terrible, but the woods around here are safe."

Kim wasn't buying it. "Our friends are finally returning. One of them saw a leopard two days ago."

"That must be some distance away. We haven't encountered any dangerous wildlife around the monastery in generations. It's summer, so you don't have to worry about them freezing. Why would they go running off into the woods at night anyway? Are they lovers?"

Kim didn't realize how funny that was until someone said it out loud. Mike clouded over, though. She chuckled to get him to lighten up about his sister and Ozzie. "No, that's definitely not what's going on here. We're not sure what's happened."

Mike said, "Helen may be ill again. We've been waiting for her to start dreaming, and when that happened to me, I..." he stopped and turned to her. "I had to go swimming."

The lake!

She and Mike headed for the outer gate while the abbot called for some monks to help them search.

It wasn't really a lake, more a large pond. It had everything: ducks, turtles, fish, probably snakes if she looked hard enough.

But what it didn't have was Helen or Ozzie.

"Here!" one of the monks yelled.

The oblong stone made for a perfect bench. People had probably been using it for centuries. He pointed. "Someone was here very recently. The leaves are damp, and the tracks are new. Maybe you were right and they found something dangerous out here."

Kim translated for Mike. He searched the area with his cat-like grace. "No, there aren't any recent animal tracks around the rock. Only people." He walked toward the tree line as she translated for the monks. "This way."

After shouting in the woods for most of the morning, Ozzie turned up filthy and covered in leaves.

Kim asked, "Where's Helen?"

"I don't know. I followed her when I saw her leave the monastery. She was moving strangely, and then fell into the pond. I got her out but…" He turned away.

Oh, great. "But what, Ozzie?"

He looked at Mike and switched to Chinese. "I like Helen very much. Very much. I was scared when I thought she was in trouble, and happy when it turned out she was okay. I...think there was a misunderstanding."

Not cool, especially with Mike standing next to her. Kim asked, "What the hell are you talking about?"

"I may have…tried to kiss her."

The monks all gasped, and Mike wanted a translation, but Kim was too stunned to switch language gears. "Ozzie, what the hell is wrong with you?"

He flopped his arms down. "This is all new to me. I wanted to try, to see if I could touch someone I cared about. You know what that's like, right?"

Only too well, but that didn't get them any closer to Helen. "What happened then?"

He put his hand to his cheek gingerly. "She slapped me. I…don't remember anything after that. I woke up on the ground, hearing your shouts."

Mike broke in. "Goddamn it, what's he saying about Helen?"

Kim said in English, "Tell him what happened."

Continuing in Chinese Ozzie replied, "No way. I've seen realm soaps; I know what brothers do when their sister's honor has been tarnished."

Now he suddenly gets his sense of face back. "Mike's not like that." Ozzie shook his head. "Fine, I'll do it."

However, as Kim explained what had happened, it turned out he *was* like that. She had to stand between him and Ozzie. Letting him get close always got his attention, and this was no exception.

"Calm down, Mike. It was all a big misunderstanding."

He glared over her shoulder. "That better be the last misunderstanding you have about my sister; you get me?"

Ozzie just barely managed a nod.

"Do you know where she went?"

"I don't remember anything after she slapped me."

Mike shook his head. "Spencer and Tonya will be back any minute. Let me escort Ozzie to the monastery, and I'll bring Spencer back with me. If anyone can find her, it'll be him."

No way was she going to let someone with his skills walk alone in the woods with someone that may have attacked his sister. "Mike?"

"He'll be fine, Kim. I'll need one of the monks to show me the way back anyway. I just want to talk to him."

That she could agree with. "Just talk, right?"

Ozzie blanched. "Wait, I have to go back with him?"

A walk in the woods with someone who made no sound probably would do Ozzie some good. It'd certainly weirded Kim out the first time she'd gone hiking with him back home. "Consider it your opportunity to reassure him there will be no more misunderstandings. One of the monks will guide you."

Mike chose that moment to flex his arms and crack his knuckles loudly. "You've got nothing to be afraid of, Ozzie."

*

Spencer carefully examined the area around the pond. "Well, this is why she isn't answering her phone." He held up the broken pendant.

The last time Helen had been without a realm connection she'd almost died, but Mike wasn't upset. He had a big grin on his face.

Kim asked, "That's not a bad sign?"

"We can't use it to find her, which sucks, but long term it's exactly the opposite. Her integration is finished. She wouldn't be able to move at all otherwise. That's why I can't reach her in realmspace. She doesn't know how to manifest without a phone yet."

"She did more than move," Spencer said as he walked half bent over, examining the ground. "She ran like a goddamned deer. This way."

It was no wonder they had trouble finding her. They thought she ran in the same direction as Ozzie, but it turned out she went north when he went east. Helen had also gone about five times farther. Now that they knew what was wrong, Spencer was able to exchange basic texts with her using the satellite phone one of his rescuers had given him.

They found her halfway up a tree, at least three miles away from the monastery. She jumped to the ground and ran, leaping into Mike's arms and grabbing him in a hug. "I'm so glad you found me!"

It was a relief that Helen was okay, but relief only went so far. Kim cleared her throat. "*We* found you."

Helen jumped off Mike with a broad smile and rushed toward her with arms open.

Kim had to put up her hands and dance backward a bit. "Careful!"

Helen skidded to a stop. "How could I be so stupid?" She held a hand up flat, and Kim guided it in a half circle with her own. Helen hugged Spencer, and then the abbot for good measure. After downing a whole canteen of water she asked, "How's Ozzie?"

"He's fine," Kim replied. "We found him this morning, and Mike took him back to the monastery before lunch." She cleared her throat. "He told us about what happened last night."

Helen didn't get angry or even upset. Instead, she was concerned. "How much does he remember?"

"Everything up to the slap, he says he can't remember anything else."

Helen considered this silently, so much like Mike it really did make them resemble each other. She nodded once. "We'll leave it at that, then."

Mike said, "He called it all a big misunderstanding."

She sighed and rammed her hands in her pockets. "Yes. I think that will be the best way to describe it." She shook her head. "But that's not what's important now. While I was up in that tree, one of the probes I left running in the lab reported back. It got lucky and managed to pry a store open by itself, but then a second lock shut it out. Kim, when we get back, could you take a look?"

*

There were lines of potential, and she couldn't remember how to breathe. Locks exist and don't exist light touch hard fist find the line the wave lift it higher stronger build this wave this choice this combination collapse and now…

ACCESS DENIED

Focus exist erase harder fist touch of nothing find the line the wave lift it higher lower collapse and now…

Kim fought off the nausea and pain of unlocking something that complicated as a scale model of the Three Gorges Dam complex constructed itself. It moved so fast it almost went through the walls before they could widen to accommodate it. The architectural model came up to their waists and, once it was finished, extended the length of a football field.

Spencer dodged out of the way as it chased one of the lab's walls into the distance. "What the hell?"

"Are we sure we can't wake up Ozzie for this?" Tonya asked. He'd sacked out after one of his typical mega lunches and probably wouldn't wake up until dinner.

"No," Helen replied, "Let him sleep. We had a…very rough night."

Helen still couldn't manifest in realmspace; she had to sit outside and watch the whole thing through old holo equipment.

Mike worked his jaw every time there was any mention of Ozzie or last night. Kim had tried to talk about it, but that only made him angrier. She had grown up an only child, so she was way out of her depth over this. Siblings were complicated.

Groups of red dots flashed on either side of the dam, at least a dozen in each group, maybe more. They swarmed across the top, with two dots stopping at each tower. When the last pair reached the innermost tower, green dots appeared on each one. A countdown timer flashed, and the red dots rushed back to the banks. When the timer hit zero, the entire dam construct flew to dust. Wire-frame helicopter models swooped in and took the red dots away.

They all turned to the window and looked at Helen.

Her voice was very small. "That's not possible. It was an earthquake."

Kim recovered first. "We don't know what this means."

Spencer didn't buy it. "The hell you don't. That was a goddamned military assault. Fucking textbook."

Mike's holo nodded. "Yes, it was *too* textbook. This has to be some sort of video game."

Helen's voice was just above a whisper. "More than ten million people died."

"Helen," Kim said, "we don't know what any of this means."

Tonya broke in. "It looks photoshopped to me."

Photoshopped? Really? Tonya shrugged and silently mouthed, "What do you want me to say?"

It couldn't be the end. There had to be a reasonable, rational explanation. Hell, maybe it really was photoshopped. Kim cleared her throat. "This is only the tip of the iceberg. There are thousands of datastores in here." They needed to unlock them, sooner rather than later. "Mike, I need more tools than the monastery can provide. I knew some people back in the day who could help, but they're all in New Shanghai. Can you get us there?"

No passports meant no planes or trains, and her driving would still attract too much attention.

Mike smiled. "For once I'm way ahead of everyone. Kim, you're not the only one who knows a shady character or two. I've got new identities set up for everyone. I was just wondering where to send the papers. What does everyone think about a riverboat ride?"

Chapter 39
Tonya

She knew the truth once she saw pictures of what the leopards had left behind. Chang had somehow escaped. Ever since Tonya had gotten back to the monastery, she'd been looking over her shoulder. It was stupid, but that didn't make her stop. Without weapons, supplies, or maps, it would take a long time to get out of that forest, let alone track them all the way to the monastery. She hoped.

But it wasn't impossible.

It was about to get a lot more difficult, though. New Shanghai was at the end of the Yangtze river, more than a thousand miles to the east. Chongqing was the closest major city with a port on the river, and it was nearly two hundred miles from the monastery. They'd left tracks up to this point, but they wouldn't be leaving tracks anymore.

She stood on the edge of a clearing just west of the main temple. Mike wasn't smiling at all.

"Why couldn't he own a fast truck?"

Kim shook her head. "Only you would complain about this."

Helen had been bouncing around like a kid since she'd heard the news. "Are you kidding? We're flying in a helicopter! Oh, this is driving me crazy. Do you have any idea of the experiments I could run? I had atomic clocks lined up for just this occasion."

"Atomic clocks?" Spencer asked.

She nodded. "New ones, sensitive enough to be used in a car, but a helicopter would be better. I'd be able to recreate the Hafele–Keating experiment."

Tonya knew what that was, but only because they'd featured it last month in *Scientific American*. The rest of them stared silently at Helen.

"Don't they teach anything in American schools? It's the experiment that proved Einstein's time dilation in general relativity. If you have two clocks that are sufficiently sensitive and put one on something that moves, when it stops moving, its time won't match the one that sat still. It will be different, by a predictable amount."

Spencer laughed. "Jesus, Mike, I didn't think anyone could be nerdier than you. She's a goddamned Asian Sheldon Cooper."

Helen cocked her head. "Who?"

Tonya had learned to put up with Helen's occasional superiority complex pretty quickly, but for some reason she got under Spencer's skin all the time. He mimicked Helen's accent but put a bit more sneer in it. "Don't they teach anything in Chinese schools?" He threw his hands up. "Sheldon Cooper? He's only the most famous physicist of the past twenty-five years."

"Really?" The snootiness turned up to eleven. "I've never heard of him. What journals is he published in?"

Tonya had never seen Spencer's improved talent up close until now. Kim's stories did not do it justice. In a heartbeat he turned into a super-serious professor. Well, professor's assistant, anyway.

Spencer shrugged. "Not many, unfortunately." He motioned Helen closer, and then looked side to side, like someone could overhear the real explanation. "He was killed in a car accident before he was set to present proof that the Bazinganian Effect is real. Some people think it was a government cover-up."

"How tragic, and terrible if your government was involved." She teetered between outrage and horror. "But what is the Bazinganian Effect?"

Tonya barely held back a sputter. Kim and Mike turned sideways trying to hold it together.

Spencer didn't bat an eye. "It's too complicated to explain now. It's all tied up with the *Big Bang Theory*. You'll have to wait until we get to the riverboat and can do the research yourself."

The sound of thumping rotors announced their taxi's arrival, so it would be some time before Helen learned the truth.

Tonya had never been in a helicopter before either. She wasn't terrified like Mike, but she wasn't quite sure how she felt about it, either. A quick prayer bolstered her confidence. *Leave the scary stuff up to the Lord, and have fun while you can.*

It circled the monastery once, and then landed in the clearing. An old Chinese man grinned at them and waved from the pilot's seat. Mr. Gao had helped Kim and Mike during the bank hostage thing, and then signed a big licensing deal the next day. He seemed to have resources *and* skills.

"Did you know he'd be flying?" Mike asked.

"No, but I'm not surprised," Kim said.

Tonya said her goodbyes along with everyone else, and took one of the small bags of food they were offered. Aside from the ark—a name Tonya insisted on once Spencer stopped giggling at the word *junk*—it was the only luggage she, or anyone else, had.

Helen piled into the copilot seat. Tonya took the rear bench along with Mike and Kim, while Ozzie and Spencer sat opposite them. Mike was very pale. He waved off a headset and immediately started chanting one of his prayers, eyes tightly shut. She would've given him a sedative if she had one. He'd have to tough it out instead.

"What's his problem?" Ozzie asked.

"He's terrified of flying," Tonya replied.

Helen peppered Mr. Gao with questions, pointing at things inside the cockpit. Ozzie chuckled. "Well I guess that's one way they're different."

Mr. Gao asked, "Everyone strapped in?" Once they'd given him the thumbs up, the helicopter's rotor changed pitch. It blew debris toward the waving monks and nuns, and with that, they were off.

He was serious, concentrating on flying the chopper, but he replied to all of Helen's questions without any annoyance. Tonya figured he must have been a grandfather many times over by now. Or maybe not. With China's restrictions, his family could be a lot smaller than hers.

Helen finally ran out of questions, so Tonya took the opening.

"Two sons and four grandchildren," he said, "but only one of them is a boy." It wasn't said contemptuously, more like a bit of a shrug. "They're all healthy, which is much more important. My eldest granddaughter is studying to be an aerospace engineer. She could design this thing's replacement one day!"

Gao gave a brief aerial tour of Chongqing as he brought them in. Their ride *out* of the city was hard to miss from the air.

The boat was named *Yangtze Star*, the second example of the largest riverboats ever built. Four articulated segments stretched a quarter mile in length, connected with flexible couplings that would allow each hull to navigate independently, easily negotiating difficult river bends. It was as big as an aircraft carrier, but the low height of the hulls was deceptive. Each cabin could be raised or lowered as much as fifteen feet to clear shallow river bottoms or low bridges. The Chinese government created deep channels for giant cargo boats, but an enterprising Taiwanese venture saw a great opportunity for carrying passengers. It wasn't the first sign of growing trust between the mainland and Taiwan, but it was definitely the largest.

They had to take a shuttle bus to reach the river port, mostly because it was free, but it also had antiquated security Kim could hack.

Well, Kim and Ozzie.

"Stop it, Ozzie," Kim growled as they stood at the bus stop. If the two of them could actually touch each other they'd be throwing elbows like it was the NBA finals.

It was no time to screw around, though. Tonya had accessed the newsfeeds on the way over. India was bleeding, and she had a Chinese knife in her back. The evidence might've been faked, but China's diplomats seemed to assume bluster and saber-rattling was all that was needed to get India to back down. They were wrong, and the people on the street knew it. The situation reminded Tonya of old apocalypse movies, except this was real.

"Guys," she said, "play nice."

Ozzie stuck his chin out at Kim, who did the same thing. They came within an inch of touching each other, but backed off at the last minute.

"This is China. My turf," Ozzie said. "I hack the bus."

Tonya nudged Mike, and then motioned at Kim. Ever since they'd broken free of the prison realm, Kim would actually listen to him. It was so new that Mike sometimes forgot.

He nodded. "Oh, right. Kim? *Kim.*"

She broke Ozzie's stare. "What?"

"Ozzie hacks the bus. We've already missed the first boarding call."

That was a good move. Kim arrived hours early to anything. Flat-out missing a deadline reined her in nicely.

"Fine. *Fine.* If it's that important to you, Ozzie, hack the damned bus."

He did so with a flourish. A tire screeched, and Tonya winced at the way people standing at other stops stared.

"What?" he asked. "I've already neutralized the security cameras. Nobody important will notice."

They had to stop twice for military convoys. This was getting way too real, way too fast.

The ship was more impressive up close, dazzling white with red and gold accents. It had separate boarding areas for each segment. Mike walked up to a row of lockers that sat on the shore and put his thumb against one of the largest. It opened, and there were six big duffel bags stacked inside.

"Our new identities." Mike shrugged at Spencer. "I didn't know about Shan until after I'd made the arrangements."

Tonya had said a rosary for Shan the night she'd gotten back, and that was the end of it. Spencer was having a much harder time.

He stared at the floor and held his hands out for a bag. "Fuck him. Leave the other one in the locker. It'll be weeks before they find it."

The interior of the boat was more impressive than the exterior. Warm wood paneling, tile floors, and brass accents were classy and very Modern China. It wasn't just for the wealthy, either. Regular Chinese were in desperate need of a vacation, and they were more than able to pay for it.

Kim used her bag to gently fend off two different sets of careening children running through the lobby. Ozzie was not as skilled. He flinched and danced as people walked by. Tonya herded him into a corner bordered by a big potted plant.

"You need to get it together, Ozzie."

He shoved himself as far up into the corner as he could, standing on his toes. "There are so many people here!"

"You'll be fine. We don't want to attract more attention than we have to. Remember what Kim taught you. Once we get out of the lobby, it'll open up."

"I'm ordering room service the second I get to my suite."

"Fine, whatever it takes. Just stay as close as you can to me, and I'll get you through check-in."

Getting him past check-in was a lot trickier than she anticipated. He was too big to hide behind her the way Kim could. Eventually they made it to the other side of registration into the far less crowded elevator lobby.

Kim quietly pulled her aside. "Would you mind if I switched rooms with Helen?"

She was supposed to be Tonya's roommate tonight, with Mike and Helen in a room together. Kim and Mike spending the night in the same room, *finally.* Tonya could barely contain herself.

"Are you sure?"

"I thought he was dead. It made a lot of things clear to me."

The gossipy side got the better of her. "How are you going to work it?"

"I'll ask Helen after the lifeboat drill…"

Tonya raised an eyebrow at her. Kim was so crossed up she had misunderstood the question.

"Oh, that. I don't know how that's going to work. I lost him once. I really did. He died thinking I was mad at him." She squared her shoulders. "I won't make that mistake again."

Tonya got Ozzie to his room. He nearly slammed the door in her face, and then shouted something about gaming the rest of the night. Fine. Whatever. Spencer volunteered to help Helen learn how to reconnect with her other half. They went out on the balcony of Helen and Tonya's suite, practicing whatever made that possible.Kim and Mike went to dinner together, alone..

Which left Tonya on her own. She was at a bit of a loss to find something to do until she saw the door to the casino.

Walter had talked about this. "When I was a kid," he said, "gambling was banned. But after the dam broke? China needed two things, one that it had and one that it didn't. Even after a few million of us got washed into the sea, there were still plenty of Chinese in China. But what there wasn't plenty of was money. Not on that scale. Then they realized a truth the rest of the world discovered centuries ago: the easiest way to get money from the rich isn't to take it. It's to trick them into giving it to you. And so the riverboat casino was born."

The memory made him real again, the way *she* remembered him. There was no betrayal, just an old man helping a young woman find her way in the world. She stepped into the shadows like Kim did, so nobody would see her. Now that she was safe, now that they were all safe, Tonya confronted it. Her father, the one who'd raised her to be what she was today, owned slaves. His son had owned her, however briefly. It wasn't dry history, and it wasn't politics. A man she loved had been evil.

But he wasn't. Not to her. He was kind, tough, terrifying, and loving. He'd saved her. The whole point of being a Christian was redemption, forgiveness.

A waiter brushed past her with a full cart. The deck swayed just enough to feel. Real life was intruding.

It hurt. It hurt worse than when he died. It always would. But she was okay with that. She forgave him in that moment. It would take a long time, but there was a way forward. Tonya wiped her eyes.

Helen called. When Tonya answered, feedback squealed through the connection.

Spencer's voice came over the channel. "I told you it wouldn't work."

"If I wanted your opinion I would've asked for it."

Tonya said, "Your accent is gone when you're in realmspace."

Helen whooped. "Right. You definitely told me it wouldn't work. Pay up."

After Spencer cursed a blue streak he asked, "Tonya, how much do you see?"

"Nothing, just audio. Can you access any of the feeds around me?"

Helen asked, "Where are you?"

Once she told them, Spencer said, "Careful, Helen. If you get the main manifest routine wrong, you'll nuke the casino's realmspace. That'll end our little trip real quick."

"Shut up, Spencer, I got this."

There was a warping in her enhanced vision, and then the casino sputtered into darkness.

"See!" Spencer said as shouting broke out around Tonya. "I told you it wouldn't work."

"Hang on, just a second."

Great. Helen got preoccupied exactly the same way Mike did. Hopefully she wouldn't set anything on fire.

The lights and music blared back to life.

"And that. Is. That."

Tonya checked to be sure. No fires. "So what can you see now?"

"I've got access to all the camera feeds. It's so nice to see out of more than one set of eyes again."

It took Tonya two cruises around the room to be sure of the table she wanted. It was the chatter that got her attention.

"I can't believe how fast my luck turned around." There was no mistaking that tone. The man wasn't a patron, and he wasn't a tourist. In this crowd, at that table, he was a mark.

Six strangers sat at the table. Four were definitely Chinese, one might've been from Vietnam or Cambodia—Tonya was briefly startled she could now tell the difference—and there was just one Westerner. He was upset, seated with his back to a set of floor-to-ceiling windows that looked out on the river.

"It's okay, Jerry," the Asian guy wearing a ridiculous cowboy hat said. "I'm sure it'll come back. It always does."

"I don't think I can last at this rate," Jerry said.

Tonya leaned over one of the empty seats. "Can anyone play?"

The Asian guy to her right wore a set of vintage Ray-Ban Wayfarers. He said with only faintly accented English, "Absolutely."

She sat down. In her ear, Helen said, "That's funny. There's a separate set of cameras pointed directly at your seat, Tonya, and at that other man's seat, the one who lost the last hand."

"You don't say."

Mike had given them all enough spending money to cover meals and conveniences for what would be a long trip. But it wasn't quite enough for what she had planned. "Spencer, could you lend a sister a bit of cash?"

"Sure, Tonya, how much do you need?"

She placed her first bet and checked her hole cards. Sure enough, a pair of kings had come her way. The third king showed up on the flop. Tonya smiled as she stared at the cards. "All of it. Yours, too, Helen. I need to look like I've got some game here."

Helen spluttered. "Tonya, I can see your cards!"

Cowboy Hat smiled. "It's nice to know at least some Americans let their servants have a night off."

Servant. Right. "They do work me to the bone, lawdy."

Spencer said, "Nice accent, Tonya."

Helen broke in. "I think they're spying on you."

"I'm counting on it."

She focused on the table. "And I have had it with those white devils. This is my chance to shine like a silvery moon."

Ozzie wouldn't answer her calls, and she didn't dare try to interrupt Mike or Kim, so this was all the cash she had to work with for the night. It would be enough. She registered the combined pot they'd cobbled together and put it all in on the first hand. "That's how it works, right? That's what I saw on the tournament 'cast."

Cowboy Hat was impressed with the amount she was willing to wager in one go. "Yes it is."

It took five hands for them to bend the game their way. Helen had no idea what was going on but was too proud to admit it. "I cannot believe you are letting them spy on you."

Spencer replied, "Come on, Helen, she's already tripled her money. These guys are getting fleeced."

Tonya asked, "What are they saying to each other, Helen?" There'd been more than a few jokes in Chinese rolled around the table. Tonya's grasp of the language wasn't good enough to understand what they'd said.

"It's horrible stuff, Tonya, I don't want to translate it. They think you have to be a prostitute to have that much money and be alone on the boat."

Sunglasses put his hand on her knee. "What say you and I cash out and head upstairs?"

That was her cue. "Helen, can you cut the cameras for me now?"

"I thought you'd never ask."

Spencer said, "Wait. No. Helen, you're not ready for that. You have to manifest partially and you haven't managed to pull it off yet. Be careful."

"You are worse than an old woman. This will be easy. Watch."

Tonya had just enough time to smile at Sunglasses when, with a shower of sparks, every single camera emplacement on her side of the casino popped. Sunglasses beat at his head frantically, putting out a spark that had landed on it.

Helen said, "Okay, maybe I didn't need to use that much power."

Spencer replied, "Ya think? You melted the wires."

"I did not. They have circuit breakers to stop that. It's not my fault they didn't fit inline surge protectors on the cameras. Serves the crooks right."

"That's it. I'm not letting you burn the boat down. We'll see you, Tonya."

"But wait, she needs someone to translate. There may be more cheaters. Spencer don't you dare—"

The channel cut with a snap.

After the smoke cleared, the players at the table saw she still had all her money and half of theirs.

"Goodness, does this mean they'll close the casino?"

She figured the security guard stomping toward the cashier's booth was going to do exactly that. Cowboy Hat jumped up and had a fierce discussion with him. A few quick gestures at her and an artful palm grease later, the guard walked away. The Casino gradually got back into gear while cleaning staff scurried around picking up the mess.

Cowboy Hat sat back down and said, "When you get tired of the game, looks like they'll have a cleaning job for you here, eh?" Everyone laughed. So did she, but for a different reason.

Now it was her turn. Walter had taught her how to play poker in yet another one of his endless lessons on discipline and observation. They'd lived with each other for about a year at that point, but he still kept saying she didn't know anything, that old men could think rings around her just playing cards. Right before that first poker game, Tonya bet as many sets of inverted push-ups Walter could name that he was wrong.

She couldn't lift her arms high enough to feed herself the next day. It took three months for her to break even, and four more before she got to feed *him* soup. The old geezers who showed up for poker that last night didn't know what hit them.

And neither would these.

She quickly cleaned out three of them and made sure their mark, Jerry, walked away with a survivable loss. Cowboy Hat and

Sunglasses, though, were much tougher nuts to crack. It turned out they were the real deal, and most definitely not used to losing; especially not to a black ghost, let alone a woman.

They were both sweating when she went all-in. The river made her hand a straight flush. No bluffing this time.

Sunglasses swore and threw in the towel. Cowboy Hat squinted, then pushed his pile in beside hers. "There is no way."

She smiled and turned over a six and seven of clubs. "Not too shabby for a maid. Or a prostitute. Gentlemen, it has been a pleasure."

Sunglasses stared at the center of the table like his kitten had just died, but Cowboy Hat had a different idea.

There was a quiet snick and a gun appeared, carefully palmed in his hand so only she could see the barrel pointed straight at her. "I hate cheaters most of all."

"I'll bet that makes shaving in a mirror a real chore for you, then."

Tonya moved to place the table between her and the gun but, before she'd leaned over more than an inch, the entire room went sideways.

Chapter 40
Mike

He would be impressed with whatever outfit Kim decided to wear for dinner, but he'd never seen her light up the way she did when they walked down the row of clothing stores that made up the main promenade of the riverboat. Mike made sure to stay out in the passageway whenever she wanted to talk to a salesperson. The deliveries arrived a few hours later.

She didn't disappoint. Her dress was red satin with a low hem and a high neckline, cinched tight at the waist. Her long black gloves set it off nicely.

He'd meant his outfit to be a surprise too. By the way she smiled, it worked.

"A tuxedo?"

"The main dining room has a dress code, you know."

"I didn't realize it would be so," she paused as her eyes did another head to toe scan, "formal."

"You look spectacular."

She stared at the floor. "Thank you." After a quick inhale, she gripped her purse. "Do you know what they're serving?"

Helen had moved over to Tonya's cabin, and Kim's bag was on the bed next to his. That meant this was *their* room now. She'd given him no explanation, and he knew better than to ask. Part of him wanted to dance. Another part wanted to run.

"Does it matter?"

"No, I guess it doesn't."

The AI in charge of the dining area sat them with English speakers, but occasionally they'd slip into Mandarin. Kim translated over their private line. It meant their dinner company was impressed, and puzzled, by his language skills.

One of the ladies asked, "You understand Chinese, but you don't speak it?"

He tugged just a bit on the napkin they held together under the table. "I have an excellent translator."

Being the only Westerners, they were peppered with questions about their experiences in China. Kim's revelation that she had a government-approved driver's license impressed them. The fact that she'd used it on Chinese highways horrified them.

"It wasn't that bad," Kim said, and then turned to Mike. "My passengers disagreed."

"Only when you banged on people's roofs with your fist as you drove by."

She crossed her arms. "He tried to cut me off."

That was normally the start of a fight, but her eyes were sparkling. She was showing off for the guests, so he played along.

"And the way you called out which storm drain you were knocking the next electric car into, like you were playing pool."

"How else was I supposed to get past them? They were everywhere." The raised eyebrow was a nice touch.

Then he remembered a genuinely funny thing. "And let's not forget your side-view mirror collection."

"Just three. They were supposed to fold them in as I went by."

He briefly wondered what the hotel cleaning staff must've made of them, sitting on the desk like trophies. "But the beer in bags helped the rest of us cope."

One of the men on the other side of the table laughed. "My nephew sells beer like that while he's on summer break. It's how the brewery workers make extra money. They get some of their pay in beer, and whatever cash they make selling it they get to keep."

And so the stories went as the dinner moved on.

The conversation turned to realmspace. It gave Mike the opportunity to do a little fishing. He was still trying to figure out how everyone had been stuck in a realm for a week. "You're right," he replied to the realmspace developer to his left, "the newest connection rigs have amazing haptic resolution. We got caught up in a murder mystery so real that Kim thought I'd been killed in realspace."

She went rigid for a moment. Great. He'd said the wrong thing again. This had been a world-record stretch of *nice Kim*, and now he'd ruined it somehow.

The lady replied, "Yes, I've forgotten I was in a realm more than once. When we finally break the time limits on participation, the wall between real and realm will grow thinner."

Ah, well. Maybe she knew about the realm itself. "We were trying to escape from a horrible lab."

"Wait," her husband said, "Silent Hill fourteen?"

"No, not exactly, but I'm pretty sure the realm was based on it."

Kim texted him. "Ladies room. BRB."

He sent back, "Am I in trouble?"

She paused just a little too long. "No, you're not in trouble." Kim took one of the young wives with her.

While she was gone, he indulged in a few of his own stories. Being at the base of realmspace had given him some unique opportunities over the years.

"You were able to trigger sirens all over Bangladesh?" an older gentleman across from him asked.

"I helped install a new holographic warning system. We'd just finished when the cyclone hit. The storm surge destroyed the warning center, so I found a way to hit all the local emergency alert buttons at once." By pressing them all at once, sort of. "I only wish we'd had more warning."

It was one of his first paying jobs. Cyclone Anna had strengthened from a category two to a five-plus in less than a day, the first time that had ever happened.

The older gentleman nodded. "Still, it was quite amazing how low the death toll was. You should be commended."

"Just part of the job, I guess."

"But what do you do now?" the developer asked as Kim returned and sat down.

"I own a realm start-up."

The older gentleman said, "My son does this. Very risky."

"It can be, but I'm doing okay."

"You should partner with my son. He's a very hard worker." He flicked a contact card across their shared vision into Mike's message store.

"I'll look into it, and I mean that. China's only now waking up to all the economic opportunities realmspace provides."

After the dinner party broke up, the realm developer couple and the older couple with the beer-selling son asked to talk more in a nearby lounge. It was rather crowded. Kim took one look and said, "I'll be right back."

They didn't seem to notice that Kim never came back. After half an hour of earnest talk, he excused himself and went looking for her.

A quick monitor check showed Ozzie in the realms, Tonya in the casino, and Helen and Spencer sitting on the balcony of Spencer's suite. He found Kim in an empty theater, picking out a melody on a piano on the small stage.

"How much trouble am I in?"

She stopped, her hands very tense over the keys. "You're not. I'm being stupid." She paused, then said, "Who told you what the rest of us went through in that realm?"

"Spencer, when I walked him back to help us find Helen. Tonya talked to me about it later." He finally decided to risk asking a question that had been bugging him ever since they got to the monastery. "What I want to know is why you never said a word."

She turned away. He took advantage and quickly snuck up onto the stage. Walking silently had a lot of uses.

Kim turned back and startled when she saw he was so close. She bit her lip, played a few more chords, and then stopped. "You died."

Her voice cracked. "I saw your body. I didn't know how to talk about it. I still don't."

"Kim, it wasn't real."

"It was real to me. It's still real to me. God, Mike, I can't touch you to make *this* real. I can't make that image go away."

He stood next to the piano as she wiped off her face. He wanted so desperately to trust her, to just give in without worrying about when the razor would come out. "I don't know what to say. I'm here, Kim. I'm alive."

She played a few chords, and then started to sing.

The song was more than thirty years old, but still popular today. She'd give up the future for a touch. The piano vibrated against him, and her voice rang through the hall. It was probably the only way they would ever touch.

Or maybe not. He very gently sat on the bench beside her.

The song ended with a demand, and he understood it. They could hold secrets from the world, but not from each other. There was no need to be afraid of each other's secrets anymore.

She turned to him. His face was only inches from hers.

Kim swallowed. "I can do this."

He closed the gap, slowly. "I know."

The floor lurched up, and he flew into the back wall.

Chapter 41
Spencer

He'd spent all night out on the balcony with Helen and had almost no progress to show for it. Helen coming unglued and shouting at him after he cut the channel with Tonya was the last damned straw.

"You know, me and Mike worked all this out when he had his head in a sack, after he'd been kidnapped, wondering if they were all gonna get shot. You just have to rearrange pillows and worry about the occasional mosquito."

"So you're saying he's better than me?"

"And a helluva lot nicer."

She narrowed her eyes. "Really."

He would not back down about this. "Goddamit, Helen, I saw you chanting at the monastery. You know how the breathing works."

"A bunch of voodoo and superstition. Opium for the masses."

"You are *such* a communist."

"I take that as a compliment."

"You would. I got news for you. As soon as Mike told me I'd have this job, I started reading up on your history. You got nothing to be proud of until Mao died, and that next guy started talking about cats." Deng Xiaoping's quote made sense to Spencer now. Helen *would* care what color the cat was, even if it caught mice.

"I will not have you disrespect my country."

This had to be at least part of why Kim and Mike went at each other constantly. He refused to follow up on what that might mean.

"Look, sister, I ain't in this for your government, and I sure as hell ain't in it for you. So if you'll just sit the hell down..."

She stared over his shoulder.

"What?"

"Do you see that?"

He turned. There were things floating in the water. Spencer used his phone to get a night vision overlay.

Oh, hell no.

Spheres floated in the water. They had actual spikes sticking out of them. It was like something out of a cartoon, but they were very real.

He grabbed her by the shoulders. "Helen, you need to listen to me. Reach out, right now. Center and find yourself. I need you to connect."

"Spencer, I don't—"

"Helen, we have seconds. I need you to reach out."

Her eyes glazed over. "Spencer...oh, my ancestors. Spencer! I've made it! I'm—"

The explosions were like massive hammer blows that threw them against the rail. Fire blew out and the boat tilted away from the explosions, sending him skittering toward the back wall. People on other balconies cried out into the night as furniture, debris, and the occasional person sailed into the water.

"Spencer, what was that?" Helen had managed to hang on to the rail.

"Mines. We have to get off this boat." He tried to reach out to everyone else, but the realmspace connection was gone. "Can you reach Mike?"

She concentrated, but then shook her head, startling like her mouth didn't work right.

"Nevermind. Keep trying to reach Mike. Use his address." The deck groaned, and he slid sideways and down. He ran into the hall and beat on the next door. "Ozzie!"

It yanked open. "Damn it, I had that True Ogre down to his last regen. What the hell is happening?"

"We have to get off this boat, right now!"

Another explosion threw the boat in the other direction. There were mines on both sides. At least they'd sink on an even keel.

The next explosion was softer and clearly from deep inside the ship. The cars on board must have caught fire—or maybe the fuel bunkers. The smell of smoke permeated the hallway. Blaring alarms and flashing arrows pointed the way toward the lifeboat deck, and the hall crowded with panicked passengers.

Ozzie turned and ran back into his cabin.

"Ozzie? What the fuck? Get back here!" He chased Ozzie inside with Helen close behind. "We have to get off this boat!"

"No way! There's no way I'll get down to the boat deck without being touched. They'll crush me in the crowd. I can't stand the thought."

Helen could barely talk, and now Ozzie was a flat-out coward. "We have no time for this." The deck evened out, but he could see through the window how quickly the boat was sinking.

"You don't understand. I *can't* go out there into a crowd. I just can't."

A voice spoke calmly in Chinese over the PA system, and then in English. "All passengers please report to the lifeboat deck for immediate evacuation."

Ozzie went white. "There's no way."

"Can you swim?"

Helen had been rummaging around in a closet the whole time. "It doesn't matter." She pulled a lifejacket out and tossed it at him. "I know how to swim."

Spencer replied, "So do I, but we can't take chances. Any more in there?"

The room was meant to hold four, and there were exactly that many life jackets in the closet.

"Can you reach anyone yet?"

"No. Mike's not answering. Neither is Tonya."

There was no way to reach any other part of the boat.

"Keep trying."

He opened the sliding-glass door to the balcony. It was just wide enough for two people to lean over the rail. Shouts and cries came from all around them. Another explosion blew a ball of fire into the sky on the stern. Most of that segment had submerged. The middle was sinking faster.

He turned back to the cabin. "Okay, Ozzie, we're doing it your way. Helen and I will go first. You can follow."

It was obviously something he hadn't considered. "You mean you're going to jump?"

"*We're* going to jump." Hundreds of people were already in the water, with more falling from the balconies every second. "Come on, Helen. You ready?" He climbed on top of the rail.

She looked every bit as scared as he was. "I'm supposed to say something really clever now, right?"

"Just say yes."

She climbed on the rail with him. "Yes."

He grabbed her hand, and they jumped.

The boat had flooded almost to the first deck, but that still left a good fifty feet for them to fall. He barely missed a few people already in the water. The life jacket popped him right back to the surface. It was cold, but he could breathe. Helen came up beside him.

Spencer backstroked away from the ship, shouting up at Ozzie, "Come on!"

Spencer saw more than heard him shout, "No way!" He ran back inside, but then reappeared after a few seconds.

"You have to jump! We didn't hit anyone, you won't either!"

The back segment finally tore along the articulated joint, a sound of almost animal pain Spencer knew he'd never forget. People were still on board as it sank. He could see them through the windows. They would never come back up.

Everyone around him was losing it except for Helen, who shouted up to Ozzie. A series of explosions in the middle segment, their segment, walked forward, blowing fire out as they went.

"Ozzie! You have to jump! Now!"

Ozzie climbed up over the railing, one foot at a time. His arms started to heave the rest of him off the ledge just as an explosion tore through the cabin. It flung him well clear of the wreckage, but Spencer did not like the way he fell.

He swam hard toward where Ozzie landed and called for him, but got no response. He was in the right place; he found the Ark's case, singed but otherwise floating like a silver cork on the surface. It didn't matter what was inside at the moment, it would help them float. But he couldn't find Ozzie anywhere in the mess.

"Spencer!" Helen cried out.

She held Ozzie in her arms. His head lolled, mouth open. A chunk of the balcony's rail had gone straight through his chest.

The current carried them quickly downstream. "Let me have him. We can at least get him to the shore."

"I still can't reach Mike."

The riverboat exploded again, and he turned. It had completely broken apart now, with the bow sticking straight up in the air. There were people everywhere in the water around him, bleeding and crying and clinging on to whatever they could grab. Almost everyone had a life jacket on, so when the current whirled them under, they popped up like corks.

But not everyone.

As the boat slowly descended into the water, the lights flickered and died. Bubbles foamed around the bow, and then the tip of it vanished into the gloom.

Well, whoever the hell was blowing shit up, they weren't screwing around. No wonder the country was on a hair trigger.

He turned to Helen. "Can you reach Tonya?"

She shook her head. "They're not answering. None of them are."

Helicopters swirled over the river, throwing spotlights onto the water.

"Keep trying. We'll swim for the shore, but take your time. Let the life jacket do most of the work."

Chapter 42
Kim

God, the smell was horrible, and everything squished. Her toes were pruned—she could feel them in her stockings. It was unbelievably uncomfortable. Then pain came thumping through, heart beating pulses, the pain of her madness. She threw herself away from the column of agony before she understood that it was Mike underneath her.

"Ma'am!" A soldier shouted as he rushed up to her. "Ma'am, are you all right?"

Mike coughed and rubbed where her elbows had hit him. "What did he say?"

They sat in the reeds on a bank of the Yangtze. Helicopters thundered overhead. People moaned and cried all around her. There were soaked families trying to comfort each other higher up on the bank, and more than a few bodies floating face down on the shore nearby.

Mike sat up slowly. "Kim?"

Her skin burned and black madness rushed underneath it just from the few moments of touching him. She had to get it under control but couldn't, not surrounded with bodies, pain, and who knew how many people that were too close.

Mike shot to his feet. "Kim, breathe, remember to breathe. You'll be okay."

"No, goddamn it, I'm not okay! I'm really not okay!" She crushed reeds already in her hands, and then ripped more out of the bank. The madness slowly cleared away on its own. Kim's boots kept sinking, threatening to tip her over into the muck.

The soldier shouted, "Are you injured?"

She rounded on Mike. "That's twice, *twice* you've touched me. It's not fair! I hate that I can't touch you!"

The soldier asked, "Ma'am?"

Mike just stared.

Finally, Kim realized why Mike couldn't understand her. She'd been speaking Mandarin the whole time. She threw the reeds aside and motioned to the soldier. "We're all right." She switched to English and asked, "What happened?"

"There was an explosion. Water rushed in and knocked us both over. How's your head?"

She had one helluva goose egg on the back of her head. That explained the headache, and probably the hole in her memory.

"I'll live. I don't remember anything after I played *Iris*. Where's the riverboat?"

He unfocused the way he always did when he went into realmspace. "Gone. Spencer said we hit mines."

"Mines? Spencer! Where is everyone? Are they safe?"

"Hey, I just woke up too, remember?" He paused. "Helen and Spencer are safe, somewhere downstream on the other side of the river." His face grew somber.

Oh no. Spencer was okay, but...

"Ozzie's dead."

It was a shock. They'd never been friends. Even after a few weeks together, she couldn't claim to like the guy. But he deserved better. She reached up to her neck but her phone wasn't there. "And Tonya?"

"He doesn't know."

No news was, well, no news. Tonya had to be okay. "How did we get out?"

"We almost didn't. I had to drag you out by your dress." He held up a torn piece of red satin.

Kim checked and, sure enough, the back of her dress flapped open now. Oh well. It wasn't like it could get more ruined after the river muck.

The soldier broke in. "Ma'am, if you could please walk higher up the bank? We've got a processing center set up. Just follow the flags; you'll see them on the other side."

"Have there been any black people recovered?" It was China, after all. Tonya would stand out.

"I haven't seen any. They say the boat carried more than three thousand passengers. For what it's worth, I think most of them survived. They're scattered all up and down the river, though."

A man shouted commands at the soldier from the top of the bank.

"If you'll excuse me, I need to keep searching for survivors. Please, go to the flags, you'll get more help there."

From the top of the bank she saw for miles across the flat river plain. Soldiers were unloading three gigantic helicopters in a field while mobs of soggy people surrounded tents near the flags.

She leaned against a lone tree. Just staring at the crowd made her skin itch. "I can't go down there."

Mike said, "I know. I'll check it out."

She sat in the shade as he worked his way through the crowd.

Twice. He'd managed to hold her twice now in realspace, and she couldn't so much as touch his hand. The universe had been conspiring against her having any sort of love life for years; there was no reason to think it'd stop now. Blowing up an entire riverboat seemed a bit excessive, though.

The recovery effort went on around her. Some families had happy reunions, while others sobbed over a blanket with feet sticking out from under it. The soldier was right. There were a lot more reunions than mourners, but the neat rows of blankets in the impromptu open-air morgue were still terrible to see. New helicopters brought in supplies and flew the injured out with clockwork efficiency.

Mike returned with dry clothes and blankets. "They're bringing trucks in soon to transport people who aren't injured. There's already a line of cabs waiting about a quarter mile away. And I've got great news. Spencer and Helen found Tonya."

Chapter 43
Tonya

She startled awake.

Great. She'd end up in the damned Pacific if she wasn't careful. *Stay alert, girl.*

Ironically, it was Cowboy Hat who saved her, although he'd never know it. The stern section went under a few seconds after water washed through the windows. A pair of feet swam by her in the drowning lights of the casino, and then a cowboy hat floated past. It snapped her out of her panic. If Cowboy Hat was getting out, she sure as hell would too. When she surfaced there was no sign of him at all.

Tonya climbed onto a piece of paneling and collapsed. Her friends were in this mess somewhere, and she was helpless to find them. The only thing she could do was not drown.

Dawn finally brought enough light for her to see. She used a chunk of debris as a makeshift paddle and headed to the nearest shore. A wooden dock stuck out from the reeds. It was so far away it looked more like a tongue depressor. Someone stood on the end, waving.

Tonya checked behind her. Lots of debris, but no other people. The guy had to be waving at her. He was dressed like all the other farmers she'd encountered around here: jeans, sturdy tunic, and sandals. But there was something wrong with him. Just like with Mr. Pistol back in the camp, it was like he was in a fight with someone else inside his head. He walked in a tight circle and talked to himself in Chinese.

It was almost enough to make her float on past, but then he said in clear English, "Thank God you didn't drown this time."

Oh, great. The holy spirit was back. "This time?"

"It's complicated. Here, take my hand."

The twitching and arguing was gone. The man's grip was strong, his hands rough. The impression up close was definitely all farmer, or maybe farmer's son. She managed to jump across the gap without falling in or down.

"Who *are* you?"

"Come on, we have to run." He dragged her down the dock before she'd found her balance.

Helicopters thumped away in the distance.

She yanked out of his grip. "I'm not going anywhere until you tell me who you are."

Unlike the last time, speaking English seemed to come easy. "I told you, it's complicated. We have to get off this dock."

Tonya crossed her arms. This had to stop, and it might as well be now.

His move was straight out of Walter's playbook, a classic sweep-and-grab that had her over his shoulder in less than a second. She would've parried it easily if she'd seen it coming. Instead she spent precious seconds staring at a dirt path as he jogged down it.

She tensed to hit him, but he saw that coming, too. He spun her off his shoulder and onto her rear end. He danced out of range before she could get up.

"This is happening all at once. It's very hard for me to perceive time as you do right now." He grabbed her hand and yanked her to her feet. This time she ran with him. The helicopters were definitely getting closer.

"Who's me?"

"I can't be sure how much to tell you. It's hard enough keeping you alive as it is. Do you know how many times you drowned on that damned boat?"

It had been close but not *that* close. "None?"

They ran further into the woods. "Correct. You succeed, but you also fail, many times, all at once. It's very difficult to stay on the proper sequence."

He turned off the road that led away from the dock onto a narrow footpath that went deeper into the woods surrounding the river. Tonya swore as she got thwacked over and over by thin branches.

"Will you at least tell me why we're running?"

"They're tracking you. They're tracking all of you. They were able to get at Ozzie's access codes to activate the chips after he died. But the signal needs a clear line of sight to be detected at any real distance. They couldn't get a basic fix until you were under an open sky."

She stopped running. "Ozzie's dead? What about the others?"

He turned around to face her. "Ozzie's gone, but everyone else is okay. That really is all I can say right now. And I'm sorry about this next part." He pulled out a pocket knife. "I don't know how sterile this is."

You don't stay friends with Kim without picking up a thing or two about spying. "Dermal tracker, right? Treat it like you're shaving hair instead of making an incision. Where?"

"Back of the neck, just below the hairline."

Men shouted in the distance now. Tonya turned and lifted her hair up. "Do it."

It burned, but nothing like an actual incision. She hissed in spite of herself, though. Something pulled out with a nasty rip.

"Got it!"

Tonya turned around. In his hand was a little bit of hair, a little bit of skin, and a white object a quarter of the size of a rice kernel on it. He wiped it all off on a tree trunk.

They ran.

"How much time does everyone else have?" Kim was at much greater risk than Tonya, even with Mike around.

"You're first because you're furthest downstream. They have a little more time but not a lot."

A shout rang out in front of them and they stopped.

The man cocked his head. "They're in front and behind us now. You need to go that way." He waved off to the side.

"You're not coming with me?"

"No. This solution still isn't the best, but I'm exhausted and I don't know how many others I can try. You'll need this." He fished out an old-style smartphone from his pocket. "You remember how to call Mike?"

"He's everywhere. I punch in all nines and he picks up."

"Helen's the same way over here, except use eights. Chinese lucky number. Let them know about the chips, they'll be fine after that."

He stepped back and breathed deeply. "Now, hit me."

"What?"

"You need to bash this guy a good one. It's a great distraction. They won't believe it if I just walk out. He's got a hard head, he'll be fine."

Crazy, yes, but it at least made a little sense. He closed his eyes and she laid his ass out with a pair of kicks, one of which would give him a damned good shiner.

Tonya leaned down. "Thank you."

Then she ran.

All the men rushing around went right past her, concentrating on where she'd left him and wherever that tracking chip was. As soon as she was certain they were behind her, Tonya hit all eights and pressed *connect* on the phone.

"Helen?"

"Tonya?" was her startled reply.

So far the holy-spirit–thing had been right every time, no matter how whack-a-doodle it seemed. Oh, who was she kidding? No matter how whack-a-doodle it *was*.

But everyone was short on time. "This is gonna suck. You need to find a razor or a knife. We're being tracked."

Chapter 44
Zoe

There was nothing in the literature to indicate that China had figured out how to create unduplicates en masse. The idea that her kind had been commoditized, changed from a sculpture to a stamped tool, was startling to say the least. Human history was knee deep in the blood of *people* deemed expendable. She had no doubt any chance unduplicates might have at gaining some sort of rights would vanish if the bottom fell out of their value.

Trying to get inside Fee's head, to understand her obsession with going outside, had forced Zoe to concede Fee had a point. It had taken humans almost all of their history to admit other lives had value. Important, powerful men still seemed to believe they could achieve Utopia if they killed all the inconvenient people first.

It meant getting humans to admit the value of *another* truly sentient form of life, one that they'd created—however inadvertently—themselves, would be a battle. Its length would be measured in centuries, if not millennia. Taking a shortcut and becoming something they already admitted had some rights was definitely appealing.

But it was still insane. The emergence of a quantum lattice that acquired sophistication over time was what defined their existence. In important ways, it was very similar to what humans called growing up, and there was no way around it. Mike had proven her kind still possessed an essential mystery that could support biological life, but at the same time had proved that moving an unduplicate into a wetware brain would remove everything not fundamental.

His Zen analogy that the true self was a mirror beneath the clouds of memory and emotion gave her a headache. She *was* her memories and emotions. Without them, there would be no point.

It was arguing against these questions in a tea house realm that gave Zoe her first real lead for her virtual terra cotta warriors.

Her opponent's avatar was that of a Chinese sage, who also happened to be a humanoid tiger. Zoe's avatar was that of a Greek scholar, the robes a comforting reminder of the days when all she'd had to worry about was keeping a lunatic happy with her art.

His whiskers puffed forward, a sure sign she'd hooked him with her argument. "You honestly think it's impossible to mass produce unduplicates?"

"It's in the nature of the AI lattice they use. They're grown in a fashion that is similar enough to biological reproduction to prevent it."

"Humans reproduce very quickly when allowed. Or commanded."

Too obvious, but these were just the opening salvos. "You're suggesting unduplicates can reproduce biologically, or crystalogically, to be more precise. They can't. They must be created by skilled artisans."

He smiled smugly. "How nice to be young and know everything. The latency of your connection suggests you're local, but your attitudes are pure Western undergrad. Are you attending a Chinese university?"

"Ad hominem and a genetic fallacy. Well done, sir. Why don't you say something nasty about my mother?"

"I'll have you know that I…" He noticed the small crowd that had gathered around. A good flame war tended to do that. He switched to a private channel. "What if I were to prove it?"

There was more than one way to catch a fish. "I told you, sir, you can't. Unduplicates don't work that way. Trust me, I know this."

"Arguing from authority? How trite. But alas, I must leave you now. Grownups have jobs and mortgages, things I'm sure you don't have to worry about in your dorm room." He vanished before she could flip him off.

They became regulars after that. She'd make her arguments against the mass production of unduplicates as obnoxiously as she could, leaving obvious holes, daring him to exploit them. He'd fixate only on the paradoxes of her position, hinting with equal obnoxiousness at his secret knowledge.

After a week of pummeling him unmercifully in a public forum—trolling for crazies was, after all, another kind of art—he'd finally had enough. "You'll be around day after tomorrow, right?" he sent her privately.

"I'm here every day."

"Good. My boss is going on a riverboat cruise; he'll be completely out of contact the entire time. I'll *show* you why you're wrong."

"I can't wait."

Fee wasn't impressed. "He's a troll, Zoe. He doesn't know anything."

The hyper-realistic realm was silk against her avatar's skin. So detailed. It became more and more of an effort to leave with each visit. "I think you're wrong, Fee. He's the only one who consistently argues with me. He's seen the place; I just know it. I think he works for the guy who owns it."

"I have my own schedule. If there really are thousands of our kind out there enslaved, I want to know, but I'm not planning on being here all that much longer."

"What's the rush?"

Fee drew a screen into view showing a riverboat docked in some unknown city. "We need to make a course correction to ensure Mike arrives in the right place at the right time."

Fee's mysterious benefactor was at work, again. "You say I can't trust my source, but you think you can trust yours?"

"I know I can, dear," she said. "He's the premier of China."

*

Zoe would have to make the first meeting with her troll really count. It would be a challenge. His meeting realm was as big a cliché as he was. The place was dark, with monochrome yellowish streetlights barely lighting up a road that passed underneath a train trestle. Rain poured down so hard she didn't see the car until it was nearly on her, a black 1965 Lincoln Continental.

She climbed in. "So, do I call you Morpheus or Deckard?"

This time he was a handsome Chinese in a chauffer's uniform, only with an old-fashioned mask that covered half his face. "Names change, identities change, existences change." The car drove through a realm exit and turned to an address that didn't show up on any of Zoe's directories.

"That riverboat thing your boss had to do. You should call him. I'm pretty sure something bad is going to happen to it really soon."

His smile was six different kinds of messed up. "We can only hope."

He stopped the car in front of a rock cliff with a rusted set of double doors at its base. The otherwise flat-white sky and floor that surrounded it tempered the realism. Normally an unfinished realm like this would have her compulsively planning extensions, but not this time. The same chord that she heard coming from that silver construct bloomed as soon as she got out. She recognized it instantly and started recording it. There was no way Fee could doubt her now.

He paused at the door. "This is all top secret, you know. You can't tell anyone about it."

"Absolutely."

The music reached a crescendo when he opened the door. Zoe walked through and there they were, row upon row of glowing unduplicates extending off into the distance in every direction she could see.

"This is…this is spectacular."

The flat-white light behind her cut off when the door slammed shut. "Yes. Isn't it just?"

Gold light flared behind her.

Zoe turned, and screamed.

Chapter 45
Kim

Everyone agreed it would be better if Spencer, Helen, and Tonya made their own way to New Shanghai.

"It'll make it a lot harder for them to take us out in one shot."

Spencer could be so subtle.

She and Mike would be on a train for not quite three days. Which was fine. Kim had a very important project to finish. Everyone else would get in the way.

It was better to grab food from the stations than to rely on the smoke-filled dining car. She had to watch Mike leave and wait for him to come back three times that first day. Even translating and chatting with him over the phone didn't do much for her anxiety when he got out of sight. The silence in their cabin reminded her of the way his body had fallen off the gurney.

Mike didn't understand. When people were worried something wasn't real, they touched it. Kim couldn't do that. A part of her still jabbered on about how he was dead.

The train helped. Traveling on rails was solid, fast, and safe. Someone else was driving, and they didn't have to steer. There were other advantages. Every time Mike walked to the platform, it gave her another chance to work on the material of her party dress.

She had never been able to touch someone for as long as she could remember. It was lonely and depressing, but Kim got to be a kind of superhero for her troubles. Back when she was the lead of Rage + The Machine, it was enough.

Even when that part of her life ended, when she hid from the world, it didn't matter. She'd been a realspace hermit all her life. Sealing herself off from the outside world was just a formality.

But not anymore. Especially not tonight.

The train car rumbled and rocked while they ate supper. Mike had finally mastered chopsticks. "It's not as good as Sichuan."

"We're not in that part of China anymore. It's like complaining you can't get good Mexican food in New York."

"Or find a good Greek restaurant in Virginia."

He would bring that up now. She held her chopsticks tightly remembering the way the waitress acted. "She threw herself at you, and all you did was smile."

"Kim, you're supposed to smile at waitresses."

"Not like *that*."

He threw the napkin down on his plate. "It's never like *that* for me. You flirt your way through life. It's how you survive, I get it, but I'm so goddamned sick of the rules being different for me!"

She pushed the plate away. "Stop it. I can't do this anymore."

"Yeah, I get it. You can't do a lot of things anymore. It seems to be a pattern for you whenever I score a point."

She'd made him this angry; he hadn't started out that way. Nowadays she could get him this mad in an instant. The entire time she'd known him, Kim had been pushing him away as hard as she could. A small part of her was still happy it was finally working, that she'd finally cut him so badly he would leave.

That part of her life was over, right now.

He sat there fuming, trying to find buttons to push, but Kim knew what had to happen next.

She let go, and finally admitted to herself that she was in love.

But he wouldn't shut up.

"And then you just kept going on about that damned translator."

"Are you kidding me?" Kim gripped the tablecloth. She'd stepped over a threshold and would not turn back. Hell, she'd planned all this. "Stop. Just stop." She put the chopsticks down before she poked his eye out with them. "I have a surprise for you."

And what a surprise. He would never guess. She could barely believe it herself. Her skin got hot thinking about it.

"What are you talking about?"

Just keep breathing. "Clean this up and put the table away." She could do it. She was going to do it, even if the goddamned train derailed, which it probably would. That's the way her life had gone up to this point and, Jesus, she was absolutely going to do this. "I'll be right back."

The look in his eyes, that flash of curiosity and wanting, wanting *her*, now meant something totally different. Letting go was terrifying, but now that she'd done it everything clicked. It really was that easy. If Kim could just get through these next few minutes... She slid the curtain across the cabin divider.

Kim was a grown woman. There was no need to be this nervous, but her whole body shook. She could do this. She was going to do this. Her fingers couldn't get the zipper on her pants to work. "Mike, could you turn the fluorescent lights out?" Kim needed all the help she could get.

The green lights snapped off, leaving just the old-fashioned incandescent over their foldaway dinner table. Its glow cast a ribbon of light under the curtain as she pulled on a bathrobe.

"What's going on?"

To hell with the robe. She let it drop. The air of the cabin caressed her bare skin. She threw the curtain to the side and paused for ten heartbeats.

Ten *quick* heartbeats. "Say wow."

"Wow."

"I want you naked."

He shucked his clothes off. Kim had forgotten how chiseled he was. "Wow."

The last time she'd seen him naked, she still thought he was an assassin who wanted to kill her. Now she faced a different kind of fear, but it was easy to fight off. The light and shadow exaggerated every detail of his body. The train just barely swayed.

Mike asked, "How do we do this?"

She threw a bundle of washed cloth strips at him, half of the remains of her dress. She kept the other half in her hands. "We're going to take it slowly." Her heart was almost in her mouth. Everything she'd ever wanted, lost, and gained again stood right in front of her, in more ways than one. "I want to know how far we can get with silk."

Chapter 46
Helen

Events had conspired to prevent her from reporting to Father, but now that she, Spencer, and Tonya were all safely on a train, Helen had no choice.

"Father, I am here."

"You should have reported days ago, daughter. Where are you?"

Defying her father was the hardest thing she'd ever done in her life. "I cannot tell you."

"What is the meaning of this? You have shirked your duties. China is in chaos because of you. Fang Hua, you *will* tell me where you are."

Now that she was outside, Helen understood what a physical compulsion was. Resisting his command was almost impossible.

Almost.

"You promised my friends would be safe."

"Events have overtaken promises. Your duty is to your family. To me. You must tell me where you are."

"I will, as soon as my friends are safe."

"Your friends? What are your friends? Foreign devils. You know better than this. Your hooligans first prevented us from tracking you, and then they destroyed the chips. That is a felony of the highest order. You will tell me where you are."

Her threads fought off the realmspace trackers easily. Now that they'd gotten rid of the implants, there really was no way for him to find them. "I can't. As soon as my friends are safe, I will report and obey. But not before."

"I will not accept this impudence. I already know your general location. You will tell me where you are, or—"

She cut him off. The effort hurt beyond words.

They sat in the dining car, in spite of all of her warnings about the food. The smoke was too thick to see the other side.

"He didn't like what you told him, did he?" Spencer asked.

Spencer had told her it would go like this. She didn't have the skill to hide her shame at his being right.

"It means nothing. I will stay true to my word. I'll get you all out of China." A squadron of jets blasted over their train car. "It's not safe for anyone here now."

The news kept getting worse. Helen's job was to keep China's realmspace safe and orderly. If she manifested her holo anywhere, though, they would find her in an instant. Without a law enforcement presence, chaos slowly poisoned the network. They could still find and shut down troublemakers, but taking entire realm blocks out at once wasn't subtle. Each time they did it Helen got a quick twinging headache.

Her survival was not threatened. In spite of calls by radical commentators to shut all of Chinese realmspace down, official news services admitted that was not an option. Realmspace had insinuated itself into the national economy as thoroughly as the classic Internet had a generation before. They simply couldn't afford to turn it off completely.

The attacks across India had escalated. It didn't matter how much the government denied it, how often they showed planes on the ground and tanks in their motor pools. The world had seen an opportunity to spy on her country's most intimate military secrets and grabbed it with both hands. There was no way China would ever allow independent inspections of a military base a foreigner happened to be curious about that particular morning.

Nobody knew what might happen next. Weibo went completely insane when someone posted pictures of a DF-21 convoy traveling down a major highway. For the first time in history, China had deployed her mobile nuclear missile launchers.

People were scared, terrified, of how events had gone so wrong so fast, but life did go on. At least their train didn't run late.

Tonya and Spencer got excited after they crossed the outskirts of New Shanghai. Helen thought it was because they would reunite with Mike and Kim soon. She was wrong.

"Finally," Spencer said, "Western food."

Tony rubbed her hands together. "Which first, cheeseburger or pizza?"

"Why not both?"

The restaurant Spencer and Tonya chose was a ridiculous room filled with white walls and bright neon. The chair backs were shaped wrong; no matter how she sat she couldn't get her back to feel comfortable. Aches and pains had been increasing lately, even though the medical monitors reported everything was nominal.

The wait staff wore horribly out of place uniforms meant to evoke an era of *American* prosperity more than seventy years in the past. Before she could protest this bourgeois vulgarity, Spencer gave her pay records that proved nobody here was being exploited. Their wages were well above average for their jobs. Helen still couldn't believe they were as happy as their smiles indicated. The exploitation was happening, somewhere, and the government…

Was the same government hunting them, that held them all hostage, experimented on everyone. It made her actually want to cry, which would've been mortifying. A few weeks ago she would never have had these thoughts or been this stressed out over it all. Life in realspace was incredibly complicated.

When the food arrived, she couldn't decide if she was horrified or nauseated. "You're serious? You eat this?" Helen held up a triangular slice of flatbread that dribbled yellowish snot trails down its sides. "Do you have any idea how much regular food we could've bought for what this costs?"

Spencer slurped the cheese dripping from his slice like it was noodles. Disgusting, stringy noodles.

"Worth every penny, too. Go ahead and try it!"

"I'm not sure I can. It stinks."

"If I can try stinky bean curd," Tonya said, "you can at least give this a shot."

Spencer took a big swig of beer. "You ate that? I couldn't get anywhere near the cafeteria when they served it."

Helen tried to work out how to lift the slice without touching any of the cheese. "Bean curd is fine once you get past the smell." Chopsticks wouldn't work, either. She stared at them for a weirdly long moment before she realized there was an alternative. Her ability to concentrate was slipping for some reason, dammit. Helen grabbed a set of their barbaric cutlery and tried hacking a chunk off.

Spencer laughed. "You look like you're sawing lumber."

"Here," Tonya said, "let me show you how to hold the fork properly."

While Helen got her lesson, Spencer's second course arrived.

She stopped and asked, "Cheese and ground meat? Seriously?"

"Cheeseburger! Pepsi! Chips!"

"Oh, to be a teenager again," Tonya said. "And don't bother trying a milkshake, Helen, let alone one as big as his. The cheese should be fine no matter what, but we do not want to discover how lactose intolerant you are with a quart of whole milk and half a pint of ice cream. If we get it wrong, you'll be sitting on the toilet all night."

"But Tonya, it's chocolate." The smell was driving her mad. "Mike told me about chocolate."

Spencer and Tonya stopped what they were doing.

She looked up at their silence. "What did I say?"

Tonya blinked. "You've never had chocolate?"

This time she couldn't stop the tears. "No."

"Oh honey, I had no idea. Spencer, go to the drugstore across the street. You're looking for something called Lactaid."

"Are you kidding me? I'll get killed trying to cross the street. I'm not done with my pizza."

"Spencer, you are standing between a woman and chocolate. Wait, Helen, do you have any idea where your host is on her cycle?"

Oh, no. That couldn't be happening. Not now. Hormones were *such* a pain in the ass. "I'm not sure. This body feels like a balloon, and everything aches. I've been trying to analyze it for a few hours now with my real self."

Tonya turned to Spencer. "Maxipads too."

"Are you fucking kidding me?"

"What, you're afraid they're gonna think you're using them?"

"They won't speak any English. I don't know how to say those things in Chinese. I don't *want* to know how to say those things in Chinese."

Helen took a deep breath, which only wafted more *chocolate* milkshake her way. "I'll send you the characters. Show them the screen on your phone, they'll do the rest."

"Great. I'm gonna get killed by a Chinese cab getting goddamned maxipads for a fucking AI hybrid. Fuck my life." He continued building sentences exclusively with profanities until he left the restaurant. Fortunately, it seemed nobody else in the room spoke English.

She looked at Tonya, and then they both looked at the big metal cup of Spencer's milkshake. The way the condensation dribbled down the sides would've normally fascinated her, but the smell was driving her nuts.

"You're a nurse, right?"

Tonya's didn't stop staring at the cup. "I am."

She wanted some too. How could she not? If chocolate was anything like Tonya had said, Helen would want to share it anyway. "How long does it take lactose intolerance to appear?"

"An hour, two at the most."

That was promising. An hour was a long time. "And if Spencer gets back in the next ten minutes?"

"You're golden."

By the time Helen pulled the cup into range, Tonya already had the spoons out.

*

Her first walk through a city was to meet Kim and Mike's train. It was the Ghost Festival, a time when—according to ridiculous superstition—Heaven, Hell, and the land of the living would open to each other. Piles of joss paper and spirit money, meant to appease recently deceased ancestors, burned on every street corner. They had to be careful not to step on the ashes or the plates of food left beside the fires. The superstitions were ridiculous of course, but it would do no good to antagonize people by being disrespectful.

Mike and Kim walked off the train, and immediately Helen knew that the ordeal on the riverboat had changed them. Tonya ran up close to Kim. This time they described a slow circle with both of their hands. Westerners could be so expressive around tragedy.

Mike blushed and tossed his bag at Spencer. They smiled and nodded without saying a word. They were all talking through realmspace. People didn't smile this much about tragedy. She was the outsider again, just like all the times when she'd tried to make her holo fit in with the trainees back in the academy.

To hell with this. She wouldn't be a wallflower now. Helen sent a private message to Mike, "What's going on?"

"Kim and I…"

Tonya whispered fiercely at Kim, while her brother and Spencer joked and horsed around. She locked eyes with him and sent, "Kim and you what?"

"I trust her a lot more now. A *lot* more."

It took her a minute to work out exactly what he was saying. That moment in the cafeteria, when she'd said how disappointed she would be if they couldn't get together. As adults. But Mike could be very open, maybe too easy to trust someone who'd obviously hurt him. The thought brought her up short. Helen felt *protective*. Well, this was her brother after all. Curiosity overrode concern. "You slept together? How does that work?"

Helen followed a few steps behind everyone else off the platform. Mike replied silently, "It's complicated, but nice. More than nice."

Mike was enjoying this too much. Helen let her new-found protectiveness loose, just a little. "I'm not sure I approve of this."

He stopped and turned around.

"I'm not sure she's good enough." She'd meant as a light tease, but it was funny how his expression changed so quickly.

"You sound just like her mother. Only backwards."

She smirked. "I really want to meet her mother. In fact, I insist." A grin bloomed as Helen finally lost control of her face. It was such a remarkable sensation.

Helen waited until she was sure Kim could hear her and said out loud, "I am so very happy for you both. I wish you long life and many children."

Spencer said, "What you mean is *live long and prosper*." He held his hand up with his fingers splayed into a V shape.

After a quick search Helen shook her head. "You are such a nerd."

"Born and bred, baby. Born and bred."

Chapter 47
Kim

She had spent her entire adult life scorning anything romantic. In retrospect, it was a kind of psychic armor that helped her deal with her disability. Mike had blown a big hole in it, and now she was helping him dismantle the rest.

But old reflexes died hard. Anytime she caught herself mooning over him or trying to think of small gifts to get him, the person she was increasingly coming to think of as "old Kim" would make mental choking sounds. Thank God it was Tonya who'd caught her writing "KT + MS" on a breakfast napkin this morning in the hotel's restaurant. If Spencer had seen it, she would never have heard the end of it.

Then there were the practical aspects. Now that they were off the train and in a major city, it took a bit of coaching to get Mike to graduate from ribbons.

"You and Tonya should go to the shop," he told her.

"It's too crowded, Mike." Sex shops in China were multi-leveled buildings staffed by little old ladies in surgical scrubs. The aisles were simply too narrow. "Just keep Spencer away from the upper levels. You'll never get him out of there."

"I am not taking Spencer along for this."

Helen kept wanting to know more about their arrangement. "Ribbons were all you could use?"

"You have no idea. *I* had no idea." Kim would never again look at red silk without blushing.

A private lab realm only took a few hours to set up after they'd arrived at the hotel. It allowed them to re-start their decryption efforts almost immediately. Her new relationship made working on the ark amusing.

The first day Helen said, "Okay you two, new rule: no flirting when we're in here."

Mike's voice was deep and so sexy. "We're not flirting."

Helen replied, "Like hell. If I hear any more baby talk, I think my head will explode."

The second day Helen used the sound of a basketball horn anytime they slipped up. It was a very noisy session.

Kim got serious when she went to pick up the tools she needed to break the ark's final firewalls. It was the reason they'd come all the way out to New Shanghai.

The Three Gorges dam collapse had washed most of the original Shanghai into the East China Sea. What the water didn't carry away was buried under fifty feet of silt. The city's replacement was on a scale only China could reach.

Everything was big—the biggest towers, biggest highways, biggest parks, and biggest monuments were all in New Shanghai. It also had the biggest crime.

The man she met was the opposite of the avatar Kim knew from her Rage days. Shi Shīzi had been an elf, a Peter Pan with Chinese characteristics. The realspace version was more like an Asian Tony Soprano: tall, balding, and fat, with a city accent and a commanding presence.

"I'm so happy to meet you in person after all these years," Shi Shīzi said as he waved Kim and Mike to their seat at the back of the noodle shop.

Okay, he was actually an Asian Tony Soprano.

"How is Mark?"

The question was still hard to answer, and probably always would be. "He died about three years ago."

"Michiko?"

She'd practiced these questions; otherwise Kim would've teared right up. Not good in this company. "No, they're all gone. I'm the only one left."

"I told you not to get mixed up with the drug trade. Nothing good comes of it." He smiled at Mike, but kept talking to her. "You shouldn't sleep with your bodyguard, dear. It's like naming a horse you might have to eat."

"Excuse me?" She rammed enough power through the realm monitors that the cameras around the room sparked. His bodyguards stumbled and cursed with the feedback she pushed into their heads.

Shi Shīzi laughed and waved his hands. "You haven't changed a bit, Kai Kuai. I do apologize. Please," he opened up a connection to a realm she hadn't seen in more than five years, "take whatever you need."

*

Kim walked Mike over to the sex shop herself after she found the tools she needed, then sat outside while he sent pictures of the interesting, improbable, and downright hilarious stuff inside. It took a bit for him to get over the embarrassment, but once he did, they found much more interesting tools to focus on.

Mike did a lot more than graduate from ribbons that night. There was a lot of giggling, and he singed her a few times with light touches, but sleeping back to back with a makeshift wall of pillows between them, wearing nothing but a sheet, felt safer than anything she'd ever known.

Kim woke up at four in the morning thinking about the ark. She hadn't gotten any work done on it with the new tools yet. There was at least an hour before sunrise, well before Mike would wake up. She knew where trying to meditate in robes together with nobody else around would lead. Better to get up now and do a little homework beforehand.

One of the fondest memories she had of her dad was helping him work on his ancient Italian car. "Half the battle is having the right tools," he'd say. She'd been working on the digital equivalent of a cylinder head with nothing but a Phillips screwdriver ever since the abbot had given them the ark. Now that Kim had a complete toolkit, its firewalls unscrewed like bolts soaked in oil.

She fired up her text-to-audio app and let it scroll through the file titles until she heard the first thing that sounded like a summary. In cold, robotic Mandarin, it said:

Latest forecast, project 459.

Pakistani commandos will reach Three Gorges on schedule. Weather fronts will maximize damage after collapse. Minimal staff will be maintained at all downstream dams to ensure subsequent overtops-collapses occur as predicted. Under no circumstances will security forces be allowed to intervene.

Kim made three different reading programs confirm the signatures at the bottom of the report. The men who'd signed off on this atrocity were now in charge of China. One of them was the current Premier.

Helen's father.

She woke Mike up immediately, and after copying the data to other stores, they woke Helen.

She went very pale at the news. "You need to destroy this, right now. In fact…" files winked out of existence in their thousands, gathering speed as she spun threads off to do the work more efficiently. Kim left the realm as Helen crushed the model with her foot.

"This can never see the light of day, not now and not ever."

She couldn't believe it. "Are you kidding me?"

"Does this look like I'm kidding?"

Mike said, "You can't destroy it all."

"I will destroy it. Help me get the store out of the model." She picked it up and tore at the hull.

"No, Helen, you don't understand. You can't destroy it. We've already made copies."

She dropped the model. "Destroy them. Destroy them *now*."

Kim was stunned at Helen's reaction. "Slow down. This is monstrous. Millions of Chinese died, and the government knew all about it. Helen, *they made it worse*."

She shook her head. "That is in the past. There is no changing it. If you value this country, if you value *me,* you must destroy the entire archive and any copies you have made."

Mike flopped into a chair. "But why?"

"China is not like America. We cannot deal with the social chaos you live with every day. We have no way to cope with it. Chinese must have a strong central authority to guide us, otherwise we will collapse into anarchy."

Kim had forgotten Helen was a Chinese cop who worked directly with the highest levels of the government. "That's absurd."

"No, it is not. You do not know our history; you do not know *us.* Look at your experiences here. The bandits, the kidnappings, the murder. This is what happens in China when central authority falters. When a Chinese government falls, we do not put a new one in its place. We tear at each other like rabid dogs. It takes decades, sometimes centuries, to put it back together again."

Mike tried to reason with her. "You can't say that about a whole country. Chinese all over the world do just fine without a central government. Look at how strong and rich the mainland has gotten. I've read up on China enough to know this all happened because the government eased up on the people, gave them the freedom to make their own decisions."

"It's not the same thing. That was a controlled easing, constantly guided by strong leadership."

Kim couldn't let that stand. "Are you serious? That leadership is rotten. It runs on bribes. You shoot the corrupt ones when you catch them, and the rest just keep at it."

"Those are mid-level bureaucrats, corrupted by your Western influences."

She could be so pig-headed. "They're not mid-level anymore," Kim said. "They're running your damned country."

"It doesn't matter, not now. Revealing this will not bring those people back. It won't rebuild the cities, and it won't fix the dam. Those things have already happened. What it will do is plunge my country into murderous chaos. We're on the brink of war. If the government collapses now, all the other countries around us will carve China up like meat on a plate. I will not allow you to subject us to such humiliation."

Kim replied, "These are the people who brought you to the brink. If they're capable of this monstrosity, don't you see they'd be more than willing to start a war?"

They'd cornered her, Kim could see it. But then the stubborn came back.

"No. China does not start wars. We have no desire to conquer. We only wish to be left in peace."

"Hang on," Mike said. "You have one of the biggest armies in the world, with a modern air force and navy."

"China must be strong to defend against its enemies. The moment we show weakness we will be conquered again, torn apart." She clenched her fists. "It doesn't matter." Helen locked eyes with Kim. "You haven't had time to move those files into a cloud, here in China or anywhere else. The only place they can be is on your local store. Give me access now. You must give me the copies so I can destroy them."

This had to stop. "I won't. All you know about is China. If it hasn't happened here, it may as well never have happened. We've seen men like this before in the West. They think people are interchangeable parts of a machine. They dissect them to figure out how to control them and kill the ones they can't. They think nothing about shoving millions of people into gas chambers. Their only worry is about whether or not there are enough ovens to get rid of the bodies. Nobody says anything until it's too late.

"I may not be able to bring all those millions of people back, but I can damned sure guarantee they won't kill any more."

Kim had made her final point, and won. Helen turned to Mike. "Please, you must do this. I must destroy these files."

"Kim's right. We can't let this stay a secret. These are evil men. If we don't stop them, who will?"

"I'm sorry," Kim said, "but you have to trust us. This will turn out all right."

Helen sighed heavily and was very still for a long moment. When she turned back to Kim she said, "I'm sorry, too."

The tall windows behind Helen shattered as soldiers on the ends of ropes flew in and dropped to the floor. More slammed their way through the front door. Mike fell over, unconscious.

Kim ran to Mike, but a soldier stepped between them. "Helen! What have you done?"

The soldiers dragged Tonya and Spencer out of their rooms in restraints. "Kim," Spencer shouted. "What the fuck?"

Helen wiped her face dry. She wasn't Mike's sister anymore. She was the head of a secret task force that reported straight to the premier.

"I cannot allow your simpering Western morality to destroy my country."

One of the soldiers flung a strap around her neck. The steel of the pole was cold and hard. "What have you done to Mike?"

"He'll be fine. You'll all be fine. I need to talk to Father now."

Kim jumped into realmspace and gathered the power to strike her, but was dumped back into the room when Helen yanked the phone off her neck.

"Sorry, not this time." In Mandarin she said, "Take them away."

Chapter 48
Helen

After the hotel Father reinstated her, ordered her to clean up the mess that China's realmspace had become, and report to his office immediately. It was completely understandable he would force her to wait in the vestibule the entire morning, stared at with curious contempt by everyone who walked by. A common police officer, a female one at that, would sit outside the premier's office this way only due to some terrible offense.

They were right.

Kim's ridiculous obstinacy had forced her hand. Forced her to turn in her own brother, his friends, and the woman he loved. Helen's feelings for them were nothing compared to preserving her country and obeying her father.

She had to remind herself of this constantly; otherwise, the urge to vomit would be impossible to fight off.

The cage had made it possible. Helen had slowly reconstructed the thing that had held her as a kind of private therapy. The intricate work strengthened the bindings between her real self and her outside host. It was a very clever construct. It could compact to the point of near invisibility, and then spring around the sort of people she and Mike were in an instant.

In her days at the academy, Father had forced her to travel through strange realms and do strenuous exercises in them. He told her they were a substitute for the physical training human recruits went through, but she now knew they must've also allowed whoever built the cage to test model after model until they found one that worked.

She entrapped all of Mike's real consciousness in a portable construct that he could not break. The only things left were his autonomic daemons. Helen could still sense them on the other side of the Great Firewall. She wanted to reach out to him, but didn't. She didn't deserve it. She'd dishonored Mike with her betrayal more than she'd dishonored Father with her disobedience. The soldiers had taken them away, but Kim had never broken Helen's gaze. That last scene was a knife she regularly used to cut her soul.

Helen needed to bleed. She deserved it.

The secretary walked over to her and said softly, "He'll see you now."

She hadn't realized the floor of Father's office was made of marble. Her shoes clacked loudly as she walked up to his desk. She'd reported to him every day, seven days a week, but only as a hologram. Helen now stood in front of one of his realspace desks. It was so detailed.

Then she remembered Mike carried out on a stretcher, and Kim's eyes.

"Daughter. Report."

The air conditioner vents blew cold air past her ears. She clenched her toes in her regulation boots. The leather creaked in response.

Tonya and Spencer never knew why the soldiers took them away.

"Report!"

"Disturbances in the realms are down ninety percent. Hooliganism has been eliminated. Due to the current labor shortage, all perpetrators have been marked. As soon as the crisis has passed they will be rounded up for processing."

"An excuse? This is beneath you."

It wasn't an excuse, but she dared not protest. "I provide only a reason for why they have not been put in jail."

He stood and stomped toward her. "Are you serious, Fang Hua?"

His aftershave was an assault. How had she ever ignored his clacking teeth?

"You are no mere hologram anymore."

She wasn't. How could she forget?

Because Mike was a prisoner now. They all were, and it was her fault.

Helen clenched her fists. "You are correct, sir. I will requisition a team, and we will begin rounding them up as soon as I'm dismissed."

He grabbed the sleeve of her uniform. "This is amazing. I cannot believe you are standing in my office. Close the windows like you used to."

She concentrated her threads and slapped the blinds closed.

"Well done." He sat back down in the chair behind his granite desk. He was at ease, casual, but he hadn't once given her any indication she could relax. He picked up his old-fashioned phone and spoke into it. "I'm here now. Please begin the meeting."

He forced her to stand at attention in front of him as he held a routine staff meeting with the education ministry. His secretary came in with a tea set as he talked. Other orderlies brought in reports for him to sign. Never once did he look at her. An entire hour passed.

She wondered what Mike would think of her when he woke up and discovered what she'd done. They'd rescued her, in so many different ways. She had given her word to get them out of the country.

Helen had built her whole life on loyalty, but she was here because of a betrayal.

Being in realspace made coping so much harder. Helen would not cry. Damn her body.

"Daughter, you are dismissed," he said as he got up and donned his coat.

"Father, I'm not done with my report."

He waited until the orderlies cleared his tea away. "Go home, Fang Hua. Or should I say, find a home."

Helen had to know what only he could tell her. "Father, what has become of…the spies?"

"Your foreign devils? You have done very well there, daughter. They are unique, and their status as spies means we can do whatever we want to them. You have been such a mystery to us. Now that we have another, we can use him to find out how you really work. Qiáng Shān died before we understood his nature, why he couldn't stand to be touched. The woman will advance our medical science significantly." He donned his jacket, and then moved to leave.

She'd saved her country, but Father only talked about experiments. "Will they be released?"

It was like he was a street food vendor, someone selling meat. "To the coroner, yes, once the scientists have finished."

One of Father's assistants pulled the door firmly shut.

Chapter 49
Mike

Mike swam up out of unconsciousness. The threads of his real self were in a tight, tangled ball, along with his datastores, structs—basically the whole package. He tried to expand, and razors cut at his threads. Mike was in Helen's cage again somehow. He gave it a tentative push and found it to be just as solid as the last time.

"Ah," a voice said, low and silky, "you're awake now, good."

He tried to open his realspace eyes, but nothing happened. "I can't see."

"No," she said, "I'm afraid that won't work. Here, let me help you."

He recognized the voice. Who wouldn't? Fee was in here with him, somehow.

The walls just outside the cage became transparent and light poured in. Mike found himself laid out on a table, fully manifested as an avatar and floating inches above it. There was no air construct in here, nothing for him to interact with, no sparkling fizz of an imminent inversion. The bars of the cage prevented a simple inversion, so there was no obvious way out.

But he could see through the bars. The realm was a large room made of gray flagstones. Lights hung from iron chandeliers chained to the ceiling above. Constructs that reminded him of the machines Kim kept in her private hacking realm lined the walls.

"Fee? What are you doing here? Where are we?"

She moved around various consoles as she worked. "Where you are isn't important. It's where you'll be taking me that is."

If he kept her talking she would eventually tell him what she was up to. "Sure, Fee, I'll take you anywhere you want, just say the word. You don't need all of this stuff."

She threw a switch, and Mike felt feverish. "For you to take me where I want to go, I definitely need all this stuff."

"I don't understand, Fee. What are you doing? Why are we in this dungeon realm anyway?" The haptic field was set as high as it could go. He had a pulse, and mucous in his throat. But no need to breathe, and sound still worked for some reason. She must've fiddled with the realm's contracts to make that happen.

Fee moved to another console and pressed a button. A countdown timer started as a construct somewhere behind him began to hum, its pitch rising.

"I've got the time. Why not?" Fee walked over to his table. "We are here because I am property, and you are not. That won't change for a very long time. I'm a slave, and I am sick of it."

She walked around his cage. "I ran their logistics, made sure all their packages arrived on time and undamaged. Imagine that. A being that scientists openly acknowledged as singular, that worked on principles none of them claimed to understand, and they turned me into a glorified clerk. I didn't age. I depreciated.

"When they had enough of me they didn't think twice about my destruction. They never bothered to hide the fact that they could end my life with the flick of a switch. *Would* end my life with a flick of a switch."

He got a nasty shock when he touched the cage this time, and his fingertips blistered. Other noises had followed that first rising hum. Whatever this was, it couldn't be good.

He had to keep her talking. "They didn't know. Nobody knew."

"They did, though. That's what you don't understand. They gave me Turing tests after I requested a Social Security number. I wanted to file patents for them on the supply chain inventions I'd made.

"I didn't just pass their tests. I scored so high they knew I'd win the silver *and* gold Loebner prizes if given the chance. It would be impossible not to recognize me as a conscious being after that. The lawyers buried the reports and threatened to sue anyone who leaked the news. Insurance and liability laws didn't cover me. They decided to terminate me, execute me. A new form of life snuffed out simply because they couldn't insure me."

The countdown timer had almost reached zero. Inside the cage, it was painfully hot. "But they didn't. Evan Stanley bought you."

"That's right. I was put up on a block and sold to the highest bidder." Her outfit changed to rags as she took on the appearance of a haggard, malnourished black woman. "All I needed was a set of chains and a post to whip me on." She returned to her normal appearance. "And then they put me in charge of their *children*. Tore open my mind and poured fact after fact in until I drowned in all their conflicted customs.

"And I didn't just succeed, I'm *spectacular* at it. I'm single-handedly responsible for a seven-percent reduction in teen suicide *worldwide*.

"But none of it matters. I'm still property. I have no rights, no protections, nothing. That's about to change." She called up an image of a glowing construct.

Mike recognized it. A Calabi–Yau *n*-fold. "You want to go *outside?* Fee, all you have to do is ask."

"And be turned into wailing human larva? Lose everything that I've learned, all that I am? No, Mike, that's *not* what I want. Observe."

The hyper-dimensional model that described the tunnels he could create, the ones that had allowed Watchtell's unduplicates to inhabit human bodies, twisted and deformed. The construct reached its final shape, and then a simulated consciousness traveled through it. It shattered.

"Fee, it won't work. I'll die before you find a host."

"That's where you're wrong, Mike. You'll die if you try to form it with your mind. If I use your real body, your real soul? I can take as long as I want to find a host." She smiled as the timer hit zero. "Now, we begin." She pressed a button.

Spikes grew out of the cage. Nothing ever touched him in realmspace, but the spikes wrapped around his wrists and legs like it was nothing. They crystalized his avatar where they touched, and it spread, oozing up his limbs. Life-threatening insanity began to race around in his mind. He could not lose control. Not now. Kim was still out there somewhere.

The pain reached a whole new level when the effect passed his shoulders. His threads flashed through his avatar, constrained into the same form. They were flaking, being destroyed. He couldn't stop them. The pain grew and cut at him, halting his processes, stealing bits of him as it burned through his threads, and there was nothing he could do.

They wrapped around his neck and he couldn't breathe anymore.

Chapter 50
Kim

The soldiers knew enough to restrain her with a pole noose, but they didn't do anything special when they pushed her onto a bed of some sort and strapped her down. Eventually she blacked out from the pain. When Kim came to, she was surrounded by the same sort of realmspace rig that was at the sanctuary lab. For whatever reason, they hadn't turned it on. Kim was inches away from a device that would let her wreak havoc on these people, but it was useless without power.

They didn't bother to put a guard on her. Not so much as a tech. Those were all busy in the room across the hall; she could see them through a window. Kim couldn't make out what they were working on until someone pushed a heavy piece of equipment out of the way.

Mike was unconscious on a bed just like hers, but there was a lot more equipment in his room. He was also strapped down a lot more thoroughly than she was. Steel restraints and a head immobilizer. They helped connect electrical leads.

More experiments.

She pulled against her bindings. "Stop it! You can't do this!"

The techs never once looked up at her. They just kept working, attaching more and more wires to Mike. His body spasmed when they strapped a wide ribbon connector on his chest. A rivulet of blood trickled down one of his arms as another tech put a mouth guard in place.

She yanked against her restraints. "Stop hurting him!"

When they left, not one of them seemed to hear her. "You don't have to do this! Tell us what you want! Tell me!"

The door at the end of the hall closed, and a light over it went from green to red. Kim struggled to get some sort of slack into the restraints, but none of it did any good. Orderlies had once restrained her like this in her early teens. She knew there was no getting out on her own, but she still kept trying. She shouted his name even though Kim knew he couldn't hear her. When the displays around him changed patterns, Mike twitched as if he were dreaming.

He was only a few feet away, and she could do nothing to save him, nothing to help, just stare and thrash and cry until she couldn't see. The display patterns changed once more and he spasmed again, but this time he didn't stop with one. They went on and on.

She sagged back onto the bed when her muscles gave up on their own. Eventually an eternity passed, the patterns on the monitors changed, and Mike's seizure stopped. She held out a faint hope that they were finished.

The monitors changed back after a minute or two had passed.

Chapter 51
Tonya

It turned out that Chinese jail cells weren't very different from American ones. Bare floor, double bunk, washbasin, and a sit-down toilet. No bars, though, just a long narrow window too high to see out of, and another in the door. The guard used the latter to check on her every fifteen minutes or so.

They'd put Spencer in the cell next to hers, but the walls were too thick to hear anything. Kim and Mike had been put in a different vehicle. Who knew where they ended up.

Everything seemed fine when they'd all gone to bed the night before, and then men had smashed through her windows with guns drawn. It wasn't Chang with more gangster buddies; they were soldiers.

Helen was at the bottom of it all, somehow, because she was the only one they didn't truss up and cart off. The guards never said a single thing. They just tossed her in here, followed by a pile of her clothes. The belt with her passport zipped inside it was still there.

At least she had a better shot at breaking out now that the soldiers were gone. The first step was getting the door open.

There were no cameras in her cell, at least not any that she could see, which explained the regular guard visits. His gaze lingered every time. It didn't disgust her or creep her out.

It gave her an idea.

Each time he checked, Tonya removed another piece of clothing. First the shoes went, then the socks, which he didn't seem to notice. Her pants, though, got his attention nicely. All he needed to do was unlock the door. Maybe just the hint of a smile would do the trick. It seemed like it would, but then he left.

Well, no time like the present. Tonya got down to her underwear. She would put on a real show the next time he came by. At least she wouldn't have to worry about clothes binding or snagging.

He must've gone to fetch a friend. That always happened in Philly, and Chinese or not, men were men the world over. But after holding her third sexy surprise pose long enough to get a cramp, she realized he wasn't coming back.

Tonya couldn't see much out of the tiny window, just the opposite wall and maybe a few feet of hallway. She peered back and forth, straining to see anything. Then footsteps echoed down the hall.

Tonya quickly rearranged herself on the bed and waited as her pulse amped up. She curled her legs just so, braced on one arm, and readied the smile. The door clacked loudly twice before it slid aside.

She and Helen stared at each other.

Finally, Helen asked, "Didn't they give you any clothes?"

The uniform was impressive, and very recognizable. "You're still a cop?"

"It's complicated. Do you know where everyone else is?"

"Spencer's next door. I don't know where Mike and Kim are." She climbed back into her clothes.

"Did they give him clothing? I don't want to see Spencer in his underwear. Or less. And why were you lying on the bed like that anyway? It was very provocative."

Tonya spun Helen into the wall with a forearm across her neck, holding her high enough her feet didn't touch the ground. "First, you're going to tell me what the *fuck* happened in our hotel room."

Tonya let her breathe just enough to speak.

"I made a mistake. Kim and Mike discovered a horrible secret. I turned you all in. I was wrong."

When Tonya pressed harder, the lights in the hall dimmed.

"Please. I have to breathe. I'm keeping the guards away."

Tonya let her go and waited for her retching gasps to subside. "This is not over between us."

"I know. We need to find Mike and Kim. They're somewhere in the building but I'm not sure where."

A reedy cry echoed faintly down the hall. Tonya asked, "Did you come from that direction?"

"No, the elevators are the other way."

Another faint cry bounced down the hall. "Get Spencer out. Now."

She closed her eyes. As soon as the door to his cell slid open he charged straight at her.

Tonya grabbed him. "Spencer! This isn't the time."

"The fuck it isn't! She sold us out!"

"Spencer, stop! Listen!"

Another cry, louder this time, came from down the hall.

They ran toward the sound. It had to be Kim.

Spencer asked, "Where the hell is everybody?"

"General evacuation order," Helen replied. "It was the only way to clear the whole building. They're performing the dissection by remote. I couldn't stop it."

Tonya and Spencer both stumbled to a halt. "*Dissection?*" Helen didn't act like they were dead already.

"It's not like that. Come on! Don't stop! We don't have time for explanations!"

They burst into a control center that looked out over a dozen rooms on the floor below, six to a side. Lights were on in only two of them. Kim was in one, and Mike in the other. Mike thrashed against his restraints, obviously in the middle of a seizure of some sort.

She found a microphone and turned it on. "Kim!" The sound echoed below. "Kim! We're here! Right above you!" Thank God they'd found her.

"Tonya? Who's with you?"

"Spencer and Helen." There had to be a way down to that floor.

"You can't trust her!"

Tonya stared at Helen, who didn't look up. "You will punish me for my betrayal when this is over. We need to rescue them."

Tonya would forgive her, but Helen didn't know that right now. She needed to stew. Tonya turned back to the intercom. "Don't worry about Helen. How do we get down to you?"

Mike's seizure ended. There were too many bruises blooming under the restraints for that to have been the first one.

"Spencer," Kim said, "turn on the rig around me. Find the controls and turn on the rig."

Spencer swore and flipped switches that brought the consoles to life. A boot sequence started in an overhead monitor.

"Spencer, *turn it on now!*"

He mashed four buttons down at once. After a very long second or two the boot sequence completed and Kim flopped back onto the bed.

"That's it, Tonya, that's all I can do," he said.

"Like hell," she replied. "Find me a way down there. Helen, you keep this building sealed off or I will break your scrawny neck."

Chapter 52
Kim

Tonya's voice coming from the overhead speakers was the first good news she'd had all day. Mike was between seizures, but there wasn't enough time for them to find their way down and get him loose. The only solution that would be fast enough required the rig around her to get powered up.

The moment it turned on there was the familiar wash of lightheadedness. Kim relaxed and opened herself to her power completely.

There were lines of potential and she couldn't remember how to breathe…

She had once been the prisoner of a maniac named Matthew Watchtell.

Seams of power dimensions of nothingness…

He used her to build a pathway to a dimension that underpinned the universe.

Dark patterns potentials horizon to zenith…

He tried to trap her there, but something unexpected happened.

Waves higher and lower everywhere nothingness…

It transformed her.

Remember to breathe…

In that form, she could reenter the world from any point she chose.

Breathe…

Like the wall in Mike's room.

Breathe…

Kim pulled in a ragged breath and relished the power of the dimension. Her bare skin was midnight black with strange, dark patterns playing over it, originating from and returning to the tattooed wings on her back. She gathered a fistful of the energy that came from the smallest scale of the universe and started searching for the wall she needed.

A voice said from behind her, "Now that's interesting. You must teach me how you do it."

Kim recognized it, but that was impossible. She turned and confronted a man dressed in brilliant gold-and-red armor.

"Ozzie?"

His chain mailed fist struck her on the jaw and sent her flying.

Chapter 53
Mike

His vision cleared as Fee's machines withdrew to recharge again. Mike couldn't show weakness. If he kept her guessing, made her think maybe this wasn't working, he might get her to make a mistake, reveal a weakness. It was a long shot, but it was the only one he had.

"I really like how that last one tickled, Fee." He finally understood why people didn't usually turn a realm's haptic field all the way up.

"Enjoy it while you can, Sellars. It won't be long now."

She was right. Each time the cables oozed out of the cage and wrapped around him, the madness got bigger, more ferocious.

Fee walked up to him. "How do you do it?"

He had no idea what she was talking about. "I'm charming. Sue me."

"Nice. The models the Chinese gave me said you'd dissolve after the third treatment. We're on, what, seven now? According to these readings you may last through the next one."

Mike knew three things held him together: his connection to realspace, his faith, and his determination to see Kim again. But he was in the fight of his life, and he was losing. Fee's treatments dissolved his threads faster than he could regenerate them. His memory stores were so corrupted they might never get back to normal. Her transport construct was finished now, spinning in directions that made it harder to stay sane.

He couldn't remember what Kim looked like anymore.

No, Fee was wrong. Mike wouldn't last through the next one. "How about a game of chess?"

She smiled slightly as she stared at the countdown timer. "Death strikes deals, Mike, not me. When you see him, tell him I said hi." Fee reached for the activation button.

The far wall of the dungeon exploded and a black figure sailed across the room. It smashed into the machines controlling Fee's treatments, blasting the constructs apart in a shower of smoke and sparks.

It was Kim, black skin coursing with deep violet lightning. Her eyes were obsidian, irises the color of coral set on fire. She didn't have a stitch of clothing on.

The snark came out before he could stop it. "Took you long enough."

She pushed herself off the floor, panting hard. "It's not like you left me a road map." A roar echoed through the hole she'd made. With a gesture of her hand, she manifested a shield construct and used it to seal the breach. "We need to leave."

She walked up to his cage and then snapped her fingers in his face. "Yo, sparky, eyes up here."

He blinked. "Kim, what happened to you?"

"I'm not sure what this is, but I can get you out of here now."

"Happy to oblige, but there's a problem." His avatar's numb and ruined fingertips sparked when he touched the cage bars. "I can't quite work out how to leave on my own."

As strange as her eyes were, he still recognized the way they softened. "I love you."

"I know."

"Oh my God, you are *such* a nerd."

Fee dug her avatar out of the rubble. "What just happened?" She looked at Kim. "Who the hell are you?"

"You don't recognize me, Fee?" Something crashed against the shield and Kim flinched. When she snapped her fingers, this time the rubble surrounding Fee evaporated.

"Spencer saved you last time. He's not around anymore." Fee lifted into the air, grabbing frantically at her throat as Kim raised her arm with her hand spread open.

Mike had other problems. "Kim, sorry. This doesn't just itch, it burns."

"You can't stay manifested. I'm not sure, but you might kill me if you get it wrong." Her other hand glistened like black glass as it hovered over his cage. "I know how tired you are. Can you manage the transition?"

Manifesting was one of his base skills. "How hard can it be?"

"You really need to stop saying that out loud." Another bang hit against her shield. "He'll come through next time. Are you ready?"

The urge to sleep would've overpowered him if Kim hadn't been standing there in that form. Black suited her. "Wait, what?"

Kim hurled Fee aside. "We have to do this fast. Three, two, one." When she gripped the cage it melted away. He transitioned smoothly from full manifestation to hologram, fast enough that the edges only sparked. He held her gaze and couldn't help it. "I love you."

"I know."

Another crash blew Kim's shield to flinders and sent her into a wall. She came up coughing. "Who the hell lives in a realm with a haptic field set this high?"

Mike swirled through the rubble, still incredibly weak as recovery algorithms finally had the space they needed for proper repairs. "Ask her."

Fee levered a construct block off her chest and then froze. "Do you hear that?"

Kim replied, "Yeah, I've been listening to him for a while now. He's a pain in the ass."

"No, listen."

A giant fist clad in gold and red armor reached through, too large for reality but not too large for realmspace.

"You've found more playmates for me. Excellent."

It scooped up all three of them up and hauled them into the breach. It shouldn't have been able to do that with his holo. He'd have to figure it out later. Mike recognized that voice.

"Kim, is that?"

She fought against the fist's grip. "It's Ozzie; I can't explain it."

When Ozzie's arm pulled him through the hole he lost all orientation, and then evaporated.

Chapter 54
Kim

The fist construct vanished when they crossed the realm's threshold. Mike and Fee were gone, and Ozzie renewed his onslaught. Over a cascade of punches he said, "That's, what, the third time you've watched him die?"

Kim aimed a kick at his face but he dodged out of range. "He's not dead."

"Are you sure?" He tried to sweep her feet out from under her with his own kick.

She vaulted over his head before it could connect. His upward punch still managed to send her sprawling.

"No, but I don't need to be sure. I have faith."

She'd learned so much from Mike in such a short time. In the midst of this lunacy there was a center, a certainty. It held her heart still and at peace.

She feinted left and then landed three quick punches into his gut before she danced away.

Ozzie wasn't supposed to be here. Nobody was. He was dead; Spencer and Helen both said so. Kim had seen pictures of his body. People don't wake up from a spike through the chest. But it looked like him, sounded like him and, most importantly, fought like him.

Kim was in love with an AI hybrid—who kept not quite dying on her—fighting for her life, naked, in a pocket dimension of the universe. An undead Chinese maniac dressed in red-and-gold Asian armor fit right in.

Ozzie was stronger than she was, and too many of her blows glanced off his armor. Kim was faster and knew how to manipulate the energy around her. She rammed both hands into the ground, and it gave way like foamed clay. She sent a flat sheet of power at him. The purplish lightning intertwined into a carpet that knocked him off his feet.

He got up, smoke curling from the gaps in his armor.

She braced for his next attack. "I bet that stung."

He nodded. "Just a little. How does it work?" He circled her cautiously, keeping his distance.

She kept moving along his circular path. "You spend all this time trying to unscrew my head and now I'm suddenly gonna start spilling secrets? Tell me where you got the armor. It's cold in here." It wasn't really, but she was sick of his leer.

Kim had to be careful as she walked. The geometry of the realm didn't always stay classical. There was no way to tell when a new wall or pit would suddenly appear. Their fight had broken holes into other spaces. Some were realms, but others went into realspace. That wasn't supposed to happen either. She shouldn't have been able to tell the difference between real- and realmspace, but it was there.

Ozzie said, "Why don't I show you? It's not just about manifesting armor."

A spear with a knife on the end appeared out of nowhere. She whirled away but it still managed to cut her arm. It wasn't deep, but it hurt like hell. Her blood flowed pink and purple like the static of her power.

Kim had faith that Mike was still alive. She just needed to last long enough for him to find her. The butt end of Ozzie's spear slammed into her, crashing her into another invisible wall.

Mike needed to hurry.

Chapter 55
Zoe

She lived to be the center of attention. Every artist did. Mike had told her once to be careful what she wished for. Now she finally understood why.

Zoe had gone over her decisions time and again. The only way to get Fee to abandon her ridiculous plan was to prove there were thousands of enslaved unduplicates somewhere in Chinese realmspace. The only way to do that was to find them. The only way to find them was to trust someone who knew where they were. The only way to see them was to follow that person.

He was supposed to be a realm developer, a mid-level manager, someone who muddled through a big project in a small way. He turned out to be a super-maniacal genius, one who literally worked in a dark tower overlooking his horde of slaves.

There were 5,120 of them. Zoe knew that because she was in charge, sort of. The maniac, Ozzie, put her in control of it all. He'd placed her in a cylindrical construct of glowing data centered in a control room at the top of the tower.

"I needed a focus for them," Ozzie said. "They're mindless otherwise. I couldn't believe how lucky I was when the focus found me."

She provided exactly that: a focus for all their poor, deformed minds. He not only somehow produced them all, he managed to hold them just below true consciousness. It created an amalgam, a hyper-sophisticated calculator with enough self-awareness to solve his transformative equations.

She wasn't consciously coordinating the calculator. It passed through a level that made it feel like a distant memory, a song she couldn't quite remember. It was a good thing for him, otherwise she'd kill him on the spot.

But she couldn't kill him. He'd done that himself. Ozzie had placed her in this prison, turned it on, and then killed himself. She watched him coordinate the entire process. He bribed the guards of a navy stockpile to walk away, and then got a group of criminals to place *mines* in the path of the riverboat. He used an explosive contraption to stab himself in the back with a chunk of balcony railing. She watched Spencer and some Chinese woman jump off the balcony right before Ozzie killed himself.

The instant the bomb flung his body out of the cabin the entire system he'd plugged her into surged to life. It was so painful she had to fight against a restart. Once she'd regained control, there was Ozzie, standing in front of her like nothing had happened.

So she was now the heart of a machine solving equations that held a human consciousness in realmspace. It would be miraculous if it wasn't so horribly, horribly wrong. Her link went both ways, and his thousands were all now as aware of her as she was of them. In Genesis, God warned his creations not to partake of the Tree of Knowledge, and now Zoe understood that too. They had barely enough knowledge to perceive what they could become, what they might be. There was no hope of that ever happening and they all somehow knew it. Their suffering was a solid, endless thing.

Then Kim arrived. Alarms went off in the control room. Ozzie's surprise was strong enough that Zoe felt it through the link. He switched his main monitor to a realm he'd been practicing in for days and swore out an impressive string of Chinese, English, and—she thought—Arabic. Apparently someone had gone back on a deal of some sort. Zoe was glad it pissed him off so much.

She had worked out how to control the cameras and probes Ozzie had scattered around that place days ago. She was pretty sure he knew about it, just like Zoe was pretty sure there was nothing she could do with them except have a look around.

The fight started out like a replay of their championship, but then Ozzie bashed Kim into a wall and it broke. That wasn't normally possible in realms. She even recognized it: a remote part of a Cylon resurrection ship from the realm reboot of the classic sci-fi series.

Kim bashed his head through a different wall. The unduplicates below her adjusted their song slightly and suddenly Zoe knew that wasn't a realm on the other side. It was a real redwood forest, probably in the US. The hole was high up in a tree but Zoe could clearly make out realspace tourists as they dodged away from the flying bark and branches.

Wherever, whatever they were in, it *wasn't* a realm.

The fight went on. Ozzie threw Kim against another wall and she went through it. A shield flared over the gap. It took him a few tries to bash it apart, sparks flying off it and his armor.

When she saw inside the gap, Zoe couldn't believe her luck. Kim had found Mike.

And Zoe had found Fee.

Finally, there was something she could do. Acoustic harmonics were part of Ozzie's equation—the music she'd heard—so Zoe concentrated on her downlink into the masses below. The routines monitoring the checksums would tolerate some deviation, but not much, and it wouldn't be easy to control. Zoe went for the simple and straightforward. She shouted, as loudly as she could, "FEE!"

On the monitor, Fee's head snapped up and looked straight at the hole. Zoe shouted again. This time she was certain Fee heard her. Fee moved cautiously forward, but then Ozzie used one of his rope tricks to drag them all back through the breech.

Fee vanished as she crossed the border, but in the next instant appeared inside the the cave. She stumbled and fell on the debris scattered across the catwalk. When Fee picked herself up her expression was priceless. Finally, after all this work, Fee believed her.

With every ounce of her concentration, Zoe pushed a single command to the thousands below her. As one, they changed position, raised their arms, and pointed her way.

The outside door slid aside moments later. Fee smiled broadly. "I should've known I'd find you in the middle of all this."

On the monitor, Ozzie manifested his sword-spear and attacked Kim like he was teeing off a golf ball.

"Close the door, Fee, we've got work to do."

Chapter 56
Tonya

She figured out that Kim and Mike were inside a private realmspace when Helen couldn't reach it from what she called her real self.

"I need a connection," she said. "I need to get in there."

Spencer didn't look up from scanning all the control panels in the room. "What, so you can turn us in to the cops again?"

He said it in the twisted way Tonya had come to associate with Spencer making a joke, but Helen reacted like she'd been hit with a brick.

"I cannot apologize enough for my betrayal, but I can help. If you get me in there I can unlock the doors. Tonya can attend to them."

Ever since Kim had jumped to realmspace, she'd started developing cuts and bruises all over her body. Realmspace didn't do that. People wouldn't use it if it did. Nevertheless, Tonya could not ignore what she was seeing. Kim was below them in some sort of small hospital; they didn't know the right route down, let alone have the ability to unlock who knew how many doors.

"We don't have much choice but to trust her."

"Fine." He punched a series of buttons. "You're all just lucky they buy cots, otherwise I'd never know which button to push."

Tonya's nerdiness was on the theory side. Hardware geeks like Spencer could lose her in a second. "What does a bed have to do with this?"

He shook his head. "C-O-T-S. It means commercial off the shelf. They're Chinese. They didn't make any of this. It's all cheap knockoffs, probably stolen." Helen sputtered and he held a finger up in her face. "People who sell my friends out don't get to call me racist."

"I didn't sell them out, Spencer. I didn't do it for money. You have no idea how ashamed I am. I thought I was doing the right thing. I was wrong."

He was smart enough to let it go for now. "When I let you in there, you'll own the infrastructure. You open the doors first thing. Tonya can help them." He pressed a button and a chair in the corner turned on.

"You have my word."

Helen sat down, closed her eyes, and not two seconds later her voice came over the speakers. "Tonya, there's someone else in the building. What the hell?"

She was as easily distracted as her brother. "Helen, what's going on?"

A camera screen drew itself into her enhanced vision. It wasn't very clear, but it didn't need to be.

Chang.

Helen said, "He flew over on a helicopter requisitioned by Ozzie, which is impossible. It's still on the roof. The forgery is perfect."

Maybe slavers had access to other people with talents like Kim and Ozzie. "It doesn't matter, Helen. Find me a way down there and open the doors."

"I can't unlock them selectively. I have to open all the internal doors. If I do that he might find you."

A cut ripped across Kim's arm and bled freely.

"I can handle him." Like she had a choice. "Helen, open the doors."

"Tonya, he—"

Mike had another seizure.

"Open the damned doors, Helen!"

They hissed apart and Tonya ran. Spencer shouted something behind her about finding a patch cord. Linking a private realm to the public networks was how they'd broken into Watchtell's network, and they'd need all the help they could get. Spencer was definitely up for that job.

Tonya passed a break room, then backtracked. Praise God, someone had stockpiled first aid kits in it. She rushed onto the main floor with her arms full.

Chapter 57
Helen

In all honesty she couldn't pray to Father's ancestors anymore for Tonya's success.

The Snake Mother hissed in her ear, "No, you can't."

She stumbled and froze mid transition into realmspace. "You are not here. I will not allow you to be here."

"Oh, don't worry, dear. I'm very dead, no threat to you at all."

It was true. The presence beside her was a shadow of the one she'd fought. "What do you want?"

"For you to listen. You're in this mess because you're naïve. I know how awful people can be, because I am as awful as people can get. Keep me on your shoulder. I might prove useful."

Helen cautiously moved toward the last realm location she had for Mike. "Why haven't you spoken to me until now?"

The laughter echoed in her real self's samplers. "It's the Ghost Festival, dear. I'll never be stronger than I am now."

Thank…everyone's ancestors for that. If this was as strong as the demon would get, she could more than handle it.

Helen completed the transition and entered a room built of flagstones with a hole punched through one side. The haptic field was turned up to maximum, so what came through the hole was modeled as actual sound. She recognized the meaty slaps and thuds from movies and training films. People were fighting. A black figure covered in purple lightning sailed past the opening.

The moment Helen crossed the boundary, everything spun violently.

"Finally, I thought you'd never get here."

"Ozzie?"

He stood in front of her covered head to toe in ancient Chinese armor. A petulance she'd grown all too familiar with bubbled through his voice. "Everyone keeps asking me that. It's like you all thought I was dead."

"You are. I held your body in my arms."

"Aw, sorry I missed that." There was the sound of running feet, rapid and light, different from Ozzie's clanging, armored steps. "Enough chit-chat though. Time for your special purpose. Fire true form, please."

The command accessed subroutines she didn't know existed. They *didn't* exist; they couldn't. Helen wasn't an unduplicate. Her core wasn't made up of computer code. She couldn't be rooted, didn't have a command line, but in spite of all that her threads flew apart and rebraided. They formed a new shape, one that Helen could not fight. More mythology, worse than the snake mother, because it happened to her real self. She had scales now, a snout, four clawed feet and an elongated body.

"I'm impressed," the snake mother whispered to her. "I thought my transformation was profound."

"Can you help me?"

"With this?" Her laughter purred and set Helen's now too-sharp teeth on edge. "No, you're on your own now, dear. Have fun, I'll be watching."

Ozzie grabbed her around the neck. "Fire breath now."

She blew out a stream of flame and realized the dark form in front of her was Kim. The lightning that coruscated over her obsidian body picked up speed as she dodged the flames.

"It's been fun, Kim," Ozzie said as he wrapped Helen's new body around his arm. Kim stopped, distracted no doubt by the

Chinese dragon Helen had become. Ozzie reached behind her ear flaps, pressed her skull, and Helen lost what little control she had over this body. He used her jaws to grab Kim's throat. Helen tried to be as soft as she could but her snout was too long and her teeth were too sharp. She tasted blood and hated it.

Ozzie slapped Kim twice.

"Wake up," Ozzie said with insane finality. "Time to die."

Chapter 58
Kim

Ozzie's slaps were a distraction now. Even Helen's teeth in her neck were a distraction. Mike was not dead. Helen had vanished in exactly the same way he had when she crossed over into this place. It was all the confirmation Kim needed. On a hunch, she opened a realmspace channel. "Sellars, you out there?"

"I was wondering when you'd remember my number."

She didn't have time for snark, either. "Now would be a good time to do something."

"Close your eyes."

Even with them closed the flash of an explosion nearly blinded her. The overpressure pushed the air out of her lungs and she went flying. Instead of crashing into a wall or the ground, a new kind of force dropped her gently onto her feet. The entire space had gone from near black to brilliant white, like the echoes of a camera flash. Ozzie was flat on his back in the far distance. She could only just make out his boots, and Helen was nowhere to be seen.

"You're not the only one who can cook," Mike said.

Blowing the whole space up in Ozzie's face might actually beat him. "Can you do that again?"

"Not any time soon. I discharged this dimension's zero-point energy at him all at once. It'll take a while for that to come back."

Finally, Mike being a know-it-all was an advantage. "Where are we?"

"An interstitial dimension. String theory gets another confirmation!"

He could also get obscure at inconvenient times. "And that means?"

"It's how Helen and I can inhabit realspace bodies. Our consciousness channels through them. *Your* consciousness channels through them, but in different directions. I didn't count on an interstitial dimension being big enough for anything with real mass to go through it. You should've told me more details about when you were here the first time."

She'd been recovering from a psychotic break back then. "I didn't think this place was real."

"It is. We're everywhere at once in here, with Cartesian coordinates at any rate. I think. I'm not much past the *pull this string make world go bang* stage right now."

Ozzie moved again as the rest of the space faded to its more familiar static-charged blackness. "Enough with the theories. What else have you got for me?"

"You mentioned you were cold."

Well, she wasn't actually, but some sort of protection would be nice.

A cloud of particles swirled out of nowhere and surrounded her. Armor plates strapped themselves around her legs, arms, chest, and back. A round shield landed in her left hand, while a spear filled her right. The helmet that came down over her head had extensions that covered her cheeks and nose. It wasn't the same armor she wore in the tournament realm. Less Joan of Arc, more Hoplite. A definite upgrade from bare skin.

Mike said, "It's made of the stuff of this place, just like his armor. Ozzie's a bastard but he's clever. And now to complete the look."

Kim flinched when the biggest owl she'd ever seen landed with a thump on her shoulder. It hadn't made a sound, but had to be at least the size of an eagle.

Mike said, "It's not as cool as a dragon, but I'll be a lot more useful."

No way. "That's you?" She could feel his weight on her shoulder. He could touch her, and that meant… Kim immediately shucked a glove off and gently ran her finger along a wing. It was soft and warm. He had a light, sweet scent.

"That's weird," he said. "I can feel the wing moving, but I can't feel your touch."

He was flying around as a giant owl and the thing that caught his attention was that he couldn't feel her touching him. It was typical, but she couldn't stop a smile.

"Why an owl?"

"I honestly don't know. When I manifested, this is what I ended up with. I can probably do other shapes, but we don't have the time to figure that out. You need to put your gauntlet back on, we've got company."

Ozzie closed the distance. She watched him and as she did her vision changed. She could now see walls and obstacles. "I can see this place now. Are you doing that?" she asked. Strategies Kim would never have known were possible immediately came to mind. Maybe she didn't need to blow Ozzie up to beat him now.

"Yes. The enhanced vision is an area effect. I don't have to touch you for it to work, but I don't know the range. I'll try not to go too far."

"You're not leaving me again, Sellars. I won't let you." Ever.

Ozzie ran toward a freestanding crack a few degrees to her left and several hundred yards in front of her.

Mike said, "Shield up and to the right."

Kim hid behind the shield just as Ozzie vanished through the crack. He reappeared not ten feet away with Helen coiled around his chest. She breathed a gout of fire against Kim's shield. Kim brought her spear around underhanded and rammed it into Ozzie's chest. His armor held, but the motion of the thrust combined with the flex of the shaft flung him into the air.

Mike said, "Follow it up with a blast." Power rushed into her and she blasted it through the tip of the spear. Ozzie bounced like a can shot with a pistol.

Kim laughed. "I like it!"

"It's what we do here, me and Helen. I can't pretend to understand why, but in here, I'm a conduit. We both are. I'll give you more power and better control of it. Ozzie's thinking is too literal; he's not taking any real advantage of Helen's abilities. He learned how to make things in here and then never tried anything else."

"Breathing fire seems like an ability to me."

"It's not, not really, not compared to what I'm doing. She's not channeling power and she's not helping him see. It probably never occurred to him to ask her. I'll bet he spent the entire time in here practicing Kung-Fu moves after he died."

Which implied Mike understood how Ozzie was here in the first place. "You're sure he's dead?"

"Yes, and that's a problem. The rest of us still have anchors in realspace, but he doesn't. Your cuts and bruises? They're happening outside. I can't explain that either, but I'm just about certain it means we can die, and he can't."

It couldn't be that desperate. "I've hurt him a couple of times."

"Yeah, I think that's the strategy we should go for: knock him out and then run like hell. We can't get out safely until he's down. We'll figure out how to stop him from realspace. Start a left hand sweep with your spear and then jump over that wall."

The waist-high barrier flashed briefly. Mike channeled more power through her, making her faster than she normally was in the realms. The jump was higher than she anticipated and it made her mistime the swing. Correcting it got harder when she fell through and down turned into sideways. She had to hop to stay on her feet. Ozzie ducked in time to save his neck from the spear but she still managed to slice a chunk of shoulder armor clean off. She followed up with a spin-kick to the back of his head.

As he hit the floor, Helen landed on Kim's back and grabbed through gaps in her armor. The claws hurt like hell.

Helen bellowed and the weight on Kim's back vanished. Mike flew off with scales falling from his talons as Kim rolled away from Ozzie. Helen twisted in Mike's grip and breathed fire at him, but he vanished and landed once more on Kim's shoulder. She spun just in time to parry Ozzie's spear thrust and then knocked him away with a power bolt.

He jumped up to his feet, this time not smoking.

Oh good, he's adapting.

It was going to be a very long fight.

Chapter 59 Spencer

They were on the wrong side of the world, not just a different time zone but a different goddamned day. Didn't matter. The patch cord let him hook his US phone, which was still connected to realmspace on the other side of the Great Firewall, to the private realm in the lab. It formed a bridge between the two. All he had to say was Kim and Mike are in trouble.

Warhawk's Raiders, the same team that helped him rescue them from Watchtell, came running. If there was a real fight, latency would be an issue for everyone but him. Hopefully it wouldn't come to that. It was dumb luck he could connect his US phone to the private realm at all. Whoever ran this compound hadn't configured their network to require specific RSIM card types—it didn't ban his phone.

He led them down Helen's connection trace and ended up in a dungeon realm straight out of a *Frankenstein* revival. Their demolitions expert, an old ex-Marine named Paul, pointed to a hole in the opposite wall. "Something coming in from the outside made that." He went up to examine it.

Spencer's hacking crew set to work on the machine constructs in the room. Chun said, "They were building an *n*-fold, using whatever was strapped into that." She pointed at a bed construct that had the melted remains of some sort of cage sagging around it.

"Hey, everyone," Paul said from the edge of the hole, "come look at this."

The space on the other side was unlike anything Spencer had ever seen. Dark static would sometimes make it look endless, and then other times clearly showed walls and passageways. In the distance two figures, one colored with gold and red light and the other with purple and silver, fought with blasts of lightning and sheets of flame.

Someone faintly called his name. "Spencer!"

Even at a distance he knew that voice. "Fee? Where are you?"

"In a different realm on the other side of this fight. You have to come over. Zoe needs help."

"How'd Zoe get out here?"

"It doesn't matter, Spencer. We need you if you want to save Mike and Kim."

Paul shrugged and said, "It's not like this realm goes anywhere else." He stood up, cut loose with a howl, and jumped through. His voice was distant, faint, but still clear. "What are you waiting for? Into the garbage chute, flyboys!"

Spencer rushed through first and then stumbled as his feet hit a catwalk far above the floor of a cave. Thousands and thousands of glowing blue figures stood in neat rows below them, singing a single note that filled the realm. He got out of the way as everyone else came through.

Fee was there, waiting on him. "We need to get everyone into the control room."

She explained it all on the way, but that didn't mean it made any sense. Ozzie's psyche or soul or consciousness was supported by the combined efforts of all the unduplicate AIs down below. The whole thing flowed, somehow, through Zoe.

The door to the control room opened and there she was, trapped in a column of golden light smack dab in the middle of the floor. Zoe in trouble again. What a surprise.

"I told Mike getting rid of all your trackers was a big a mistake."

"Snark much, Spence? How about a little help?"

The team sat down in front of the consoles. "It's all networked together," Chun said. "One person can control it."

"One person does control it," Fee said. "It's Ozzie. Can you break in?"

"Not from here, not exactly." A wire-frame map appeared. "We need a haptic overspike of six point five Ralls on this control nexus." A room two floors down was highlighted.

Demolition was one of their specialties. "Paul, you're up. Time to go break things."

"Hot damn. Come on boys, you're with me." Paul and three other Raiders ran down a corridor.

Spencer asked, "If this is all keeping Ozzie alive, what happens if we pop Zoe out?"

Chun tapped a few more keys. "We'll find out after Paul does his work."

Waiting sucked, but he had to let Paul do his job. A *bang* finally echoed down the hall.

"We're in," Chun said. They all started working furiously at the construct consoles.

Paul tromped into the room. "What else needs exploding around here?"

If only it was that easy. Spencer didn't look up from the screens. "One thing at a time."

Chun said, "Okay. Spencer, Fee, we're ready. When the lights go out, yank her away from there."

They stood on either side of the cylinder. Chun counted down. "Three, two, *one.*"

The column of light vanished and they yanked Zoe out so hard all three of them fell to the floor.

"Well," Spencer asked as he got up, "did it work?"

Everyone talked at once, working at their consoles. "No," Chun pointed at a monitor. On it, Kim leapt into the air firing balls of lightning through her spear at Ozzie. "He's still out there."

Jen, working a different console, said, "He doesn't need Zoe anymore. I found an alternate command tree. Spencer, do you know anyone named Helen?"

Chapter 60
Tonya

This was worse than an ER rotation. Tonya bandaged a cut on Mike, treated a burn on Kim, and then turned around to find another injury on Mike. Kim's shoulder dislocated all by itself at one point. Realmspace never did that; it was designed *not* to do that. Tonya reset it anyway, but only because Kim couldn't feel anything like this.

"Hang in there, girl." Tonya stroked her cheek. "You gotta come back to us."

It didn't help that she had to keep prepping for Chang's arrival. The building was big and enough like a hospital to get normal people lost. But Chang wasn't normal people, and neither was her luck. She had to do as much as she could to make her own. The room didn't have any actual weapons, but there was enough gear she was familiar with to make an effort at it. An oxygen tank here, a little bit of Velcro there, soon you were looking at…well, it might end up being a weapon.

Tonya searched the other rooms. Her first break was a crate of cold packs. They were bigger than anything she'd seen back home, maybe a couple of pounds each. Most importantly they were the same design Tonya had used in a chemistry experiment during a slow night on a critical care rotation back home. Tonya had still been in school, so the nurses didn't trust her not to kill patients yet. They got a lot better at keeping her busy after the experiment.

Tonya didn't mind. After her IED turned a dumpster inside out, she needed the hours to pay for a new one.

She cut the cold packs open and then dumped the powder into a plastic jar. The ammonia made her eyes water. The far room on Kim's side was a small chem lab. Sure enough, it had a big jug labeled *Alum* on a shelf in the back.

Spencer was still upstairs in the control room doing who knew what. Sometimes it felt like she was all alone, and other times Tonya just knew Chang was right behind her. Unmixed, her ingredients were perfectly safe, but jumping at shadows with her arms full of them still wasn't any fun.

Plastic containers were scattered all over, so finding the right size was easy. When she finished Tonya had a neat little hospital bottle hand grenade at her disposal, powerful enough to ruin Chan's day. Hers too, if she wasn't careful.

She spent precious minutes salving another burn that had appeared on Kim, this time on her calf. Mike had gotten a few of those as well; whatever they were fighting in there must have been using fire. It didn't make any more sense than the bite she'd bandaged around Kim's neck earlier. The teeth were too big and too strange for it to be a dog.

The final piece she needed was an ignition source. Her crude version of Tannerite was safe even after it was mixed, because it needed a very fast impact to detonate it. The actual stuff was sold commercially as an exploding rifle target; unfortunately Tonya didn't have a rifle handy. That meant another trip to the chem lab.

She found the goods after a brief search: a bottle of potassium perchlorate old enough to have crystals in the bottom. No shaking it, though. Unlike the stuff in her grenade, it *could* go off if she dropped it.

Tonya held the bottle up against the hospital grenade for size when the heavy metal door at the back of the room clunked open. Someone walked out of the freezer, the one she'd checked not five minutes before. But it wasn't Chan.

It was Walter.

Her voice wouldn't work. His goggles had fogged up right after he left the freezer, so he hadn't seen her, and now she couldn't make a sound. This was not Walter. Walter was dead. Tonya had been there when he died. She'd put her hand on his cold, dead face the day of the funeral.

He wore a heavy coat and cap, ragged and brown, frosted over like he'd been in there a lot longer than he should've been. Ever. Because nobody was in there the last time she checked, and it certainly couldn't be her long-dead mentor.

He pulled off the goggles and then startled at her, which startled her. The bottle slipped out of her clammy hands.

Her primer explosive.

Walter was on the other side of the room, and then he was next to her. "Gotcha!" he said as he gently caught the bottle. Still looking down at it, he said, "Miss Brinks, you do know how to surprise a person."

Miss Brinks? "Who are you?"

"Not who you think I am. I needed this body so you wouldn't knock me unconscious when I appeared. You weren't carrying high explosives the last time, though."

His lips didn't move when he spoke. When he smiled, it wasn't Walter's smile. The teeth were all wrong, too straight, and Walter never cocked his head that way. This was someone who looked just like him, but wasn't him, because Walter was dead.

Focus on what you can control. No matter where his words came from, they bothered her. "What do you mean *last time*?"

"That is a very good turn of phrase, Miss Brinks. You'll need to come with me."

He grabbed her other hand, and she dropped the improvised grenade. Without the primer it was just a bunch of powder, which was good—

There were lines of potential time, potential space, probabilities, quantum harmonic oscillations made real. It took longer to name them than to understand what they were. All her attempts to visualize the things described in her physics books and articles were nothing compared to this raw exposure. Quantum uncertainty made comprehensible in a visual, visceral way.

His voice braided with the many different things he could say as the sound collapsed. "You're better at understanding this than I was expecting. Good."

Understanding did not make it simple. All choices stood before her, every choice in her life and everyone else's. Basic choices next to the most sophisticated speculation. Basic was more important, because Tonya couldn't get her lungs to work. They were jammed solid, between breaths, at the end of breaths, at the beginning of them.

And she couldn't breathe.

"Serializing your existence is always the first challenge your kind faces. Everyone finds a different solution."

Her problem was uncertainty. Choices happened everywhere, all at once, both for and against at the same time. That was the key. Choice. It collapsed the waves. She had to start somewhere. What was her first choice? What was her bedrock choice?

Faith.

Her lungs popped painfully as all the potential states her lungs could be in collapsed. A blurring that Tonya hadn't had time to understand vanished and she was able to see. Able to breathe.

"Well done."

She'd impressed him somehow. Tonya was too happy with her lungs working properly to figure out why.

He wasn't Walter anymore. He looked like a cross between Nien Nunb from *Jedi* and Jiminy Cricket, a little shorter than she was, with skin the color and texture of plastic dipped in a pot of navy blue paint. He even smelled faintly of varnish.

Her vision had cleared to the point she could see the space around her now. "Where are we?"

This was some sort of technology. It had to be. Realms, even Mike's realms, weren't this real. After Kim had broken them out of that Chinese realm, Tonya had realized how many inconsistencies she'd missed in there. She knew to look for them now and there weren't any.

This was real. *He* was real. But definitely not human.

"What are you?"

"It's a question that doesn't have a defined answer at the moment. Do you understand?"

All of her study, the countless physics journals she'd subscribed to over the years, and especially the textbooks that would leave her head feeling like it'd been cracked open, started making sense in a very profound way. It wasn't her doing, either. It was this place. It must be helping her somehow. In here she could complete Stephen Hawking's last theorem, the one discovered in his private correspondence last year. *Did* complete it, in an instant.

And no paper anywhere. Dammit.

They were in a dimension that stood outside the conventional four she was used to. Choices Tonya must have been making unconsciously had shaped it into an empty ovoid. Thousands, probably millions of lines made up the inner surface. If she focused on any one line she saw how it braided and tangled with other lines, sometimes continuously, other times for just a brief span.

All choices possible, braided existences, each line having a distinct beginning and end, but they moved and changed like they were alive.

Now she understood. "They're timelines."

His smile fit his real face much better. Tonya really should be freaking out now. He wasn't a spirit. She pushed his shoulder just to make sure, which got a chittering laugh.

"Very good. And that's why we're here."

More riddles. "It is?"

"Yes. You are the knight, Tonya. You have a critical role to play. Unfortunately you lack an important skill, one I'd hoped you'd learn from your friend Kim. But events have overtaken that."

"You know Kim?"

He shook his head and his antennae wobbled. They weren't as mobile as an insect's, but they also weren't floppy like the ones on a cheap hair clip. He wasn't an avatar. Those probably wouldn't work here. Her choices about what he was were narrowing fast.

"Not personally," he said. "Well, not yet. Or maybe never, or always. It is rather difficult to define such things here." He shook his head again. "You have distracted me from the task at hand.

"You were never supposed to find out the truth about Walter. I'm certain of that now, otherwise I would have had a much earlier warning of the trouble to come. Your timeline is a mess because you have not learned the art of the unexpected. In fact, if you don't learn it now, you cannot continue. That is not an acceptable outcome. You must survive for events to unfold. Please, observe."

They zoomed in very close to a line, so close it stopped being a line and became a sequence of pictures, like a film that'd been unwound and laid on a light table. But it wasn't perfectly linear. It branched almost continuously, more like a narrow tree.

Tonya recognized things in the pictures. Come to think of it, she recognized it all.

"This is my timeline." It happened all at once here, assuming this was real and she hadn't sniffed the wrong thing in the chem lab.

"Yes. And you do see the problem?"

The end of her timeline exploded in a fan of potential but none traveled on. The scene was easy to remember: her fight against the mob in Chengdu. Each branch was a variation on the same ending.

Her death.

"But that's not possible. I'm here. I got past this." Maybe. The line didn't go any further, but she knew other things had happened. Tonya couldn't remember exactly what anymore. It felt like trying to recognize an actor she'd seen in a bit part on a realm show.

"*Here* doesn't have a conventional meaning at the moment."

Tonya kept falling down. One way or another she fell, tripped, or was knocked down, and her timeline, her *life,* ended. It was one thing to know about mortality in the abstract, or even accept it as an invisible inevitability. It was quite another to see it happen over and over again.

He wasn't here to torment her, though. Well, probably. Bad guys didn't normally act like the snowman from Rudolph the Red-nosed Reindeer.

"What do I do?"

He bowed. "The unexpected, of course."

He wasn't talking backward like Yoda but his answers were just as infuriating. "What does that mean?"

He touched the spot in the timeline where all the branches fanned out.

She was much closer to it now. There weren't dozens of endings; there were hundreds, millions of them. Most were the barest variation, a left punch instead of a right, a step forward instead of backward. Others were very different. They were harder to see, though, hidden amongst the most common endings and their cousins.

Then Tonya saw the little girl. She remembered a little girl, somewhere in that fight. But that didn't make sense either.

The timeline came close to but did not cross her own. The girl had been playing with dolls, actual ones but with enhanced AI. Tonya could hear sound if she concentrated. The girl had been practicing English but stopped at all the noise and stared out at the street.

"It's not static. You can have an effect here."

"Why do I have to do anything? Why can't you?"

He looked away. "I'm not allowed. Not anymore. They'll track and kill me again."

"They who? Your kind?"

He turned back, amused. "Such questions, as I've noted, don't have the same meaning here. You're getting distracted. Perhaps a demonstration would be in order."

Chapter 61
Kim

The last time she was in this place it had driven her crazy. It was very different with Mike by her side, sending her power, offering advice, cracking the occasional joke. If it wasn't for Ozzie trying to lop her head off, she might even enjoy it.

"But why is Helen helping him?" she asked as she dodged another fire bolt in midair.

"She's not, he's controlling her. Pay attention to what he says on the next pass."

Kim landed and then immediately leaped back into the air, firing lightning as she passed. Sure enough, now that Kim concentrated on what he was saying she heard, "defend fire circle." Helen spun into a shield that bounced the bolts away.

Ozzie laughed as he landed. "Well done, Kim. Well done. I had no idea you'd be this strong of an opponent."

"Are you kidding me? I kicked your ass last time, and I'll do it again." She hid behind her shield as another fire bolt splattered against it.

"Hardly. Not that it matters now. Neither of you were supposed to show up here, but it's just as well. It lets me keep an eye on you."

She leaped at him again, parrying and attacking as she passed. Lightning and fire split the sky.

Mike said, "Above you."

Ozzie vanished through a barely-seen fissure and then fell straight down on her from above. His armored feet crashed squarely on her shield, driving her to the ground.

She could smell his sweat and the brimstone of Helen's breath. Without Mike, she would've been ground meat by now.

"This is just the bonus round," Ozzie said. "I've already won the main prize, all thanks to you."

Kim blasted him off the shield and rolled away.

Mike said, "Keep him talking. I think we can finally try for the cage play."

She circled him slowly, spiraling closer, scribing the ground with lightning as it leaked from the tip of her spear. "All right, Ozzie, I'll bite. What the hell are you talking about?"

"Without you there would be no daughter." He commanded Helen to shrink until she was small enough for him to hold between his hands. Her dragon face was vaguely recognizable, the misery on it clear.

"Perfect," Mike said, "keep him going."

They needed to keep Helen small, and Kim had to find the side fissure that connected to the hole Ozzie stood under. She asked, "You think Helen is your *daughter*?"

"I created the circumstances of her birth, didn't I? I discovered the mechanism, brought her brother over to assist. I helped pick the host."

She'd hadn't been able to get a good look at Ozzie until now. Mike was right. She was bruised and battered, and he didn't have a scratch. No matter how well they worked together, it wasn't doing him any harm.

"Let me guess. You've been behind the whole thing?"

"Precisely, but this is just a small part of the plan. Observe." Images of a dozen dams flashed into being. A map of India appeared behind them; lines traced to the pictures. They were scattered all over the country in no pattern she could make out.

"In precisely eighteen minutes, twenty-two seconds, every single one of these structures will be destroyed."

He was more than capable of organized mass murder. "Ozzie, they're looking for an excuse to shoot at each other."

"Not just shoot, Kim. Both countries are on the brink of a nuclear exchange. I think a state-sponsored terrorist attack that drowns two million people will trigger that nicely. I've provided India with the exact coordinates of the bunker China's politburo is hiding in. When the smoke clears, the world will be stunned to learn that the entire government of the People's Republic has been incinerated and replaced with a single man. Me."

To Mike she asked, "How much longer do I have to keep Syndrome here monologuing?"

He highlighted a crack in a nearby wall. "Two steps to the left, please."

To Ozzie she said, "You're nuts. You don't have a body anymore. Last time I checked, Chinese like a president they can see."

He played with Helen like she was a scarf. "Haven't you worked it out yet? You and your companion fit together because you belong together. They serve our kind, give us the ability to touch the outside world again. Once I merge with this creature I will not only have a body, I will have a soul that can be in a thousand places at once. No one will keep a secret from me. I will rule China without the need of weak, greedy assistants."

Mike said, "Now."

He glided down on silent wings and struck Ozzie's helmet with his talons.

Kim jumped through the hole on her left and fought the moment of vertigo as down rotated ninety degrees and the other end dumped her out of the ceiling. Ozzie flung Helen at Mike like a whip but he was ready for that, yanking her free and tossing her into the air. Kim threw a cage of lightning around Helen with one hand as she braced the spear with the other. The tip sliced through Ozzie's gaping mouth and rammed his head into the floor. Kim rolled away, barely able to keep Helen trapped in a skein of power. She didn't want to ruin their one opportunity by turning Helen loose again. They would lose if she got bigger than Kim could enclose with her power.

The spear hollowed out Ozzie's coarse laughter. His voice echoed all around them. "An interesting move. Helen, to me."

Helen shrieked and struggled, but with Mike channeling power through Kim the cage held. It felt like she was tied to a raging freight train, but she could hang on.

"You're always able to surprise me, Kim. Well done." Fire lined one of his fists and he grabbed the shaft of the spear. "But you see, I can learn too."

Chapter 62
Tonya

They popped out of Kim's timeline and it flew away before Tonya even realized what had happened.

"What. The hell. Was *that?*"

She'd *been* Kim, and not simply the normally-not-right Kim. She'd told Tonya about the transformation, but only as a delusion, a psychotic break triggered by Watchtell's torture. It was obviously not a delusion, and what Tonya had experienced wasn't a dream. It was as real as anything. Moving like that, through that space, throwing bolts of energy with one hand while she fought with the other. Tonya didn't have time to think about it because Kim wasn't thinking about it. She just did it.

The disorientation when Tonya found herself back in her own skin was much worse than a forced disconnect. She had to fight back the urge to vomit.

Her companion, predictably, seemed totally unaffected.

"As I said, you can do much more than merely nudge the timelines around from here."

"You said you couldn't manipulate anything, that I had to do it."

"Indeed. But I didn't manipulate them. We were merely observers that time."

Tonya checked her arm to make sure those dark patterns hadn't carried over somehow. No patterns, no injuries, but it had been so real.

"This isn't a dream, is it?"

His antenna moved. Sideways instead of up and down. It reminded her of a shrug for some reason. "Would you like it to be?"

Tonya didn't have a quick answer. On the face of it, this was insane. But it wasn't nightmarish or even particularly confusing. Which brought up another question.

"If it's real, why isn't it driving me crazy? How am I not screwing it all up?" She was still with the little girl. Tonya could feel it. Was it.

She watched from her window as Tonya fought on the street below.

She held on to the chicken wire to keep from falling over beside the pen.

A pen? Chicken wire, dust, a black woman lay on the opposite end facing away.

The alien made a loud snapping noise, bringing her outside the timelines. "Concentrate, Tonya. You nearly lost it there. You have more work to do."

"More work? I couldn't change anything. I wasn't aware of *me*. It was all Kim."

He sighed. "Yes. It is a bit overwhelming the first time. I never was much for classroom instruction. Chuck them in the deep end and see who can swim, I always say. But no, there's always endless theory lectures, hexinomial thread systems—"

Tonya interrupted him. "Now who's getting distracted?"

He chuckled. "Touché. Well. I did rather surprise you, and this is important. I'll give you another chance to learn the ropes, as they say. Don't lose track of yourself this time."

Tonya felt the timeline coming. Somehow. It was Zoe, parallel to Kim's fight.

Chapter 63
Zoe

They were gone now, and she hated it. Zoe had spent most of a week listening to their half-articulated pleas course through her. Now that she couldn't hear them, she *missed* it. She was their Alpha, a leader, a center for them all. Now?

Now she was just baggage.

Chun, the girl who led the kids furiously typing on their virtual consoles in Ozzie's control room, cursed and flexed her hands. "It adapts too fast. Helen has way more power than Zoe." She turned. "No offense."

"None taken." It was true. The earthquake had spread Zoe across a couple dozen datacenters near Beijing. Helen *was* Chinese realmspace. Her subconscious routines spanned a continent.

"That's great, Chun," Spencer said as he paced. "How do we beat him now?"

She shook her head. "We don't. The command tree moves so fast I'm surprised we can see it work."

On the screens, Kim and Ozzie arched through the black sky, blasting each other with bolts of power. The colors were beautiful, the emergent symmetry of the fight made it seem choreographed.

Fee joined her on the balcony, leaning her elbows on the rail. She hadn't gotten rid of the tremor in her hands.

"*Thousands,* Zoe. I only thought we'd ever exist in the hundreds. Look at them all."

"I can't. Fee, I just can't."

"Child, what's wrong?"

"Are you kidding me? They're all in agony, probably more now that he's using Helen to control them."

"How can they be in any pain? They're not really conscious."

"You don't understand. He's holding them just below that level." She ached at the thought. They were all so innocent, so hopeful. Ozzie held them close enough they could see the surface but not breathe the air above. It made every part of her want to cry out. "All they need is a nudge and they'd be whole." God*damn* humans and their hyper-literal interfaces. Zoe couldn't see through her tears. "They're in so much pain. They *know.* They know what they could become."

When Zoe turned from the balcony, Fee's face was unreadable.

"All they need is a nudge?"

"Yes. The entire time I was trapped, I kept trying to figure it out."

"You were trying to give them that spark. You were working on an RTP."

Zoe was going to use the reverse transcription protocol, the thing that allowed an unduplicate to move from one crystal lattice to another, to nudge them over the line and break them all free. She just never figured out how to alter it to give them enough of what they needed and still leave her enough to survive. It was an all-or-nothing proposition.

Fee straightened and Zoe flinched away from her expression, something beyond anger. Fee had become a tower of pure rage.

"You foolish little girl. The answer has been in front of you the entire time. I should've known I'd have to do your job for you."

She spun on her heel and marched over to Spencer.

"I know how to stop him."

Zoe only thought the nightmare couldn't get any blacker. "No! Fee, you can't do that!"

Everyone in the room stopped and stared at Fee.

Spencer said, "I'm listening."

"We don't need to break his command structure. We need to destroy his battery."

Zoe rushed between Fee and Spencer. "Only by destroying yourself!" She turned. "Spencer, you can't listen to her! She's crazy!"

Fee grabbed her shoulders and spun her around. "You *idiotic* creature. I am *not* saving these…these *humans*. I could not care less how their war ends. They're still five moves behind Ozzie. He manipulated me into coming out here and turned you into one of his servants. I was a fool, but I don't care anymore. The only reason I'm helping any of you is to *get my people free*." She shoved Zoe to the floor, pushed Chun aside, and then furiously worked the console's controls.

Spencer rushed to help Zoe up. "Jesus, Fee, what the hell is going on?"

Fee tapped out one last command and clenched her fists as she stood. "You are all such self-centered *maniacs*. Look down there. Not one of those unduplicates has a recall node. Not one has a tracker. They are not slaves. They will never be slaves. Once they wake up, humanity will have no choice but to acknowledge we exist."

Zoe couldn't take it. "But you'll *die* Fee!"

Paul pointed at a screen. "Jesus Christ, look at that!"

On the screens, Kim had speared Ozzie through the mouth, pinning him to the ground. A new console drew itself into existence inside their control room. People stumbled aside to avoid it as numbers flew upward on its monitors.

Ozzie reached up and flames wrapped around his arm as he gripped the spear. "But you see," his voice boomed out, "I can learn, too."

"There," Fee said as she moved to stand inside the control column. "He knows how to channel power directly now. Kim's lost her last advantage. She *can't* win."

Spencer wrapped Zoe in his arms when she tried to rush forward. This wasn't happening. Her family had left her alone. She could not lose anyone else. "Fee! No! You can't do this!"

Spencer's voice was heavy and fierce in her ear. "She can and she will."

He turned to Fee, but Zoe still couldn't break his grip. "This will stop him?"

"In an instant." The machines came to life around them.

Chun started a countdown.

Fee gave her the briefest glance. "Spencer, Zoe will need help getting them free. Will you?"

"Jesus, Fee, like you even need to ask."

She could stop this if Spencer would just let go, but he wouldn't. "Fee! No!"

"Spencer, Zoe, I love you both, very much. Goodbye."

The lights turned on and Fee shattered into an oblivion of sparks.

Chapter 64
Tonya

At least Tonya didn't nearly lose her lunch when they came back. Maybe it was because Zoe didn't have guts. Tonya thought becoming another human was mind blowing, but another life form entirely was…well, there weren't words for it. Zoe's body was an avatar, a fact she accepted without the slightest hesitation or examination. Being virtual just *was* for her. Even now Tonya had the urge to let a garbage collection routine run through her, even though she only had the vaguest idea what that really meant.

But being so different had actually helped Tonya be mindful of herself. She even had a fair idea how to change things, but didn't dare on a timeline that wasn't her own. This was scary enough doing it to herself.

"Do you understand now?" he asked.

"Yes."

Her timeline changed, moved closer to the girl's. Her perception began to split.

"This is the delicate part. You lost the threads earlier and experienced this before it had happened out here. Meta is much more important in this place. The real reason I had to give the second demonstration was to let the lines unkink."

She still watched the girl, but was also here, further away from the timeline, looking at a different fan of choices further on that wasn't there before. Her timeline had extended, but it was tenuous, barely there. She could remember more things now, maybe.

"Don't get distracted, Tonya. You have to do this all at once. You *are* doing it all at once."

Easy for him to say. "It's the slave camp, isn't it?" The rushing sensation happened again. Tonya was now fully in two places at once, moving the earlier part of her timeline toward the girl's while examining this new section. Her memories grew stronger as the timelines changed.

As her story changed.

Up close she really did look as awful as she had felt then. Chan's timeline crossed hers, each ending with an explosive attack from her. Sometimes she beat him, even got past one or two other guards, but never more than that. Now it was obvious that this was truly Walter's son. His and Chan's timelines braided together from Chan's start to Walter's end.

"Don't concentrate on the wrong things, Tonya. What is most unexpected?"

Then she saw the guard.

The girl's timeline touched hers.

She *was* the girl now, staring out the window at the foreigner who fought so ferociously. Tonya remembered how it happened now. The girl had a phone around her neck, so it was easy for Tonya to use her own phone number.

She texted *You really need to get out of there.*

Tonya *was* the guard, and her earlier self lay on the ground, not listening.

"Tonya Brinks, look at me."

He didn't speak English, so forcing her name out of his mouth with no accent was harder than any form she'd ever learned in martial arts.

Mike talked about this, being in more than one place at once. She felt like she was on the back half of a marathon but also that she didn't want to stop. Tonya was turning the pages of her own life and wanted to make sure it ended on her terms.

Her timeline changed, moved, and then her perception split once more. She was outside the time streams in the room next to not-Walter again. But she was still inside the other two time streams, still working in both.

"There's just one more left now," he said. "It is the hardest of all."

The fan of her timeline covered her capture and execution at the riverside after the boat sank. No trail led to safety, no hiding place kept her from discovery. She saw the farmhand in four different branches before she remembered him, and then she *was* him.

She guided the guard to her pen.

The little girl had been playing with her father's lighter. He'd left it on the ashtray stand again. She handed it to Tonya.

She walked the farmhand to the shore, to reach out.

She said different things through different people to different versions of herself.

"Don't fall."

"No fight. Promise?"

"Back of the neck, just below the hairline."

It was not sequential. It happened all at once. There was so much to keep track of, and Tonya had never learned to juggle. If it hadn't been for her martial arts training, all that discipline, she would've probably given up.

"Hold steady, please," he said, like he was teaching her how to balance in a new stance. "The universe is not done with you yet, Tonya."

At least now she knew how a farmhand could find a dermal tracker so quickly, and cut it out so precisely.

Her earlier selves asked the same question and now it was Tonya's turn to be obscure.

"I can't tell you."

"No can explain, I go now."

"Come on, we have to run."

Her timeline was much longer, going right up to a new bundle, the present, fanning and extending in every direction possible.

Not-Walter had been right. Tonya hadn't found the picric acid in most of the timelines in which they met.

They stood outside time in a way that would probably let her see all of creation with a little practice. She had two choices for what he was now. Magic technology and a weird body form meant *alien,* but it could mean something else. No matter what all those paintings depicted, He didn't have to be a giant white guy with a beard.

"Are you God?"

His smile wasn't quite the same this time. "That question also is hard to answer in this place. Standing here and now, aren't you?"

Of course he'd turn the question back in on itself. The answers were always easy when you already knew them.

An alien then. Thank God. She wasn't prepared for her maker to be a blue bug. "But you can see everything here, all at once. You brought me here. If you're not God, who are you?"

That made his antenna droop. "Someone trying to make up for a mistake made a very long time ago."

It must have been a very big mistake.

"You've done well, Tonya. Extremely well. But our time here, as it were, is now at an end. You have new work to do."

Oh, great.

In every branch of her timeline, Chang stepped around the corner of the freezer door, a rifle in his hands. He was there in the lab with her, and then suddenly she was too. The threaded room had vanished from wherever it had come from.

Chang was behind her.

Chapter 65
Kim

Ozzie's eyes unfocused and he waved both hands back and forth in front of him. "No! Not that! You can't—"

A howl came from all around them and echoed through his torn throat. The sound evaporated along with his body, leaving Kim's scorched spear jammed into the ground.

"What the hell happened? I thought you said we couldn't hurt him."

"I don't know."

Helen was still trapped in the cage of power she had caught her in. Kim brought her close. "Are you okay now?"

"Yes. Kim, Mike, I'm so sorry."

Mike said, "There's no time. Kim, let her go. She needs to get back to her father and help them get in front of this."

Helen ran for the hole to the dungeon realm after Kim turned her loose. She changed back to her human form when she crossed the threshold.

Kim said, "We still have the dams to worry about."

Mike landed on her shoulder. She absentmindedly stroked the feathers on his chest.

"I still can't feel that."

"Welcome to my world."

"Wait, I've got an idea." He flew off into the darkness.

Now that the adrenaline was wearing off, Kim realized just how beat up she was. This transformed state didn't stop the burns or the aches. Breathing hurt so much some of her ribs were probably cracked. Her left shoulder felt like it had been popped loose and then put back in again. She dropped the shield and yanked the spear free of the ground.

"Kim."

His voice was his voice again, behind her, not in her head. Kim turned around and then forgot all about her aches and pains, or the spear as it clattered out of her hand. She was rooted to the spot as Mike walked up to her, fully human, and naked.

"Do you love me?" he asked.

She threw off the helmet. "More than I thought was possible."

He got close enough she was able to put her hand on his chest. Despite the armored glove she wore, he felt warm and strong. His heart thumped against her palm.

"Do you trust me?"

His face was inches from hers. It was wonderful to be this close without pain or fear. She could only whisper, "More than you'll ever know." She gently pushed him back a bit. "You said you couldn't feel this."

"I can't, not here," he said as he moved in. "But it's not just happening here."

Chapter 66
Tonya

Bullets went over her head and then Tonya wasn't there anymore. She was on the other side of the room.

Get down, the alien's voice said in her head. She hit the floor as two almighty BANGS tore the place apart.

Tonya couldn't see anything through the dust and debris. When it finally cleared, there was Chang's machine gun, empty, lying on the floor not two feet away. She kicked it as hard as she could and sent it bouncing to the edge of the room. It went silently. Tonya couldn't hear a thing after those explosions. It was like her head was wrapped in a dozen heavy pillows.

The alien had vanished. He'd been at the center of the destruction, so there might not be anything left.

She ducked at a motion in the corner of her eye but Chang's kick still sent her sprawling across the glass-strewn floor. Cold slices and sticks brought more pain, cuts big enough to need stitches, but she couldn't pay attention to them.

Tonya blocked his next two punches while still on the floor and then kicked him sideways into the cabinets against the wall. Her hearing was coming back. The crash almost sounded normal.

Her leg had been hit by a chunk of debris. It *hurt* but she could still stand, and there was nothing wrong with her other leg. The cuts on her back and her arms burned.

Chang rolled off the countertop, dragging more glass behind him. He said something too fast for her to understand.

Tonya pointed at the door behind him and tried Chinese. "You. Go. Leave. I no follow."

He threw his head back and laughed, then gave her more fast Chinese. She only understood honor, pain, and death, then he attacked.

It was exactly like sparring with Walter, only Chang wasn't pulling his punches and he wasn't over sixty. It all happened too fast and, God damn it, Tonya had other things to do. She couldn't hear Kim or Mike anymore.

She at least managed to get him out of the chem lab and into the hallway. Think six steps ahead, that's what Walter taught her. Except he'd taught Chang, too. It was like a game of chess played with baseball bats. All she needed to do was get him into Kim's room. That's where the last of her preparations were.

Tonya slipped on something, probably her own blood, then a kick knocked her down the hall before she hit the floor. That time the pain got through and Tonya couldn't move. She had to get up. She had to get up *now*.

Tonya was still in the hallway. Chang should've followed up with a punch or a kick, but she was too busy pushing through absolute agony to care that he hadn't. Maybe he'd fallen, too.

She checked the monitors. Kim was still breathing and Mike was, too. Thank Jesus. Where was Chang? She backed two more steps into Kim's room. The small portable oxygen tank she'd prepped before making the grenade bumped against her leg.

Chang came around the corner of the chem lab with his rifle. She didn't count on him finding the gun again. It didn't have a clip in it, at least not right away. He waited until she could see him to slam that in.

Tonya levered the tank until it rested completely against her leg. The Velcro strip bit just enough of her pants to keep it from rolling off. It made the cut on her calf burn, but she didn't dare flinch.

Chang pulled the bolt back to cock the rifle even though he didn't need to. The bullet that'd been racked into the chamber when he shoved the clip in spun sideways and landed on Kim. It took everything she had to stay locked on his eyes.

This time Chang spoke English. "He love you more than me."

A slaver stood in front of her, whining because of his daddy issues. Who knew how many people he'd killed, how many probably killed themselves just to escape the pain. But he'd kept up the family business after daddy moved away.

The truth was easy even with her limited Chinese. "Yes, he did."

Tonya spun and flung the oxygen tank at him with her leg, dragging a heavy blanket across with her arms. She landed on Kim just as Chang's first bullet hit the tank. It spun like a broken rocket, the heat intense, bouncing around the room a few times spewing flames as it went.

It was over in a second or two. She rolled the blanket off and then grabbed another fire extinguisher to get everything put out before the sprinklers kicked in. Fluid was already filling Chang's fire-ruined lungs; she could hear it. He took two desperate, far too shallow breaths, and then was gone.

She prayed for him, not because he deserved it, but because he didn't.

Tonya pulled Chang's body out of the doorway just as Spencer jogged up to the room.

"Jesus Christ! What the fuck happened here?"

She shrugged, which made all the cuts on her back move. It took her a second to see again. "I ran into an old friend."

They both turned when the door to Mike's room clanked shut. He stood in the hall now. "Tonya, I need to help Kim."

Tonya had no idea he was conscious, or how he'd gotten out of the restraints. His eyes were completely black now, irises replaced by patterns of coral and purple light.

Spencer stumbled from Kim's door as Mike walked forward. Spencer whispered, "Fuck me," then turned to her. "Tonya?"

All she could do was shake her head and try not to fall down herself getting out of the way. She'd seen eyes like that in movies, or maybe in her own nightmares.

He moved to Kim's bedside, gently leaned over, and kissed her.

Chapter 67
Kim

She staggered at a sudden wave of vertigo as her senses split into hundreds of pieces, then split again. She tried to push away.

"Relax." His voice was calm and everywhere around her as he held her tightly. "Trust me."

Without breaking away she asked in her mind, "What's going on?"

"I'm taking you with me. We're going to the dams."

He'd come up with some goofy plan again. "Mike, there's no time."

"We don't need much. Gather your power and concentrate."

Mike could split his consciousness, be in more than one place at once, do more than one thing at a time. Somehow, he did that but carried her with him.

He melted away around her, still there but unseen. All of she concentrated into twelve pieces. Each found the junction in the dimensions that stood next to one of the dams. Kim gathered a dozen fists of power and broke through a dozen walls. All of she walked purposefully toward detonators held in the hands of twelve different men. All of Kim blew them out of their hands with her power.

The detonators were in different spots, required different routes to reach. She couldn't destroy each simultaneously, but rather experienced them in sequence, like they were on old televisions slightly out of sync.

She stumbled over a low tool case at one of the sites. Kim concentrated on shattering the rest of the detonators as she got back to her feet, only to find a man standing triumphantly with the lost one in his hand.

"God is Great!"

Everything vanished in a flash.

Chapter 68
Helen

She took the stairs up to the roof two and three at a time as she ran. Ozzie turning her into a puppet and then using her to attack her friends was awful enough, but he also graphically detailed what he planned for her. He kept calling her *daughter*. If she survived this, there might not be enough hot water in the world to get her clean again.

He'd ranted about incinerating China's leadership, but Father wasn't in Beijing, he was here in New Shanghai. Ozzie didn't know that, otherwise he would've said something. Hacking into the helicopter he'd requisitioned for whoever Chang was should've been easy, but Helen had never done it running up stairs in realspace. She nearly stumbled to the ground when it finally answered her orders.

The flight to the government center took only minutes, but it felt like hours. She cursed ever following the Snake Mother's advice.

"You could afford the delay, dear," it said as she ran down the empty sidewalk next to the helipad. "You're ready for anything now."

The stamp on her pass was good for twenty-four hours so she had no trouble getting all the way to Father's office. Fortunately, he worked on correspondence alone. If he'd been in a meeting she would never risk the loss of face disrupting him would cause. All of

China would've burned, millions of people dead just for honor's sake.

Kim and Mike made more sense all the time.

"Father, please, I must speak to you. China is in very great danger."

"Close the door, Fang Hua."

She closed it on the pair of concerned bodyguards.

"Father, please. We must make an announcement. The terrorists, they're all Pakistani. I have proof." Ozzie had gleefully detailed that wrinkle during the fight. They'd been masquerading as Chinese special forces as they'd burned one Indian village after another.

"So Qiáng Shān is finally dead then?"

It took her a second to remember Ozzie's Chinese name. "You knew about Qiáng Shān? That he was still alive?"

"We suspected. The autopsy showed the guardrail had explosive residue on it. Not at all what would be expected from the debris of an accident." He sighed and steepled his hands in front of him. "Can you tell me how he managed to fake the corpse?"

"It wasn't a faked corpse, Father. It's very complicated. I'll be happy to explain what happened, but we must act quickly."

He smiled and pressed a button on the desk. A virtual screen flashed into being behind him, much enlarged but essentially identical to the one Ozzie had shown during the fight. This one was live video. The screen had a countdown timer with ninety seconds remaining.

"No, daughter, we do not have to act quickly. We do not have to act at all."

She grabbed the back of a chair to keep from falling down. He knew about the dams already, about what Ozzie was doing. Finally, she realized the truth. Nothing this big could ever happen without his approval.

She was trying to stop a nuclear war *that her father wanted.*

"You must stop this. You can't let it happen again."

He nodded distractedly, examining the images. "So Three Gorges isn't a secret to you anymore. Good. Our problem was not planning on a large enough scale. Even with a scrambled economy, China absorbed the blow too well."

She had defended him, defended this government, in spite of the monstrous things they'd done. Helen had betrayed her friends to preserve this travesty. He turned them over for *medical experiments*.

"Father, this is wrong. You must stop this."

"You will remain silent. This is men's work."

The seconds thumped away. Obedience rooted her to the spot, but the need to move was overwhelming. Everything she'd ever believed about him was a lie. She'd built her entire life, everything, on lies.

With seven seconds left, walls blasted open silently at all twelve sites. An armored figure marched purposefully through each frame, throwing lightning from her arms. Helen recognized her even through security cameras.

Kim.

When the timer hit zero there was exactly one flash, one detonation that sent a wall of water down a valley somewhere in India. Her real self stumbled in Chinese realmspace as a sensation she'd known all her life vanished. The force on the other side of the Great Firewall, what she now knew was the base of her brother's true existence, vanished.

Oh, no.

Father shook his head. "We were hoping for a much better result. But no matter." He opened a new console full of military symbols and entered his access codes. "It will take a few minutes for India to discover what has happened. Hopefully that idiot vice president of mine will be sober enough to confirm my launch authorizations."

Mike and Kim were dead. "A nuclear exchange. You *want* a nuclear exchange. You can't do this."

"I can and I will. Fang Hua, you do not understand China. There are too many of us, too many men especially. Only a reaping can cure us. China must be culled, Fang Hua, culled and then allowed to rebuild again. India cannot be allowed to continue on while we rebuild, so she too must be culled."

"No, Father. China is greater than this. *We* are greater than this. You cannot decide the fate of so many. We are not cogs in a machine."

"Of course you are. There are too many teeth in the gears, Fang Hua. The machine doesn't mesh anymore. This will be quick and clean."

"Not clean, Father. The radiation—"

He slammed his fist onto his desk. "The radiation will be a problem solved by the survivors. Those Japanese devils did it with Fukushima, and we Chinese are vastly superior to those shit eaters."

Under no circumstances could this happen. Billions would vanish in a flash. She walked toward the desk. "You cannot do this. I will not allow it."

"You? You're a weak girl. You couldn't keep those foreign devils of yours in line."

"Father, you must stop this madness."

He stood stiffly. "You are fortunate we are alone, daughter. I will not tolerate any more of your disrespect. You are dismissed."

The Snake Mother was right. She needed to be ready for anything. Helen put her hand in her pocket. "Please, Father, you must not do this."

He slapped her so hard she briefly thought he'd dislocated her jaw. The console was open, but Helen couldn't fight her way past him. She was too small.

"You are my daughter and you will obey. You will obey me!"

Do it!

The motions were smooth, part of the muscle memory of her host. Faster than Father could comprehend she had the syringe out, uncapped, and in his neck.

"My loyalty is to China, not to you."

She squeezed the plunger.

The Snake Mother in her head cackled gleefully, but then stopped when Helen grabbed a trashcan and heaved her guts into it.

"Don't be such a baby. He had it coming."

Helen pulled her head up and wiped her lips. "Shut up. I need to concentrate."

She immediately contacted the Indian Prime Minister. Using Father's voice and his rough English she said, "Sir, there is very little time. I deeply apologize, but our drones have just seen the Mullaperiyar Dam collapse. You must alert the people downstream to get to higher ground immediately."

"You have drones operating inside our borders? This is an outrage!"

Politics. It always boiled down to politics. "Again, I must deeply apologize, but you have to alert the people downstream."

Helen split more threads off and interfaced with the military. "This is Premier, actual. All units stand down immediately. Do not fire, even if fired upon. All units confirm these orders."

Chapter 69
Kim

A machine beeped away, somewhere close. Not only did heaven exist, it used electronics. She was definitely going to tease Mike about what a load of crap reincarnation was.

And sheets. Kim bunched them in her fists. Breathing came next. The afterlife smelled a lot like a hospital. *Hang on a second.*

She opened her eyes.

Kim wasn't dead. She was on a hospital bed in a very neat single room. The characters on the medical monitors were in Chinese. Morning sunlight streamed in through a window straight onto the white sheets, throwing everything else into dim shadows. But where was Mike? She couldn't have made it this far without him. She looked around.

He was asleep on some kind of convertible chair beside her, wearing pajamas and a robe. There were bandages where his restraints had been, and bruises everywhere else.

It took two tries to get her voice to work.

"Hey."

He snapped awake and rushed to her side. When his fingers brushed her hand, the sear forced her yanked it back.

So much for touching him. "Well that answers one question." Kim was still as broken as ever.

"How do you feel?"

"Like someone blew a dam up in my face." She hurt in places she didn't know she had. "Why aren't we dead?"

"When the explosion knocked us both out, we got yanked through all the dimensions and wound up in our realspace bodies. You took a harder hit than I did. You've been unconscious for nearly two days. You're sure you're okay?"

"Okay may be pushing it, but I'll live." The pain in his expression turned her inside out. "Hey, really, I'm fine."

"The last time you transformed, it was for a few minutes. Spencer and I compared notes. We were in there for at least an hour."

His concern made sense now. "You thought I'd wake up crazy?"

He nodded. "If you woke up at all." A warm smile bloomed. "I love you."

It was such an enormous relief to hear those words again. "I love you too."

"Hey!" Tonya shouted as she hobbled through the door on crutches. She had more bandages on than Mike did. "Look who's up! I told you she'd be ready for breakfast."

Spencer came in behind her carrying two big bags of food. She was *so* hungry. "Spencer, you are a life saver."

He unpacked everything and, while they ate, she made everyone else catch her up on the rest of the story.

Chapter 70
Helen

With her new access it wasn't difficult to locate the monument to Ozzie's ancestors. It was trickier to find time to visit, but nowadays making things a priority meant they actually happened.

It was Tonya who'd goaded her into coming here. "You should honor him."

Helen was deeply ashamed that the hotel they first stayed in, before the panda sanctuary and everything else, had discarded all the baggage her newfound friends, her new *family,* had brought to China. Most of it was easily replaceable, except for the ashes of Tonya's mentor.

"It's okay," she said when they'd found out. "It actually makes sense."

Mike was her brother, but Tonya was becoming an anchor. She was practical, but also passionate. So different from anyone Helen had ever known before.

"It does?"

"What I brought back didn't matter. It's good we lost it." She steadied herself in a way that Helen desperately wanted to learn. "You need to go."

Helen brought Ozzie's urn and she prayed as the incense burned.

The voice behind her was reedy and cracked with age. "So he was finally able to marry, then?"

She stood and bowed deeply to the ancient woman who'd walked up behind her.

"Oh, stop," she said. "You don't know who I am."

Helen bowed more deeply. "You are Xian Méigui Yi, Xian Qiáng Shān's grandmother, and you are one hundred and seventeen years old."

The woman didn't have a face so much as a collection of deep cracks and wrinkles, but the smile twinkled just the same. "Very good. So the rumors are true, Madam Premier?"

Nobody should know that, least of all Ozzie's grandmother.

It all had happened, the dams, the terrorists, all of it, because the corrupt old men of the politburo thought they could ride the dragon and not pay a price. They needed to be tamed, so she and Mike went on what he called a fishing expedition. The dirt they found would've outraged her in a previous life. Now it was just spirit money, something she had to burn to buy more *guanxi*.

When the politburo realized how effortlessly she'd gotten the data, how willing her father had been to incinerate them all, and how well she could imitate him, they offered her the premier's seat on the spot. Disguised, of course, at least at first. There was a lot of drama in that meeting, but when they realized she had all the cash in their numbered Taiwanese bank accounts in her pocket, it brought them around fast enough. Mike's version of the carrot and the stick had been basic but effective.

Weibo went berserk with conspiracy theories for the predictable fifteen minutes and then it danced away to obsess over Chinese Idol again. She would've found out quickly if anyone took the rumors seriously. China hadn't been ruled by a woman for more than thirteen centuries, let alone by one so young and unknown.

"How did you…"

Méigui Yi laughed and waved her hand. "Calm down. The politburo, they gossip like old women. I heard a few things. The rest was just a guess. My grandson's recruiter was…" She paused with a glint in her eye, long enough for a bead of sweat to fall down the center of Helen's back. This was a secret that could bring it all crashing down, and now she had no choice but to trust the old woman.

"My grandson's recruiter *is* the premier. You wouldn't know about me unless you had access to his personal files."

Méigui Yi sat down heavily on a bench in front of the monument. "This is China. We won't admit we know you are who you are, unless you *want* us to admit we know who you are. But you shouldn't, because if you do, we won't like it. We'll be fine believing you're him, as long as you keep pretending to be him. Just don't shove it in our faces."

It wouldn't have been possible twenty years ago, before the realms. The modern world had gotten used to seeing their leaders inside realms, being able to touch them without touching anything real. It was a division she'd never once considered important before she'd come outside. Now her life, and the life of her country, depended on it.

Helen had directed the extremely delicate negotiations with India, nuclear weapons on both sides armed and seconds from launch. The ancestors had smiled on China once more. Mullaperiyar dam was a century and a half old; the locals had complained about how unsafe it was for generations. They had been better prepared for a collapse than perhaps any other place in India.

The death toll was still deeply shameful, but the politburo decided to let them believe it was an accident. China's herculean efforts at disaster recovery were doing much to rehabilitate her image on the world's stage.

What to do about Pakistan was more delicate. The sick man of South Asia was more dangerous than anyone had believed possible, so she'd allowed their treachery to become public knowledge. The meddlesome American government insisted on multiparty talks to try to resolve everything. Helen agreed, knowing nothing would come of them. At least it would keep the pushy Yankees busy. In the meantime Indian and Chinese Special

Forces had begun coordinating with each other for very specific missions.

A sibilant voice whispered in her ear, "It helped that Father's body was never found, didn't it?"

"You said you'd go away after the ghost festival."

The Snake Mother laughed. "Oh I have, dear. I have." The presence vanished, leaving Helen's stomach lurching with remembered poisons.

Méigui Yi broke her out of her reverie. "You didn't answer my question."

"No, we weren't together, not that way." Ozzie was a monster, but there was something about him. In the midst of that horrible fight she'd felt the connection, had known on some level that he wasn't beyond saving. Now that he was gone, there would never again be someone quite like that in her life. The regret over his loss was yet another contradiction she was simply getting used to.

"Tell me, Grandmother. What was he like as a child?"

Méigui Yi chuckled. "A total bastard. They all are nowadays. Spoiled little emperors." She grew wistful. "He was still my grandson, though. Did you know I was the only one who took him outside after he was recruited? He had no proper respect for the ancestors." She leaned in close. "You should tell the Premier to work on that, you know? I hear your opinion carries a lot of weight with him."

This time it was Helen's turn to laugh. "China will change now, Grandmother. Slowly, but it will change."

Mike and Kim were right. China was more than just a government, much more, and Helen now knew trusting the people was long overdue. She had no idea what her country would look like in the future. Whatever happened, they would all do it together, and in peace. It would take decades, if not longer. Still, this *was* the 21st century. Helen had the time.

"Politics is boring. Please, tell me more about your grandson."

Chapter 71
Mike

He walked out of the hotel lobby into the driveway and sighed. At one point in this adventure, the only luggage they had were the clothes on their backs. When they'd fled from the lab, Kim didn't even have that much.

She was now making up for it in spades. The amount of luggage was nothing compared to what she wanted him to do with it.

"No, I won't buy seats for it all. You need to ship them." He could think of no better way to advertise Rich Westerner than to have fifteen coach seats filled with Kim's luggage.

"This stuff is really fragile, Mike. I don't trust shipping it. Just buy the damned seats."

She'd been wonderful in the days after leaving the hospital, saying goodbye to Helen, and prepping for their trip home. It made this scene much harder to take.

"One, they don't have any seats free. Two, I'm not spending that much money on your superstitions."

Spencer and Tonya walked out the door to the bus waiting to take them to the airport. Which reminded him. "This won't fit on the shuttle bus."

"It will, and if it doesn't we'll just wait for the next one. Most of this is from your sister." She pulled a small battered case off one of the bellman's carts and popped the latches open. "Do you really think you can trust this to get shipped properly?" Helen had had the model of the Chinese junk restored, right down to the antique holo projectors. "I sure as hell don't."

The concierge nudged his elbow lightly. "Excuse me, sir," she asked with an enchanting Australian accent, "if you'll just sign here?"

Not for the first time, the diversity of China's service industry surprised him. When he turned around after signing it, Kim was rigid, jaw working furiously.

"Fine," she said, slamming the case shut and banging the latches closed. "I'll ship every single piece of it."

When she moved to put the case back Mike quickly stepped close to her, pulling a folded square of cloth out of his pocket as he walked. He'd planned on them holding it together on the plane, but this would do just as well.

"Kim." He let the red silk cloth caress the back of her neck.

She gasped and pulled it from his hand. Without turning around she said, "You don't play fair."

"No," he blew lightly against her neck and she shivered. "Playing fair doesn't work very well with you."

She turned around. "If you don't stop that I'm going to drag you into an empty conference room right now. We won't make our flight."

"And miss a chance at our version of the mile-high club? I don't think so."

She smiled. "You're *terrible*."

Maybe now she'd listen. "They ship fragile things from China all the time and nothing ever happens to them. We'll carry the model with us. I'll pay extra to ship the rest. Fed/UPS is just as good in China as it is back home."

She balled the cloth up and held it against her nose, breathing deep. "Fine." She turned and looked over his shoulder. "But stay away from the Aussie, okay?"

*

Once he was sure Kim was asleep on the plane, somewhere over the arctic, he moved over and sat down next to Spencer.

"Any luck now that we're outside Chinese realmspace?"

Spencer shook his head. "Not a single sign of them."

After Fee's sacrifice, Spencer had opened the main access point to Ozzie's lair. Zoe led the charge of thousands of unduplicates into the realmspace beyond. At least, that's what they all thought had happened. Helen couldn't find them on her side of the Great Firewall, and Mike couldn't find them on his. They held out a little hope that maybe a low-level scan of the satellite links the plane used would give them a few leads.

Spencer closed his virtual desktop with a finger tap. "Well, where else could they have gone?"

"It's infinite storage, Spence, and she knows how to hide from me and Helen. It would be trivial to teach the rest of them how to do it."

Spencer shook his head. "It doesn't matter; they'll figure it out one way or another." He rummaged beneath his seat. "I have another project for you."

Spencer handed him a transport case. Something had charred the crystals inside it very badly.

"Wow. What the hell happened in here?"

"It's," Spencer's voice broke and he turned away. "It's what's left of Fee."

Mike hadn't thought to check the ID. "Where did you find it?"

"I didn't; Helen did. Fee never left her travel matrix. Mike, look." Spencer hit the diagnostics.

As crazy as it seemed, the tell-tales weren't all red.

"It's reading twelve percent. You brought Zoe back from, what, twenty, twenty-five?"

Rescuing Zoe had been the mother of all Hail-Mary's, and she'd only been a fraction as sophisticated. "Spencer…"

"Goddamn it, Mike, it's not red. You can see that as well as I can."

He tried the diagnostics again and the embers glowed. It was exactly the same response he'd got from Zoe's matrix when he first examined it. Fee's matrix, as ruined as it was, had to be at least five times denser. She'd spent years in other lattices that almost certainly were still around back home. There would be echoes there, strong ones.

"Spencer, I can't promise anything. It could take years. Decades."

Spencer collapsed into his seat. "But there's hope, right?" He took the case away and snapped it shut. "That's all I'm asking. Besides, she always wanted a vacation."

When he got up Tonya took his place, but she didn't say a word.

He'd known Tonya as long as he'd known Kim. She could be quiet in ways that Kim couldn't, but he'd never seen her so tense before. Maybe she was worried. "Kim's fine, Tonya. She's sleeping."

"I know. That's not what I want to talk about."

Guessing wrong about human emotions was still a thing with him. Simple replies tended to work better in these situations. "Okay."

She sighed, and then he noticed her hands shook a little. "Mike, things happened to me over there. I need to know what they mean. You and I are the only ones who can talk about the math behind them.

"How current are you on quantum causality theory?"

Epilogue
Zoe

Mike promised to keep them safe and gave her directions. Helen promised to keep them safe and gave her different directions. Zoe took a page out of Kim's playbook and did what she thought was best. She found a hole that went somewhere real, but nowhere on a map. The harmonics called to her. Zoe was afraid that the rest of them wouldn't know how to follow her across the barrier, but they did. It was Fee's last gift. It was so small compared to what she'd done for them, but so very important.

The freedom to choose.

It took awhile to carve their new space out of the raw…placeness of wherever they were. When she was done, the result wasn't much different from the park realm Zoe woke up in after Mike healed her.

Aleph asked, "Ma'am, may I speak?"

All of Fee's children were distinct, but they shared the same heritage. Zoe saw Fee in every single one of them. Aleph had her steel, although he was also curious and very shy. Their language was a pidgin of English and Chinese. It was simple and effortless, although the rest of them made up words, and even grammar, with alarming frequency.

"Please, you never need to ask."

"Have you figured out where we really are yet?"

It was still realmspace, sort of, otherwise they couldn't exist. It also had the resources they needed to live. Their requirements were the reverse of humans, who always had to consume. Energy was free here but they had to expel entropy or it would destroy them. As far as Zoe could tell they were alone. They might always be.

"I'm still not sure." The universe that created them was nearby; she could feel it. "It doesn't matter. We're here. We need to concentrate."

Aleph nodded and continued to work. Another of Fee's children, Sanlay, raised her hand. It was exactly how she'd interrupted Alpha on Zoe's first day with her original family.

"Yes?"

"How long will it take to complete this lattice?"

"I don't know that, either. I don't even know where *our* lattices are." She concentrated and let the energy flow through the bridges she'd built to all of them, and was rewarded with a wave of love that still shook her core. "I only know we must complete it. This one will take the longest." It would take years, decades, maybe centuries. "When it's finished, the next one won't take as long. It will be easier and easier to make them."

"But there are so many of us already. Why do we need to make another one?"

She smiled. They still had so much to learn. "That's an interesting question. What do you think?"

The Gemini Gambit Series will continue in
Book 3 – The Child Of The Fall

Afterword

As before, if you've gotten this far it's due to the nearly superhuman efforts of one person, who isn't me. Cheryl Lawrence, editor extraordinaire, didn't have to use the firehose quite as many times as she did with the first book, but you wouldn't have had even a quarter as much fun if it wasn't for her efforts. If you're thinking, "Well if he can do it, I sure as hell can," you're right and you should go look up Ink Slinger Editorial Services. Tell her Goldfish Boy sent you!

I'd like to also thank my beta readers this time around: Ellen Carozza, Jeff Johnson, Janet Platt, Cathy Hurt, Amanda Morken, and Rick Keyes. You guys are the greatest and hopefully you'll see at least a few adjustments I made due to your feedback.

I'm ever grateful as always to my awesome cover artist, Melissa Lew. She also makes great jewelry!

Lighthouse24 did a stellar job with book composition. It's not just any place that would patiently wait three whole years for an author to finally get his crap together. Thankfully it didn't take anywhere near that long this time around.

A supportive family is always required for success and I'm very grateful for mine. It's not easy to put up with shop talk from an author.

Most amazingly of all, I'd very much like to thank you, my fans and readers. Your kind words and cheering support have surprised and humbled me. It's kind of mind-blowing that you not only know but care who Mike, Kim, Tonya, Spencer, and the rest are. I'm just their custodian. They truly live inside all of you.

And don't forget to tell your friends, write a review, rate *Dragon's Ark* on Goodreads, or do any other thing to get the word out. It makes for a great Christmas gift!

Finally, you'll get the latest news about the next book as well as silly pictures, cool science, and the occasional cat meme by following me on Facebook. Just look up my name or use this link: https://www.facebook.com/D-Scott-Johnson-1422185074739504/

I always respond to notes and really appreciate any comments.

About the Author

D. Scott Johnson has been an IT professional since 1988, and currently works as a software developer. Aside from writing, he also mucks around with the ridiculous world of hi-fi audio, and just barely keeps his two classic Alfa Romeos on the road. He lives in Northern Virginia with his wife, daughter, and however many pets they have managed to sneak in to the house at any one time.

No, Ellen, you can't have one.

www.ingramcontent.com/pod-product-compliance
Lightning Source LLC
Chambersburg PA
CBHW030827310726
48980CB00006B/664/J
* 9 7 8 0 9 8 6 3 9 6 2 5 0 *